Temporal Gifts

Whitney Hill

BENU
MEDIA

TEMPORAL GIFTS

Benu Media

6409 Fayetteville Rd

Ste 120 #155

Durham, NC 27713

(984) 244-0250

benumedia.com

ISBN (ebook): 979-8-9873785-3-3

ISBN (pbook): 979-8-9873785-4-0

Library of Congress Control Number: 2023906534

Cover Designer: Pintado (99Designs)

Editor: Jeni Chappelle (Jeni Chappelle Editorial)

Content Warnings

This book contains strong physical violence and gore, on-page death, swearing, slurs (not toward any real racial or ethnic group/identity), alcohol use, knife violence, threat of sexual violence, mention of past abuse by a guardian, deadnaming, state-sanctioned violence, blood-drinking, consensual on-page sex scenes, and brief mention of off-page/past sexual assault.

For those who have had to reclaim their power from people who refuse to see it.

Chapter 1

A storm raged in a desert, winds whistling through tall stone spires and clouds blocking out the moon.

Or I thought it did. I was asleep. Dreaming. I knew I was dreaming. I knew the storm wasn't real, that it was just a figment of my subconscious. The stirred-up agitation brought on by being presented with the weight of what I had to do in waking life, bringing the elves and the djinn together once more and restoring balance in Otherside.

So I indulged myself in a way I couldn't in the waking world. I became the storm.

Fell into the gale and pummeling rain that sent a deluge of sandy mud streaming around me. Wrenched every drop of moisture out of the sky, then drew more in.

I would see this desert bloom.

A cramp tightened my muscles. Odd. I shook my head and ignored it. I needed this release.

Another cramp. This time, a stronger one. Then another when I tried to push it away, strong enough to drop me to my knees.

I lost control of the storm.

My eyes snapped open, and I gasped awake.

I was drenched, and so was the bed—and a deathly serious-looking Troy and everything in the damn bedroom. Sand was heaped in the corners, and the lamps had toppled from the nightstands. The space reeked of burnt marshmallow. Those cramps must have been him trying a spell to get me conscious. Underlying that was the dry scent of the desert though, like I'd somehow pulled even that part of my dream into the real world.

My heart stopped as I took in the trashed room. When I brought my attention back to Troy, he lifted his brows, expression still hard.

I shook my head. "I have no idea what— This has never happened before. Nothing in my dreams is real."

"Nothing in your dreams *was* real." His quiet, even tones said he was controlling a strong reaction. The bond was locked down, so I couldn't tell what.

"Did I hurt you?"

"I'm fine. Are *you* okay?"

"Physically, I'm fine." I shuddered and disentangled myself from sodden sheets. A puddle splashed as I got out of bed. "But this? What the hell."

"What happened?"

"I was dreaming. A storm in the desert. I knew it was a dream, so I just...let go. It's not real, Troy." Maybe if I kept saying it, it'd be true. Even if I knew life didn't work like that.

Sighing, he got out of bed and dragged his wet T-shirt off before throwing the window all the way open and peering outside. "Looks like the effects were limited to this room."

I went to check the kitchen, finding it dry and sand-free except for the trickle of water making its way under the crack of the bedroom door. It smelled like dinner, not the desert.

"Yeah. Okay." I reined in the rising panic.

I'd cast in my sleep before but only ever Air. I'd never just created sand—or pulled it from the dream?—or drenched a room. There wasn't even sand like that in this area. It *felt* wrong. Or at least different, like the sand at Wrightsville Beach had felt different from the sand at Jordan Lake. But more. A completely different composition. Nothing that was around here.

Think. I needed to think.

Troy was still looking at me like he was trying real hard not to demand answers I might not be able to give. I couldn't call Duke; I still got the twisty feeling in my stomach at the idea of asking him what this was about.

Duke. I couldn't call him, but I had spoken to him. He'd said something that I had no idea what it meant. But I couldn't figure out what else this could be.

"Chaos spheres," I said. "I told Duke about dreams of the forest and the beach and that you were there sometimes. He swore and told me I should have said something. Said it was a talent and implied it required a certain amount of strength. That's the only thing I can think of, but I have no idea what it is or what it means. And he refused to tell me."

Troy stiffened. "Wait. You dream of a forest and a beach? Tall redwoods? Cliffs? Like something on the West Coast. Seattle."

I nodded. "I mean, I don't know what the Seattle area looks like but yeah. Big trees. Cliffs or mountains or something. And you're always there. But I only have the dream when we're separated."

He went very still. "I wonder if that's why I stopped dreaming of you there when I moved in."

Flushing, I nodded and looked around the bedroom again, trying to distract myself from the idea that he might actually have been in my dreams for real—or I was in his. Some of those dreams had been...interesting.

"Lemme clean up. We'll figure it out," I said.

He kissed my cheek as he passed to the bathroom, telling me he'd only been scared for me, not mad.

Or maybe a little mad. Frustrated. I could see it in the line of his shoulders. As my bondmate, fiancé, and sometime bodyguard, he didn't like when things got out of his control, and while he didn't try to control *me* these days, he did like to have some control over the environment.

Nothing for it.

Centering myself, I surrendered to Water and pulled all the excess moisture in the room into a ball. That went out the unscreened window with a splash before I embraced Earth and did the same with the sand. The water-damaged papers on my nightstand and the fried jamming device Troy had in the one on his side got a sigh. I could only manipulate the elements, not magically restore paper and electronics. Fortunately, the laptops were in the kitchen, and our phones were at least a little waterproof. I gathered them up and headed to the kitchen to bury them in a bowl of rice, just in case, before changing my clothes.

The first light of dawn was peeking above the trees when I peered out the window. Far too early to be up, but my heart was troubled enough that I didn't think I'd make it back to sleep. Certainly not tonight. Sleeping had been hard enough when the gods of the hunt kept pulling me into the Crossroads, but that was almost better than this. At least then I had someone to blame then.

Now there was nobody to blame except myself.

I didn't know what was going on or how to fix it. All I knew was that if I went to sleep, I might do some magic that could hurt Troy. And while he had some auratic talent, I doubted he could stand against this new power. He'd been born a Monteague, and they leaned heavily toward mental manipulation.

He came back out of the bathroom while I was changing the sheets. He dressed in the cut-off grey sweatpants and T-shirt that said he'd be going for a run after this and helped me finish with the bed before asking, "What's on your mind?"

Of course he picked up that I was noodling on something. "Two things. We can't tell the djinn about this. Duke gets squirrely every time dreaming comes up, and you heard what he said about Dreamwalking. He's mentioned problems to be contained in the context of my mom before, so now I'm wondering if it was really just her relationship with my dad that was the problem like I always assumed. Second, we really need to talk to *your* dad."

"Why my dad?"

"Because I think he knows something."

Troy's expression shuttered. "About djinn dream talents? Or yours in particular?"

I shrugged. "Sight doesn't work like that for me. I just know it's something to do with him."

"I don't think I like that. He's up to something."

This time, I bit my tongue. Troy's feelings about being reunited with his father were complicated, and it'd only been a few days. None of us could get a read on the man, and neither Troy nor Allegra could recall him acting as erratically as he did now. None of us knew if it was a consequence of being in solitary imprisonment for twenty years, a residual effect of having been tortured, something to do with his trickster patron, or all of the above. Or something else entirely. Either way, Troy would need time and space to work through it.

When the bed was done, he grabbed a pair of socks. "Moon's making me itchy, and now I'm up again. Will you be okay if I go for a run?"

"Yeah. I need to have a think about how to get the elves and the djinn to agree to this new House structure. I don't want to leave it until the last minute."

He gave me a long look that said he knew I was avoiding sleep again but just said, "Okay. Back in a bit."

I threw myself on the bed as he headed out.

Step by step, I went through my memory of the dream, trying to figure out at what point it had gone from just a dream to something that could be pulled into the real. That and how I'd done it. I hadn't even known it was possible for dreams to be real.

When that line of thought failed to produce answers, I turned to what it might mean. That my magical strength was growing, obviously. But Harqil had been concerned yesterday when I told them about the prophecy, or whatever it was, and they'd suggested someone else might have been naughty.

Was this power even mine?

That soured my mood another lemon. The last thing I needed when I was already battling imposter syndrome was to doubt whether the things I was doing were even mine to control or if I was as much a puppet to some unknown god now as I'd been when Neith's gift had taken over my mind. If that was the case, I needed to know how they were influencing me. Harqil's gem was the only new gift I'd accepted from the gods, but that was in a lead-lined neutrality box. I'd had to be holding the knife Neith had given me for it to influence me. So if it was outside influence, it was by some other means.

Shit.

Whatever it was, I had no answers and no way to begin to get them unless I wanted to call Duke, could get Cyrus to talk to me, or Harqil dropped in for another visit.

I shoved the worries in a mental box to deal with later. If I had no answers, I had to focus on something I had a chance of controlling or at least influencing. Top of mind just now was the safety of my home. The boundaries might have been secure, but I was still pissed that the Sons of Seth had dared to attack and more so that the Bureau for Supernatural Investigation had apparently authorized it. Acting Director Sinclaire had also made threats against my people, which I needed to do something about. The kidnapping attempt had failed, and now her little shadow op hadn't managed to take me out, so the smart option would be to try weakening me by going after one of the local faction heads next since I was proving too much to handle. It almost made me miss the days of being a private investigator, when my biggest concern was finding my next client and keeping Callista happy.

My head spun a little at that thought—the near-nostalgia for Callista as a simpler problem. Life really had taken a strange turn.

Restlessness drove me to get up and make a cup of tea, mulling over what angle to take with the mundane issue. I might be pissed about my home, but I kept having to remind myself it wasn't all about me anymore. I needed to restore balance within Otherside and between Otherside and the mundanes, and I needed to protect everyone while doing so. Harqil had said balance was the price of magic, and we were currently in debt. Deep in debt. I had to work fast if we were gonna have any chance of keeping magic.

The wereleopards were going to be the most vulnerable. But Maria was still struggling to regain control of the vampires in Raleigh, I had elves acting out on my borders, and I hadn't heard anything from the werewolves in the mountains in far too long. If I didn't get Otherside in line, fast, our best chance at achieving balance and keeping magic was fucked.

I couldn't let that happen. Which meant I needed to set aside the damn mundanes for a minute and get this House restructure done. The Otherside population was too small for any one faction to establish a balance alone. We needed all of us, united.

Calmed somewhat by having something to do and somewhere to start, I took my tea to the deck out back to keep plotting and watch for Troy's return. I called a gust of wind to clear the remaining sand I'd chucked out from the bedroom, pushing away the unsettled feeling that tried to rise again.

Nothing I could do about it right now, no matter how much my stomach clenched.

A nudge in the bond pulled my attention to the tree line.

Troy vaulted the fence rather than using the gate. From the steady look he gave me, he wasn't at all surprised to find me still up and, at the same time, was swallowing a scolding.

Once upon a time, I would have been annoyed at that. Felt like he was treating me like a spoiled child. Now I just understood

that it was born out of the depths of his care for me and the effort
to let me be me, even if he thought I was hurting myself, because
he knew me well enough to know pushing me would draw out
my contrary streak.

Instead of pissing me off, a different heat lit in me.

He paused then inhaled deeply as he slowly mounted the stairs.
His dilating pupils said he was fully aware of the shift in my
mood as much from my scent as the bond, probably.

"Where did that come from?" he asked.

"I want you." The words jumped from me with no thought,
let alone grace. Just pure sentiment.

He smirked. "You had me all last night."

"Well now I want more."

"I know that. What—"

"You're the one constant I have. I cannot catch a single fucking
break. Shit just keeps changing. And the only time I feel like I can
breathe is when I'm with you. I—I need you. Please." I shut my
mouth so hard my teeth clacked, trying to stop the gale of words
as my face flushed.

I was usually more reserved than this, but lately, I was so afraid
of being too much. Afraid that all the growing I was being
forced into would push him away, no matter what he said about
growing alongside me. I was feeling insecure as hell because I
couldn't even fucking sleep without possibly ending the world,
and I just needed to know he was still my anchor.

I dropped every wall on my side of the bond, a dirty emotional
play, but one I thought he'd understand.

On silent feet, he approached until he towered over me. With
a single finger, he tipped my chin up. A darkly playful grin curled
his lips. "If you want me, you'll have to catch me."

I was up before he finished, but he was still too fast for me.

Despite his earlier run, he led me on a wild chase through the
woods and back to the house before finally tiring enough for me

to bring him down when he stumbled after jumping the fence again.

I straddled his hips and trapped his wrists against the ground, hesitant and still worried about being too much at first, then harder when he moved to throw me off.

"I love you," I whispered against his lips.

He kissed me as he dropped the walls on his side of the bond, signaling his surrender. "And I will always love you, no matter how scary your powers get. Never doubt it, cariñamí."

With those comforting words, I got off him and dragged him inside to claim my prize, determined to carve out a little something good before throwing myself into the new set of problems that'd landed on me.

Chapter 2

Those problems apparently would not be abating anytime soon, as I discovered when I dragged myself into my office at the bar. Of all the shit I thought I was gonna have to deal with this month, turning a mundane into a wereleopard was definitely not it.

I stared at Terrence, seated across from me, hoping he'd say something, anything, else. As if I didn't have enough to keep in balance between the elves and the djinn, and Otherside and the mundanes. Now he wanted to add something that would piss off the werewolves?

Terrence stared right back, eyes the color of tiger-eye gems giving even less away than usual. Worse, he said nothing to expand on the bomb he'd just dropped.

I had to crack. "Let me get this straight. Lola. Your second. Revealed herself to a mundane, in contravention of leap law and custom and the agreement you specifically made with the alliance. Said mundane now wants her to bite him in the hopes of being turned and joining the leap as her mate. Did I hear that right?"

"Yes, Miss Arden, that you did."

"Not only that, but you want me as Arbiter to sign off on it, given that it's flat-out forbidden to grow were populations by bites rather than births."

"Yes, ma'am."

Terrence was always respectful, but this was exceedingly formal even for him. There wasn't a hint of the catlike amusement that usually lived in the curl of his grin or the glint of his eyes. In his steady gaze and stiff posture, I finally saw the Marine the tattoo on his forearm said he was.

I leaned back in my chair, mind racing. Trying to figure out the political pitfalls of this request.

Maria's reaction, I couldn't even begin to predict. The vampire Mistress of Raleigh was a friend, especially to me, and was dating Troy's sister. But Maria had always been jealously protective of her territory and her resources, and while there was more leeway for vampires to turn humans given their ability to glamour any accidental witnesses, she'd be testy about adding more predators to the area. Troy was unusually open-minded for an elf and dedicated to doing the right thing, especially for those who'd been historically excluded or harmed. But he was currently feeling the pinch of a significant drop in the local elven population, which was ultimately my fault, and had been touchy lately on territory matters.

The djinn were rarely too bothered with earthly concerns, but that might change with my proposal to djinn and elf representatives yesterday to rebuild the local elven Houses as jointly elf-djinn led. The fae mostly kept to the Summerlands, but more of them had migrated to this side of the Veil and to Durham in particular of late. The witches, who tended to live and let live, were directly concerned with my dramatic growth in power and the shit I could now do with it—like change entire weather patterns for a hundred-mile radius. I'd had to deal with a terse visit from Janae this afternoon, which would have been the worst of it, except that the elementals were furious with me to the point of even my friends not taking my calls.

All of that wasn't even considering Vikki Volkov, alpha of the Red Dawn werewolf clan. Like Maria, I considered Vikki a friend...usually. Territory questions had gotten tense lately, and adding a wereleopard would set off an argument I'd had to put firmly to bed a couple months ago.

Saying yes to Terrence would piss off a lot of important people.

Saying no wouldn't be fair, given the historical mistreatment of both wereleopards in New World Otherside communities and Black folks in the United States. It might also worsen the imbalance in the Otherside community, which was what I was supposed to be fixing.

I bowed my head and closed my eyes, searching for the right answer. The Sight gave me nothing, even with the ring that let me see the unseen.

Because at its root, the question wasn't about Fate or Fortune.

It was about Justice.

The Lady of the Scales might be blindfolded, but that was because the heart knew. We could lie to ourselves, but the ancient Egyptians had it right: an unjust heart would weigh heavy when the time of reckoning came. Some folks might pay for absolution in this world or the next, but the heart would always know.

If I wanted to restore balance and call myself a protector, I had to be willing to make unpopular decisions and take risky actions in favor of those who needed it most. Otherwise, *my* heart would be the one weighing heavy.

"Granted," I whispered.

"What?"

When I looked up, Terrence had lost his stoic expression. Pure shock widened his eyes and opened his features.

"Granted," I repeated. "And may the tricksters take joy in the trouble it's gonna cause me."

His eyes narrowed. "What's this about the tricksters? We leopards keep right with Aunt Nancy, but I thought you were one of the hunters' children."

"Oh I am. But they're not the only ones with an interest in primordial elementals." I left their interest in Troy as a now-disorderly elf out of it. "Regardless, Terrence, you're the smallest faction, locally or nationally. Correct me if I'm wrong, but neither your leap nor Ximena's prowl have had a birth in years. Your faction is several times wronged going back to the time our ancestors all arrived here. Change and justice have to start somewhere. If that means taking the hit for breaking the Détente when me and the vampires have already beat it to shit and the Richmond elves thought they could work with the mundanes..." I shrugged.

Terrence tilted his head, studying me. "If I can be blunt, you continue to surprise, Miss Arden." He raised a hand when I stiffened. "Nothing personal, but you know as well as I do that Callista was egregiously unfair and that skinfolk ain't always kinfolk. In either skin."

I nodded, having had experience with both situations. "That's true. But the Acacia Thorn leopards and the Jade Tooth jaguars have always led by example. A good example. Troy told me about your aid to Lydia Desmarais."

A smile cracked Terrence's face. "Stubborn little thing. I liked her. Had that five-century vagabond wrapped around her pinky finger even when she could barely stand." He sobered. "But I hope you didn't agree just for that."

"I didn't. There's admittedly a strategic aspect in that I need more people who might at least consider being loyal to me when the shit hits the fan. But the bulk of it is like I said. Y'all are owed. If nobody else will acknowledge and pay, I will."

He pursed his lips. "Conditions?"

This was why I liked Terrence. No bullshit. No games. Forthright acknowledgment that, even when we were on the same side, there had to be guidelines. "Same as for births. The turned one is your responsibility. He loses his shit and kills someone he shouldn't or draws the wrong kind of attention to the territory, it's on you to put him down. Or I have to make an example of the whole leap. Ximena's prowl as well, if she steps in."

"Fair." He grimaced. "I hate it, but it's fair. Special circumstances and all."

"Exactly. Does Vikki know?"

"She's been occupied."

I frowned. This was the first I'd heard that the clan alpha of the local Red Dawn werewolves had something going on, but I'd been far too busy with elf, djinn, and elemental concerns in the weeks since my birthday. "With what?"

"Far as I can tell, those brothers of hers out in Asheville are acting out again."

With an effort, I suppressed a sigh. One of those brothers—the elder—was my ex-boyfriend, Roman Volkov. The other was the baby brother of the family, Sergei. The youngest Volkov was the biggest pain in my ass out of the three of them, but all of them—and especially the two men—had a heaping helping of entitlement. To make matters worse, the family and pack had the kind of money and influence that made it everyone's problem, even with the Blood Moon clan supposedly bowing to Red Dawn now.

Which meant it would probably be my problem before long, especially if Vikki had failed to mention it during our last girls' night. And if I was being real honest, I still hadn't forgiven Blood Moon for their role in temporarily severing my bond with Troy. That had more than sucked. It'd nearly killed both of us.

"I'll speak to Vikki," I said. "And deal with Troy and Maria, if they look up from their own factional issues long enough to pitch a fit."

Terrence's usual cat-smile came back. "Much obliged, Miss Arden. Gotta say, it's much more pleasant dealing with the elves and the vamps with you in charge. Makes me feel like we're part of a team. And like we made the right choice early on."

"Good. I appreciate hearing it. Was there anything else I can help you with?"

He tilted his head and gave me a long look. "Seeing as you're being so accommodating today, I wonder if I might trouble you with another matter."

"I can certainly hear you out at least."

"Okay then. You were there when Vikki made her initial offer with regard to moving to the Triangle."

I thought back to the meeting between Vikki, Terrence, and his werejaguar partner Ximena on the banks of the Eno at my place. "Ah. She promised to cede the land taken by the wolves back to the pride once there was an opening for her to go back west."

"In the name of justice." Terrence's cat-grin was ironic now. "And yet..."

"The wolves are still here."

He tipped his head and flashed his brows. "Now, we ain't fixin' to make a stink about it. You've been plenty busy with the vampires and the elves. And the trickster gods apparently." That got me an arched eyebrow. "But I'd be doing my people a disservice if I didn't remind you—respectfully, of course—that we're still hereabouts and have concerns too."

I couldn't help my flush. "Of course. Point taken, in the spirit given. What are you specifically looking for?"

"If you'll recall, another part of the agreement with Viktoria was that she couldn't grow the wolf population via bites. Now, she might mean well and say the right words, but if we're turning consenting mundanes and she's not allowed to..."

I sighed, seeing what he was getting at. The same thought I'd had earlier. "She has been vocal about wanting to get hers in the past. Roman tends to blunder. And Sergei's been even louder with less sense."

"Glad to see we're on the same page."

"You want my assurances that I'll step in if any of them kick off."

He nodded. "Yes, ma'am. I very much do. And eventually, I may be calling upon your assistance in arbitrating the fulfillment of the agreement Red Dawn made with Acacia Thorn and Jade Tooth."

"Understood. Since that is technically my main duty, you'll have it."

"Much obliged."

"Okay then. As always, I appreciate your candor, Terrence. Anything else?"

"No, ma'am. I'll be taking the good news to Lola. We'll keep you posted on what happens next." The musky tang of cat filled the space. Terrence might put on a neutral face, but he was excited about this opportunity for his leap.

Good. The werecats, both locally and in general, tended to be overlooked in Otherside, when they weren't outright kicked. Like most weres, they minded their business. Being minorities both in Otherside and in their human skins meant they had a vested interest in keeping their affairs within their communities.

Which reminded me of something, given we couldn't all just stay in our own spaces anymore, not and keep ourselves and the rest of Otherside safe.

"Last thing before you go—I want everything in writing," I said. "The mundane makes a new will and signs a contract stipulating the expectations of his behavior. If you need a template, ask Iago Luna about the House adoption contracts the elves draw up. Tell him you'll need language added for possibility of death, et cetera. He'll have a better idea of what's needed than I do."

Iago was a bar-certified lawyer in addition to being my Chancellor. He'd have something. And he wouldn't screw over the weres like some of the other elves might.

They might be my people to lead now, but that didn't mean I would be as naïve as I used to be when it came to elven political machinations.

Terrence nodded, pursing his lips. "Appreciate the resource. We don't have a lawyer of our own."

"I know. I want this to be airtight for when it eventually gets out. Especially if he dies or has to be put down."

"Fair." He sighed. "The world ain't what it used to be. I just hope we come out alive on the other side of all these changes."

"I'm trying to ensure that."

"I know, Miss Arden. I know." Rising, he shook my hand and headed for the door. "Stay safe."

With a grimace, I said, "I do my best."

He snorted. "Nobody makes it easy on you, I'll give you that. Good night, ma'am."

After the door closed behind him, I turned back to the reports I'd been digging through prior to his arrival.

A quick update from Matthias, the vampire Master of New York. The people he'd sent to Jacksonville, Florida to grab territory from Santiago, Master of Miami, were doing well, despite Santiago having finally noticed their presence and making a first push to get them out of the state. Charity, Mistress of Atlanta, and Renaud, Master of Charlotte, remained content with the arrangement; apparently they'd been concerned about Santiago encroaching on their territories, and any distraction from that aim was both welcome and made them more inclined to think well of me as Arbiter of the Carolinas and the Dominion demesnes.

Nothing from the djinn or the Richmond and Charleston elves yet on my offer to re-establish the Chapel Hill Conclave with two new Houses headed by reps from each of the other conclaves, *if* they accepted having djinn as equal partners in leadership and management. It'd only been about twenty-four hours, but I was still anxious to hear what they said.

I wanted them to say yes, badly.

Not just because it would be a step toward bringing my parents' dream to fruition but also because Harqil, a celestial messenger of the trickster gods, had flat-out told me that balance was the price of Otherside's magic.

We were badly out of balance, both within Otherside and between us and the mundanes. If I wanted to achieve both my goals—protecting Otherside from rising human aggression and fulfilling my parents' dream of healing the rift between elves, djinn, and elementals—I had to find a way to achieve balance. It was a mess I had no idea how long I had to fix. I just knew I had to fix it or we'd lose magic. All of us except, apparently, the elementals.

Troy had already made it clear that wasn't an acceptable option. Not because he was against elementals but because the elves were so reliant on their magic to give them the upper hand among everyone else while their population plummeted amidst a slow reproduction rate, inter-House power struggles, and assassinations.

I hadn't had a chance to ask the rest of the alliance yet, but based on the reactions to having them hold the gem that'd given me the first clue, none of them would find the loss of magic acceptable either.

So yeah. I was pretty damn anxious to have the elves and the djinn agree to my plan.

Then there were Darkwatch reports on mundane police and federal law enforcement comm chatter. The human supremacist terrorists, the Sons of Seth, had attacked my home two nights ago. I'd destroyed eighteen down to the elements making up their blood, bones, and souls. Troy and the gytrash guarding my home had stopped another six and turned them over to the Ebon Guard for questioning. It was technically too early for the mundanes to file missing persons reports, but the federal Bureau for Supernatural Investigation had signed off on the attack on my home. They'd be looking for a return on their investment.

My blood boiled at the memory of the attack. That anyone would dare—

The buzz of my phone pulled me out of my thoughts.

Troy: *We'll get answers. I promise.*

I was a little embarrassed that I'd gotten so pissed so fast that he'd not only felt it in the bond but knew exactly why.

Then again, it was his home that'd been attacked as well. I'd put his name on the deed, partly to get him to understand that it really was his home and he was welcome to live as though it was, and partly because I kept getting attacked and didn't know who else to leave my stuff to if my luck ran out.

The morbid thoughts dragged my mood down, and suddenly I was tired of sitting in a windowless office, poring over reports. I could do the same at home—and given the recent attack, I wasn't keen on leaving my land undefended.

An Arbiter was only as strong as her territory, and mine was shaky enough even without the threat of losing magic hanging over us.

Chapter 3

I walked the borders of my land when I got home, still bothered by how out of control my dream had gotten last night. The new moon hung dark overhead, an eye closed to any evils being carried out on the earth below.

I might not be an elf, whose power waxed at the lowest ebb of the moon, but it still suited me. The magic I'd used to clear my land of invaders had been dark enough when it came down to it. And I certainly wanted it all kept hidden. Which was why I was prowling the edge of the trees, sweeping with all my senses for anything my magic hadn't been able to break down—the plastic the Sons had been carrying, mostly—and driving it deeper into the earth.

As I reached the part of the yard farthest from the house, something felt off.

A presence in the dark, watching me.

I stiffened in alarm, looking for it, and caught a shift in the air molecules the second before an iron grip banded around my arms. A hand clapped over my mouth as a scream tried to burst free.

With a snarl, I fought as I'd been trained—by the very man who'd just snuck up on me, probably after stalking me from the woods, given the scent I belatedly caught.

Knowing it was Troy who'd ambushed me didn't make me take my reaction down a notch. We never gave each other quarter, not until and unless it was asked or strictly necessary. Both our survival counted on it. No enemy elf would take pity on me, an elemental, when elementals were still considered bounty hunts by most elves in the world. And no enemy power, elf or otherwise, would leave a king of Troy's strength alive at their back once they'd decided to attack. We were the only ones we could both trust to go all out with in training and to have the knowledge of when it was too much.

I broke free. Grabbed Air and sent a punch at his ribs, the ones on his left flank I knew were a little soft from having been repeatedly broken. His whole left side was a terrible mess of healed injuries that occasionally gave him a twinge, for all they'd been healed with Aether, but the ribs and shoulder were the worst.

Somehow, he dodged. Elemental magic affected the physical world, and physical attacks could be dodged, but most people couldn't manage it.

Most people weren't Troy, who'd been terrifyingly fast even before he'd grown more fully into his power.

Rather than running, I stepped into the space left by the dodge and attacked.

He blocked easily then countered with magic of his own that I barely cut through with a scythe of Chaos.

Round and round we went, until I lost track of my footing in the dark and tripped backward over a fallen log. I landed hard, fortunately on sandy soil rather than rock or a sharp stick, and tried to scramble to my feet.

Troy was on me in half a breath. His rough grip pinned me to the ground.

I wrestled free and managed to break away, only to be tackled down onto my belly this time. The ground was his domain. Stars danced in the darkness behind my eyes as the arm he looped around my throat tightened.

Frustrated as hell, I tapped out, slamming my hand on the ground three times as I dropped the walls between us in the bond. He released me immediately, pulling away far more slowly than usual and retreating to crouch a few steps away.

Savage pleasure echoed through the bond, and as frustrated as I was, I wouldn't deny him the enjoyment of a fair win.

"Name your forfeit," I gasped when I had some of my breath back.

Troy's dark chuckle sent chills over me. "I think I'll keep this one for later."

It wasn't until he said that that I realized how much I'd hoped he'd claim it now...and physically.

"Really?" I asked. Heat pooled between my thighs and spread through my core. Elven hunting games or not, I wanted him. Again. Bad.

"We have other things to do tonight. Leadership things."

Frustration heated my skin. "Then why'd you—"

He moved with the deathly silent speed of a hunting elf at the new moon before I could track him, pulling me to my feet, gathering me in, and stealing a kiss so thorough I lost my breath again.

"Because I damn well wanted to," he growled when he freed me. "And because the moon makes me itch if I don't hunt *something* when it's new."

"Keep kissing me like that and I might forgive you scaring the fucking bejeezus outta me then."

That got me another kiss, somehow better than before, one that didn't end until I'd melted against him.

I wavered, resting my hands on his chest when he pulled away. "You are a very dangerous man, Troy Solari."

"Not to you, cariñamí. Never to you."

"No, especially to me. Because I can't keep my head around you."

Pleasure echoed through the bond as he tucked me under his arm and turned us toward the house. "You say that like you had sense to begin with."

"Hey!"

"Hey yourself. I'm not the one who voluntarily dove into Jordan Lake last month."

We bantered back and forth as we headed back to the house. The new moon itch he'd mentioned had him in high, almost wild spirits—this one more than most, for whatever reason. It was bringing out a side of his nature he usually spent a lot of energy to keep tamped down, certainly around other elves, who were inclined to think a goldeneye king was feral for indulging in hunts under the new moon. Especially hunting his own queen. Pretty sure that'd be a killing offense in the rest of the Houses, but there wasn't much else that'd give him a decent challenge these days without risking a problem with the other alliance factions.

To me, it was no different than a were feeling called to run in the woods under a full moon, and I'd done that often enough with Roman. If Troy needed a hunt and a fight to feel good, I'd give him both. He gave me so much more, as far as I was concerned.

"Stop that," he murmured as we got inside. "I give you what I can and want to give. You help me see how much is healthy and when to stop. You don't owe me."

I just went up on my toes to kiss him again then plucked a dried leaf out of the loose wave of his raven-black hair and flicked it back out behind us before shutting the door. "What leadership things are so damn important that we can't fuck?"

He grinned at my desire for him, and a teasing curl of Aether snaked through me before he sobered. "Preparation for an Otherside without magic."

That cut right through my horniness. "Of course. And I thought Terrence's request was a big deal."

Troy frowned, suddenly all business. He was on excellent terms with the wereleopard. With Terrence's Marines background, I suspected they both understood the strain of controlling their wild sides under violent pressure better than most. I'd even call them friends, and Troy didn't have many of those.

"What's wrong with Acacia Thorn?" he asked.

"Nothing's *wrong*. Terrence just had an unusual ask." I filled Troy in.

His gazed unfocused as the gears in his brain started turning. "That's not just unusual, Arden. That's potentially hugely problematic. Especially if we lose magic. What does a new wereleopard do if he can't reach his leopard?"

I winced. I hadn't thought of that.

Troy just sighed and shook his head. "I want to object to this."

"I thought you might."

"But you were counting on me seeing it as the right thing to do."

"Honestly, yeah. Was I wrong?"

"No." He leaned on the half wall dividing the front entry from the dining area, arms crossed as he looked out the back window and scowled. "But, Arden, I can't offer elven resources for a cover-up if something happens. Not with the feds and this deal pending with the djinn and the local Houses. Or with my father disappearing this evening."

"Excuse me?"

Cyrus Veisi had sworn an oath to my mother to protect me for reasons I still wasn't entirely clear on, but it'd ended up costing him his family and nearly his life. The man had a grudge against queens and also one of the trickster gods as a patron. He was definitely not someone I wanted unaccounted for in my territory, especially not given the little nudge of the Sight I'd gotten on meeting him, even if he seemed inclined to hold to his oath. For now.

"What did Brielle have to say?" I asked.

Troy snorted. "Profuse apologies. If she hadn't seemed convinced that I was going to behead her, I'd have come down on her harder."

Probably that and his deep-seated concern about how his people perceived him as a goldeneye king. The general perception was that any elf, but especially a male, who was close enough to what they'd once been to regain the gold flecks they all used to have in their eyes, was dangerous and needed killing.

So much killing with the elves. If they hadn't been so keen to kill me, I might have pitied them. Nobody should live in constant fear when all they did was exist.

I scrubbed my hands over my face, suddenly way too tired. "I want him found, Troy. Fast."

"I know. The Lyon elves are working on it."

Not much else to say or do there, and picking at Troy wouldn't get his father found any faster. "Fine. What other leadership things need covering?"

"We need to apply pressure to the elves and the djinn on our offer."

"It's only been a day." Even if I was eager to hear back.

"It's *already* been a day."

Apparently, there was some nuance I was missing because we hadn't had to do this when we got the summit together. My stomach chose that moment to growl, and I waved him off when he moved toward the kitchen. I was perfectly capable of reheating leftovers for myself and didn't want him to feel like he always had to be serving me, cultural upbringing or not.

He nodded when I held up one of the plastic containers with single servings of venison stroganoff and held up two fingers. I grabbed two more and got the contents of all three into a pan on the stove to reheat.

"You know better than I do that the djinn will spend their three days bickering in council," Troy said. "The elves know it too. They'll be waiting to hear something from the djinn via us because they don't want to lose face looking too eager to partner with djinn."

I let that roll through my mind. "You're saying that, because they can't have the rule of the new Chapel Hill Houses outright, they need to be able to say that they were bullied into it by the big bad Arbiter and her King."

"Something like that."

"Even though they get to offload any troublemakers onto us and said troublemakers will be elevated beyond the opportunities they would have had in their birth Houses."

Troy shrugged. "There's also defending elementals."

And there was the real problem for the elves. Maybe not just for them though.

"I need to talk to the other elementals," I said. My stomach twisted as I tried to imagine what they'd say, hard enough that I almost didn't want the food that was starting to smell real good on the stove.

"What are you afraid of?" Troy asked gently.

"That they'll be pissed because I didn't give them the option to lead the Houses. Val flat-out said that part of the reason they're so furious with me already is because I've been working so much more with the elves in particular."

He held himself very still, like he was suppressing any natural reactions he might have had to that statement. "They haven't exactly given you a chance or any indication that they'd be willing to work with you, right? I thought it had been completely the contrary."

"I know, but what if I blew my last shot by bypassing the Collective and going straight to the djinn and elves?"

"Again, my love, they've had two years to give you some sign that they'd be willing to work with you. Have you had a single word from anyone other than Val, Sofia, or Laurel? Anything from any of them indicating that the Collective would allow you to make any sort of case for them to join the alliance more formally?"

I turned back to the stove and stirred the food then grabbed plates, avoiding answering as long as I could under the pretense of preparing to eat. "You know I haven't."

"Okay."

There was more he wanted to say. I could sense it in the tautness of the bond. But he knew the other elementals were a sore point for me.

The djinn tolerated me. The elves were either forthright in hating me, or they swung in completely the opposite direction, seeing me as the solution to their problems with their cultural death cult and offering rabid loyalty.

But the elementals—my own people, for all I was the trueborn daughter of a djinn-elf pairing rather than wildborn like the rest of them—had gone from wanting nothing to do with me to outright ostracizing me and cutting me off from my friends.

It hurt. I didn't want it to because I had my own little family now, such as it was, with Troy and Allegra and the faction heads of the alliance in a weird way. But I was always alone in every room I went into because the other elementals didn't feel safe enough to join.

And that was on me.

"It's not on you," Troy said in response to the feeling that was probably throbbing through the bond. "I keep telling you, you can't own everything."

I didn't bother to answer, focusing on plating the food and getting it to the table.

He huffed a frustrated sigh and sat opposite me. "Thanks for the food."

"Thank *you*," I said. He'd cooked it, originally. "But yeah. If nothing else, I need to give them fair warning. Maybe they'll be more pleased at the potential of more trueborn elementals."

I didn't need Troy's aborted grimace or heavy silence to tell me that was a long shot.

Not wanting to dwell on it, I updated him on everything else that'd been in the evening reports. As we compared notes between factional intel and what the Darkwatch had gleaned, I tried to refocus on business and not on my feelings. Now more than ever, I needed a clear head.

Eventually though, we had to come back to the elf-djinn negotiations.

Troy pushed his clean plate away and leaned back in his chair. "I did have one idea about how to bring the elves in line. And tempt the djinn."

"Let's hear it."

"The Book of the Damned."

I stiffened, having forgotten all about the horrid elven book that'd somehow made its way into Torsten's library, which was now Maria's. My parents' names were in it, sealing their death notices and those of everyone in the original House Solari.

"I thought that only covered the sins of the Chapel Hill Conclave," I said.

"Mostly. Not all. We could blackmail the entire East Coast if we had to. Some of the records were pretty old, but we have long memories."

Which raised the question of how I wanted to lead. Again. I was tired of these tests and out of words to express myself. Rising, I gathered our plates and silverware and dumped everything in the sink.

"Not yet," I finally said into the long silence. "I have to believe what we're doing is important enough and impactful enough that it won't come to that. Leave me my illusions for another twelve hours if we can."

Troy's only response was to meet me at the sink, gather me into a hug, and kiss the crown of my head. We both knew the odds of getting this done that easily were low, but he knew when not to bother pushing me.

Chapter 4

Turning a mundane did indeed come with a ceremony.

Shortly after midmorning, I stood behind the ring of wereleopards and werejaguars in the backyard of Terrence's duplex north of Durham. Most of the pride had moved farther out in the last year, but Terrence and Ximena had maintained their residence close to my seat of power, as much to keep their fingers on the pulse of things as to provide an anchor for any new weres arriving in the area. They lived in one half of the building; the other was maintained as guest lodging.

After today, it'd be temporarily occupied by Lola and her prospective mate, Darnell.

Ximena had hurriedly explained that Darnell was formerly incarcerated. Instead of finding religion or learning a trade, he'd come out with a desire to learn more about Otherside. He'd met Lola at a community service event, they'd hit it off, and a whirlwind courtship had ensued.

Fair enough, even if I was a little suspicious of it after all the trouble we'd had with the feds, the Sons of Seth, and conservative politicians in the last two years. He could be a plant, a spy of some kind. Terrence had vetted and vouched for the man though, and he'd signed the paperwork Iago had rushed over. So it wasn't my business as long as the pride kept their newest member in line. And Darnell seemed decent enough—just someone who'd gotten a harder lot in life than some and was trying his best to turn it around. Maybe being welcomed into a community and starting a new life would be that chance.

So we stood in a circle around Lola and Darnell—or rather, the weres did while I stood under the enormous tree shading the yard—heads bowed. My presence was a risk, given the Sinners or the Sons were probably trying to track my movements, but the pride preferred that to the risk of attack. I'd done everything I could to obscure my trail here, leaving my car at the bar, exiting via the hidden backdoor in my office, and taking a van registered to one of House Solari's shell companies. Troy quietly did his part by drawing attention away from Durham with a visit to Maria and Allegra in Raleigh.

Terrence spoke. "We gather here today for a solemn rite that has not been carried out since the time of my granddaddy's granddaddy. We welcome a new member into our leap not by birth but by bite."

A few members of the pride, leopards and jaguars both, glanced my way at that. My presence should have been enough to signal my explicit acceptance of what was happening here, but I nodded to them anyway. Postures loosened, and chins lifted at the confirmation of my favor.

Nice that I could still make some people happy, at least.

Terrence continued. "Lola, you bring this man to us. You consent to step down as second for a year and a day to shepherd him through his transition?"

"I do." The small, lightly brown woman nodded solemnly. "I step down uncontested and unforced for a year and a day."

"As has been agreed, so it shall be, with the blessings of Aunt Nancy and our ancestors." Terrence turned slightly to catch the eye of one of the bigger weres, a dark-skinned, bald man. "Malik, you've been nominated to serve by the leap. Do you accept?"

Malik stood taller, looking around the circle. All of the leopards and a few of the jaguars nodded or smiled. He smiled back. "If it pleases the leap—and the pride as a whole—that I should serve as second, then I'm honored to do so with the blessings of Aunt Nancy and our ancestors."

"Good man." Terrence clapped Malik's shoulder before turning to Ximena. "Jefa of the Jade Tooth prowl, do you consent to this arrangement? Birth by bite and second by proxy?"

Ximena stalked forward and circled Darnell.

To his credit, he didn't react. No posturing. No flinching. Just a quiet calm that suggested he'd seen or been through much scarier things and, to me at least, boded well for his new life as a leopard.

Seemed Ximena thought so too because she nodded. "Malik has proven himself time and again. He has earned my trust. And this Darnell..." She studied him again, eyes flashing to the red-gold of her cat, and smiled slightly when he still didn't react. "I'm willing to give him a shot."

"As has been agreed by leap and by prowl, so it shall be," Terrence said. "After you, Lola."

"Yes, Terrence." She led her man into the house with Terrence coming after as everyone in the yard settled in to wait.

Apparently, the ceremony was a private one, even for the rest of the clan. I could have ordered that I be allowed to witness it, but that would go against the point of my not being like Callista.

Joachim, Ximena's second, ambled over to me. "May I ask you something, ma'am?"

"Sure."

He hesitated, eyes still on the house. "We're at a sensitive time. Everyone knows it. Why agree to this? Why take a risk on us?"

The last question caught me in the heart and squeezed. It was spoken in the tone of someone who'd been overlooked and looked down on for most of their life, a blend of outright disbelief, cautious hope, and the anticipation of disappointment that I knew very well.

Something about it moved me to give him the truth. "Because we're out of balance. Otherside. The mundanes. Between and across us all and with all of us and the Earth. I can't fix it all myself. But I can help with small steps. Y'all are owed. It's in my power to give, so I do."

I pressed my lips shut before I could rattle off more, belatedly realizing that I was nervous as hell about whatever was going on in that house.

His sharp inhale said he hadn't expected me to say that much, although it could have been equally a Flehmen response to taste my scent. "You honor me with the truth."

"Y'all honor me with your trust. You always have. I said I'd be a different Arbiter than Callista was, and I intend to prove it."

Joachim nodded. "It's just hard to believe shit could really be that easy. 'Scusing my French, ma'am."

I snorted. "And again, y'all are the only ones who are willing to take it at face value that it's possible. That we can have this new future, a balanced future, if we imagine better and then make an effort to implement it."

Swallowing past a lump in my throat, I strove to keep a neutral expression befitting a bad-ass Arbiter. I'd needed this conversation. I'd needed to hear that I wasn't some addled idealist for believing that this was all possible. The elves and the djinn kept looking for tricks and catches, betrayal and lies. Apparently, the rest of Otherside found it completely outrageous to hope and to strive for something different or better than what had brought us all here.

I blinked as that thought hit me like a lightning bolt.

That was my first challenge: giving my people something to hope for. I'd forced Otherside into a Reveal. We'd all done it thinking it'd make us safer, and it hadn't. We'd taken a big step together and had the mundanes fall on us with violence and hate. Trusting to hope in a better future had backfired. Homes and businesses had been targeted. People had been hurt, even killed.

I'd pushed too much change all at once. The Reveals. The breaking of the Détente that followed. The mundane backlash as Otherside made baby steps toward societal legitimacy and legal equality.

I could deal with change because it'd been a requirement for survival, even if I didn't like it. I was continually having to adapt myself to dance between Otherside and the mundane world as a private investigator and Callista's Watcher. The rest of them had watched from the shadows, interfered and hunted and killed from the shadows, but never engaged as deeply as I'd had to.

I blew out a heavy breath. "Thank you, Joachim."

"For?"

"Helping me see something just now."

He saluted, fist to heart. "Happy to be of service, ma'am. Especially if it means we might get to turn a jaguar next."

With a last grin at my sharp look, he shoved his hands in his pockets and ambled over to whisper in Ximena's ear.

She glanced back at me and gave the barest nod.

I nodded back and leaned against the tree behind me. I had no idea how long it'd take to turn a mundane, but I wasn't gonna leave until I'd seen my decision through. Being here to defend the leap, one way or another, was the least I could do. I just hoped that defense wouldn't be destroying a body.

△▽△▽

Hours later, after noon, Terrence came out to tell everyone that, for now, the rebirth was a success. There was a lot of quiet hugging and relieved, happy tears around the plates of barbeque Ximena had cooked up and brought out. Then people started cleaning up and filtering home. After a last check-in with both were alphas, I joined them, stopping to swap the van back and leave the bar in my own car.

I got home to find Troy's car still gone and Cyrus sitting on the top step of my porch, his cane beside him. The gytrash had him under guard, Bás sitting in front of my door, glowering at the elf's back with Marú sitting in the yard.

"Motherfucker," I muttered as my eyes met Cyrus's.

From his grin, he could read lips. He didn't move other than that though, watching my car and me with cool grey eyes.

A quick peek in the bond told me Troy was too far away to reach telepathically, so I sent him a text as I got out of the car and raised my auratic shields to their highest, tightest level.

Found your dad.

Where?

Home.

The flash of irritation in the bond said that wherever Troy was in his discussions with the Raleigh coterie, he wouldn't be there much longer.

Take your time, I wrote. *I can handle this.*

If I can't get out of this meeting, I want updates every hour.

K.

I shoved my phone in my butt pocket as I reached the foot of the porch steps and stopped, crossing my arms and cocking a hip beside Marú. "Fancy meeting you here, Cyrus."

"Brielle's good, but she doesn't have a patron. And I've learned the habits of all my guards." His eyes twinkled. Which meant he knew that I'd set someone to watch him and who, even if he didn't seem particularly offended that I'd done so.

I studied him, trying to figure out how to play this. "Doesn't explain how you broke through my wards."

"They only work on people who mean you harm." He shrugged. "Easy enough to circumvent when I'm oathsworn on your behalf."

That implied there were improvements I could make to the wards, but that was a secondary concern for me just now. "So you slipped the Darkwatch and my wards to...do what, exactly?"

Shifting, he pulled a leather messenger bag around from behind him. "Are you going to blow me to Kansas if I reach in here?"

I didn't bother hiding my suspicion. "Depends on what you're reaching for."

If anything, I think it amused him. Or challenged him, given that his passive power was to put people so at ease in his presence that he could charm just about anyone who wasn't fae—and literally without even trying. No wonder the queens had kept him strapped with lead and silver for the duration of his imprisonment.

He tapped his fingers on the bag, a quick ripple. "A book."

Not what I was expecting. "What kind of book?"

"The kind your mother wrote."

I stiffened with a small hiss before I could stop myself. "I have nothing of hers. How the fuck do you have a book? One that she *wrote*?"

He gave me a too-patient look that was eerily close to one of Troy's. "Let me take it out, and I'll tell you the whole story."

Reminding myself of what I'd told Troy—that I could handle Cyrus—I nodded tightly even as I set myself on the edge of reaching for Air.

Cyrus reached into the bag and slowly withdrew a small book bound in tattered leather. From the tiny, smooth pores I had a sick feeling it was human leather, but I really didn't want to think too hard about how or why my mom would've made that choice—assuming it really was a book she wrote.

When Cyrus held it out to me with a solemn look and a slight bow of his head, I snatched it and flipped it open to the first page.

"Cuneiform?" I asked. "How the fuck—"

"Flip the book over and read from the back."

I did as Cyrus said, finding Latin characters...and Latin words.

He sighed at my flat look. "They didn't teach you Latin."

Ignorance was something I tended to take as a personal offense and a failure, so I just gritted my teeth. I hadn't been taught any language except English, and the one time I'd tried looking at an elvish book from Callista's library, she'd smacked me to shit and filled my brain with horror stories about what the elves would do if they caught me. Troy and a few of the Ebon Guard were working on teaching me elvish, but it was slow going. I wondered what'd happened to that library before refocusing on the possible threat in front of me.

"I suppose Callista had a vested interest in your ignorance." Cyrus held out a hand, and I reluctantly passed the book back. He flipped through it, running a hand over a page a third of the way from the back. "It's on Dreamwalking."

I went cold.

A quick flick of his gaze took in my rigid stance and utterly blank expression. "I thought you might start having trouble with that."

"Why?" I snapped. "How?"

With another of those long, too-patient looks, he handed the book back and said, "Because dreams are the realm of the tricksters. While she was still carrying you, Ninlil said—and I quote—'The promise of the stars will be the harvest of the heavens, but only if she learns to part the Veil without crossing it.'"

I just stared at him. That meant nothing at all to me.

Cyrus pinched the bridge of his nose. "Of course Callista kept you ignorant of the Veil and the way of dreams as well. Fuck. This is going to take a while. Do you even know about Chaos spheres?"

That, I could answer affirmatively. Or at least I thought I could. Assuming I could trust Cyrus. But then, why would the Sight have nudged in his direction if I wasn't supposed to at least talk to him?

Another quick glance from Cyrus and a subtle sniff. "Look. I am rooting for you, both as an Ebon Guardsman for an elemental and as a father who sees what you've done for my son. But that doesn't mean I can't have my own goals. If those goals conflict with yours, it's not personal. Just the gods and my own pain."

"The gods. And the future of everyone on this plane."

His eyebrows flashed as he grinned. "Exciting, isn't it? The best gambles are always the ones with the highest stakes." When I didn't smile back, he sobered. "Come on, Ar—my queen. I know we got off on the wrong foot. But can you blame me? When I wouldn't bend the knee to Keithia, she broke it. We both have trust to earn."

I studied him. The man's frustration was palpable. I imagined he was used to getting his way much more easily than he was with me now. In a childish way, that satisfied me, and I had to get training from somewhere. I couldn't keep dumping a whole fucking desert in the bedroom or drenching Troy while he was sleeping because of a bad dream.

"Fine." I waved off the gytrash, making the fae hand signal Zanna had told me was a gesture of appreciative dismissal.

Without any noise of complaint, they rose and stopped menacing Cyrus directly, although it was clear they wanted to stick around. I nodded at Bás, and she curled up on the porch like she was just another big black dog. Marú trotted around to the back of the house.

I slapped my mom's book against my hand. Definitely human leather. I did my best to pretend it didn't make my skin crawl. "Yeah. I know a little about dreaming. And Chaos spheres. I might have made one last night."

At that statement, all of the blood drained from Cyrus's face.

Chapter 5

"Please tell me that's a bad joke," Cyrus said.

I shook my head.

"And you're still here?" He snatched his cane and pushed to his feet, fury giving him a dangerous mien. "Where's my son?"

"He's fine. He knows you're here, and he'll be home soon."

Cyrus looked like he wished he could throttle me but brought himself down to the edge of his usual charming self with a deep breath. "What happened? Exactly what happened, no hedging."

His harsh, judgmental tone was making my contrariness kick in. It died quickly though, as it occurred to me to wonder what—who—Troy might have been, had his father not been exiled and had Keithia not traumatized the hell outta Troy.

I had to make this work. Even if there was anyone else who could teach me about Dreamwalking and Chaos spheres, Troy had only the one father. If that relationship was broken, it needed to be his choice. Not a result of my actions. On top of that, I couldn't have wild dreams coming to life and throwing everything even further out of balance. I had to do this—now, with Cyrus.

It made my jaw clench, but I took a breath and backed down. "I thought I was having a normal dream. A desert, with a storm coming. I joined the storm, like I would while awake. Most of the bedroom got covered in sand, and the storm drenched the bed. Desert sand and water. Not local, not something I pulled in from outside. It...felt different."

I didn't know how to explain the elemental sense of things, the subtle difference in taste and texture to everything from soil composition to the wind itself.

"So Omar did teach you restraint," Cyrus said.

That sent my temper right up again, given Omar had unsubtly called me a bully. Enough that Bás looked up with baleful eyes. "Are you trying to be the most difficult fucking person to work with, or is that just another talent?"

Cyrus's grin threw me off. "Bit of both. If I'm going to train you in a djinn talent, I have to know what I'm working with." He sobered, flipping to grim in a mercurial flash of moods that could have confused even Noah. "Especially given we're going to need Troy for this. I'm assuming you can pull him into your dreams with this" —he waved his hand in the general direction of my head— "Aetheric bond you two have."

"Yes. It certainly seems that way." I glared. "And it was a combination of Callista and your son who taught me restraint. He's very good with me."

From Cyrus's small flinch, that slap landed.

I wanted to feel victory. All I felt was gross and sick at what I'd allowed myself to say in my irritation and my frustration with him. "I'm sorry. I shouldn't needle you with him."

"Again, a queen apologizing." At my flat stare, he raised a hand. "Accepted. I honestly don't know what to make of you, but...at the end of the day, I can't deny that you saved him when nobody else could have or would have. I have to believe that means you know his value. You won't throw him away like Keithia or a wife of her choosing would have."

"Never." I bristled at the thought of it. "He can leave me if he wants. I won't force him to stay with me. But I want him to stay. I love him, Cyrus, and I value him. If you believe nothing else about me, believe that. And believe that I understand the responsibility I have as his bondmate. Or, at the very least, that I'm trying."

For the first time, Cyrus's cold edge thawed. "You'd die for him."

"And live for him."

His brows flew up, like he heard exactly what I was saying. Hell, he probably understood better than most what it felt like to want to completely give up some days. In a lot of ways, living was harder than dying.

"That certainly does say something," he murmured. Sadness flickered in his expression for the smallest moment before he settled back into the usual wry amusement. "Well. Now that we've bared our souls to each other, where do we go from here? How do we make this work as teacher and student? Because Goddess save us all but you cannot continue creating Chaos spheres like that."

"You clearly don't want to acknowledge me as your queen," I grumbled, as much for the concession to Cyrus as for the realization that I'd started getting used to my pedestal among those elves who'd sided with me. Not good. "Let's start here: just call me Arden."

That got me a long look with narrowed eyes and another sniff. "You mean it. You don't like it, but you mean it."

I shrugged. "Troy needs space to figure out where he stands with you. If he's busy defending me, that pits him against you by default. I won't do that to him. I won't be another Keithia, at all but especially to him. He's fought enough battles, with more than enough to come."

In his baffled look, I finally found the satisfaction I'd been wanting. I could choose the better path. And I could enjoy the way it fucked with people.

Maybe I really did belong to the tricksters as well as the hunters.

From the sudden return of his grin, Cyrus seemed to come to the same conclusion. "I suppose you are one of us."

"We'll see."

"That's all I ask then. Keep him safe. Keep him alive. Not just in body but in spirit. There's a darkness in him, Arden. Beyond what most elves carry as beings of shadow." His gaze darted to my right hand—or rather, the ring on it. "Seeing the truth of things is another of my talents. He came too close to the edge at least once. I can see that. I just pray you have enough of Ninlil's light in you to bring him back when it's needed."

That explained Troy's truthreading ability. I wasn't about to tell Cyrus about the rough periods last year, when Troy had indeed sunk into somewhere dark as he worked to confront patterns ingrained by Keithia's abuse and understand his new situation as a king and valued bondmate. But it was good to know that my perception wasn't just me being a worried fiancée.

"I'll keep him safe and alive. You do the same for us both and teach me Dreamwalking. No tricks. No fuckery." I took a step closer and got in his space. "Because Cyrus? If I die, Troy dies. That's not a threat. That's the nature of the Aetheric bond. You and me are both on the hook for his life with this. Even if you can trick your way out of your oath to my mother, there's no getting rid of me and saving him. Allegra and Iago have both tried to untangle the bond, and the one time it was severed was really fucking bad for us both. Then when I died at the Wild Hunt, he sank part of his aura into me to bring me back. Another severing could kill one or both of us, with no guarantee it'd be him who lived."

The blood drained from Cyrus's face again, and a savage part of me was sickeningly pleased. Nobody could figure him out, but for one reason or another, Troy was important to him. As son, as legacy, as a pawn, who knew. But the onyx ring was hot on my finger, and this was a truth I'd bet my life on.

"Understood," Cyrus said hoarsely.

"Great. Let's go inside and discuss a training plan."

We hadn't been talking long when the wards pinged. I looked out the window, straining to hear what'd tripped them. Engine. SUV. Troy's MDX came up the driveway too fast.

I sighed. "He's lucky Zanna spends most of her time at the bar these days. She'd curse his breakfast again for throwing gravel like that."

Cyrus's chuckle followed me as I rose and went to the door, opening it to lean against the frame.

Troy parked up and practically threw himself out of the car. His gaze lit on me immediately, flicking over me from head to toe.

"I'm fine," I called, hoping I'd preempt the more urgent questions. "Your dad and I have come to an understanding. He's gonna teach me Dreamwalking."

Didn't stop Troy from blowing past me and into the house like the storm I'd conjured in my dream.

"Where the hell have you been?" he snarled.

"Here and there." Cyrus leaned back in his chair and crossed his arms. "Your queen said I was a free man."

That pinned Troy between my authority as High Queen of the House and his own security concerns.

I squeezed his arm, giving Cyrus a tired look. "He went to see his patron."

That made the irritating man sit upright and give me a serious look in turn. "I didn't tell you that."

"No. But you knew we were having you watched. That's the only thing important enough to give away that you could slip our Watchers."

Consternation painted Cyrus's features. "That wasn't the Sight?"

Troy relaxed. "No, that was the deductive reasoning of a private investigator." He leaned down to kiss my cheek then went the rest of the way into the house. "So, you're going to teach Arden to Dreamwalk."

"Yes."

"What's in it for you?"

"I can't help my future daughter-in-law save the world?"

Troy looked sharply at his father. "So the tricksters are after another apocalypse?"

"Some gods are always after an apocalypse." Cyrus shrugged, like it truly didn't matter. "I would like to keep living, now that I've gotten my freedom back and you with it. But the gods are...the gods."

"I'm going to ask you one more time," Troy said. "You answer me directly, or you won't be doing this. What's in it for you?"

Cyrus sighed and looked away, hedging for a few moments before bringing his gaze back to his son's. "You're my only child, Troy. I help her to honor my oath, yes. But helping her in this keeps you alive. It's a wonder she hasn't trapped you both in a Chaos sphere, from what Ninlil said once."

I bit back a comment when something in the bond wrenched, and I couldn't help a questioning look at Troy.

"I always wondered," he said. "If..."

Cyrus shook his head. "No. The queens haven't denied you any other siblings by me."

The bond gave me Troy's wave of confused relief and sadness before he boxed it away.

He turned to me. "How do you feel about this?"

"I can't ask Duke. Or Iaret or any of the djinn." I glanced at Cyrus. "He had a book of my mom's. Oh hey, don't you read Latin?"

Troy nodded, and I handed him the book. He didn't seem anywhere near as bothered as I'd been by the human leather as he took it and flipped through the back of it.

"Goddess." He looked at his father. "Is this real?"

Cyrus flashed his eyebrows. "You see why I'm here."

Being ignorant stung again. "What?"

"Apparently, we got lucky last night," Troy said. "According to your mother, it's as easy to take people from the real into a dream as it is to bring elements from a dream into the real."

I went cold as my stomach clenched. "I could have trapped you there."

"You wouldn't."

"I wouldn't *mean* to!"

Cyrus sipped the coffee I'd made for him, his expression closed and hard. "Which is exactly why we're starting today. I don't know why you two insist on keeping human hours, but I'll deal with it."

Troy was already shaking his head. "We need to attend to House business today."

I sighed when Cyrus shifted to look at me and tilted his head, already annoyed at being caught between father and son. "How long will it take to do a crash course in Chaos spheres?"

"How quick a learner are you?" Cyrus countered.

Troy crossed his arms and gave me the distant, evaluating look of a trainer. "She's quicker than most to pick up new concepts in hand-to-hand combat. Anything magical is fast and hard when it's the deep end. Usually painful as well. Raw power is her strength. Control needs work."

I bit back a sour *gee thanks,* untwisted the reflexive grimace on my face, and settled into the parade rest that would signal to both elves that I was ready to take a subordinate role and be trained.

Cyrus arched an eyebrow at that, like he didn't believe me, but kept quiet for once.

"Excuse us for a minute, Dad." Troy steered me to the back door with a hand at the small of my back, where we could step outside and be out of his father's hearing range but keep an eye on him through the sliding glass door. The last thing we needed was for him to wander the house like Troy had on his first few visits as a Darkwatch agent and find the interesting goodies I kept in my closet. It made me want to tie Cyrus down with Air, but he'd been a prisoner for twenty years. I didn't think he'd take even another five minutes very well.

"He reads lips," I said when the door was shut.

I know. Troy turned me to face the woods and half turned toward me. *Give the djinn the archives.*

You're serious?

"Yes. I cannot afford to lose either party on this," he said in a low voice, lips unmoving.

Is it the weres?

It's the possibility of losing magic. If balance is the price of keeping it, I have to do everything in my power to pay it. Losing elven dominance in Otherside is unacceptable.

This was the first time he'd full-on insisted that the elves retain their status, and it clashed with what I'd told Sonia in Richmond—that some folks were gonna have to give up some of their power. That might make a mess out of the need I had to restore balance. I wanted to ask who was pressuring him, but he was almost as stubborn as me. Nobody really pressured him anymore, not with Keithia gone, so it was probably just his sense of duty to his faction.

That didn't sit well with me, but now wasn't the time to argue it. "Fine. Go distract your dad. I'll make the call."

As Troy went inside, I held my callstone and connected with Duke.

"What now? I'm busy negotiating your outrageous demands." Despite the tiredness in his tone, Duke chuckled, rich and deep, when I told him the elven archives were on the table. "Shit just got interesting, little bird. How lovely of you to make today worth my while."

"Just get it done," I said. "I want a positive outcome by sunset tomorrow. I gave permission for Terrence to turn a mundane, and that means I'm gonna have to deal with the wolves again sooner or later. Maybe Maria as well."

This time, he outright cackled. "I'm going to pat myself on the back for instilling the virtues of chaos in you, my dear. Lovely. What a splendid time to be rejoining the earthly plane."

If it was anyone else, I'd think they were being sarcastic, but the djinn always saw opportunity—and amusement—in chaotic situations.

"Fantastic," I said. "If it brings the Council around, use it. I need balance, Duke. Now. The djinn and the elves are one of the biggest sources of *im*balance."

"Oh, I certainly will use it. To prove my influence as your advisor, if nothing else."

I spluttered. He'd had nothing to do with it.

"Politics and that," he said. "Speak soon, little bird."

The connection broke.

After a few calming breaths, I went back in the house.

Cyrus eyed me. "How's Duke?"

"Just peachy," I muttered. "Are we good now?"

Troy scrubbed his hands over his face. "I don't like this."

I held up a hand to stop whatever quip Cyrus had on the tip of his tongue, from the sparkle in his eyes. "I don't love it either. The timing sucks. But—"

"Yeah. We talked about it," Troy said. "Fine. Dad, I need to make a few calls. I assume there are basics to run through? Safety protocols?"

Cyrus nodded. "Go take care of your business. Your queen will be safe with me."

The look Troy gave him then was not friendly. "She'd damn well better be."

"One last thing." Cyrus looked between Troy and me more seriously than he had up to now. "You're sure you want to learn this together? Some of it will take you deep into each other's psyches. We're not really meant to know that much about each other."

He had a point, but I didn't have options. "Who else can I trust?"

Cyrus grinned. "Nobody. Not even me. Because frankly I would love to see my boy free of all queens." He raised his hand as I stiffened. "Our agreement and my oath to your mother notwithstanding."

"Dad—"

"Don't worry, boy. I told you, I won't hurt her. Oaths aside, she's explained the nature of your Aetheric bond, and I won't lose you. Not again." The fire that sparked behind Cyrus's eyes showed a hint of what his plan might have been without that bond: Troy as High King, no queens in the picture. "Besides, it'll be a grand trick to have a Dreamwalking elemental. The djinn will shit themselves. My patron's delighted."

The knife in his smile made me shiver in spite of myself, and I asked myself again who and what exactly we'd freed when we'd agreed to the deal that'd brought Cyrus Veisi out of exile.

Chapter 6

Despite the djinn's training, it turned out there was a whole lot I didn't know about dreaming. Or maybe worse, there was a whole lot I'd have to unlearn.

"They told you to do what?" Cyrus said. The intensity of his grey gaze pinned me to my chair.

"Step out of the dream. Just leave it."

"Of all the irresponsible—first lesson, don't do that."

I frowned. "Why?"

"Because if you really are creating Chaos spheres, you're crafting a magical entity that is then left to do whatever it wants in the Veil."

"Whatever it wants. How? It's not real."

"Wrong. Dreams are as real as the real is, especially in the hands of a trained Dreamwalker. That's why the Chaos spheres are so dangerous. If you pull Troy in too much, you'll kill him with a nightmare."

"Then why would Duke and Grimm—"

"Grimm would steer you wrong purely because she is an outrageous bitch."

I couldn't help my flash of surprise. Cyrus had commented on my "letting" Troy talk like that before. At the same time, I couldn't disagree. Cousin or not, she'd tried to kill me out of spite and hatred.

Cyrus held up a hand in an absent apology for his language. "Where is she, by the way?"

"Troy killed her, about two years ago now." He didn't need to know she'd been trying to kill me.

That got a savage grin. "Good boy. Now, back on topic. Duke, for all his charming personality, is still a djinni. And the djinn do not like Dreamwalkers, even when they're other djinn."

"I gathered that. Why?"

He shrugged. "Who knows why the djinn do or don't like anything? I'd think they'd want more chaos in the world. Maybe it's that this is Chaos magic controlled by an individual, rather than random effects that anyone can benefit from."

Made sense.

"How often does he pop over here?" Cyrus asked.

I grimaced. "Not often, but he can and does with the blood tie."

"Not much we can do about that, but it will be a problem. I assume you're keeping him busy?"

"Yeah. Busy enough."

Cyrus held out a hand. "Callstone."

"What? No." I gripped it. Before Cyrus had given me the book, it was the only djinn thing I had—my one tie to my mother and her vision for what the world could be. Or at least, what I'd understood of her vision. Apparently uniting the elven Houses with the djinn had only been step one in a larger plan, assuming I believed Cyrus. Which I didn't. Not entirely.

"You can't wear it while we practice. It's too easy for djinn to join us, whether as eavesdroppers or as accidental guests. Most djinn don't have the strength or capability to manipulate Chaos, but your mother managed it once to my knowledge, which means others might as well. Take it off."

"How the hell would she do that? Chaos comes from blending both halves of Aether."

Cyrus gave me a look like he was seriously regretting offering to teach me anything. "Ninlil was old. Older than Atlantis and much older than Duke or Grimm. There was a great deal that she knew how to do or had trinkets to help her do. All of it lost when Keithia killed her. Now. Take off the callstone."

Glaring, I slowly did as he said, feeling the sting of the knowledge lost with my mother. Rather than give the stone to him though, I went to the bookcase next to the fireplace and put it in the lead-lined box I had tucked behind some of the books. It nestled alongside my other djinn-related items: the cuneiform-etched bone, the iron railroad spike I'd found, and a few gems that could be used for divination. Duke would be suspicious if he turned his attention my way and couldn't reach me, especially after I'd been so insistent lately that I be able to reach *him*, but he'd also been very clear about the djinn position on Dreamwalkers.

I held in a sigh, praying that I wasn't about to ruin my relationship with the djinn the way I had with the elementals. Why was it that the more I stepped into who I really, truly was, the more it pissed people off?

Not the time or place for that. I returned to the table.

"Now what?" I couldn't help the grumble of my tone.

To my surprise, Cyrus didn't take the opportunity to needle me for it. "Arden, I need to know that you're not going to balk when I tell you to do something."

I narrowed my eyes at him. Nobody told me what to do. Not anymore. And I'd be damned if I let someone who actively had an agenda that didn't serve mine get me to just follow orders. I saw where that'd gotten Troy.

"You don't understand the dangers yet," Cyrus said.

His solemn tone almost scared me. But Troy was a good actor, and Cyrus had to be better to have stayed with his wife and hidden as an Ebon Guardsman in Keithia's court as long as he had. He could probably make himself look or sound any way he wanted.

He rose abruptly. "Fine. If you can't trust me this far, we can't do this."

I almost let him leave. Almost. Troy could read Latin. He could translate the book for me.

As though he'd read that thought, Cyrus leaned on the table and said, "Yes, Troy can read the book for you. But if he knew how to manage a dream—how to wake you properly—you wouldn't have had the desert in your bedroom. The book could tell him. But from what I've seen, he takes more strongly after the Monteagues than the Veisis. He might manage it. He might get both of you killed. *You* might get both of you killed." His expression softened. "Let me protect my son."

"From me."

Troy had been taken because of me. Tortured nearly to death. So many of the hurts he'd taken in the last two years were because of me, and a lot of the stress he carried had me as a source. My heart sank, and my stomach twisted.

What's wrong? Troy sent from outside.

Nothing. It's fine. Some hard truths.

Do you need me?

No. Thanks, cariñomí.

Suspicion coated the bond in a heavy layer of prickly ooze, but he refocused on his calls.

"You're not the only one who needs to make amends for the harm done to him," Cyrus said. "Let me do this. I couldn't be there to protect him from Keithia. But this, I can do. Besides, why would Ninlil have left the book with me if she didn't intend for me to teach you?"

I didn't know that she'd left the book with him at all. For all I knew, this visit to his patron had included a detour to some stash or other.

Whatever the case, I couldn't risk hurting Troy. Not again. And if this talent, or even just the threat of it, would give me an edge in forcing Otherside to get its shit together and unify, it would be a tool that wouldn't require bloodshed or death. I hoped.

It had to be enough.

"Okay," I said.

"Okay what?"

"I'll do as you ask." I gave him a steady look. "As long as the Sight doesn't nudge me in another direction."

He stared at me. If I didn't know any better, I'd have thought there was frustration there. For what, I didn't know, but I didn't back down.

"Agreed," he said.

For the next hour, he talked me through how to dispel a dream. It was all theory until I had a chance to actually do it, but at least it was something. Cyrus refused to teach me how to do anything else until I could do this correctly at a bare minimum. But it was Aetheric metaphysics for djinn magic explained by an elf. Some of it made no sense whatsoever to me.

To his credit, he tried a few different metaphors until one clicked.

"Try this," he said. "What do you do when you want to split a breeze?"

"Oh! I just...find the seam. In the flow of the molecules."

"Okay. Think of the Veil as a breeze. You're going to want to detach it with Chaos then step to the edge—just outside it, not yet waking—and then split it like you would a breeze."

I mulled that over, trying to remember my sense of last night's dream and how I would have done that. Just as I thought I had it, my wards pinged.

Troy, I sent. *Visitors.*

He sent an acknowledging nudge back as my sense of him sped to the woods and around to the front of the house.

"We're about to be interrupted," I said to Cyrus.

"How— Oh. Your wards."

Viktoria's at the gate. Troy's sending a few moments later was grim. *Not happy. You want me to let her up?*

No. She can wait at the bar. I didn't need her or Cyrus being more in my business than they already were, and I was already irritated at Cyrus turning up unannounced today. I had boundaries, and I needed them respected. People didn't just get to turn up at my house and be mad.

Cyrus was studying me when I refocused. "You can talk to him. To Troy. Telepathically. Can't you?"

Somehow, I kept the wince off my face and managed to give him my version of Troy's blank hostility. I hadn't meant for him to know that. Bad enough that Harqil knew. Apparently, I wasn't as resistant to Cyrus's talent as I'd thought because I was usually much more careful than that.

He raised his hands, but another flicker of interest lit his eyes.

I steered us back to our conversation for the few minutes it took for Troy to come back up to the house. His grimly satisfied expression as he mounted the porch made me frown.

"Shit," I muttered. You could take the elf out of the Darkwatch, but you couldn't take the Darkwatch—or the fight—out of the elf.

"What?" Cyrus said.

Before I could answer, Troy slipped inside.

I leaned back to look at him upside down. "That pissed?"

His lips twisted in something that might have been a grin. "She's been needing to be taken down a peg." He leaned over to kiss my forehead before coming around the half wall to sit beside me. "And to be reminded I won't tolerate threats to my queen on my land."

Cyrus frowned. "King or not, don't get cocky. This isn't your land, son."

"Isn't it?" Troy gave him a steady look until his father dropped his eyes. To me, he said, "In any case, she'll be waiting. No promises on the state of the bar when you get there." This time the grin was more of a smirk.

I sighed.

He kissed my temple. "Sorry, cariñamí."

"Don't be. How long?"

"Give her twenty minutes." He wrinkled his nose. "Long enough to make the point that you're in charge. And let her get over the reminder that, here, I am too."

"Great. Have one of the Guard meet me there." I might not allow bodyguards beyond Troy and the gytrash at the house anymore, but I wasn't about to put Troy's patience to the test now.

Satisfaction and approval curled through the bond as he swiped out a text.

"Cyrus," I said. "I appreciate the lesson, but I need to deal with this situation. Are you free tomorrow?"

He shook his head—not negation but bemusement. "A queen asking rather than telling."

I just cocked an eyebrow at him. We'd been over this, and it was getting boring.

With a shrug, he rose. "Certainly. Not like I have much else to occupy myself with."

Somehow, I doubted that, but I kept the comment to myself. "Sunset?"

"I'll be here."

"You need a ride?"

"I'll get Brielle to bring me tomorrow, but a lift into Durham would be appreciated."

Troy rose as well. "I'll drop you off."

As soon as the two men were gone, I went for my callstone. It was quiet as it hung around my neck, which was a relief. Duke was still busy with the sweetener I'd offered. After another ten minutes, I headed for the bar.

When I got there, Pascale, a former Sequoyah fully adopted into House Solari, was waiting in her blue Honda HRV. Her blond hair was pulled back in its usual severe ponytail, blue eyes sharp and more on the surroundings than on me.

"Ma'am," she said seriously.

"Pascale. We've got at least one pissed-off werewolf to deal with this afternoon." I kept going for the door, and she fell in behind my left shoulder. "I'll handle her."

"Yes, ma'am."

That's why she was one of my new favorites on the Ebon Guard. No silly questions. She might be a high-blood elf, but like Thana Luna, she'd gotten over the elemental thing real fast if it meant the chance at safety and a family with an elf of her choosing.

It gave me hope that I might win over the Richmond and Charleston Houses for my new arrangement here in the Triangle.

All conversation stopped when we stepped inside. A few people toasted me with their drinks, and I nodded back. I rarely came in the front door, but I needed Vikki and everyone else to see I wasn't afraid of her, bodyguard or not.

I scanned the room and counted it lucky there was only one broken chair. Vikki glowered at the door—and at me—from over her pint in a corner booth. My brows lifted at the bruise around her throat, the clear imprint of a hand the size of Troy's. She must have tried to get out of the car, only for him to pin her in it. Pin her hard, given how fast weres healed. He probably would have killed a mundane.

Interesting. Outside of sparring, Troy only got physical when he had to these days and only enough to bruise or draw blood if it was absolutely necessary. The alternative was a spell, and he was smart enough to know Vikki would claim magical trespass, even if she'd trespassed on our land first.

In the name of making a point, I checked in with Zanna behind the bar first. "What's the damage aside from the chair?"

"A Modernist vampire with a sore head." She kept her attention on Vikki, looking like she was considering cursing the werewolf's beer. "If the vamp hadn't started it, she wouldn't be here."

"Got it. I'll talk to her."

"See that you do." She thunked a highball of soda water with lemon on the bar harder than was strictly necessary. "This is a *peaceful* establishment."

I snagged the glass, saluted her with it, and headed for my office. Pascale trailed me, taking up a post beside the door.

I wasn't waiting long before angry voices rose outside.

"If you don't get the fuck outta my way, elf—"

"You'll do absolutely nothing at all because you know better than to come at the Arbiter like that."

I put on my bitch face and opened the door to find Vikki bristling at the much taller Pascale.

"Vikki," I said in a softly dangerous tone. "You're not threatening my security, are you?"

"And so the fuck what if I am? Your *bondmate*—"

"Viktoria." When her attention stayed locked on Pascale and her hands stayed fisted, I dropped my shields.

She flinched as my power signature blew through the hallway.

Pascale stiffened, but she was more accustomed to it.

"Back. Off." I pressed power into the command with a hint of Chaos. Not enough to be magical trespass but more than enough to cow even an alpha werewolf. "I know what you're here about. We can speak civilly, or I can remind you how I came to be Arbiter. Your choice."

For a minute, I thought she was gonna make me remind her.

Then, with a low growl, she stepped back from Pascale, crossed her arms, and cocked a hip. Still far too much attitude, but she was a werewolf. Attitude carried the day and saved face. Better that than a fight with me that she couldn't win.

I let her compose herself a few moments more before saying, "Thank you, Pascale. Vikki, step into my office. Sit down. And shut the hell up."

I hated being the bitch with people I normally considered friends. But I couldn't be Arden today. I had to be the Arbiter. And if Vikki was here like this, her brothers were going to be even worse when they got wind of everything going on in the Triangle.

Chapter 7

I sat behind my desk and waited for Vikki to take a seat on the other side.

Of course, she wasn't inclined to listen to orders. She stormed in and tried to slam the door behind her.

I caught it with a chord of Air and shut it quietly but firmly. "I know you did not just come in here like that."

The glow of my eyes did as much to give her pause as the unexpected lack of a dramatic bang from the door. "It's not—"

"I said sit down and shut the hell up."

She started to speak again.

I lifted my eyebrows and drew harder on Air, spiking my power signature another notch.

Her face flushed a deep red, and she flipped her long, brown ponytail. But she sat, mouth closed.

"The next time you come to my bar, I expect you to comport yourself with the dignity befitting a wereclan alpha. Not this spoilt brat shit. You'll send your apologies to Maria for the injury to her vassal. And if you haven't already apologized to Zanna for disturbing the peace, you'll do that too. Humbly, Viktoria."

The flush deepened until it was almost purple. "May I speak, Arbiter?"

I gave her a hard stare even as I ignored the clench in my stomach. I hated when my friends put me in this situation. But everything in the Triangle territory and two demesnes relied on my maintaining control over the unusual mixed-faction power-sharing agreement here. Otherside as a whole required me to find the proper balance. I wouldn't be Callista, but I still had to be in charge.

When the silence had stretched long enough for her to start fidgeting, I nodded. "Speak. Civilly."

"You allowed Terrence to turn a mundane."

Normally I didn't answer statements, but I'd make an exception now. "I did."

"That's not fair."

"Maybe not. But it's justice."

She frowned, clearly not expecting that answer. "I'm not here about justice, I'm here about—"

"You want the same thing Acacia Thorn has been permitted. You're not gonna get it. And before you even think about running to tell Maria or the Farkas pack, let me just assure you in the strongest terms that'd be a very damn bad idea."

Vikki's expression twisted to bitter rage, and the heavy scent of musk and cedar flooded the room. "You've always given them preferential treatment."

"You weren't around for what Terrence said about equity when we formed the alliance, so I'll give you the highlights. Some folks—some factions—are gonna be getting a little more than others to catch them up to the rest." I held back a comment that she should have understood that, given her little speech at my place when she, Terrence, and Ximena had hammered out the agreement that gave her sanctuary and land here. "Do you have a problem with that?"

"Yes! Red Dawn needs more wolves. Blood Moon is still a threat."

That was interesting, given the general lack of communication from Asheville. And clever as Vikki was politically, she should have known better than to give me that opening. This really had her thrown.

I arched an eyebrow at her. "Then woo some more of Blood Moon's wolves over when you go home. Or absorb the whole pack. Up to you."

"Excuse me? Home?"

"Yes. Home. You made an agreement with Terrence and Ximena, on my land, with me as witness in my capacity as Arbiter. The lands ceded to you in the name of Blood Moon were to be ceded back if your father was removed and you had the opportunity to claim ascendancy. It's been a year and a half since you got your aims."

She gaped at me. "But we're settled here."

It was all I could do not to scrub my hands over my face in frustration. "Settled or not, you made a binding agreement. Red Dawn needs to head back to Asheville and adhere to the promise you made to bring the clan into being."

"My brothers—"

"Submitted to Red Dawn as the alpha clan in the Blue Ridge Mountains. You're not in the mountains. You're here, in territory that rightfully belongs to the cats. Any problems that have developed in the time between then and now are of your making and for you to deal with."

She scowled. "I thought we were friends."

Now I wanted to shake her. "My friends don't put me in positions like this. They see that I need some fucking allies out west, and they jump at the chance to repay some of the help I so graciously offered them. And before you make this any more personal, Maria had to learn it the hard way as well. I'm not singling you out."

"Did you have Troy rough her up too?" she said, tone nasty. "Or did she get a pass for fucking his sister?"

"You turned up on our land unannounced with a bad attitude. You're lucky a little bruise is all you left with. He was within his rights, both as my bondmate and as a faction head defending his territory from another, and we both know it." I put more steel in my tone. "We also both know what Callista would have done."

Vikki blinked and paled, leaning back in her chair. "You wouldn't."

"I'd rather you didn't test me. For all our sakes. We need a strong werewolf clan as allies in the demesne. The *western* half of the demesne, holding that border. I'd rather it was you, but I'm Arbiter over the Dominion demesne now as well. It could as easily be the Farkas pack of Blood Moon if the Volkovs can't get their shit together."

Her political acumen snapped back to the fore. "I'm primary alpha. Ana already agreed. You can't use her family against mine."

"And you can't decide which agreements are convenient or beneficial for you to honor. Get your ass back to Asheville within the month so I don't have to handle this personally. I have too much to deal with right now, Vikki. If you make me settle this as Arbiter, I will do whatever ends it fastest whether you like it or not."

"So help me bring Sergei and Roman around."

I gave her a flat stare. From what the werecats had shared, Vikki hadn't even made the beginnings of an effort to deal with her brothers. And I'd be damned if I was gonna go to Asheville and give Roman any kind of opening with me just because Vikki wanted the easy way out.

"Come on, Arden."

That was the last straw. "No. I've tried to treat you like a friend, and you've taken advantage of it. Of me. That's not how friendship works." My expression tightened with all the disappointment stewing in me at yet another friend thinking proximity to power meant special privileges. I shook my head. "You're dealing with me as Arbiter now. So as Arbiter, here's my ruling: Get your shit sorted out with your brothers and uphold your deal with Acacia Thorn and Jade Tooth. You have until the full moon to deliver a plan and until the next new moon to execute it. Or I'm gonna have to arbitrate a bit more forcefully. And publicly."

The look she gave me then promised trouble. I'd need to let Etain and Omar know to have the Ebon Guard and the Darkwatch on alert for shenanigans. Vikki could be fun on a girl's night or when she was getting her way, but she had a nasty streak to accompany the Volkov entitlement. As with Maria, I'd let my desperate need for connection get ahead of my responsibilities as Arbiter.

"As the Arbiter orders, so do I obey," she said.

I ignored the growl under her tone, the one concession I'd offer, given Troy had already bruised her pride worse than her throat today. "Thank you. Was there anything else you wanted to discuss?"

"No, Arbiter."

"Great. Keep me posted. And don't forget those apologies to Zanna and Maria on your way out." I doubted she'd call Maria, but I'd deal with that if and when Maria complained. She might be glad to have a Modernist roughed up. The younger vampires were giving her hell lately.

Vikki left in a more subdued mood than she'd arrived. I still sent Terrence and Ximena a texted heads-up though. Eventually, Vikki would cool down and realize I hadn't picked now as the time to raise the wereclan territory issues for shits and giggles, and she'd probably try something with the cats. I hoped not. I hoped she'd remember the spirit she'd come to the Triangle in, looking to do the right thing by her people and theirs. But the last year and a half had been trying for all of us. We were running out of everything as more Othersiders flooded into the Triangle and had to be absorbed or managed by the local factions: territory, prey, good-paying jobs, even goodwill. Everyone was feeling pinched somehow, and it was gonna keep falling to me to deal with it. Getting the werewolves out of the Triangle and back west would help, but it was only one part of the solution.

I tried to remind myself that it all fell under the umbrella of being a protector. That was why I was taking on all this headache—to do everything I could to shelter all my people, whether they'd been here from the start or fled here from places even less friendly to Othersiders. It wasn't their fault ambitious faction heads made it hard sometimes.

With Vikki handled, I turned my thoughts to my other big territory problem: the other elementals. They were entitled to their feelings about me and the risks I was putting all of us in by consorting with elves and being open about my magic. But the conversation with Vikki reminded me that, as with Maria, I'd given them enough space when I'd stepped back from my duties last year. They were the only faction in the Triangle I was still allowing to outright avoid me. Even the damned fae king was speaking to me via Zanna.

It had to stop.

Just on principle, for one thing, but with what Harqil had confirmed about the possible disappearance of magic if I didn't get Otherside back in balance, we'd need them. As much as it stung to admit, I couldn't carry all of Otherside's magical needs alone. And if nothing else, I needed to warn them.

Sighing, I kicked to send my chair wheeling back and spun to unlock one of my file cabinets then withdrew a slim manilla folder. Last autumn, I'd gotten fed up with the Elemental Collective's hedging about meeting me and used my skills as a private investigator to track them down. I'd never used the information—it was a gross invasion of privacy for some very private people—but I was out of options, and it was within my rights as Arbiter to act.

My big question was who, if anyone, I could take with me when I showed up on the outskirts of Hillsborough. Troy was out of the question. An elven king and known Darkwatch agent would set everyone in a panic, which was exactly what I didn't want. I wasn't sure any of the half-elves would be any better. Duke and Iaret were busy with negotiations. I needed the gytrash on Cyrus. If he could slip the wards at my house, he could get inside and cause all manner of mischief. The witches were keeping themselves apart, dealing with the uptick in threats they always got whenever the mundanes kicked off against Otherside.

But if I was honest with myself, I was mostly trying to avoid having witnesses to whatever was gonna go down with the elementals. They were already ostracizing me. That meant they thought they had power over me.

As Arbiter, I couldn't allow it. Shit was gonna have to come to a head one way or another.

Alone. I had to go alone.

I called Troy.

"I'm not apologizing for Vikki's throat," he said when he answered. "She started shifting and moved to get out of the car when I told her to go home."

"Not what I was calling about."

"It's not?"

"No." I snorted. "I told her she was lucky that was all she got and that she needs to get the hell back to Asheville to honor her agreement with Terrence and Ximena. If she was doing all that, she earned what you gave her."

Even at this distance, a little knot of worry unraveled in the bond. "Oh. Thanks, my love."

"Thank *you* for defending my boundaries and our land."

This time it was pleasure that curled through. Troy loved hearing it acknowledged as ours and loved getting praise for taking care of it and us. He stuck to business though. "What hare-brained thing are you about to run off and do that I'm not going to like?"

Of course he'd anticipated me. "I need to go talk to the Elemental Collective. Alone."

Silence dragged out on the line long enough to make me fidget almost as bad as Vikki had earlier. I needed to do this. I didn't need his permission, and I'd go either way. But I really didn't want to have to fight over it. Not when we needed to be a united front for the ongoing elf-djinn House negotiations.

"Okay."

"Huh?"

"Okay. I want to tell you to take someone. But that'll be counterproductive. It'll piss off the elementals." He snorted. "And you'll feel like I'm punishing you for doing me the courtesy of calling."

"I mean…you're right. I just didn't think you'd see it that way."

"Nice to know we can still surprise each other."

That was delivered in a dry tone that said maybe it was, maybe it wasn't, but I knew to quit when I was ahead.

"I'll check in when I get there," I said, "and let you know when I'm home if you're not there when I get back."

"I won't be. I'm heading over to Chapel Hill. Charleston is stalling, and I need to play the monster."

"As long as you're only playing at it," I said softly.

"We need this deal, Arden. If I haven't done whatever it takes to try showing the tricksters that we'll bring things back into balance—"

"It still wouldn't be your fault that we lost magic. You don't get to own this when it's been centuries or millennia in the making."

"It's here now. I'm king. I have to own it."

I squeezed my eyes shut and took a breath as quietly as I could. From the clipped words and hard tone, he was going to be stubborn about this, and I didn't want to fight him over the phone. "All right. I'll keep you posted. Oh, and can you let your dad know we're not available for Dreamwalking training?"

"Of course."

"Thanks. Love you."

"Love you too. Stay safe."

I ended the call and shouted for Pascale to come in.

"My queen?"

"I need to go out to Hillsborough. Alone." I paused, waiting for the objection, but she just waited. "You know what's in Hillsborough."

"The Darkwatch was reasonably certain, yes. They just weren't enough of a threat to bother hunting down while we were dealing with other concerns." Her gaze dropped before meeting mine guiltily. "Unlike you, ma'am."

"That makes things easier then. I've already called Troy, so you won't have to explain this to him. I just need you to make sure I'm not followed."

The slight drop in the line of her shoulders telegraphed her relief at that, which made me less annoyed at feeling like I'd just asked my fiancé for permission. I was part of a team now. That was all. Teams needed to communicate. At least, that's what I told myself when these little things stung at my sense of independence.

Welp. Troy knew that about me, and he'd just given me enough rope to hang myself if I wasn't careful. As I headed out, I prayed I wasn't about to.

And as it had once before, ethereal laughter echoed in my wake.

Chapter 8

I didn't go straight to Hillsborough. That would have been faster, both timewise and logistically, but Val had been a good enough friend to me over the last couple of years that I felt like I owed her a heads-up. I had a feeling she'd been ordered to keep tabs on me, and my turning up in Hillsborough unannounced might get her in trouble.

Her expression when she answered the door of her modest ranch and found me on the doorstep would have been hilarious if the situation wasn't as serious as it was.

"You've got to be shitting me. You can't be here," she said. Quiet enough that the words wouldn't carry to the neighbors but firm all the same. Firm enough to put my back up.

"I think you'll find I can be wherever the hell I damn well please in my own territory." My voice was equally as quiet and a great deal harder.

That caught her off guard. "Arden—"

"Arbiter." As tired as I was of correcting friends, it came out more sharply than I'd intended.

Val stiffened. "Arbiter. With all due respect, if you've led—"

"Guess you better let me come inside then. Or get in the car so we can continue on to Hillsborough. Your choice. As a friend."

Friend or not, the look I got wasn't friendly. I gave her the same bland face Troy gave me when I was being difficult.

"Fuck," she muttered. "Lemme grab my shit."

"Don't call ahead."

With a tight-lipped nod, she stepped back long enough to grab her phone and purse before coming out and angling for her car.

"I'm driving," I said. "We need to talk."

A hesitation then another silent nod.

Fine.

She said nothing as we hit the road, just kept staring out the window. I bit my tongue until her temper snapped.

"What the hell is this? What is so damn important that you decided to risk blowing my cover? Somebody has to be following you. Following *us* now."

A deer stuck her nose out from the trees lining 85, and I sent her—and the small herd waiting to follow her lead—back into the safety of the forest with a nudge of Chaos. Sunset was a dangerous time for them to be trying to cross a west-bound freeway.

"Arden?" Val pushed.

"The Ebon Guard is taking care of any tails I didn't shake. The tricksters are why it's important."

"What about them? Wait, are the gods fucking with you again?"

"Something like that."

"Like what? What is this mysterious hard-ass shit?"

"If I can't do as they've asked, Otherside is going to lose magic."

Shocked silence met me before the explosion. "What? Why wasn't this brought up in a parliament meeting?"

I took my eyes off the shadowed road long enough to glare at her. "I just learned it. And it's hard to tell people something when they won't even speak to you."

As quickly as she'd flared up, she deflated. "I wanted to take your calls. Grandad said I'd be cast out if I kept associating with you after the press conference though. I have to protect Sofi."

I gripped the steering wheel and stewed. Val was my friend, but her sister always came first. Understandably, of course, but when combined with the rest of the elementals trying to treat me like I was just some wayward child, we got this mess.

"Look, I'm sorry," she said. "I just don't have much else. Not since my parents passed."

I didn't know what to say to that, so I didn't address it. "There's more. All of Otherside will lose magic. Except us."

"Huh? 'Us' who? The elementals?"

I nodded.

"Why?"

"Because of the nature of our magic. A magical loophole that either makes us the saviors or the ultimate threats in this game."

By the time we reached the small, unincorporated town outside Hillsborough, I'd managed to fill her in on everything: the tricksters, my plans for the local Houses, the promises I was demanding from all of the incoming elves to protect the elementals like the Ebon Guard did.

She sat in shocked silence, jumping when I pulled up to her grandfather's house. Then she glared at me when she realized where we were. "You investigated me? Investigated us?"

"Just independently ensuring my information matched what the Darkwatch had."

"Fuck," she whispered. Then she turned to me. "Troy wasn't just being an ass then, when he said the Darkwatch already knew where we were. We really can't keep hiding."

"He's a good liar when he wants to be, but he knows better than to lie to you. Even back then, he did." That felt like over explaining, but I needed the tenuous trust between Troy and my elemental friends to hold now more than ever. "I gave Terrence permission to turn a human by bite. The mundanes know about my abilities with the weather. And frankly, Val, I'm sick of being punished by my own faction when I've done everything possible to keep the focus on me as a one-off freak of nature. Otherside is going to need us soon—all of us elementals—and I am fucking sick of taking every crisis on my shoulders. Y'all can help me for once."

Embarrassed by my outburst, I moved to get out of the car. Resentment and anger boiled in me, and this time I couldn't push it back down.

Val grabbed my arm. "I'm sorry."

I pulled free. I'd had enough sorries lately. I didn't need more. I needed support, and I was tired of waiting for it to be offered. "Let's just get this conversation with the Collective done before Troy feels the need to come looking for me."

Speaking of...I swiped out a quick message confirming my safe arrival.

Val's agitation heated the air enough to shift it in a small eddy as we approached the door. She knocked on the door in a pattern I committed to memory, just in case.

Swift footsteps approached. I was shielding too hard to read the telltale signs of a functioning organic body, but I could tell from the sound—the timbre, the step length and heaviness—that it was a shorter person. Hardwood floor, rug in front of the door. The porch light flicked on, but I stood to the side where it'd be hard to see me from either the peephole or the front window unless we'd been seen coming.

The door swung open.

"Val?" Older. Masculine. Probably the grandfather. "Whose car—"

I stepped to stand beside Val. "Hi, Mr. Pérez. I decided it was time we talked."

Val's grandfather, a white-haired man with light brown skin and green eyes, paled then flushed as his hand moved.

Even as Val flinched, I pulled on Air to catch his hand and stop the slap before it could land on her cheek. "None of that. She was following your orders. I already knew where you were and made her come out with me. And if y'all'd had the sense to meet with me sooner, it wouldn't have come to this." I forced a smile. "Now, invite me in so I don't have to do something drastic. Because I'm damn tired of all of this."

From the taut hatred heating Pérez's gaze, he was thinking real hard about doing something to force that drastic measure. Fortunately for everyone in the area, he nodded. "Won't you come in, Arbiter?"

I released him and preceded Val in. I'd had to drop my shields to use Air, so I scanned the house quickly, finding it otherwise empty, before heading to the parlor and making myself comfortable.

The hatred flickered to awe at my casual use of elemental magic but snapped right back when he saw me watching.

Still, he gave the formal greeting. "Be welcome in my home. My table is yours, my hearth is yours, and my roof is yours, while you are here."

I gave the formal reply and then kept going before he could get a word in. "This bullshit with the Collective effectively ostracizing me ends tonight."

"Just on your say-so," Pérez said. "*We* are the Collective."

I arched an eyebrow. "*I* am the Arbiter."

"You're a disaster."

Val's gasp made me wonder if she was shocked at the rudeness or if they'd been saying things about me that should have made it dangerous for him to say that.

I pushed down the roil of anger and sought the cold tones Troy would use. "Okay. I'll bite. Why am I a disaster?"

Pérez stared at me.

"Well, don't let your courage fail you now. I came all the way out here when I have much bigger issues to give y'all your say. Say it, and then we'll get to the important bits."

"Our concerns aren't important enough to you, Arbiter?"

"On the contrary. They've been so important that the Collective is the only governing body I haven't steamrolled one way or another in getting the Triangle under my protection."

"Protection," Pérez spat. "You call admitting your powers to the world in a mundane press conference protecting elementals? When the elven bounties are still active? When more elves are coming to the territory every day and I have to spend my waking minutes wondering if one of them will find my granddaughters?"

"I call it protection when I'm forcing the djinn and the elves to unite in a new House system, potentially creating new trueborn elementals to strengthen us and grow our numbers," I said. He tried to break in with an objection, and I spoke over him. "And when the trickster gods are going to strip magic from everyone except us if I don't manage to wrench Otherside and the mundanes, and all of us and the planet, back into balance as soon as possible. Starting with the demesnes I control, of course."

That finally shut him up. He stared with a blank expression I assumed was shock.

Then he said, "Val, go gather the rest of the Collective." She left, and his gaze would have skewered me if it was physical. "If this is true, all of us are both at great risk and have great opportunity."

I flashed my eyebrows. Good to see that at least he was intelligent, even if he was hateful. That, I didn't get.

"What did I do to you?" The question jumped from me before I could really think about it.

"You drew attention to my girls. Now Sofia is permanently maimed. Putting the faction and our community at risk is bad enough. But you had to get the people I love most hurt. Both my girls and Laurel were traumatized by what they went through." His lip curled. "That's if your taking up with an elf—a Monteague, no less—wasn't enough."

Despite the flash of guilt over the harms Val, Sofia, and Laurel had taken from the lich and the outrage at his judgment of my relationship with Troy, I almost liked the old man. Unlike so many of the other people around me, he didn't mince words or play games.

"I can respect that," I said. "I don't like it and I don't particularly like you, but I can respect where you're coming from."

From the confused anger on his face, I could guess why Val had gasped earlier.

His fists clenched, and he drew himself up. "I won't bow and scrape to you."

"Not many people do. I'll settle for you not being an asshole when I have multiple crises on my hands, some of which do need greater elemental involvement."

"We'll see what the rest of the Collective elders say," he said.

Nope. Wasn't letting that one fly, Val's grandfather and elemental elder or not. "Regardless of what they say, you don't get to block and avoid me for two straight years and then get mad when you're not included beyond whatever meetings y'all allow Val or Laurel to attend. Elders and their wisdom will always have their place. But respect is earned. Involvement is earned. And people can't know what they haven't been told." I shook my head and let disgust curl my lip. "You have to know I was raised by Callista. I didn't even know other elementals existed until I ran into Val. You don't get to blame me for that. Not when I've been trying this hard. Effort is a two-way street, and being an elder doesn't make it a one-way just for you."

Pérez glowered. "You wouldn't have dared speak like this to Callista."

The snort that ripped from me was almost big enough to blow the house down. "I went to the gods' plane to stick a knife in her throat. Maybe don't try telling me what I would or wouldn't do about her. And maybe don't try setting yourself up as a superior power to me simply because I'm an elemental too." I finally let the nastiness spoiling inside me fully into my expression, and he quailed. "I've killed three elven queens and severed a fourth and her heir. I don't take well to challenges to my authority. Not anymore. I've had to learn the hard way too many times. By now, most of my friends have too."

A knock in a slightly different pattern came at the front door before it swung open to reveal a pair of white-haired women, one dark-skinned with a short cloud of curls and the other pale with straight locks hanging loosely to her waist.

"Benjamín," the lighter-skinned woman started. "What on earth do you have Valentina— Oh!"

I nodded to her politely but kept my seat as she noticed me. After two years of bullshit, I'd show respect when it was shown first.

The darker woman nodded slowly. "I thought it might be you, Arbiter." She turned to Pérez, and her tone sharpened. "And you, Ben. I told you she knew where we were."

"The Darkwatch does as well," I said lightly. "In case you were wondering. I didn't tell them. But they know. My bondmate has been keeping tabs on any elven movements this way to ensure y'all remain safe."

"Your bondmate," the lighter woman said flatly. "The Monteague prince."

"The Solari king now. But yes." I knew who they were from my investigation, but better to let them introduce themselves. Less threatening that way. "In any case, we have Benjamín Pérez and...?"

Both women exchanged looks first with each other then with Pérez. He shrugged.

The darker woman approached slowly, like I might bite her. "My name is Rose. It's an honor and a pleasure to make your acquaintance at last, Arbiter."

Given the dirty look she shot at Pérez as she said the latter bit, I guessed I might have an ally here. Rising, I shook her extended hand. A hint of dry heat danced along her aura and warmed her hand. A dea.

"Thank you, Rose," I said. "A pleasure to meet you as well."

That brought her chin up in a self-satisfied way, like I'd proven a point for her, and she sat down in the armchair next to me.

The other woman introduced herself as Tara, but she stayed where she was, next to Pérez. Fine by me. Made it easier to see who I needed to convince or, I thought with a mental wince, bully. I pushed Omar Monteague's admonishments aside and focused as more elderly elementals knocked and entered.

In the end, we had two from each element, as far as I could tell. Rose and a man named Samson were dea. Pérez and Tara were undines. Juliette and Roland were oreads, and Nathaniel and Olive were sylphs. Those last two surprised me. Air was the rarest type. Then again, these might have been the only two in the demesne for all I knew, now that I was a primordial and not a sylph myself. My investigative research had been limited to where they were, not which element they held.

After introductions and a few sips of mead, Pérez kicked us off by repeating what I'd said so far. He was fair in it, to my surprise, if a little more emotional than I'd expect from an elder. Those fears for Val and Sofi had to be riding closer to the surface with me sat in his parlor.

When he'd finished, he waved to me. "Tell us what you want, Arbiter. What's the ask?"

"I need to know the elementals will stand with me if the tricksters do take magic back," I said. "I may be a primordial, but I've been humbled before, trying to stand alone. And something like this?" I shook my head. "I can't do this alone."

"You can shift a weather pattern for a hundred-mile radius, but you can't handle this," Nathaniel said skeptically. "And you want us—wildborn elementals a great deal weaker than you—to...what? Help keep elves and vampires and weres in power?"

I shook my head, already kicking myself for not anticipating that and scrambling to get ahead of them. "No. Help me keep this territory safe from mundanes."

"When you drew their attention here in the first place," Tara said.

I did my best not to huff with frustration. "I mean, sure, if you want to blame the gods of the hunt looking this way on me. I didn't ask to be born here or at all. Nobody makes that choice for themselves. We just do what we can with it once we're here."

That got a few sage nods and a few mouths twisted in sourness.

"It's too dangerous," Roland declared. "Callista kidnapped and disappeared or killed half the elementals in the state looking for her. Then more left in fear, and a few of those were murdered by elven bounty hunters. No. We can't risk the gods or another celestial's rabid attention."

Probably best not to mention Harqil then. They weren't rabid, but I did have their attention.

"Callista's dead," I said as blandly as possible, trying not to be dramatic in a room full of people I needed to impress with my level-headedness. "I killed her myself. The East Coast Darkwatch answers to me now. The Ebon Guard is sworn to protect elementals ahead of all others and has been for millennia. And any new elves or djinn coming into the territory are required to swear to actively protect all elementals, not just obey me."

Olive frowned. "Why is this the first time we're hearing of this?"

From the corner, Val stirred, subsiding when Pérez gave her a sharp look.

"We all agreed it was safest for all of us if the Arbiter was kept apart, given her...connections," he said with a sneer. "We can't trust any of them. Not with our safety. Not with our lives or our children and grandchildren."

Rose scoffed. "*You* insisted on it and got enough of a majority to force the rest of us into unanimity. It's time to change course now, Ben. You talk about the grandchildren, but what our young people need is opportunities. Opportunities the Arbiter can offer them."

"Opportunities to die," Juliette said with dry bluntness.

"Everyone dies," Rose snapped. "Every*thing* dies. Fires burn down to embers and ash. Hurricanes blow out. Mountains crumble. Seas dry up into salt and dust. Do not act like it would be better for our people to go out in passive complicity with what the elves have done to us, rather than fighting and proving that we are owed a place in this world. This is our chance! Now, when a primordial lives among us!"

I liked Rose. A lot. But I needed to let them focus on themselves rather than continuing to use me as either a punching bag or a distraction.

"I need to be on my way," I said as I stood.

It took an effort to steel my tone, despite the sinking feeling in my heart. I don't know what I'd expected in coming here, but I'd hoped to impress upon them the need for unity.

I'd failed, and now it was time to figure out a Plan B.

"I've imposed on your hospitality long enough, and I need to let my bondmate know I'm safe. But I will return. I hope to have your support when I do, for the sake of all Otherside." I glanced pointedly at Val, still silent in the corner. She shook her head. I guessed she'd find her own ride home. "Y'all know where to find me and how to reach me."

Only Rose acknowledged me as I departed, a fierce, tight nod that told me she'd keep fighting for me after I left.

At least someone here would. After years of being kept apart from my own faction, it was almost enough to bring a tear to my eyes.

Chapter 9

As I pulled out of the driveway, Harqil manifested in the passenger seat.

I jumped and nearly swerved off the road. "Fuck's sake, I can't fulfill y'all's stupid mission if I drive off the road and die!"

They chuckled. "I'd say not to shoot the messenger, but I'm pretty sure you'd do it out of a combination of contrariness and pique."

"Don't tempt me."

"I'll get right to it then. Anansi sent me with a message."

This was only the second time they'd mentioned a trickster by name. It also implied Cyrus's patron wasn't Anansi—possibly not Laverna either—given Troy's dad seemed to be working toward entirely different goals to Harqil and that was the only other god Harqil had named.

"Stop trying to reason it out. The message is, 'The webs we weave draw ever tighter. Being trapped is being free.'"

I waited for more, but Harqil just watched the landscape fly by in the dark.

"Is that supposed to help?" I asked.

"It is what it is. Before I go, there's also a task for you."

"I'm a little busy for tasks."

"I want you to look into the Court of Nightmares for me," they said as though I hadn't answered. "Find someone on this plane who knows something about them."

"Are you kidding me? Iaret knows of them. Go ask her. What does this Court have to do with anything anyway? Can't it wait until—"

"Who, by the nine hells, do you think sent you that dream?"

A jolt ran through me. I didn't have to ask which dream they were talking about. The one that was more vision than dream, accompanied by freaky words that might be prophecy.

I forced myself to refocus. "Ask Iaret. Job done."

"If I ask, the wrong people will know I'm interested. Besides, it's not just asking her, it's acting on the information."

Something about this wasn't right. The Sight nudged me. "This isn't a task from the gods. This is a personal favor for you."

They grumbled something under their breath that sounded like, "Gods-damned prescients."

"You want me to interrupt what I'm doing to save magic in Otherside—my actual gods-given task—to track down information about some people I've heard of once and are, as far as I know, minding their business."

"If they're not minding their own business, you'll have more dreams like the other."

"And if they are, I'm inviting trouble from beings you think are powerful enough to hijack my dreams and set the leaders of every other Otherside faction running scared! No, Harqil. I'm sorry. I'm curious as hell, but I have more than enough on my plate right now."

With a sigh, they slumped in their seat. "I had to try."

Before I could answer, they disappeared.

"Fuck's sake," I muttered again. I had plenty enough to do as it was. I wasn't the main character in a damn video game, and I didn't take random-ass side quests. When I could help it anyway.

My phone rang. Troy's name popped up on the car's HUD, and I answered. "Hey, I'm just heading home."

"Good." His clipped, terse tone set me on edge.

"What? What happened?"

"Darkwatch intel. We're about to have trouble with the mundanes."

My stomach plummeted as the Sight flared. "If you say they're kicking off over our visit to the Senator—"

"It's Verve."

Nine flaming hells. "The test they were trying to push Doc Mike to use on the vamp victims?"

"Partly that. Possibly worse. I ordered Zadie and her team to hack them, and they found some files. Arden, they might have gotten their hands on some werewolf blood. If they have it, you know the Bureau for Supernatural Investigation is involved. Or will be soon."

"Goddess burn them. I do not have time for this."

"None of us do. I've got Keeya Bedoe in agreement for one of the Houses, but Charleston is still holding out."

"And I haven't heard anything from the djinn since offering Duke the archives."

"We need to push, Arden. If the mundanes make any more moves against us, Otherside will have to push back. That undermines everything we're doing with the new Houses and with Matthias in New York. We—you and me personally—need to show we have the mundanes under control. We'll look weak if we don't."

"And looking desperate doesn't?"

"Long game. We need to lock down as much as we can. Before we're forced into a worse position."

"Fine. I'll call Duke when I get home."

"ETA?"

"Fifteen minutes? Ish."

"See you soon." His tone softened. "Love you."

"Love you too."

The call ended, and I pressed down on the gas. It'd been another day where I'd been up way too long, doing way too much high-pressure work. Fog was creeping in at the edges of my mind. I'd be paying for this later. But if I didn't push now and shit hit the fan, I'd always wonder what might have happened.

Troy was pacing and snarling down the phone in elvish when I walked in, looking scary and forbidding and somehow completely hot in a black T-shirt that hugged his muscles and a pair of dark-wash jeans. He cut off as the shift in my scent hit him in the backwash of air from the door shutting, and some of the scary flashed to smoldering before he shook himself and returned to his call.

I took the excuse for a quick shower. As much as he turned me on, I was running on fumes. We could have fun in the morning, assuming everything didn't manage to go to shit in the few hours remaining until dawn.

Troy was still on the phone when I got out, so I went to sit on the couch. I needed to call Duke, but it could wait for a minute while I caught my metaphorical breath.

Gravity dragged at me. I was so damn tired. Too long a day. Too much going on.

My head hit the cushion.

According to Troy, I frequently did a thing where my body would sleep but not always my mind. Or at least not my subconscious. He couldn't quite explain it beyond saying I often "woke up twice."

I might finally have understood what he meant.

His call ended, and his presence neared. "Shit."

I stirred, trying to convince my body it was time to wake up again. We had work to do. Troy needed me to help with the negotiations.

"Shh," he said. "Stay down, my love."

I was lifted by the shoulders for a moment, and then Troy's lap was under me, warm and firm. Nice. I shifted, getting comfortable.

He pulled the blanket hanging off the arm of the couch over me. "That's right. All the way under. Sleep."

"No," I managed. Fear spiked. There was work to do...and if I went all the way to sleep, there might be dreams. If there were dreams, I could hurt him.

I couldn't risk hurting him. Cyrus had said—

"Yes. I didn't mean for you to run yourself ragged with the Verve news or the Houses." Troy's hand cupped the back of my skull, and the barest thread of Aether slipped through my mind. "It can wait. Sleep."

First went the small pains of the tension headache that'd started after Harqil's visit. Then went the fear. And then went me.

I opened my eyes on the gods' plane.

At least, I thought it was the gods' plane. It had the same old-old feeling as on my first and last visit, the towering ferns and the even taller trees. In the distance, the surf crashed, and the breeze brought the scent of salt, driftwood, and seaweed, blended with the rich, earthy scents of an ancient forest. If Troy hadn't been touching me when I'd fallen asleep, I'd think it was the Chaos sphere I apparently created whenever we were apart.

"Imagine seeing you here," a voice said from behind me. "And what's this? A lifeline?"

A thread tangled around me as I spun. That'd never happened before—but the mottled brown-green-gold color reminded me of Troy's eyes. Was this a link back to him? What the hell? And why was I dreaming of being on the gods' plane instead of the In-Between?

When I completed my turn, my gaze fell first on a tree, stretching so far above the others I couldn't see the top of it. A hiss brought my attention back down—to the biggest damn snake I'd ever seen, coiled atop a cloud of black wool set among the roots. A black zig-zag pattern danced along its back in a striking contrast to the burnished bronze scales covering the rest of it.

It watched me with red eyes, rising up taller than me to speak. "We had heard you had a Hunter. Seems he's a great deal more than that, if he can keep you anchored to your own plane while you Dreamwalk." The snake's jaw dropped to show long fangs. "What an excellent trick."

I scrambled to gather myself.

The tricksters were shapeshifters. This could be any one of them, but the vertically slitted eyes and wedge-shaped head said this form was venomous. I couldn't assume whoever this was meant me well.

"A talking snake is a good trick as well," I said. "May I ask who I have the honor of addressing?"

"You may ask, but I may not tell." Again, a hissing noise but rhythmic. Laughter? "Don't worry, girl. I won't hurt you. Yet. I have not decided which of the available options would be most entertaining. So far, you create enough chaos in everything you do that it's more interesting to watch than to set you a trick."

"I suppose stripping Otherside of magic would be entertaining for you." I couldn't help the bitterness in my tone. The hunters had been bad enough; they had shit they wanted to get done. An agenda. So far, the tricksters had been maddeningly difficult to deal with purely because everything about them was so indirect and they seemed to lack the hunters' unity.

"It would," the snake agreed. "But so would, say, giving magic to humans. We could do that, you know."

"I didn't know," I said breathily. That would be a disaster of epic proportions.

"Of course. And you in the middle, spinning like a top trying to fix it all." Again, the hissing laughter. "But no. For now, let's see how you do. Off you go."

Without warning, the snake struck at me, fangs bared.

I woke, jolting upright with a scream as Troy woke with a shout.

We stared at each other, me horrified at what had almost happened, him flooded with my fear and wrestling for self-control, sharp teeth out.

I wanted to holler at him. How could he be so foolish as to put me under with Aether?

But we couldn't have known. Neither of us. We'd done it before with no consequences.

"It was the gods' plane," I said when I'd caught my breath enough to speak. "Apparently them taking magic from Otherside isn't the only option."

"The gods' plane? I thought it was just the In-Between?"

"Not anymore. And Troy, there was a cable. Or an anchor. A metaphysical one. The god I met said it went back to you."

He stared at me and blinked his way past me meeting a god to get to the heart of the matter. "To me. From another plane."

"I don't fucking know how it works! It's Aetheric, we're bonded, your aura is blended with mine." I grimaced, remembering my original fear about falling asleep. "Your dad said I could hurt you. That dreams are as real as reality. Maybe...maybe just let me rest. No Aether. But you need to stay nearby."

Troy frowned at the mention of his father. "What happens if I don't?"

"A Chaos sphere, apparently. Like the one that dropped the desert into the bedroom, but you get pulled into it, in every way except your physical body. Enough that you could die. I'm sorry. I meant to tell you all this earlier, and then Vikki came and my whole afternoon went to shit." I pulled away—tried to anyway.

He caught me and pulled me back. "Don't you run from me. This isn't your fault."

"What if I hurt you though?" I shuddered, remembering him on the bedroom floor after I rescued him from Keithia, broken, bleeding, and half a breath from death. "I keep getting you hurt."

"No." He pulled again, dragging me into his lap and wrapping his arms around me. "And even if you did, I accept it. It's the price of power. More importantly, it's the price of being with you."

The imposter syndrome I'd been wrestling with roared to the fore.

"Don't you even think that you're not worth it," he snarled. "We've been over this. I might not be able to turn you upside down with Air, but I can sting the fuck out of your aura if you need a lesson."

I settled for hunching closer to him. If that was how he felt, all I could really do was be worthy of it. Every time I gave him a chance to leave, he dug his heels in and anchored himself a little deeper in my heart and soul.

And if I was honest with myself, I needed it.

The bond told Troy when I'd shut down my internal argument. He gave me another squeeze. "We're going to bed."

I tensed.

"I know you're scared to sleep. But, cariñamí, your exhaustion is making me exhausted. We have to try. No Aether this time, but we still have to try."

For him, I would.

Not just because I loved him. I'd need someone to bring me back if saving magic for Otherside took me over the edge, and I didn't trust that anyone else could do it.

Chapter 10

S omehow, I managed a dreamless sleep. Maybe exhaustion finally took me past the realm of dreaming. Maybe it was just that the gods were tired of messing with me for one night. In any case, I slept late the next day, waking around noon.

To my surprise, Troy was still asleep next to me. One of his hands curved over my hip, and from the way his head was pillowed on his arm, he'd fallen asleep watching me. I checked his pulse, concerned that something about the gods' plane had pulled vitality from me and I'd pulled it from him in turn. The last time I'd gone, I'd come back drained.

He jumped as my fingers brushed his neck, snarling to drop the sharp teeth before he realized it was just me.

"Sorry." He squeezed his eyes shut before rubbing the sleep from them and hiding his teeth again.

"Don't be. I was just scared that I'd—"

"I'm fine. What time is it?"

"'Bout noon."

"Damn it. I need to call Savannah."

"What's the problem? Will she even be up?"

"She's being a brat. Half again my age and acting like she's never had to compromise in all that time. Please tell me you're ready to use the Book of the Damned."

His frustration boiled through the bond, so I straddled his lap.

"Let her stew," I said impulsively. I needed this done, but I did not need more elves thinking they could walk all over me—or him. "We need to start as we mean to go on. If Keeya will play and Savannah won't, I'll offer the other House to the elementals. Save the blackmail for something worse. If we lose magic, worse will come soon enough."

Troy's hands bracketed my hips and pulled me tighter against him—mostly, I think, to show me he was physically happy for me to be there, even if we were both distracted by politics again this morning. "Will the Collective go for it?"

"One might." I filled him in on what I hadn't stayed awake long enough to tell him last night. "And if not them, then we can put out a call to whoever the next nearest demesne is."

He leaned back and frowned. "You'd be willing to let Charleston break away from the Carolinas?"

"I know it'd look bad, but I can't afford to make this about saving face. I never can. The priority is proving we can balance Otherside, at least on a small scale."

"And thereby proving that we're still worthy of magic." He sighed and frustration spiked again. "I knew this wasn't going to be easy. But with the gods involved, it starts to seem impossible."

It wasn't like him to be that pessimistic. Sure, he got grouchy as fuck and fell into moods related to personal matters when his demons got too loud, but he usually had more patience with political matters. This frustration might have just been a consequence of my exhaustion and stress draining him—maybe literally—but I was concerned all the same.

I couldn't soothe him with Aether the way he could me, but I could soothe him physically. Get some of the social hormones flowing that'd balance him out a bit.

I leaned forward to nibble his ear.

"Arden."

The growl of my name made me smile against his skin. I nipped harder.

His sharp inhale was accompanied by the pinch of his hands on my hips. "Goddess, Arden, we have…"

"Deals to make and a world to save. Again. And if you go calling Savannah while you're short tempered and grouchy, what do you think is gonna happen?"

Another growl rumbled. He was fixing to be stubborn.

I kissed his neck then his chin then his lips. "Taking ten minutes to ground yourself now might save you an hour or more of fighting and wanting to cut throats."

"I'm supposed to be reminding you of that."

"Yeah, well…we can take turns."

Troy's hips rolled. "You're making a compelling argument."

"May I take care of you then?"

He tipped his head back, like he was trying one last time to convince himself that politics and the House and the elves, all the day's needs, came before his own.

The taut cord of stress in the bond snapped. "Fuck it," he said. "Yes. Please. I'm drowning, Arden. Trying to keep all these damn plates spinning. I need…I don't know. Balance. A few minutes for myself in all this."

"I know the feeling." I kissed him again, long and deep, a reward for breaking out of his habit of putting the world and everyone in it before himself and for speaking up. "Thank you for telling me what you need."

His only response was to reach between us and work his briefs down.

I didn't make him wait. It was tempting—I'd found I liked when he got frustrated enough to take control—but it was my fault he was this drained and off-kilter. I needed to take responsibility and focus on him.

With quick kisses, I made my way down his body and took him into my mouth.

His immediate groan of pleasure was exactly what I'd been looking for. With all the extra pressure of the last few days, he needed this grounding.

I reached up and dragged my nails down his chest and abdomen, feeding him the extra little bit of pain that would spice his pleasure, before shifting to nibble the insides of his thighs while jacking him. When I shifted to wrap my mouth around him again, his breath hitched, and his groan had more of a growl to it this time. I used every little trick I could think of, dragging him closer to climax with a mixture of focused pleasure and light pain.

Troy tugged my head up. His eyes were unfocused as he said, "I'm close, and you haven't—"

"I know how close you are. Let me take care of you. You can give me mine later."

Guilty satisfaction flashed in the bond, and he guided me back onto him. He'd been trained to serve, not be served, so the minor taboo was another goad to his pleasure.

He set the pace and came hard. When he'd finished, I gave him a last few licks then rested my head on his thigh.

"Thank you," he said, voice gravelly.

"My pleasure, cariñomí." I wanted to tell him that we could take a few minutes to remind ourselves what all of this was for—so that we could live well together—but I didn't need to rub the point in. He knew. He'd just needed permission to focus on himself and experience it for a short while.

After another minute or two, he took a deep breath and blew it out. "I don't want to drag us back to business, but we've got maybe seven hours before this deadline."

"Back to work then." Despite the words, I shimmied back up and cuddled in beside him, resting my head on his chest. "What are your priorities?"

"Savannah. If she won't accede, then I reach out to contacts in upstate New York."

"And shore up the northern connection we established with Matthias?"

Troy grunted a yes.

"Good plan. If that falls through, I'll try again with the elementals."

"Fine. Either way, I'm getting Keeya set up tonight. Her terms were that she would be queen. I might be out late taking care of that. She came around first, so she gets her choice of the Sequoyah property at Jordan Lake, the Luna property near Morrisville, or waiting for the last touches on the rebuilt Monteague mansion in Chapel Hill."

That made me lift my head to look at him. "You're not—"

"No. I want nothing to do with it." He shuddered. "This is my home now. Solari can claim whichever of the three properties is left as a base of operations and living quarters for adoptees. But I want nothing to do with any of those places unless I have to."

"I guess I was afraid this place was a little small for you." I would have said a little down-market, but despite growing up royal, he'd never complained about the size of my house or the age of the fixtures and kept the snobbery he'd had when I'd met him restricted to the food we ate. That was always top quality, no exceptions.

Troy glanced at me. "It's just the two of us. For now."

"Yeah." We wouldn't be able to fit the usual two kids most elven families seemed to shoot for in my little one-bed house.

Then he surprised me. "Plenty of space on the land to put on a couple of additions. If we need to. And if you're okay with it."

"Oh." I hadn't even thought of that.

If I was honest, I'd kind of been dreading the family thing because I knew we'd need more space and had assumed that'd mean moving into something bigger, more opulent, and less...me. The reassurance that I could stay here as long as the land was mine and the house was standing eased something I hadn't realized had been squeezing me.

"Sorry," he said. "With all this House business, it's been on my mind. What happens next. How we make it work for both of us."

"It's fine. It's good, actually. Looking ahead to what comes next reminds us why we're doing all this." I kissed him and got up. "Speaking of what comes next though, I haven't heard from Terrence about how his new leap member is doing, so I'm gonna do my job today. Surprise inspection."

"Is my dad coming back for more Dreamwalking?"

I couldn't hide my grimace. "He probably should, given last night. I just don't know when I can fit in Dreamwalking lessons alongside dragging the djinn to the table, getting the elementals to see reason, and now dealing with Goddess-burning Verve Health."

"You know what Omar would say."

Annoyance flared, and I didn't bother trying to mask it from him. "Yes, he'd have me order somebody assassinated but somehow not be a bully about it."

Troy raised his hands. "Just saying. It's an option. We can send Alli."

Somehow, it hadn't ever occurred to me that my future sister-in-law was as much of an assassin and murderer as my fiancé. Allegra didn't have Troy's sometimes-grim bearing, especially now that she was with Maria. Half the time, I forgot she was Darkwatch at all, which I guess was part of what made her good at it.

Fortunately, Troy found whatever that thought did to my expression or the bond funny. He grinned and got out of bed, kissing my forehead on his way to the kitchen.

"We're not assassinating anyone, Othersider or mundane, until I have proof they've actually done something punishable by death," I snapped.

"Okay, my love. Just don't wait too long to be sure."

I glared at his back, mostly because his attitude and posture said as much as the bond that he was completely unruffled by everything about this conversation.

"You knew who I was when you saved me from Keithia," he said over his shoulder. "And what I was. The only thing that's changed is my title and having you to keep me level. Well, that and not being punished on a regular basis."

"Yeah." I sighed. At least he hadn't outright called me his leash. I hated when he saw himself as a monster that needed to be reined in by a stronger hand. "We just have very different approaches sometimes."

"That's why we'll win. One way or another."

The return to grounded equanimity was an improvement over his pessimistic outlook when we woke up, so I decided to let it go. After a quick shower and brushing my teeth, I snagged the to-go sausage biscuit breakfast Troy had waiting and left for Terrence's place.

On the drive over to the bar to swap cars, I mentally ran through everything else I hadn't heard about. Verve might be kicking off, but the Bureau for Supernatural Investigation had been silent aside from Sinclaire's visit, despite the stunt me and Troy pulled at Senator Wright's house. That couldn't be good. The Sons of Seth were still quiet too. A smile twisted my lips as I wondered how bad they were all panicking at not being able to find two dozen of their people. I'd hated using my magic like that, but I refused to be a victim. I refused to let people think they could come to my house and hunt me as easy meat.

Of course, the disappearances would mean something would shift in how the Sinners or the Sons dealt with Otherside. Maybe that was why we hadn't heard anything. I'd need to be ready for that, but the Ebon Guard was still interrogating the six Sons I'd left alive. Apparently ordering them to dig deep meant they were being extremely thorough. Troy had warned me there might not be much left of their minds when the elves were done with them. I wondered how much of their digging was retribution for threatening me or Troy, but I kept that to myself. I didn't really want to know the answer.

I shook my head and tried to find comfort in the wind blowing through the open windows to tug my curls under the cap I'd thrown on.

One thing at a time.

Maybe I should leave steering the mundanes to the Darkwatch or the Ebon Guard while I dealt with the gods. Samarre and her triad were still keeping an eye on the remaining Sons down in Raleigh. Troy would have said if the Richmond Houses had continued their interactions with the Sinners. Apparently, my example had stuck. Shame that it took severing from Aether for those Houses to take me seriously, but that'd been their choice, not mine. Or at least, it was their consequence to own.

With those tired and guilty thoughts in mind, I pulled my borrowed van into the parking area at Terrence's body shop. At mid-afternoon he might be working, or depending on the situation with Darnell, he might be home. But I didn't want to risk surprising a new wereleopard. If he had to be put down, I didn't want it to be because of my ignorance.

Ximena sauntered out of the shop's welcome area as I parked, head tilted. "Well, look who it is. I wondered how long it'd be till you came to check in on us." She leaned against the van's door and spoke in a low voice. "Terrence is at the house. I'm handling the shop for the next few days."

"Is everything okay?"

Her hesitation put me on alert. "Could be better. Being turned is rougher than being born. Puberty's a shitshow but..." She grimaced and shook her head. "Put it this way. Finding your cat when you've never had to look for one before, having a second aura develop and smother the only one you were born with rather than them growing and twining together over time—it's not something everyone takes to well. Not to mention we're out of practice with shepherding someone through their first change. You heard what Terrence said."

"No bites since his granddaddy's granddaddy's time." I leaned back against the headrest, hoping my pursuit of justice for the pride wasn't about to turn into administering justice instead.

"Yes, ma'am. We'll get him through it."

"But?"

Her gaze darted to me, flickering to the red-gold of her cat for a moment, like I wasn't supposed to have heard the "but" at the end of her statement. "Not so much a but as, we'll get him through it alive, whatever it takes. Even if that means driving Vikki out ourselves."

"Shit. What did she do?"

"Came round here last night. A little drunk. A lot mouthy. Calling us cowards for not addressing the territory issues with her directly and running behind her back to talk to you." Ximena shrugged. "My feeling is we shouldn'ta had to talk to her about it, let alone involve you. If she'd had the honor to keep her word, it woulda been a non-issue, but a drunk Volkov isn't much of one for sense."

"The Volkovs aren't much for sense even when they're sober," I snapped before I could manage something more political.

Ximena grinned. "See, there's a reason we like you. Anyhoo, we had a little tussle in the shop. I won. She went home tail tucked."

"Goddess burn it. That's two beatings in a day for her. She's gonna act a fool over it."

"Two beatings?"

"She came up to the house and made some poor choices. Troy set her straight. Violently. I judged him in the right of it when she came to the bar and got nasty. Which, of course, only made her nastier."

Ximena's whistle skipped with the laughter under it. "Well. Says something that she'd come here after and try picking a fight."

I rapped my fingers on the steering wheel. To me, it said Vikki was feeling like she needed a win and had come here thinking she could get it out of the numerically smaller and politically weaker werecat pride. That she'd been trounced again would only damage her ego further, maybe especially given she was technically in the wrong just maintaining a presence here instead of getting a plan together to head back to Asheville. On top of that, she'd done the opposite of what I'd wanted when I'd told her to apologize to Zanna and Maria for disturbing the peace—she'd come here and disturbed it further, for no damn good reason.

Putting all that together, the political savvy that'd gotten her, as a beta female werewolf, stationed here as a clan rep in the first place would be spinning on revenge of some sort. She might not be happy about her brothers right now, but she'd have no problem using them.

Ximena sniffed and tasted the air. "What's got you so grim, Arbiter?"

"Make sure you know where your people are and post up extra guards at Terrence's place. I got a Darkwatch report last night that the mundanes might have access to werewolf blood."

She hissed, lips lifting in a catlike snarl. "That better not mean what it sounds like it means."

"So far, I don't have any confirmation on what it means. We just know there's been a development with some test they wanted to run. The Darkwatch is still digging."

"May the gods burn them all."

"Yeah. Keep it within the pride for now until I can confirm it. But keep your people safe. And call on me if you need help. If they catch wind that there are more weres than just wolves, they might come looking."

"We'll be careful." She straightened. "Go on over and see Terrence. I'll just let him know you're on your way so you don't scare the cub."

Sounded like I'd made the right choice in not surprising them after all.

Chapter 11

Terrence was waiting for me in the grass out front, arms crossed and posture stiff, when I pulled up. "I appreciate you showing the good faith and better sense of not coming straight here," he said as soon as I was out of the van. "I can think of a few people who'd try to surprise us."

"I think I know of one of them. I'm surprised Vikki didn't come to the house last night."

His lips thinned, and his expression hinted at danger as he shook his head. "I think she would have, except that a newly turned were has none of the boundaries a born were would put on their second spirit's reactions and none of the control we develop over a lifetime. If she picked a fight with Darnell and he broke free and managed the shift, she'd have to kill him or die herself. She's too clever for that much mess."

"So she just picks fights at the shop?"

Terrence shrugged. "I said she was clever, not reasonable." He turned toward the house, gesturing me to follow. "I'ma need her gone sooner than later, Miss Arden. She's riling the pride. It's bad energy to have around a turned cub, and it's taking too much effort to keep folks at a simmer."

"I told her she has until the full moon to present her plan and the new moon to get gone."

"That'll have to do, I suppose." He sighed, like he was seeing a long month ahead. "Much obliged for your assistance either way."

"Terrence, it's not just Vikki we need to consider." I repeated what I'd told Ximena about Verve as we mounted the porch steps and went inside. "Believe me, if I can get this resolved faster, I will. Meantime, I have some ongoing shit with the djinn and the elves—new Houses balanced between them—and I've got news about the gods. And the other elementals."

He halted just inside the foyer. "This the part where you tell me why you've been worried about the tricksters?"

"Yeah." I explained about the risk of losing magic, the elemental's role, and my trip to Hillsborough.

Terrence's gaze went the bright peridot green of his leopard. "I want to ask you to tell me this is a bad joke, but you're just not that funny, Miss Arden. Fuck."

Like Troy, Terrence kept a civil tongue, especially around me. He was even more strained than he let on to be slipping like this. Doubly so not to excuse himself.

"What's that mean for your...cub? Gonna take it badly if that happens?" I asked.

"Yeah. It's gonna be bad. Real bad. We can't have this. We can't lose magic." His expression got real hard real fast as he rubbed his Marine tattoo. "I could handle the loss of my cat. Ximena as well, as an alpha. The rest? I just don't know, and I'm not optimistic." The hard expression somehow got harder. "What do you need off your plate to focus on this entirely? I have someone who can go north and take care of whatever feds might be pushing this."

"That's the second time today someone's suggested killing one of them," I muttered.

"I'ma assume the other person was Troy. You oughta listen. He has a good head for strategy and politics. And with you keeping him focused on what really matters and not just elven dominance in Otherside, he's looking out for all of us."

"That's not who I am."

"Then your reign as Arbiter is gonna be a short one. All of us faction heads have had to make difficult, bloody choices. You're gonna need to join us in getting comfortable with it real soon." He winced, like he remembered who he was speaking to. "Ma'am."

I just massaged my temples to stave off the headache trying to build. "Let me see Darnell. Then I'll go and figure out the rest of this."

Terrence led me through the living room and turned left, passing a small bathroom and stopping outside a room at the back of the house.

When he knocked at a closed door, Lola's voice called, "Terrence?"

"It's me and the Arbiter."

The door opened to show Lola, looking tired and drawn. A stink of old blood, fetid musk, and rotted cedar woven through with human body odor hit me.

"Arbiter," she said. "Please don't—"

"She's not here to put him down," Terrence said. "Right, Miss Arden?"

I resisted the urge to wrinkle my nose at the disturbing scent. "As long as he hasn't killed anyone or exposed Otherside, I have no reason to."

Lola wilted. "Good. Okay. Good. Thank you. It's just... He's—"

I peered around her as she moved back to the chair alongside the bed. Darnell was bound to the frame, wearing only a pair of black briefs, his dark skin sheened with sweat. The clear bite marks of a big cat were deep punctures in his throat and thighs. Silver shone in a band on his wrist, and the sheets were twisted around him like he'd been struggling. As I slipped into the room, he snarled, his eyes the same peridot green of all the leopards.

"Is this normal?" I asked, horrified.

"Yes. For a new moon turn."

"He can reach his cat that much even with silver?" I swallowed against the knot in my throat. This was bad. There was no hiding it if the mundanes discovered it. And if we lost magic? This was gonna be real, real bad.

"Yes," Terrence said solemnly. "He'll be a strong cat, a good addition to the leap, if we can get him through his first full moon. Doing the change at the new moon is hardest on the individual because it's a hard, slow shift and adjustment but easiest for us to control them if we can't be discovered."

"We just don't know if we can afford him the time to get there now," I said softly.

A sudden burst of sadness tugged at me. I was supposed to protect these people. I was supposed to offer opportunities, not make shit harder. Drawing so much mundane attention to the Triangle was what had necessitated this man's suffering, on top of whatever he'd already been through in his life. Otherwise, they could have turned him at the full moon and gotten the chaos of the first change over with in a big, wild burst. I should have said something about the tricksters, about the possibility of losing magic, earlier. But I'd been so caught up with the other troubles that it hadn't really occurred to me what that would mean for everyone else.

It was a failure on my part. Unforgivable.

Terrence squeezed my shoulder, a tentative pressure that he withdrew almost immediately. "I smell your pain at his pain, Arbiter. Thank you. For caring."

Lola nodded. "Thank you. For giving him a chance. Not many others in his life have."

I couldn't answer, so I jerked my head in a nod and left the room. A low growl, shushed by Lola, followed me out.

Terrence escorted me out of the house. "I meant it. About the feds or the Sons or whoever else is fixin' to cause trouble."

"I know. So did Troy. But I'ma tell you what I told him: I don't kill people for what they might do. We do have the Darkwatch on this though. If action needs to be taken, I'll take it myself."

"Getting Viktoria moving would be a good start."

"Are you asking for her to be disciplined for the fight at the shop?"

He studied me, hands on his hips. "Would you?"

"You know I don't involve myself in factional skirmishes. Not without a direct request and a good reason."

"I know." Terrence looked at the ground, thinking, then back up at me. "I want her warned. Normally, I'd let this go, but I won't lose Darnell. He's not just Lola's mate now. He's a symbol. And for us wereleopards, it's work twice as hard to get half as much twice over. We have to prove we can do this."

"Okay." I got in the van and turned it on. "I'll warn her. But, Terrence, you need to be ready for her to pitch a fit."

"Permission to engage? If it comes to it."

My guts twisted. Someone I respected was asking if they could potentially kill someone I considered a friend—most of the time at least. The parliament was supposed to have prevented shit like this. But my choices kept fucking shit up.

I shoved imposter syndrome back into its box and put on my High Queen face. "Granted. Keep it quiet, or it's gonna be you I have to punish for breaking the peace. And I will give her fair warning."

"Understood. Thank you, ma'am." He gave me an honest-to-Goddess salute.

I returned it before backing out of the driveway, hoping against hope that I hadn't just signed off on factional war in the heart of my own territory.

Resentment curdled in me as I got back to the garage where we kept the van and waited for a couple to pass before dropping into the manhole that led to the tunnel ending in my office's backdoor. First the vampires and their dominance battles, then the elves and their death cult, now the weres and the ongoing impacts of werewolf colonialism and imperialism. If it wasn't going to hurt so many of the people I cared about, I'd happily let Otherside lose magic for a while just to set everyone straight. We couldn't continue like this, not now, not with the mundanes all too keen to exclude or outright exterminate us. What was it going to take for people to see that and do something?

But objects in motion would stay in motion, and a culture revolving around death was as much an object as a Mack truck running down a mountain with no brakes. It'd take crashing, burning, and mass destruction to get it to stop. Callista had kept me out of the depths of Otherside politics and society in her effort to keep me ignorant, so while I'd been aware of the violence that underpinned Otherside, I'd never fully grasped what it meant. The choices it forced otherwise good people to make to preserve themselves and their people.

I had to do something. I had to stop it or at least get everyone to tap the brakes until our populations had evened out.

More than that, until I had at least the local area unified and working toward the same goal.

When I slipped into my office, I texted Troy to let him know I was okay then Etain to let her know where I was. There'd probably be a bodyguard outside, keeping up the appearance that I was here and working, but I wasn't in the mood to talk to anyone.

I needed something resolved.

My callstone was warm when I grasped it. "Duke. I need an answer from the djinn. Right now."

After half a minute of a distracted buzz, he came back. "Busy, Arden. Besides, we have until sunset."

"Y'all are stalling, and you know it. Keeya Bedoe has agreed to the terms unreservedly. Troy's making preparations to get her installed as queen as we speak. If y'all can't get your shit together, she's gonna reign as sole queen."

"That wasn't the deal," Duke hissed.

"Then I guess it's up to you to get the other half completed, isn't it?"

Outrage boiled through the stone. "Arden, this isn't—"

"Everything is what I say it is. This is my territory and my deal. If I thought everyone was negotiating in good faith, I wouldn't have to be the bitch. Get it. Done. You advise me. You don't control me. Not anymore."

"Somebody hasn't gotten laid in a few days," he grumbled. "Very well, *Arbiter*. I'll get back to you soon. Don't smash your callstone again, hm?"

Before I could do more than sputter in outrage of my own, the connection shut down.

I channeled my anger into a fuck-off big fireball, the kind I didn't make around Troy lest it set off some of his trauma. Then I split it into two, then into four, then into eight, and sent the balls whirling in the complex patterns I used to practice my control. The heat of my temper diffused into the fireballs, and keeping my attention on not burning my office down brought my focus back.

After a few minutes, I was calm enough to let go of Fire and slump in my chair.

A knock at the door made me straighten. "What?"

Haroun stuck his head in. "Everything okay now, ma'am?"

"Now?"

"The spike. In your power signature. Half the bar emptied out." He glanced away, toward the door leading to the main bar area. "Zanna's not happy."

I scrubbed a hand over my face, annoyed with myself. "I'm fine. If she comes back, tell her I'll talk to her later."

He gave a fist-to-heart salute and closed the door.

It took me another few minutes to calm down enough to call Vikki.

"Don't tell me the cats tattled again," she said in lieu of hello.

"Which part of 'quit disturbing the peace' was unclear to you?" I asked.

"So they did tattle."

"Aside from your own self-incrimination just now, I went to the shop. There'd been a fight."

The line hung silent as she tried to suss out what that meant. I hadn't admitted that, yes, it was the cats who'd told me she'd been there, and I'd heavily implied that I'd discovered the evidence on my own.

"I just wanted to talk to them," she finally said. Her petulant tone grated on my nerves.

"Unless you're talking about how to hand back their land, you stay away from Acacia Thorn and Jade Tooth. Their people, their homes, their places of business. Physically, digitally, magically, all of it. If I discover so much as a one-star Yelp review, I'ma be looking at you, and you're not gonna like it."

"This isn't fair."

"What's not fair is you disregarding an agreement that was your idea to begin with." A flashback of arguing with Maria about releasing her vampire hostages hit me. I didn't have time for a weeks-long resolution. Still...diplomacy. "I understand you're disappointed. I get that it's tough to have a friend come down on you like this. But, Vikki, as that friend, please don't put me in the position of enforcing this." I hardened my tone. "Respect me that much."

"Fine. I'll be in touch with my plans. As ordered."

In her cutting tone, I heard that I'd lost a friend. Maybe just for now, maybe permanently. I couldn't tell yet, and there was a rocky road ahead before I'd know for sure.

The call ended before I could scrape together a response.

"Goddess damn the werewolves," I muttered.

As though She'd heard me, my phone buzzed. Troy's number popped up, and I answered.

"Hey—" I started.

"Arden? Where are you?"

"At the bar. What—"

"Stay there. Do not leave without Haroun or whoever else is there. I'm on my way."

The bottom fell out of my stomach. Adrenaline surged. "What the fuck happened?"

"Omar got a high-ranking corporate Darkwatch informant into Verve. He's just texted me. This informant is at an all-hands company meeting right now, listening to the CEO holler about defending humans against the scum of the night and developing the technology that will save them from murderous supernaturals. Using werewolf blood."

Chapter 12

After telling me to stay put again, Troy hung up. He'd be here soon; a threat like this in our backyard demanded his immediate attention. I wasn't waiting long before he blew in.

"We need to handle this," he said without preamble. "Now. I cannot have this level of risk in the territory when the situation with the elves is this precarious."

I went cold. I hadn't even been thinking about the elves, for once. "Fuck. I really do not need this right now, not with what's going on with the weres."

"What happened?"

I recounted what I'd learned from Ximena and Terrence this morning: The fight at the garage, the new were's struggle with the transformation, Vikki's continued refusal to honor the agreement she'd made. My coming down hard on her. Terrence's insistence that we could not lose magic in Otherside and, reluctantly, his offer to send someone to assassinate mundanes.

"He said I oughta listen to you," I admitted. The sick feeling in my stomach was rising to give me green gills, the nauseous tightness in my throat making it hard to keep my voice level.

The look Troy gave me held a hint of sympathy but was mostly just hard. "I know it's not what you want. But, cariñamí, we cannot let the demesne fall into chaos. If anyone else finds out they have blood, that's what will happen."

"Oh, believe me, I know. Because aside from the risk to people we're supposed to be protecting, that will show the gods that I can't keep order, let alone balance, and magic will almost certainly go."

A string of elvish expletives rattled from him in a low growl and the gold flecks in his eyes flashed. When Troy switched back to English, his voice was ice cold and his expression hard. "Let me handle this."

"It's not that simple."

"Why not?"

"We know the humans have blood. Definitely werewolf. Who's to say they don't have another faction? The Darkwatch can get into a morgue easily enough," I said. I'd run into Troy at the Raleigh morgue once, when we were still on opposite sides. "They have to have some kind of failsafe or something in the event that their test doesn't work on werewolves."

"Or it could be simple blackmail. We don't know the circumstances. Only that they have the blood."

"Or that. Fuck." I clenched my fists, trying to will away the urge to summon a zephyr—or a ball of fire, which would only set Troy off. "We need to know exactly what they have. Everything. Samples. Records. Financials. Everything we can get." Something else occurred to me. "What are the odds they're the only ones with samples?"

"Closest facility to Asheville, assuming they didn't get the blood from one of Viktoria's people or elsewhere. Vendor of record. Close enough to DC. They'll want some kind of exclusivity if the test they developed is proprietary. Good odds. They might have more elsewhere, but for the immediate concern, that's our best bet if we're going to shut down whatever experiments the mundanes are running." He eyed me. "You want to go in."

"I want to make a fucking point. They can't take away all the rights we deserve and call it democracy, and then use us to further their own agendas. That's not balance, and I'll be damned before I allow it. And not just because I'm High Queen and Arbiter. Because they don't get to treat us as being outside the law when it comes time to protect us and then insist we're under its control when it suits them. No. I won't fucking have it."

Heat built under my skin, and I pushed Fire away.

Troy's gaze went distant, and the small slip of him I was getting in the bond was heavy on mental gears turning.

"If we go in, we can stall their work," I pushed. "Maybe completely derail part of it. Buy ourselves time to get Otherside under control and stop this factional bullshit."

He looked at me for so long that I started gearing myself up to fight for it. "Okay."

I blinked. "Okay?"

"Yes. But this time, we don't stop at sabotage. We take Zadie in to hack any data they have stored on prem or in the cloud. Then we burn the facility to the ground."

"Troy." I tensed. "They might know I was involved in the last break-in."

"They can't prove you did anything."

"That makes no difference when two dozen humans go missing after being sent to my house. Especially not after a bizarre and completely random environmental disaster when, oh, there just so happens to be a weather-controlling supernatural in town. That's not to mention us threatening a US Senator."

"I know all that. We can't escape it. We don't know if or when we're going to be able to hide anything like this with magic in future. So, we make it very clear that you're not to be fucked with."

Frustration burned in me. "What the hell happened to queens moving in the shadows? Isn't that what you've been wanting from me?"

"That works when there are shadows to move in. We're naked here, Arden. The Darkwatch is good. But I'm not foolish or arrogant enough to pretend the government doesn't have their own strong players. Aside from that, they have numbers. Magic gives us the edge. What happens if that's gone?"

"We get it back."

"And if we don't?"

This time, I did give in to the frustrated swirl of a zephyr. "You're choosing to see the worst-case scenario."

"And you're insisting on seeing the best. We balance. As always."

He wasn't wrong. I just didn't want to admit that my grand goal of a united Otherside balanced with the mundanes was being completely thrown off track and that the only way to get it going again would be more destruction, maybe more killing.

No matter how I turned the situation in my mind though, I couldn't see another way forward. Verve had been a thorn in my side for years now. And it wasn't like I could make things any worse as far as the Bureau for Supernatural Investigation was concerned. I'd broken into the home of a US Senator, for fuck's sake. This was small potatoes in comparison.

I hated it. But I didn't see another option. Too many plates were spinning, and some were just gonna have to crash to the floor.

"We go in. We steal information. And we burn it to the ground," I said. "Tonight. If we don't hear from the djinn or Charleston on the Houses, we'll deal with them after we take care of the more immediate threat."

"Yes, my queen." The faintest curl of a nasty smile tugged at the corners of Troy's lips. "Fast strike. Small team. You, me, Zadie. Ebon Guard on standby for extraction if needed."

"What's Omar going to say about both sovereigns of House Solari going in?"

"He doesn't get a say. I'm King. And he sent me on suicide missions despite my being a prince with the House heir-apparent underage." The smile twisted into a harsh snarl. "Maybe Dad will get the memo as well if he sees his actions could put me in direct danger regardless of what he thinks should happen."

I wanted to stop this head-on collision he was on with both father figures, but the bond was rock hard with resolve. I had enough battles to pick from without inserting myself in this one right now. In any case, it wouldn't change what needed doing or that we were the only two who could realistically get it done if I was determined to physically destroy the organization without explosives or whatever else could be traced back to the Darkwatch.

I studied him. Debating what I could do to keep him out of this. Keep his identity—his name—safe.

"What?" he asked. Suspicion tinged both the word and the bond.

No. I had to take him. If I was going this big, he'd be dragged into it, even just with the mundanes thinking he was my bodyguard. Besides, if I went down or if my magic got the better of me again, he was the only one who could take command and hold it.

"Nothing," I said. "Make the plans. We go at full dark. Hopefully that minimizes human casualties."

His grim satisfaction zinged through the bond. "Good. I'm proud of you, Arden. I know this is a hard choice, especially when you've worked so hard to find other ways to work with the mundanes."

I closed my eyes and rubbed my temples, praying I hadn't just made a massive mistake that would cause more imbalance between Otherside and the mundanes, then started filtering through the reports in my inbox while Troy started making calls to organize tonight's mission.

△▽△▽

Full dark found us standing in the parking lot adjoining Verve's. Same place we'd parked the last time we'd infiltrated it. This time, both of us were dressed in Darkwatch black, as was Zadie Monteague, a shorter-than-average elfess with dark wavy hair in a bob cut and light brown eyes that sparkled with anticipation. She might be a desk-bound hacker most of the time, but she carried herself with the same confidence as any of the field-tasked Darkwatch. I had no doubt she could handle herself in a physical confrontation.

Hopefully, though, we wouldn't need to find out.

Unlike before, I had no need to hide what I was. There were no elves hunting me—or if there were, they'd be completely ineffective and hunted by elves of my own. Bitterly, I figured any would-be assassins were probably still arguing about the Houses. Sundown had come and gone without any word from any of the holdouts.

I'd deal with them later. Maybe my actions tonight would demonstrate that I was no longer fucking around.

On impulse, I reached with blended elements to see if there were any life signs in the building.

"Shit." I scowled. "We've got two live ones inside. Night guards, maybe?"

It'd make sense. After videos of me in action at the Wild Hunt and elsewhere went public, they must have put a few pieces together and gotten sabotage. Two guards were nowhere near enough, but it was more than the other buildings in the area had.

"How do you want to play this?" Troy asked.

I glanced between him and Zadie. The quiet option would be to send two of us in to deal with the guards while the third played lookout. The safe option would be to knock out power to the building, but that might make it impossible for Zadie to do her job. The data was a secondary mission but still important.

"We go in. All of us. Quietly," I said. "If you two can focus on finding or distracting the guards, I can slag the building's security system." No need to cover our tracks this time.

Troy nodded and made a hand signal to Zadie. She ghosted away, silent as all elves were, toward the south side of the building.

As Troy started to lead us toward the entrance to the east—facing us—I grabbed his arm.

"No deaths," I said.

The old him stared down at me with cold eyes. "We'll see."

"Troy—"

"This is who I am, Arden. It's what I was made to be."

I wanted to shake him. "But is it who and what you want to be?"

"I'm a royal. The only time 'want' has ever factored into my life was when I decided I wanted you." His smile chilled me. "Now I have you. And I will do whatever it takes to keep you until and unless you want to go."

There were a million ways that could go wrong, up to and including pre-emptively murdering mundanes to keep me safe. I forgot sometimes, with all the work we'd both been doing, that I effectively had a leashed assassin. His monster might always be there, lurking, waiting for when he was needed.

Maybe it was selfish of me, but I needed that monster too much to keep fighting him on this. At some point, he was gonna have to decide for himself what his relationship with his own darkness was gonna be. I could only put up guardrails and try to help him channel it in a way that wouldn't leave him hating himself when this was all over.

I squeezed his arm. "No *unnecessary* deaths."

He must have heard the reluctance and resignation in my whisper because he leaned forward to kiss my forehead. "I see what you're doing. I'll thank you for it later. When I have the luxury of feeling again. Now let's go before Zadie gets too far ahead."

Holding in my sigh, I hustled after him. At the edge of the trees, I focused and, with zaps of lightning, took out the cameras I remembered being on the roof then the new ones watching the doors.

"We need to hurry now," I muttered. It wasn't hot enough yet for heat lightning, and there was a residential area just the other side of this office park. There'd been an uptick in shootings on 15-501, running half a mile east of us, and the folks on the Chapel Hill side of the city line tended to be affluent enough that they might call the cops if they'd seen those flashes or heard the small pops of the cameras blowing.

Troy grunted his agreement, and we sprinted for the doors.

I slapped a hand over the pad that would have required a keycard in more subtle times and pushed lighting into it to overload it while Troy picked the physical lock.

Zadie's voice in my earpiece: "In position at the south entrance."

"Copy," Troy whispered. "Hold."

I pulsed with elemental magic once more. "Life signs are on the second floor and the basement. Moving."

Troy got the lock and pushed forward, putting himself in front of any danger we'd missed.

Footsteps in the stairwell accompanied a grumbling male voice. "...the hell is going on with this damn security system."

A second voice, tinny, coming over a radio most likely, answered. "I'll meet you on the ground floor."

Without hesitation, Troy surged toward the footsteps and reached the stairwell to the lower level right as the mundane reached the top.

The guy—a security guard in a rent-a-cop uniform—never knew what hit him.

In beautifully smooth movements, Troy grabbed him by the throat, dragged him forward, pinned the wrist dropping the radio to go for a gun, and growled, "Be still," as the scent of burnt marshmallow spiked in the small space.

The guard dropped like the sack of potatoes he resembled.

"Larry?" the radio squawked. "What was that?"

I ran for the radio and used my passive vocal mimicry to sound like Larry. "Nothin'. Tripped on these damn stairs."

"Any sign of trouble?" the other guard asked.

"Nothin' on this floor. I'll take another look," I said, still mimicking Larry.

"Fine. Be down in a minute."

I left Troy to handle him while I went to the side door to let Zadie in, relieved that we hadn't killed the guy. We'd have to drag both guards outside and out of range of danger before I brought the building down, but I couldn't risk losing the mundane allies Otherside had managed to gain and keep so far. If Troy wasn't being pushed to his limits worrying about me, he'd remember that too.

The security panel on the second door fried as easily as the first, and Zadie had already picked the lock. When we returned to the front desk, Troy had subdued the second guard.

Still breathing.

I gave him a tight smile, grateful he'd kept his monster leashed.

Zadie studied the fire map. "I need a computer. Something networked. Not that." She waved a hand at the front desk.

"Upstairs," I said. "Assuming the layout is the same, I can take you to where the C-suite had their offices."

She and Troy followed me up the stairs. None of us wanted to risk getting trapped in the elevator during all this. My footsteps were the only ones that made any noise, but they were quieter than they'd been before Troy's training.

Another fried panel and picked lock. We were making good time, and there were no sirens yet. But we had to be fast. Fortunately, the CEO's office was where I remembered it.

Unfortunately, he'd taken his laptop home for the night.

"Fucking workaholics," I muttered. "Gimme a minute."

With a lighter pulse of Air and Fire, I got a hit off everything electronic on this floor. Desk phones, printers, one of those secure shredders. Maybe if...

There.

"This way." I led them to the north side of the building. In a locked desk drawer in the section with a sign reading "Marketing" hanging over it was a laptop. I picked the lock on the drawer, pulled it out, and scooted out of the way.

Zadie grinned, looking more than a little wild, and pulled out a USB drive. "Here we go!"

Now for the part that was gonna be hard for me: waiting.

Chapter 13

Zadie was one of our best hackers, and between whatever she had on that USB and her own skill, she made short work of the login screen.

"Somebody didn't pay attention in security training," she sing-songed before dropping down into an offended growl. "Seriously shitty password. Eight characters? Only one special symbol? Insulting."

I was too jittery to say anything. Troy was too focused.

"Okay, connected to their network. Just need to override...that."

Troy half turned toward her. "I want physical backups before you destroy the cloud files."

"Yes, sir." Zadie kept her attention on the screen.

I couldn't help bouncing on my toes. Too much adrenaline. Nothing I could do until we left.

Easy. Troy sent a soothing wave through the bond to accompany the word. *We've got this.*

Minutes seemed to take years to pass, but finally Zadie said, "Got it. Files downloaded. Deleting backups of the backups, the main backups...and there. The original files are gone from the network too."

She grinned, pulled the USB out of the laptop, and tossed it to Troy, who caught it in one hand without really looking for it and shoved it in his pocket.

"I took down the firewall and seeded the network with some fileless malware and a few viruses that'll hit any computers that log into their VPN. And I'm taking this." She hefted the laptop, yanking the power cord out of the drawer as well. "Just in case."

"Good work," Troy said. "Let's go. Zadie, get the guards outside. Arden, you're up."

Time to take down the physical servers in the basement and destroy any new samples they might have gotten since we'd been here last.

We rushed down the stairs, leaving Zadie to handle her part while Troy shadowed me to the basement level. Our first stop was the room that'd stored samples before. As I'd feared, it'd been not only repaired but reinforced. The door was thicker, there was a new button-code input on the lock in addition to the keycard pad, and the room itself had new storage units that locked.

If we'd been going for stealth, we'd have been in trouble.

I grinned, glad for once not to stay in the shadows.

With a chord of Fire, I slagged the metal door around the lock and kicked it open, just to be dramatic. Then I zapped the alarm that screeched at the bypass.

"Nice," Troy muttered as he flowed past me into the room. "Clear."

I'd guessed that, given nobody had complained about a melting door, but let it be. "Anything interesting?"

He sniffed, nostrils flaring. "Yes. Werewolf blood. Lots of it. The intel was good."

Frowning, I inhaled deeply. Under the smell of antiseptic and the static smell disinfected air took on was the faintest hint of cedar and musk. I would have missed it if he hadn't said something.

"Elf too." Troy's growl came from deep in his chest this time. "The fucking Eads. You were right about them having more factions."

I wanted to find a sample and confirm, but we didn't have the time. Zadie's data and the laptop she'd stolen would have to do. Troy's nose was still better than mine, and he had more practice using it in situations like this. If he said there were werewolf and elven samples here, then there were.

"Out," I said. "This room goes first."

He obeyed but hovered outside the door.

Again, I found myself grateful not to move in stealth this time. Whatever the circumstances of gathering biological samples from Othersiders, it couldn't be good. People could talk about "just give it up if you haven't done anything wrong" all they wanted, but there was never any good goddamn reason to voluntarily give up privacy like that. Especially bodily privacy. My time as a private investigator had shown me too many instances where law enforcement would create a reason to match DNA with a story.

I wasn't having it for Otherside. This was one aspect of being a protector that I was two hundred percent aligned with.

I closed my eyes and coaxed Fire again, drawing it high and hot. Hotter. Hotter. There. Laid the chord across the back of the room, limiting it to this space with a thought. When I opened my eyes, hairline cracks had formed in the concrete wall. As I backed away, still feeding the chord, it started melting.

Cool.

Or rather, really fucking hot.

I threw a wall of Air up to block the sudden oven blast from scorching us then expanded the chord from the back wall to the whole room.

Everything wood burst into flame. Steel cabinets glowed, and I poured more Fire into them until they glowed white-hot and started sparking, gobbets of melting metal dripping ominously to the tile floor. Epoxy resin lab tables buckled as they burned and electronics disintegrated.

Complete destruction.

A scuffle behind me pulled my attention.

Troy had Harqil pinned against the wall, sharp teeth bared, punchblade under their throat.

The celestial stood with arms spread and eyes wide. If I didn't know better, they were surprised to have been caught.

"I'm not here to hurt her," Harqil said. Their voice was unusually tight, lacking the musical quality it usually carried. "Just observe."

"It's okay." I hurried over and squeezed Troy's shoulder. "They're on our side. Right?"

Harqil smiled tightly at my look. "Right."

The moment stretched as the sounds and smells of burning and breaking came from behind us. Firelight danced across Harqil's face and Troy's back as the heat grew, despite my wall.

"If you try sneaking up on me like that again, I'll kill you." Troy let them go but didn't get out of their face. "Celestial or not. Messenger or not. Count yourself lucky she seems to like you." He tipped his head in my direction.

"Duly noted." Harqil's attention flicked to the room that was now in various stages of burning or melting. "You surprised us with this, Arden. I don't know if that's a good thing or a bad thing."

"It's not vengeance," I said, remembering what they'd told me about the stamp of Regulus—whatever that meant. Another thing to research. Someday. "I'm protecting my people."

"I see that. Anansi's delighted. Others, not so much. If nothing else, you're certainly chaotic enough to be one of ours."

Troy was out of patience. "We need to move. The damage to that room is going to cause a structural weakness." He eyed Harqil. "Unless you want to find out what happens when she's trapped underground."

They swept a bow. "By all means. Don't mind me."

The bond snarled with Troy's conflicting thoughts and emotions.

Leaving him to do whatever he was gonna do, I hustled to the server room. We'd already been pushing time before, but Troy's comment reminded me that we now ran the risk of the building coming down and put extra pep in my step.

The burst of cold air was shocking when I got the door open. Inside, servers hummed away behind the metal lattices of their storage racks.

Usually, I'd use lightning. This time, I needed something more specialized: a lightning-driven EMP discharge. Massive current. Ionized air molecules. Repeating pulses.

"Troy?" I whispered.

"I'm here."

I managed not to jump at his voice coming from directly behind me, sounding like he was facing away—likely keeping an eye on Harqil.

"This one might take me down."

"How?"

"EMP. Bigger than I usually attempt for a blended working. More control."

"Do it. I've got you."

No hesitation. No fear, either in his voice or the bond. Just steadfast faith and determination to get us both out alive.

That was all I needed.

Power and strength, I had. But whenever control entered the mix, there was a good chance it'd exhaust me. Alone, I'd be overwhelmed. There was a lot a body could do alone, but nobody could do everything.

With a trusted ally? All things were possible.

Reassured, I drew Air and Fire together, weaving them so tight and strong it made the elegance of a lightning bolt look sloppy. Set up one big pulse then a descending series of smaller ones. Set up another chord of elemental safeguards as sweat rolled down my face, as much from the effort as from the heat my wall of Air was no longer able to contain down the hall. The last step was weaving the trigger.

"Done," I gasped. "Stairs."

Troy caught my elbow when I staggered as I turned.

I let him keep it and help me away from the room.

Harqil watched with the most worried expression I'd seen on them, their gaze darting between the fire that was escaping the sample room and the ticking elemental time bomb they might actually be able to see the shape of, being a celestial.

When we reached the stairs, I whispered, "Fire in the hole."

Troy tugged me behind him as I let go of the trigger chord.

Blue light flared from the server room.

Pulse.

Building...building...

"Shit," I gasped. I barely got a wall of Air and lightning up in time to shield the three of us as my EMP scrambled and then destroyed not only the servers but everything electronic outside my wall. I might have slightly overdone it in my effort to be sure everything would be erased and unrecoverable.

The moment the wave subsided, Troy was dragging me up the stairs.

I tried to help, but my legs didn't quite want to cooperate. My thighs burned. My ankle turned.

The world spun as Troy threw me over his shoulder and hauled ass up the rest of the stairs and out of the building. I got a flashback to the lich's lair and thanked Ishtar we weren't trapped underground again.

If I lost my shit this time, I might take out the equivalent of a city block.

We stumbled out the door on the north side—the one we'd hacked on our last visit. Troy nearly crashed into the trash can sitting obligingly across from the entrance, catching himself in time to avoid jolting or hurting me, then kept going away from the building.

His shoulder bumping into my stomach didn't make talking easy, but I thought I could stand.

"I'm okay," I managed.

He set me down when we reached the small picnic area.

My legs buckled, and I went down hard on the bench Troy had positioned me in front of.

Maybe I wasn't quite okay.

His knowing look was the only reproach I got, fortunately. I wasn't in the mood or headspace for commentary.

Movement in my peripheral vision was Zadie then Harqil. I waited for her to notice them, but apparently, they were doing their whole be-unseen celestial shit.

Fine. I wouldn't draw attention to them.

"Guards out?" I asked.

Zadie pointed deeper into the darkness of the trees ringing the picnic area. "They're both here. Still out. Tied up."

I nodded and took a breath to steady myself. "Goodbye, Verve. You've been a pain in my royal ass for far too long."

The knowledge the people held would still be a danger, but I could destroy the tech and the physical capabilities to harm us and make it expensive and risky as hell to rebuild. Locally at least.

Troy's hand on my shoulder steadied me as I wove a chord of Earth and Fire. Sank it into the foundations of the building, latticed it up the sides, laced it across the roof. Another wall of Air around all that to contain the damage, the shockwave, and the sound.

And boom.

The earth rumbled as the building came down. Lava consumed what didn't burn or melt, and I compressed it with my bubble of Air until all that was left was a solid, jagged heap of impure obsidian. There would be no recovering anything from this site except glass and rubble.

The sirens I'd been dreading finally screamed into the night.

"Zadie, get," I snapped.

She was staring at what was left of the building with jaw dropped, and I realized she'd only heard rumors of what elementals were capable of before tonight. I had a feeling Atlantis was about to become a whole helluva lot more real for a new generation of elves.

Zadie scrambled to grab the messenger bag with her stolen laptop and sprinted off into the night, keeping to the shadows offered by the trees to expand the cover of her own.

As I dragged myself to my feet, Harqil slow clapped. "A victory with no mundane deaths. You keep to the letter of the bargain, if nothing else. Impressive."

"I know I need to restore balance," I snapped.

They grinned, not thrown off in the least. "Good. Maybe you want to hurry up on it then. The hunters aren't the only ones who know how to fight, and if you don't keep your eyes open, you'll never see the tricksters coming."

"What, no hints?" I asked sourly.

"Anansi gave you the hint you need to see you through all of this." With a shimmering twist of reality, they disappeared.

"Fuck," I said. I wanted to repeat it louder, but we needed to get the hell out of here. Red and blue lights were painting the distance, drawing nearer.

Me and Troy barely got to the car and away before the first police unit spilled into Verve's parking lot. I'd've paid a lot to see their reactions, but sticking around wasn't smart. We hadn't preserved the lives of the security guards only to have to kill cops. Chapel Hill PD weren't my favorite people, but more than that, I needed to avoid the high-profile clusterfuck a police death would bring.

As I slumped against the leather of Troy's seats, I wondered if Tom Chan was at the scene. What he'd make of it. If the impossibility of what I'd done would shake a memory of my abduction loose.

No use considering it. That was over and done, years ago. With the Darkwatch maze that'd been laid on his mind, odds were good there was no recalling anything other than that I was an odd chick who lived in the woods and occasionally freelanced for them as a PI.

My thoughts blurred, and I shook my head. Too damn tired. That'd been a big working. Or rather, two big workings one after the other.

Troy hit I-40 already going seventy and only went faster, muttering spells under his breath as the waxing crescent moon watched us overhead.

Elvish switched to English. "Stay with me, Arden."

"I'm still here."

"You're...fluttering. In the bond. Like you're on the edge of passing out."

"Oh." My phone ringing forced me to wakefulness.

"Fucking Sinclaire," I growled before answering it. "Finch."

"What the fuck just happened?"

"Language, Director. That's just rude."

She spluttered. "I'm looking at breaking news and police reports out of Chapel Hill. A building is *gone*."

"And?"

"And it's been replaced by volcanic glass! I know you know something about it."

I grinned, feeling the sloppiness of it. I sure as hell did know. And I wasn't gonna tell her shit.

Troy took a hand off the wheel to pull my arm, tugging me upright and giving me a little shake accompanied by a sting of Aether.

My mind cleared. Fuck. I felt drunk. Power drunk though, not booze drunk. I couldn't remember it being this bad, not when it wasn't maenad magic.

"Are you listening to me?" Sinclaire screeched.

I really wasn't. "What do you want, Sinclaire?"

"I want to know if you were involved in the incident in Chapel Hill."

"I can neither confirm nor deny a Goddess-damned thing." I couldn't help the smug note to my tone. "As I said before, you'll need to direct all communications to my lawyer."

"So be it."

The call ended, and Troy sighed.

We were almost home when I got a text from Iago.

"You're being investigated for kidnapping, conspiracy, trespassing, and murder," I read aloud. I scowled at the phone and spoke my reply as I swiped it. "On what fucking grounds? They have nothing."

Troy just kept driving, the heavy feeling in the bond saying how much he didn't like this.

My phone buzzed with Iago's reply, and again, I read it out loud for Troy's benefit. "They're pinning the disappearances of the Sons of Seth on you. Say they have proof some were last known to be heading for your property and with the destruction of a building, you could easily destroy a body."

"Predictable," Troy murmured. "Gate."

I hopped out to get the gate, locked it behind us when he pulled through, and got back in. The fresh air combined with outrage to clear my head somewhat.

Troy spoke again as he drove the rest of the way up the driveway. "Hopefully, tonight showed them that at best they can smear your reputation. Between their disappeared Sons of Seth and this, coming after you in person isn't worth it. They'll have to try something else."

Gaping at him, I put the pieces together. "You knew they'd do this."

"I guessed."

"It's what you would have done."

He shrugged. "One option."

"And you didn't tell me?"

The look he slanted at me said everything. I was a big girl. I had two years of experience with how the Darkwatch meddled. I needed to be able to see these things for myself. To think for myself, beyond my immediate goals and needs.

Damn all of this.

"Leave it with Iago," Troy said as he parked. "He loves this kind of thing like I love a hunt. Gets absolutely bloodthirsty."

"Really?"

"The relaxed demeanor is for everything outside court."

I didn't know what to say about that. I was having a hard time imagining my perpetually calm and easy-going Chancellor doing anything aggressive. What I did know was that I had two new problems right now: a very visibly destroyed building and a mundane murder charge.

With the Sight twisting my guts, I had a feeling the murder investigation was the least of my worries.

Chapter 14

The moment I closed my eyes after falling into bed, I tumbled into the In-Between. Only this time, instead of a single voice taunting me, a dozen called for action. Or mitigation. Or vengeance. They debated my actions, if my strike at Verve counted as attacking humans—or not, given I was defending Otherside, had preserved human lives, and only destroyed a building that wasn't even something important, like a house of worship.

The only common agreement was that I was sowing chaos and disorder, and that, on the whole, was a good thing, even if they couldn't quite agree on the particulars.

At least, I thought that was what was going on.

I hovered at the edge of the starry blackness. Trying to sort out the voices. Attach them to beings. But the snake from before was the only voice I knew for sure. They were against me.

Harqil appeared at my side.

"I warned you," they whispered, as physical as I was in this space outside existence, which was to say, not at all.

"Does this mean I have a chance?" My voice echoed with a fraction of the eternities of the gods...but for the first time, it did echo.

Did that mean something? For me? And if it meant something for me, would it mean something for Troy as well?

Because fuck immortality if I couldn't take him with me. Fuck life in the stars as an undying constellation if he wasn't part of my endless story. I'd pledged my life to him, as he had his to me. Some promises went beyond death.

Harqil started to answer. Hesitated. Started again and aborted a second answer.

"I don't know," they finally said. "There hasn't been a debate like this since they decided to give magic to Otherside in the first place. And Orion was simple in comparison. Earth and Fire, even after he became a primordial. Lust for a goddess. A volcano that one merely needed to move away from in a timely fashion. You? With your Hunter? A man you've already defied the death gods to preserve?"

I waited for them to continue the thought.

"You might actually present a challenge," Harqil whispered. "Something to upset the balance of ages. Claim celestial power for yourself rather than being granted it, even. And that, even the tricksters don't know what to do with."

"The hell does that mean?"

"It means, darling girl, that your love for an elf might well bring the spiral of Fate back upon itself. Not just your Fate but that of all."

I didn't know what to say to that.

"Are you familiar with Adhara?"

"No," I said.

"One of your forebears. And Orion's, come to think of it. A dea. She destroyed ships at Atlantis and then seduced the Darkwatch triad sent to capture her. Made them hers. Became a primordial in the process."

Forebear. Made them hers. Did that mean she'd had children by these Darkwatch agents?

An Atlassian elemental? Having children by the Darkwatch? Had my father really been part elemental, so far back that it didn't matter? Was that even possible? Or did Harqil simply mean she was an unrelated primordial elemental who had existed before me in a similar role?

"Stop obsessing," Harqil said before I could decide which question to ask. "All you need to know is that Adhara had a choice to make as well. Like you, she was trapped. And while it remains to be seen for you, she took her trap and freed herself with it."

A flash of pain exploded into my ethereal being. I tried to answer Harqil, but all I managed was to wake, gasping for breath.

"Arden!"

I took another gasping breath. Searched for the source of the pain.

Troy stared down at me, locking my gaze with his. "Are you back?"

Blinking, I scrambled to gather the pieces of my dream and my fiancé's question. "Back."

He kept me pinned, physically and visually. "Arden."

"It's me." I inhaled deeply, as much to remind my body which plane we were on as to convince Troy. A thunderstorm raged outside, not of my doing this time. I hoped. "Harqil had insights. What happened? What time is it?"

"Noon. The news networks have been wall-to-wall coverage of what's left of Verve. It's even more impressive in daylight." He smirked before sobering again. "Jo has been ringing you for two hours."

I jolted upright, jerking away so fast I fell out of bed, hitting the floor as hard as I had when the Sons of Seth attacked but not bouncing up this time, given the sudden headache the movement engendered. I groaned. "Two hours?"

"Cariñamí, you were gone. Nothing I did could call you back. I even called Dad. He said to leave you be, but I can't quite bring myself to trust him. So I gave you a little more time and then used pain to pull you out." He peered over the edge of the bed but wisely withheld comment about my remaining on the floor. "I'm sorry about that. I don't like hurting you."

"No, I'm glad you did." I sorted through what he'd said. Troy had access to my phone; I'd given him my passcode. "Why is Jo calling?"

"She wants commentary."

"On Verve?"

"I told her you'd consider her request after speaking to your legal team."

I blinked. The arguing gods had thoroughly distracted me from more earthly matters. "Uh. Okay. Good. Iago first, I guess."

"Iago first, while I get food going." He gave me a stern look. "You don't quite have a power hangover, but I don't like the peaky feeling I'm getting from you."

"Thanks." I dragged myself to my feet, feeling too shitty to argue with him. Food would probably help a lot.

When I got Iago on the phone, there was a cold sharpness to his voice I'd never heard before. Maybe Troy was right.

"My queen," Iago said. "Shall I catch you up on the specifics?"

"Please do. Thank you." My head spun, and I picked at the scratch the godblade had made in the dining table.

He rattled off charges and what they meant, ending with, "If I may make a recommendation, my queen?"

"Be my guest."

"We bind them with their own choices."

"Explain, please."

"The human conservatives and their terrorist allies wanted to strip us of the laws protecting us by arguing we're not human."

"With you so far."

"If we're not human, how can they charge us with human laws?"

"I—" My brain seemed to short circuit. That seemed too easy. And very dangerous.

Troy turned from the stove where he had steaks on the griddle pan and lifted his brows.

I'm fine, I sent then put the phone on the table and put it on speaker.

To Iago, I said, "Troy can hear you now as well, Iago. I have a concern. If we go along with their argument that we're not human and therefore unchargeable, that will signal that we should rightfully be put in the only other category they have for us: animals. That's dangerous. That's how we get hunted."

"That's where the second part comes in. We force a new designation."

I grimaced. I'd spent too much time masquerading as a Black mundane woman to be okay with that. "So-called separate but equal caused loads of problems for historically excluded mundanes."

"Hmm. Okay, I can see that." In the background, Iago was clicking a pen—highly unusual for him. "What if we frame it as a rebellion instead?"

"As in, we retain our rights to dignity as equal and sentient beings but refuse to be governed by a state that doesn't recognize us as such?"

"Exactly. Similar argument, but rather than setting ourselves apart as non-human, we simply reject unjust governance. It's what the country was founded on after all."

"For wealthy, Protestant, land-owning white human men," I reminded him. "They only consider that argument fully valid when it comes from the same."

"Plenty of elven Houses with a cast that fits that mold. We could use them as spokespeople," Iago said.

I scrubbed a hand over my face. My elves were good people, but most of them had a number of privileges that populations like the wereleopards lacked and didn't always consider that in their choices and recommendations. Whatever path I chose for myself and my House had to be one that would make paths for my more marginalized populations easier, not just get me out of this mess.

"No," I said. "The argument comes from me. I'm the one accused. I'll have to deal with the fallout."

From the stove, Troy spoke loudly enough for Iago to hear. "What about sovereignty theory?"

I frowned. "What, declare Otherside territory a sovereign state?"

"Effectively," Troy said.

This time, it was Iago who objected. "Too difficult. We're completely enmeshed with the human population. It'd require either an entire holding—a town, more or less—under our control and fully defensible or the strength to hold any individual piece of property."

Troy flipped a steak. "Fair point generally. But Arden's land, we could do."

Iago was quiet, thinking. "We have bought out a fair amount of the surrounding land, true."

I blinked. "We have?"

Troy snorted. "My love, you now own all the private land adjoining this property, two parcels in every direction, and the buildings standing on them."

"I do?"

"Where did you think the Ebon Guard was living?"

"Um. Chapel Hill?" I said. Troy maintained an apartment there under an alias, a safehouse. I assumed the elves had plenty. I shot him a look.

"Can we update the queen on property and security later?" Iago asked.

You said to buy whatever property we needed to house newcomers, Troy sent. *We decided to keep them close.*

"Okay," I said. "Let me talk this out. We've rejected two options: one that would risk positioning Othersiders as animals, one that creates a separate but equal stance. I refuse to even

entertain being tried for murder when they were the ones who
sent people to attack me. So, we have two more options on
the table. The first frames my refusal to be tried as...what?
Conscientious objection?"

"Yes!" Iago said. "There's precedence there we can lean on."

"That precedence sent people to prison," Troy pointed out.
He plated the steaks and brought them to the table then went
back for the fries and a bowl of salad.

I rapped my fingers on the table. "They can't send me to
prison. It won't hold me."

"It will if they know about bronze, which they do," Troy said
in a dangerous tone. "We can defend your land, but then you'd
have to stay here."

Anansi might have said that being trapped was being free, but
I wasn't gonna go for it. Unless...unless it bought time for me
to get Otherside in order. I might have dealt with Verve, but the
weres were still an issue just waiting to explode. I pushed that
thought into another mental column.

"Iago," I said, "You mentioned a plea deal?"

"They'll withdraw the charges if you agree to work on behalf
of the US government."

Troy rolled his eyes as he sat opposite me and snagged a steak
for me then a rarer one for himself. He shared my opinion on the
idiocy of playing superhero for hire.

"Gimme an hour to think, Iago," I said. "I don't want to be
reckless about this because it's not just me on the line."

"Understood, my queen. I'll await your call and assemble
a dedicated team more practiced in criminal trials in the
meantime."

"Sounds good. Thanks." I hung up and dug into my lunch.

Nudging a small bowl of chimichurri across the table for the
steak, Troy said, "Whatever the decision is, know that I'll stand
by you."

"I love you for it." I offered him a smile and spread the green sauce over my steak before taking a bite. "Mm. Damn, that's good stuff. Thanks."

Pride and satisfaction spiked in the bond before Troy refocused. "Please just tell me you'll be careful."

I started to make a quip then sobered. This was serious. In destroying Verve, I'd openly shown my powers and called out local, state, and federal government. There was plenty I could be charged for.

But only if I accepted the rulership of mundane courts over me. Unless forced by overwhelming strength, I would only do that if I had a full and equal status, protected by law, in this society. Not that it would matter much or keep me particularly safe. Black folks were extrajudicially murdered on a regular basis in this country. It was the attitude shift I was trying to force. The better path, the upward spiral rather than the downward one. I wanted to be a protector. I wanted to make my parents' dreams live...and my own.

I wanted a world where I could feel safe enough to take a shot at the family Troy wanted so badly that he could barely even speak about it.

That made my breath catch. I froze, fork and knife and lunch forgotten.

"Arden?" Troy's hand covered one of mine.

I jerked and looked at him, feeling lost. I dug deeper in my heart. Did I really want a family? When I was too afraid to rely on anyone but Troy and under so much stress that my body had shut down my fertility?

Surely, a family was another trap. It'd gotten my parents killed. It'd nearly gotten me killed when I was just days old.

"What's wrong?" he asked softly.

"How can we have a family? I don't know what it feels like to be safe. How do I know— What do I need to do to feel safe?"

His indrawn breath accompanied a jolt like he'd been slapped.

My thoughts came tumbling out in my rush to reassure him. "It's at the root of everything. All my fears. I lost my family. So, I've been denying myself everything that even looks like it. But then you made a home in my heart. And the parliament, the local faction heads...they're like family, even when we're fighting. And I want that. Maybe it's enough to have friends who are like family. But I'm starting to think...maybe not. So, I have to be a protector—not just for everyone else, but so that I can finally feel safe enough to find out. To even just think about it properly."

"Okay." Troy studied me, mulling that over. "You're bringing the elves into line. Your action at Verve will give the holdouts something to consider. Regardless of whether or not magic goes, they'll have to rethink their strategies. You have breathing room there." His thumb stroked across the back of my wrist. "Would getting the mundanes to back off be a good next step? Once we've gotten the weres squared away, at least."

I thought about it then nodded jerkily.

"So, that's what we do. But, Arden, I have to ask. Do you want a family for yourself? Or for me?"

"I— For me. For us. But I'm just so afraid of what we'd bring them into." I brought my gaze to his, praying that I'd made sense and that I hadn't hurt him somehow.

The gold flecks in his eyes almost seemed to shimmer in the dull light from the rainy sky, but his expression was full of sympathy. "With that in mind—that we need to get the mundanes to back off so that you can feel safe, I'll ask again: what would make you feel safe? What would ease the pressure?"

Anger bordering on rage built in me. "I don't want files or records on us. The Bureau for Supernatural Investigation think their information and their strike teams give them power over us, and I hate it. As long as they think they have the upper hand, like they do over those of their own people that they've pushed to the margins, they'll keep coming. I want it to be too dangerous, too expensive, too whatever the fuck it needs to be to come for me. For all of us."

By the time I ran out of words, I was shaking with the passion of them.

I hadn't even dared to consider those ideas before Troy drew them out of me. I'd allowed myself to be boxed in, trapped by following the rules other people had put into place. I'd allowed them to strip rights and protections away from my people because that was apparently the will of theirs.

But when the will of some people was to destroy other people, I'd be damned if I accepted that outcome as valid. There was no negotiating with terrorists, and it wasn't me who was the terrorist. It was the Sons of Seth, burning Otherside businesses, harassing and even killing people they thought might be Othersiders. It was the dark money that'd brought populist politicians to power with poisoned words stoking fears about us.

My destroying Verve might be painted the same way by the humans. But I'd tried to do things the "right" way. Now there had been so many final straws that I was buried in them. And I had the power to do something about it, both within myself and in what I could inspire in others.

I wasn't sure how Anansi had meant his message, but being trapped was freeing me.

Troy's gaze had brightened, the gold flecks now seeming to shine as he smiled like the apex predator he was. "If that's what you want, my queen, then that's what we'll do. But first, we need to talk to Josefina. And then we'll need to find out how Verve got access to werewolf blood."

Chapter 15

Troy's plan, as elven plans tended to go, depended on an infowar as its foundation. Unlike typical elven plans though, he wasn't out to sow FUD—fear, uncertainty, doubt—and stir negative emotions. He wanted to build on the foundations I'd already laid with Jo, combine that with my insistence that we had to give people something to hope for, and use the data we'd stolen from Verve to build common ground.

"The court of public opinion will matter as much as, or more than, the actual courts," Troy explained to Iago when we called back. "We show there was a reason for us to attack Verve. It was an infringement of our right to privacy."

Iago stewed on that. "If release forms were signed for the genetic material destroyed at Verve, the right to privacy was waived."

"Legally, maybe. But we need to spin it as coercion. Coerced consent isn't valid consent. We leak limited evidence of Arden's kidnapping and whatever Zadie has managed to dig up from the Verve data. We demonstrate that there was no choice but to take the actions we have." Troy's expression hardened. "I don't like the security risk of leaking the kidnapping, but I'm planning on her blowing up that van in self-defense to deter further attempts."

Both of us knew it might spur greater attempts instead, attempts that came with bronze, but so far, we'd either held them off or outmaneuvered them. There was no perfect way to be safe here.

"What about the murder charge?" Iago asked.

"Tie it up with discovery. They have to have proof, or this is a scurrilous case that should be dismissed, no?"

"That could work. If we can find a sympathetic judge, which will be a long shot. Or if we can mindmaze one into sympathy." A silence from Iago was punctuated by the clicking of his pen. "Unconventional. But that seems to be how you two do things. This mundane journalist though—you trust her this much? To give her that much access to our queen?"

I grimaced, stomach tightening as the weight of all this—not just the actions but also the faith I was putting in a mundane to treat with us fairly—crashed down on me. "I trust that she wants the truth. Her paper is independent and leans progressive. They put out some balanced but pro-Otherside pieces when we were doing the initial negotiations. Focused on the equal rights perspective and what it meant for mundane rights."

A small smile curled Troy's lips. "And if we offer her exclusives, that puts her in the running for a Pulitzer."

Iago barked a laugh, a taut, savage sound I'd never heard from him before. "Which you will be sure to hint at, won't you?"

"I'm not above using all the tools at my disposal," Troy said easily.

"Of course, my king." The sound of rapid typing came through. "As your legal counsel, I do have to advise against the evidence leak. If it were to hypothetically implicate our queen in a different set of adverse, illegal, or questionable activities, they'll simply pivot to charge her with those."

"With their own culpability exposed and Arden having done nothing to provoke it other than existing, they'd take their own agency down with them. They're pretending it didn't happen, they outright buried news coverage on it, and they haven't tried arresting Arden for the murder accusation. So, somebody stepped out of line to run the op, and they might not even have a warrant to go with the accusation." Troy looked at me. The corners of his eyes pinched with concern as he took in my agitation. "But, Arden, you have the final say."

Mouth dry, I nodded once. "I'll take the risk. The way out of this trap is putting everything out in the open. That was the point of the Reveals. I have to assume that, between getting werewolf blood and Sinclaire's arranging the attack on my home, there's something going on behind the curtain. Something they don't want people to know about, but that they think they need us compliant or under control for. Otherwise, they'd simply set up with a sniper somewhere in Durham. I want the mundanes asking themselves if they want their government to have werewolf supersoldiers or supercops under their control, pointed at them, under the auspices of their government rather than under the controls of the Détente. I don't care if we make that part up. Get the mundanes to see the danger of their own government is bigger than the danger of us."

Troy's expression hardened at my threat assessment, but he didn't deny it. If anything, he seemed proud of me for thinking politically and strategically.

"As my queen commands," Iago said. "I'll get the various pieces of paperwork filed and aim to delay everything by at least a week while you deal with the other matters."

"Thanks, Iago. Appreciate all this," I said.

His tone finally warmed. "Oh. Of course, my queen. It's my pleasure to be of service."

We said our goodbyes and ended the call. Then I pivoted to contacting the parliament.

They were not as sanguine as Iago.

We didn't have the time to get everyone together in person, nor did I want to take the risk of having volatile personalities together with everything balanced on a knife's edge as it was, so we met virtually. Telling them I wanted to share information and update everyone on my plans got the full parliament together—including Giuliano and Maria, who wasn't delegating to Noah this time.

When I explained what I'd done at Verve and why, shocked faces stared back at me on the screen.

Then a haggard-looking Maria said, "Well, I don't know if Arden found Troy's stick or he found her—"

"Mistress." Noah placed a restraining hand on her shoulder and squeezed, as assertive a warning as I'd ever seen from him to her. It made me wonder how much he was running the coterie just now. Maria might be Mistress of Raleigh, but she'd burned a lot of her credibility when the coterie fell under attack and was probably working overtime to repair human relations in town.

She waved him off. "Fine, fine, yes. Decorum. In any case, setting the mundanes back a step is the first bit of good news I've had in days. If nothing else, I can hold it up to the coterie as action to give us breathing room. What's this about plans, then?"

"Iago is going to do what he can to delay action on the murder charge," I said. "We're gambling that they won't come for me here, given I blew up six kidnappers and disintegrated eighteen of the Sons of Seth the Bureau sent to try taking me, with another six still in interrogation and reconditioning by the Ebon Guard. And now Verve, of course."

"All that?" Giuliano murmured. "By herself? Matthias was sun-addled to try taking this territory."

"Make sure he knows it, dumpling," Maria said in too-sweet tones.

Giuliano glanced at her, his expression tightening like he wanted to say something before he nodded tightly.

"Great," I said. "Keep your people in line while I deal with this. That's not a request." When I had an agreement from everyone, I added, "Last piece of business. I am restoring the Chapel Hill Conclave." I held up a hand to forestall another snappy comment from Maria or whatever Vikki was going to say with the ugly scowl she had going on. "The gods are stirring again. They're demanding balance, between Othersiders and between us and the mundanes. That does not mean I'm making the elves stronger. It means I'm working to rebalance them with the djinn and potentially bringing the elementals into the alliance formally, rather than just as observers. That's why I've been harder to reach lately."

Disbelieving silence met me.

Maria arched an eyebrow as her eyes shifted to Troy's side of the screen. "And what does our dear King of Solari think of this?"

"Most of us were there the last time the gods made demands of the Arbiter," Troy said coldly. "I don't find it to be in the greater good to allow the matter to escalate. If that means welcoming the djinn to the Triangle to restore balance, I will support Arden in getting it done."

Terrence and Ximena nodded, as though they'd expected nothing less. Vikki looked cunningly thoughtful, which sent up red flags for me given she should have been planning to get the hell outta town. Something was wrong there, but I had to set it aside for the moment.

The vampires looked frustrated—not a surprise, given the elves were their biggest competition in the area for power and influence. Zanna looked bored, Doc Mike confused, and Janae pensive. None of the elementals had answered my call; apparently, they were still debating. Same with the djinn.

"I need to get going," I concluded. "Remember what I said: keep your people in line. Nobody talks to the mundanes, especially not about Verve. Understood?"

A chorus of agreements met me, with varying levels of enthusiasm.

"Good. I'll be in touch." I signed off and turned to Troy, bracing myself at the decision I'd just made at the expression on Vikki's face. She'd been as genuinely surprised as the others about the werewolf blood, which increased my suspicion about where it'd come from. That, combined with her reaction at the end of the meeting, worried me. "I need to find out what's really going on in Asheville. Now, while Vikki thinks we're focused on the mundanes and the new Houses."

Troy gave me a hard look. "*You* need to find out."

"Yes."

"Why does that sound like you're planning to head west?"

"Because I am."

"Then I'm going with you. You are not going to confront the Volkovs alone."

My kneejerk reaction was to reiterate that no, that I'd handle it. Then I second-guessed myself. I'd been trying to do things my way, and they kept devolving into bloodshed before they got better. Callista would have sent Watchers immediately for an assassination, but all I had at this point were the gytrash and a few foreign elves.

What was the right way forward?

"Arden," Troy said. "Answer me."

I leaned into the ring Janae had given me. When nothing happened, I pulled on Chaos and pushed at it, mentally demanding it tell me *something*.

Then it did with a certainty that twisted my stomach.

"No," I said.

"Excuse me?"

"No. I need to go. And I need to go alone."

"I don't care if the Sight told you that. The last time the Volkovs got like this they sent a squad here. To kill us both. It's not happening."

"Troy, I've had to pull rank on half the Triangle in the last month. Please don't make me do it to you."

"Don't ask me to let you go west alone." Under the anger and dogged persistence was fear. "You can ask me to do just about anything else. But don't make me agree to this."

"I'm sorry," I whispered. "I have to go. You have to stay here. I need the agreement between the djinn and the elves finalized, or I need an alternative solution. Now, since they're already testing me with this delayed response. We don't have enough Watchers to send someone else to Asheville. If you send the Darkwatch or the Ebon Guard—the only teams we have who really stand a chance against a werewolf clan and its alpha on their own lands—that will be a declaration of war between the elves and the werewolves. You know as well as I do that we can't add more fronts to what the elves are already being asked to handle right now."

"Fuck. Fuck!" Troy started pacing and glared at the cabinets like he was fixing to throw something. "I hate this."

I waited for him to vent. The bond was roiling.

After a few more heartbeats, Troy took a shuddering breath. "As my queen commands, so do I obey."

"Troy—"

"It's fine. It was going to happen sooner or later."

He might say it was fine, but all the emotion was gone, both from his voice and from the bond. He'd shut it down—shut himself down—reverting to the cold safety of the Darkwatch agent he'd been and not the king he'd become.

It was my fault. I'd hurt him. Again. Fuck.

I had to do this though. Even if it wasn't for the Sight and the ring, Roman was in Asheville. For all there'd been apologies and such, Roman had been dead set on killing Troy out of pure jealousy. Troy still hadn't forgiven or forgotten it. I suspected he considered it all the worse because he'd made such an effort to be gracious when it came to Roman's prior relationship with me. If I let Troy send elves west, Roman and Sergei would know who'd given or at least approved the order. Vikki's refusal to leave the Triangle and her anger at me meant she was potentially a dagger at his back if she and her brothers decided to stop fighting each other and unite against the elves and the werecats. So I had to pull her attention west.

I'd said I wanted to be a protector, and as always, the first person I was going to protect was Troy.

He was going to need space to see that though and then to deal with it.

"Hopefully we can get the Houses settled before I have to leave," I said gently. "I pushed Duke on getting an agreement."

"Yes, my queen. If you'll excuse me, I need to go to HQ to make arrangements."

"I—" At the deadened look on his face, I swallowed my protests. "Okay. Keep me posted."

He grabbed his longknife and his jacket and left.

Guilt ate at me, driven deeper by the abrupt, formal end to the conversation. He wasn't doing it to be intentionally hurtful, I was sure of it. He wouldn't do that to me. But after the flash of rage, he'd slammed back down into his old pit so fast he probably hadn't even realized what he'd done.

Which meant I was about to leave an unstable elven king alone, under high pressure, when he needed his mate. Or at least a supporting triad.

A triad.

Allegra. I needed to call Allegra.

Fortunately, she answered. "Arden! That parliament meeting was something. What's going on now?"

"Nothing good. I'm gonna need you to come up and stay in Durham for a few days."

"What? Why?"

"Because I need to go to Asheville to deal with Sergei fucking Volkov, and Troy is not taking it well."

"Oh. Oh, splintering fuck." She sighed. "I was afraid this was gonna happen eventually. You can't send anyone else because politics and resources. He can't go with you for the same reason, plus him and Roman would murder each other if they were in the same room and that would set Blood Moon at war with the elves in three states. But Troy's still recovering from how bad Keithia fucked him up by keeping him isolated, and he was already under pressure to get this House deal done even before they refused to play ball. Do I have it right?"

"*Thank* you." I blew a breath out. "I was beginning to think I was being needlessly cruel."

Allegra snorted. "Sometimes I wish you were capable of it. Shit wouldn't have gotten here if you were. Anything else?"

I hesitated then pushed forward. "I want to recall Darius from exile."

"Dari? I'm glad to hear it but why?"

"Troy is gonna need to be part of a proper triad again if I'm not there. He trusts you. I think he trusts that Darius was magically compelled to hurt us. We could try adding Thana or Pascale, but you two know him."

"You mean we know his moods, the root of the forced hormonal imbalance that causes them, and his propensity to throw shit if he gets real set off, which is not a good look for a king with the oyëoro."

"That part. How soon can you get to Durham?"

"Give me a couple hours to wrap a few things up and come up with an excuse for Maria."

"Tell her I've ordered you to put in an appearance to help with the new Houses."

"That'll work."

"Thanks, Allegra."

"No, thank you."

I frowned. "For?"

"Having the foresight to know T shouldn't be alone and the care to do something about it, even if he's gonna insist he'll be fine and try to order me away. He hasn't had someone with the power or heart to care for him like that since Aunt Sareena died."

I sighed, a huff to try releasing some of the guilt. "That means a lot. I worry."

"I know. That's why I let you stay with him."

The smile in her tone made me roll my eyes, even if she was serious. "Bye. See you in a bit."

"Bye, sis. Leave Dari with me."

Even ending it on that somewhat reassuring note, I was still too agitated to sit still. I needed the river. I changed into exercise clothes and headed out. As I made my way down the slope, kicking the occasional storm-downed branch from the path, I let myself feel everything boiling under the surface. If I didn't get it out now, I'd be taking it with me to Asheville. Sergei was infuriating even when I was having a good day, and it was never a good day when I had to deal with his smug, scheming ass.

It wasn't just Sergei. It was everything and everyone.

Seeing Roman again was going to suck. I was dreading having Troy come home because I didn't want to see his face when he saw me again and thought about me going out west alone. I was past tired of dealing with the elves and the djinn and afraid they wouldn't take the offer I'd laid down. I was fed up with this bullshit from the other elementals, especially Benjamín Pérez's bullshit about being an elder.

I was sick of it. All of it. And I couldn't take any of it past this moment.

The only outlet I had right now was my magic. I closed off the bond then drew deep, first sparking Fire in the pit next to the river, given the now overcast day blocking the sun, then connecting with each of the other elements in turn. The ground shook beneath me with how fully I embraced Earth. The Eno splashed, frothing with the depth of my surrender to Water. The wind whipped around me as I pulled on Air and fueled the fire in the pit, pushing it to leap higher.

Balance. I needed balance. Air and Fire were, as usual, supercharged, and Earth and Water were underpowered. Closing my eyes, I sought the fine edge of harmony between all the powers. Water would always be my weakest, while Air would always be my strongest, but I'd had enough practice now to make the subtle shifts quickly.

With a metaphysical twang, everything snapped into equilibrium.

For a moment, the universe sang as everything around me stood still. Birds stopped calling, squirrels stopped moving, fish and turtles stopped swimming. The trees, with their slow, sap-driven attention, turned my way. The rocks, always so deep in time that they would have seemed dead to most, quivered as they woke.

When I had the attention of every being, animate or inanimate, I loosed my magic.

A wave of power burst outward, sparking Chaos in a crackling wave.

The animals hunched lower before scrambling into mad activity. The trees burst with new leaves or blossoms or leakages of sap, depending on where they were in their cycles. The earth rumbled again as a rock cracked and the river surged. Overhead, thunder rumbled.

That used to worry me, the whole deal where storms gathered whenever I practiced with my full magic.

Not anymore.

Let everyone in the area remember what I was capable of. Because I was done reminding them, and fuck all of them if they thought this was a temper tantrum. I was done telling friends and loved ones to fall in line for the greater good. I was—

The scuff of a foot against rock pulled me around. I opened my eyes, already reaching for Air and Fire. A ball of lightning crackled threateningly around my clenched fist.

Troy leaned against a tree, kicking his toe against the ground in a pointed way. If he'd been an enemy, I'd have missed him, an unforgivable lapse in my situational awareness. I must have been practicing longer than I'd thought, for him to make it to HQ, run a briefing, and come back.

Fuck. Situational awareness was just one more thing I had to be better at. My control was getting better—nothing had exploded or burst a blood vessel this time. It hadn't actually started raining. I hadn't unbalanced the humidity that much. But I was still a disturbance whenever I embraced my full self.

It stung.

Troy opened his mouth to speak, pausing when I dropped the walls in the bond.

If he wanted to argue with me about going to Asheville again or if he used that Goddess-damned modulated tone with me right now, I might just summon a tornado. Or at least dump the Eno on him. I was feeling far too shitty right now for that.

The infuriating man smiled. *Smiled*. After all his moods earlier, after all my running around to make sure he would be okay, he was amused now.

Oh, hell no.

Chapter 16

I snarled back. Troy's amusement was almost worse than his disappointment in my lapse or an attempt to soothe me. I didn't want soothing. I wanted—

His secondary teeth flashed, sharp as a mako shark's.

I tensed. If he really thought now was the time to hunt me—

He turned and ran for what might be the second time I'd ever seen.

I stood there like a fool, completely shocked. Then Chaos gripped me, the maenad's hunting instinct took over, and I was after him.

The forest passed in a blur. He was faster than me. Stronger. He made the run through these woods regularly and knew when and where to jump, duck, or pivot to make it over a rivulet or fallen log or between a rock and a tree.

But the land didn't love him as much as it loved me.

I switched off the conscious part of my brain and let the elements, dirt and stream, breeze and sun, guide and fuel me. Troy moved soundlessly through the woods like the elven hunter he was, but I moved like I was the forest itself brought to terrifying life.

Finally, I brought him down.

He'd tried to leap one of the small feeder streams heading down to the Eno, but the mud had betrayed him even as it stayed solid under my feet.

"You really thought that would work." I bared my teeth at him, letting my hormonal instincts have control. "You know the river loves me."

"It's worked in the past." Troy's punch caught me in the short ribs.

I gasped a cough, shocked at the sudden lack of breath, then let him go and rolled to avoid the follow-up to my face. He hadn't pulled it—it would have knocked me silly. That was what this was about. He was still pissed about me leaving, but rather than him throwing things or us arguing with words, we were going to fight it out.

"Son of a bitch." I snarled and pulled on Air, pinning him. When he tried an Aether sting, I sliced through it with Chaos.

Silver glinted at his wrist, catching my attention. The small knife from my nightstand. I snatched it out and held it under his chin.

He dropped his hold on Aether and went still. "Haven't been in this position for a while."

My mind flashed back to the lich's lair then to our first formal training session together, in the bar's basement. The latter time I'd gotten pissed and bested him, but lost control until he surrendered and I realized what I was doing.

This time though, the sexual tension was something I could act on.

"I want you," I said.

"You've won the hunt, so you can have me. But only if you claim me."

Of course. It wasn't just the argument. It was his fears of being alone again. He could handle his shit—with my help. And this was his way of asking for that help when he was already in the pit.

I was happy to oblige him.

I hadn't realized that he'd led us just about back to my rock, the one I'd overturned with Air when I was still growing into my original power, until I looked up and oriented myself. Keeping my grasp on the knife, I let go of my magic, got a grip on his hair, and dragged him to his feet then to the rock.

It was as much his as mine, after all the hard talks we'd had sitting on it. Might as well give us both something else to remember here.

His pupils were wide when I released and straddled him. The scent of smoked herbs and his sweat were intoxicating.

I held the knife against the meat of his shoulder, the place on my body where he usually bit me, and dropped the walls in the bond to find arousal and searing desire on his side. "Tell me no."

"Yes."

I was too riled, too hungry, too full of Chaos, to question or doubt him.

"Make the cut where you want it," I said.

With a smooth movement, he locked his gaze with mine, took my hand, and pressed to slice through his shirt then into the meat of his shoulder. The herby scent of elven blood hit me, and hunger surged.

He groaned as I dragged the fabric aside, fixed my mouth to the cut, bit down, and pulled. His hips bucked against me, and he had to try twice before he managed to say, "Fuck me. Please, Arden. Don't go without giving me everything."

I hadn't had a drink, but something like the maenad's madness roared to the fore with the power in his blood, riding the Chaos I was already holding. Even without booze, the intensity of the hunt had combined with my raw emotions to draw the maenad magic much closer to the surface than usual. I pulled away long enough to get out of my pants, undo his, and pull out his dick before sinking onto him and latching back onto the still-bleeding cut in his shoulder. The scent of burnt marshmallow flooded my nose, and then I was shot to the heights of pleasure right before he bit me in turn.

I lost myself in him. Forgiving the fight, apologizing for leaving. I wasn't sure if I rode him or if he fucked me, but both of us ended up bloody and satisfied, climaxing with our blood in each others' mouths. I came so hard I almost ripped my own shoulder on his teeth trying to arch back. He held me in an iron grip as he followed me.

Mine echoed in the bond, although whether it was my thought or his, I couldn't tell. I was barely hanging on to consciousness.

I couldn't focus. I tried. Managed long enough to get off him, get my clothes right, and stumble to the ground at the base of the rock before dropping to my knees.

My legs didn't want to work.

Not that I felt bad, just...drunk. I pushed myself to my feet, only for my knees to buckle again.

"Whoa, there." Troy caught me and eased me down. Worry came through the bond as he checked my pupils and pulse then laid a hand across my forehead and sent a pulse of Aether rippling through me. His expression cleared as he scented me. "Ah. Poor thing. Come on, let's get you to the house so you can sleep it off."

My mouth didn't want to work now. As he scooped me up, I sent, *What's wrong with me?*

"Nothing's wrong. You're just coming down from the hunt."

Coming down?

"Hormonal rush. Usually, it's me hunting you, and this didn't happen the other day, so it didn't occur to me that you'd get the comedown if you were the huntress. Probably happened because you took my blood on top of the hunt. Don't worry. It'll pass soon."

I felt too good to argue with him and let myself loll in his arms. This was great. This was fucking amazing. Like a vampire bite but better, because I could taste Troy and feel him in so many ways that it was sending my brain into a meltdown of pleasure.

This is...

"I know. Stay with me. We're almost to the house, and then you can take a nap, okay? I'm sorry, my love, I didn't realize a hunt would trigger this for you."

Sorry sorry sorry. So many sorries. From Troy, from Val, from everyone. I wanted to be mad, but my thoughts were spun into a skein of chaos and euphoria and lust.

Somewhere in the back of my mind, a god giggled. Or maybe it was me.

A concerned woman's voice—Allegra?—cut through the fog of good feeling.

"What the fuck is going on out here? I come for orders and—is that blood? Is she hurt? Are *you* hurt?"

"We're both fine," Troy said, his voice a rumble against my ear. "Or she will be in about twenty minutes. I think."

I tried agreeing with him, that I was fine, but all I managed was another giggle. No wonder Maria had wanted to bite him so bad on that first mission we all went on together, to kill Leith. Troy had powerful blood. My blood now because he was my mate. Mine. All mine. Him, his blood, and his power.

That felt really good, having something I was that certain was mine.

Allegra was carrying on about something, and Troy was getting agitated in the bond. So I pulled on Air, looped a coil around her, and picked her up before she could ruin the good feeling.

The words cut off in an indignant squawk.

Next thing I knew, Troy laid me on the couch and kissed my forehead. "I think Alli's got the point. Put her down please. Gently."

I stretched languidly and did as he asked, feeling too sated now to argue.

Air molecules danced as Allegra stormed into the house and slammed the sliding glass door. "What the fuck, T? What—"

"I gave her a hunt. Her hunting me this time."

"That's how a hunt affects her? She wasn't like that at the Darkwatch trial."

"She's been under a lot more stress. You know how much harder the mellow phase hits then. Plus, there's the maenad thing. Probably more that than anything else, now that I'm thinking straight. She was working all the elements and Chaos when I found her. Had been for a while."

Mellow phase? Troy did always seem calmer after a hunt, but he'd never been like I was now. I frowned, as much for that as for Allegra's long pause.

"I hadn't realized she was under that much pressure," she said. "Goddess, Troy—"

I tried sitting up, but my body was still too wobbly.

"I'm fine," I insisted anyway.

"Like hell." Allegra peered over the back of the couch, and I resisted the catlike urge to try swatting at a dangling loc. She must have caught the impulse because she tucked it behind her ear and over her shoulder. "Is she gonna be okay to go to Asheville?"

"Who told you—"

"She did. Because she was worried about you. She wants Dari back as well."

A pause. From the spiky feeling of the bond, Troy was giving Allegra a dirty look.

"Don't get mad," she said. "She's trying to take care of you, and she knows you'll need to be in a full triad without her. She can't stay here. She can't devote resources west. So she's doing what she can. For you."

Aww. My future sister-in-law was defending me. That was good, right? Even if it was pissing Troy off. Had I done the wrong thing?

I reached up with a wobbly hand, trying to pat his cheek. "Don't get mad, Troy." My voice was too breathy, and I swallowed, trying to make it stronger. "I love you. I just want you to be okay. I want you to live. And be happy. Even if I'm not here." The bond twisted from anger to guilt so fast I blinked with the dizziness it sent ratcheting through me. "No, don't be—"

"It's okay, Arden." Troy smoothed a few curls away from my forehead. "Will you rest if I don't put you under?"

Rest meant sleep. I didn't want to sleep. I didn't want to dream. But something about the hunt and his blood and my imminent departure had thrown my body chemistry completely out of whack, and I had a feeling I didn't have much choice.

"Yeah," I whispered. Now that I was laying down, I really was tired. Between the needs of Otherside and the fear of the gods, I hadn't slept properly in weeks. "Rest."

Troy started humming, something low and soothing in the deep bass of the singing voice he so rarely used.

My eyelids flickered, and then the exhaustion of rage and grief, of a hunt completed and one yet to come, dragged me into unconsciousness.

△▽△▽

Something smelled delicious. Incredibly delicious. I nuzzled closer, wanting a taste. Salt and blood, rosemary and sage, and under it…Troy.

I inhaled sharply, coming all the way awake.

"You're okay. We're home. In bed." Troy's arm tightened around the small of my back, keeping me pressed against him.

"Did I hurt you?"

"No. No dreams either, as far as I could tell."

"How long have I been out?"

"Couple hours. Longer than I'd thought it'd be. But we both needed the rest."

"Hours?" I reached for my callstone. "Did Duke—"

"Nobody's tried to reach you."

He would know if we were touching like this. He'd get at least the echo of the call.

I glanced at the window. Sundown was almost here, a day past my deadline.

My heart twisted, grief for the outcome that was apparently too much to hope for. "They're not going to agree, are they?"

Troy hesitated, but he was too much a realist—and he would never lie to me. "I don't think they are. Keeya was desperate to start fresh. The others think this is just another power game."

"And I've thrown my weight around too much in the last few days for them to be comfortable bowing."

"That's my read." He hugged me closer to his side. "At least I'll have my work cut out for me while you're away. Staying busy will help."

I swallowed against the lump in my throat and blinked against the hot tears forming. It wasn't just grief; resentment was in there as well. I'd really thought this would work. And I'd really been arrogant enough to think my raw magical strength had given me the power Callista had amassed over centuries of fear-based rule.

Troy squeezed me again but said nothing. He was too well-mannered and considerate to say "I told you so," but I knew it was there. He had told me. Allegra and Omar had told me. Terrence had told me. Duke had mocked me more than once for being a pushover.

I kept thinking that, finally, with this or that example—killing the queens, forcing Maria to give up her hostages, severing the Eads, the whole Wild fucking Hunt—I'd shown Otherside what I was capable of. Clearly, they still saw an up-jumped child with ambitions bigger than what she was willing to do to achieve them.

In a way, my decisions might have made it worse. I was trying to show Otherside that there was another way, one that didn't involve killing each other. But it had only been two years since I'd stepped into my power, and I was still only twenty-eight. Most of the people I was up against were two or three if not dozens of times my age. My power base was entirely made up of people like me as well. The young and the gifted but also the broken and the fearful—those who'd fled situations elsewhere and had nothing else left.

How could I protect people like this?

Troy's kiss to my temple freed one of the tears. "I know this isn't the outcome you wanted, cariñamí. I'm sorry."

"They're the ones who're gonna be sorry." Bitterness nearly choked me. "The gods of the hunt walked this plane, and they don't believe the tricksters can visit their own kind of hell on earth?"

"Arden..." Troy sighed, and the bond gave me the sense that he was gathering his thoughts. "Can I be blunt?"

"You might as well."

"You're an idealist."

"You're saying I'm naïve."

He took a breath to answer, paused, then winced. "Maybe a little."

I'd thought my mood was shitty before. It was worse now. That was something I'd thought I'd gotten over—being the naïve little idiot.

Troy caught where my mind was spiraling to. "Stop that. Look, in a way it's a good thing. It's why you keep seeing paths most of us reject out of hand when we see them at all. It's why, vision-wise, you're the best choice to lead Otherside forward. But you keep thinking this time will be the one that people will listen to you, when nothing in our experience has proven that will be the case."

"You listened to me."

He grunted. "Helped that I saw you as my only way out. The only person who had both the power and the leverage to free me from Keithia." Another kiss to my temple. "And it helped that you'd stolen my heart."

"I've shown my power and leverage to everyone else as well though."

"Yes. But not in a way they'll respect. They're used to power being force. Or outright brutality. Things done purely because one can. We're a day past the deadline, and there've been no consequences."

I wanted to keep arguing with him, but it would go nowhere. It wasn't that he was wrong. It was that I didn't like what he was saying. Arguing would just sour the time before my heading west.

This was a problem to solve. One that might force me to reconsider my personal morals and viewpoints if it meant saving magic for all of Otherside. But that made me feel trapped between what was right and what was necessary.

Trapped.

Anansi's message.

"'The webs we weave draw ever tighter'," I murmured. "'Being trapped is being free.'"

Troy stiffened. "Please don't tell me that's another prophecy."

"No. Harqil popped in after I visited the elementals. They said it was a message from Anansi."

"Anansi? Why would he send a message?"

I winced at having forgotten to tell him sooner and started to say that I didn't know. Then it clicked. "Terrence. He said the leopards 'stay right by Aunt Nancy.' By Anansi."

"And you're doing what you can to support the leap."

"Which is creating chaos but the kind which apparently pleases Anansi." I blew out a breath, feeling some of the fog of defeat clear from my brain with it. "Okay. My actions against the Sons of Seth pleased him, and helping Acacia Thorn must as well. He's letting Harqil bring me hints and gifts. So, by extension...maybe he's my patron? Like Neith was among the hunters?"

"It's a trap." Troy's voice had gone flat, and his grip tightened on me, hard enough that I grunted. He didn't seem to notice because he didn't relax. "Something's going on with the wolves, and it isn't just Sergei's usual arrogant idiocy. Everybody knows by now that you'll go and face a threat to your authority. Verve having werewolf blood is more than a threat. It's a trap. That's what the message means."

But because it wasn't in the nature of the tricksters to give advice or wisdom—they weren't the sages, after all—I got a riddle. One that was making Troy squeeze me breathless.

"Troy."

He shifted like he was looking down then relaxed his grip. "Sorry."

"It's fine. I still have to go though."

"Let me send someone with you."

"No."

"Even Callista had Watchers," he growled. "Do not slip back into doing things all by yourself."

"Callista was able to lean on Watchers after four hundred years in power. And she was a celestial."

"Arden—"

"I told you." I firmed my voice, even though I knew it would hurt him. "No. I'm sorry. I know it hurts. But we both have our roles. You need all the elven strength we have here to push this new House arrangement through. I still want that done."

From the twist of the bond, the finality in my tone was almost enough to send him spiraling again, but instead of arguing further, he shifted against me so that his body blanketed mine and buried his nose against my neck, inhaling my scent before whispering in my ear.

"If anyone hurts you, I will be in Asheville." The coldness in his voice sent chills over me. "And I will kill them. Slowly. And exceedingly painfully. With every single lesson Omar taught me."

I rubbed my hand along his spine and didn't bother trying to rein him in. If that thought would give him comfort, so be it. We'd both need all the grounding we could get tonight. Especially since I was going to have to call Cyrus for a crash course in Dreamwalking before I left so my extended absence didn't create the kind of situation that would potentially have Troy dead at my hand.

Chapter 17

Dreamwalking lessons went as well as I'd expected. Which was to say, not at all well. Cyrus was in nearly as foul a headspace as Troy and I were, and none of us was in the mindset to share secrets.

Cyrus caught the mood as soon as he walked in the door.

"What is it?" he asked in a flat tone that was more demand than question.

I glanced at Troy, only to find him looking at me. I barely managed not to sigh. "I need to go to Asheville. Alone."

Glancing between the two of us, Cyrus began to speak before closing his mouth and starting again. "From my previous understanding, that will invoke a Chaos sphere. An unintended Chaos sphere."

"Seems so," I said. "That's why you're here."

Troy just crossed his arms, grinding his teeth so hard it was nearly audible as the muscles in his jaw bunched.

Cyrus shook his head. "No. It's too soon. You're only just learning how to manage Chaos spheres properly."

"She'll be fine, Dad," Troy said. "She hasn't killed me in the two years we've been Aetherically bonded."

"Don't act like you're okay with this, boy. I smell the blood on both of you. How close are you to feral?"

"Hey," I said, jumping in before Troy could go off at the accusation. "Enough. We invited you here to help. Not to judge."

"You invited me here because you don't dare to call Duke. That means I have the power here and—"

Troy stepped close enough to start a fight and spoke in a low, threatening growl. "You can help. Or you can leave right now and pray your nightmares don't come true. Feral or not, I know my heart and my duty. I choose her. What's your choice?"

Blinking, Cyrus started to answer then inhaled and froze. Swallowed hard. Took a step back, cast his gaze down to the floor, and bowed his head as he settled into a parade rest. "I apologize, my king. I overstepped."

It was my turn to blink in surprise and more than a little confusion. Something had just shifted, something the elves understood but I didn't. I sniffed as subtly as I could, trying to figure out what had changed in Troy's scent, but all I could make sense of was agitated elf: heavy on smoked herbs. The bond said Troy was feeling...implacable. Not crazed or whatever the hell they meant when they said "feral."

Implacability came out in his voice as well. "That's right. You did. I'm not ten years old anymore. She is my bondmate and our queen. Remember that."

"Yes, my king," Cyrus said.

This was really fucking weird, watching Troy pull rank on his dad. Which meant I needed to keep my mouth closed, my shields up, and my attitude hard so I wouldn't undermine him.

"Does that mean you'll be doing lessons?" Troy asked.

"It does." Cyrus looked up, and there was no missing the spark in his gaze. "I will do whatever it takes to keep you safe."

"Even if I am feral?" Troy spoke the last word with complete disgust.

Cyrus flinched then looked pissed that he had. "You're not."

"And if I am?"

The way Troy pushed made me look at him with worry. He hated the topic. I hated when it was raised because of how it made him spiral afterward.

"You're still my son," Cyrus said without hesitation. "And I'm still oathsworn to your mate."

"Good. What does she need to know for when we're separated?"

The elder elf studied me. "Pulling you in and releasing you safely. Intentionally, not just because your souls miss each other."

My brows flew up. "That's what's happening?"

"That was one theory in Ninlil's book." Cyrus shrugged. "One of the more romantic ones. Most of the others were more theoretical in a way I couldn't follow. In any case... Where would you two like to be asleep?"

"No," Troy said before I could answer. "I'll be staying awake. No offense, Dad. You explain the concept. Then I put you both out."

Cyrus darted a look between us then spoke cautiously when I didn't countermand Troy. "It will work better if she learns with you."

"She can already pull me in. That's not the problem. And if you can't teach her otherwise, I see no reason for you to be here."

I struggled to keep my expression neutral. Troy had a point. I just hadn't expected him to set himself against his father like this. He'd been tormented by the memory of what Cyrus had suffered at Keithia's hands for twenty years and then by the whole internal struggle with whether to bring him here. My heart wrenched at the feeling that the discord was because of me.

It's not you, Troy sent without taking his gaze from his father's. *I've seen him like this before. With Keithia. He wants something. I'm only holding him off by tapping your natural resistance.*

Shit. Cyrus was here trying to use magic against us both? Even if it was passive magic, from what I'd seen with Troy, they were well aware of it and could tamp it down. Passive magic didn't quite stray into magical trespass, but it was a very near thing.

"Very well." Cyrus didn't look happy about it but inclined his head. "We'll do it your way."

Definitely wants something, Troy sent again.

I'll follow your lead.

With my agreement, Troy pointed to the bedroom. "My queen." He pointed to the couch. "Dad. After you explain, in plain English, how to pull someone in and how to let them out safely."

Cyrus wasn't easily derailed. "You give your queen orders?"

I was starting to understand the tired look Troy gave me sometimes, and I turned it on his father now. Whatever wedge Cyrus was trying to drive between us wasn't gonna happen. "Pretty sure I've already mentioned he's an equal partner. In all ways. I meant what I said, Cyrus. Troy isn't a pet or a toy. This relationship isn't a game to me or a power play. It's justice, and it's what he's more than earned."

Troy was smirking when I turned back to him, the Cheshire Cat's shit-eating grin. "Told you, Dad." His expression hardened. "Now, stop stalling or get out."

Frustration flickered across Cyrus's features almost too fast for me to grasp before he settled into a neutral stance and expression. "As my king commands." He turned to me. "This would be easier with Troy because you're bonded to him at least twice over. From what I've seen, likely more." Something ugly darted through his expression before he smoothed it. "As it is, the blood tie between me and him, and the ties between you and him, should be enough for you to find me."

"Find you how?" I asked. "I never intended to find him before."

"That's what I'm afraid of." Cyrus forgot himself enough to glare before shaking his head and continuing. "There are threads, if you know what to look for. Especially if there's a connection between you. Preferably Aether, blood, or aura. Shared oaths and bodily exchanges are too weak, usually."

Me and Troy had all five between us. I bit my tongue to stop from mentioning the thread I'd seen connecting me back to Troy before, even as I wondered if it was the number of ties we had now that had made it so obvious. I hadn't looked for it, and I didn't know what it would look like with someone I wasn't bonded to. But at least I had something of a starting point.

That said, I'd never sensed any kind of tie between Troy and Allegra or Darius. Maybe this intentional Dreamwalking shit wasn't that easy.

"So, I find a thread and...what? Pull?" I asked.

"Something like that. Think of it as welcoming someone into your home. There's an energetic exchange, right?"

I frowned, never having thought of it that way. But the rituals that bound Otherside might serve that purpose, to shift energy using intention rather than active magic. It was a level of academic metaphysics I'd never had to consider and honestly would rather not. I liked my instinctual elemental magic better.

Instinct might hurt or kill Troy and unbalance Otherside though. I had to do better.

"Okay," I said. "I guess I can see that."

Cyrus just looked like he wanted to smack me with his cane.

Troy prompted, "Then what?"

"Then she maintains the sense of welcome until I'm there," Cyrus said.

"There how?" Troy asked.

Cyrus's mood flipped, and his eyes twinkled. "You begin to see the challenge. You can protect your queen's body in the real. Or you can protect her mind and spirit in the dream."

"If I feel the need to protect her from you in any way, I won't hesitate," Troy said in such bland tones that I shivered. That voice only came out when he was truly dangerous.

Cyrus noted my reaction and inclined his head. "Of course. As to how—mind and spirit, as I've said. But that much mind and spirit can be dangerous. Injury in a dream would be reflected in real life. Death in a dream could mean death in real life."

I couldn't help a horrified look at Troy. That was more, and worse, than Cyrus had explained previously.

"And that," Cyrus said, "is exactly why I've been so concerned about my son being bonded to an untrained elemental Dreamwalker whose mother was at least six thousand years old when she died and probably didn't think most of her knowledge was worth documenting."

We spent the next hour talking through theory.

Intellectually, I only understood half of it, if that. I was intelligent enough, but this was like a crash course in advanced postgraduate metaphysics taught by someone who only knew the theory itself, not the practice.

Cyrus couldn't answer all my questions, which made him cranky.

Troy disliked not having exact answers, which made him cranky.

And being in close quarters with two agitated elves made me cranky because the house reeked of smoke and herbs and bad feeling and I couldn't wall out Troy's feelings in the bond without blocking him from communicating with me telepathically.

A whole Goddess-burning mess.

Finally, I said, "I think I just have to try it to understand."

Cyrus scrubbed a hand over his face in a gesture reminiscent of one of Troy's at his most frustrated and resigned, but rose from the table and moved to the couch when Troy pointed at it. He wasn't quite as tall as Troy but would still be uncomfortable, so we shifted the coffee table so Cyrus could stretch out his bad leg, propped on a pillow.

The two men shared volumes in a look that I couldn't interpret, and then Troy put him under with Aether.

"Are you okay?" I asked quietly as we walked to the bedroom together.

Hesitation. "No. But this is part of what we need to do to retain balance for Otherside and keep magic."

So, he'd get it done.

I held back a sigh as I climbed onto the bed and settled against the pillows.

Troy pulled a throw blanket over me and slid his hand to the back of my neck, prompting a flashback to when he'd pulled me out of Maria's vampire glamour once. He leaned over to kiss me and murmured, "Sleep," as his Aether twined through my mind.

The scent of burnt marshmallow chased me into unconsciousness.

I woke almost immediately in a dream of my clearing near the Eno. Kind of like the Crossroads place Grimm had formed on the first visit, only this one was complete with scent. I knew I wasn't still awake in the way I knew that all my lucid dreams were dreams and always had. I was half surprised not to have been pulled into the In-Between, but maybe someone was watching to see if I could do this. That almost made me dispel the dream and wake up, but I refused to risk Troy or Otherside because I was afraid.

Threads. Cyrus had said to look for threads.

I settled on one of the fallen logs that stood in for a chair and focused, closing my eyes and falling into my intuition.

Threads...there. One pulsed in the same color as before, mimicking Troy's eyes. Weaker this time to my third eye. Because he was awake? How did I use that to find Cyrus?

Troy's thread had been the color of his eyes, mottled green, light brown, and gold. Maybe Cyrus's would be the same...and maybe it would feel similar to Troy's somehow because they were related? That was the theory at least, but I couldn't see—

Oh.

Even as I wrestled with it, I found Cyrus's thread. Not what I was expecting though. A graphite grey, like his eyes, but with a fiery tinge to it. That was weird. Cyrus struck me as more like gathered water: fluid, shifting, being whatever shape he needed to be and filling a container only to spill out of it or seep through the cracks. Troy was more nuanced, river and soil, a little of the fire in a torch. Hmm.

Not something to worry about now.

Steeling myself mentally, I reached for Cyrus's thread and gave a tentative metaphysical tug.

Nothing happened.

Frowning, I tried again. Cyrus had said I needed to imbue the tug with a sense of welcome, but I didn't really want to welcome him here. I wanted to know what he was hiding and why he was being so weird with Troy. More than that, I wanted them to have some kind of happy ending. It wasn't like I'd be getting one with my parents.

The thread slipped. I sighed and muttered a curse for my own distraction. It took three more attempts before the thread tightened and, with a pop, brought Cyrus to me.

"That was one of the most uncomfortable experiences I've had," he grumbled. "But I'm here and in one piece."

I was too busy staring at him in shock to answer. There was something overlaying him. I couldn't see auras like Troy could, so I didn't think it was that. But *something* hovered over him like a fiery shadow, and it gave me a bad feeling, a clench in the gut and a twist in my heart. I was lucky he was too busy investigating the clearing to notice me.

By the time he pulled his attention to me, it was gone and I'd fixed my face.

"Now I send you home?" I hoped he missed the fainter than usual quality of my voice.

He tilted his head. "You saw it, didn't you."

"Saw what?"

"Don't play games."

I swallowed then firmed my stance. "There was an overlay of some sort."

Cyrus's expression didn't change in any way that I would be able to describe, but something about his mien became dangerous. "My patron's protection. When you're playing with gods and rogue Dreamwalkers, it doesn't do to wander alone."

I couldn't help but doubt that was the full answer. With the vibe I was getting from him though, I was not about to push. Not with his open warnings about things happening here affecting us in the real. "Now I send you back?"

After a long look at me, like he was deciding whether I was going to be a problem, Cyrus nodded. "Gently. Find the gaps in the weave of the dream and the Chaos in me. Or whatever it is elementals sense in people."

"Then twist."

"*Gently*," Cyrus repeated. "Forcing it could eject someone somewhere nobody wants them to be."

"Okay." I focused, trying to find the space between the edges of the dream, like I'd been practicing. When I found one, I reached for Cyrus with Chaos.

Right as I twisted the thread of Chaos to send him through the weave of the dream, he shouted, "No! Not like—"

He was gone.

Fuck.

I split the dream to sunder it and gasped awake. My head was killing me, but I had to see what I'd done to Cyrus.

"Arden?" Troy said.

"Something went wrong." I stumbled to my feet.

Troy caught me then darted past me to the living room right as Cyrus gasped awake and started coughing.

"Gods damn it!" Cyrus pushed himself upright, snatched his cane, and got to his feet. "You cannot leave if that's how you're going to send Troy out of a dream."

"It's not like I did it on purpose," I shouted back. He'd given me barely anything to go on, couldn't—or refused to—answer my questions properly, and had objectives of his own. He seemed to blame me for the wedge between him and Troy when all I'd done was try to bring them together. My temper wasn't just lost; it was full-out gone. "How do I know it wasn't your patron messing with it? Maybe if you weren't hiding so much, we could figure this out."

Cyrus just shook his head and looked at Troy. "You say you've made your choice. I can't save you from yourself, boy. If you want to stay bonded to a primordial who could kill you in your sleep as easily as she breathes, on your head be it." To me, he added, "If you do get him killed, you'll face my vengeance. My oath to Ninlil be damned."

He left before I could answer or Troy could do more than snarl at the threat, slamming the door so hard in his anger that the house seemed to shake.

Chapter 18

I retreated to my armchair, pulled my knees up, wrapped my arms around my shins, and buried my face. That was exactly what I hadn't wanted to happen, and now I couldn't escape the feeling that I'd just damned Troy. Cyrus hadn't even told me how it'd gone wrong or how to fix it. It was like he wanted to force me to stay in the Triangle or to break up with Troy. I didn't know which, I didn't know why, and the whole session had made me utterly miserable.

Shifting air molecules warned me that Troy was near, and the light clack of a mug hitting the table was followed by the herby scent of chamomile.

"You won't hurt me," he said over the sound of his weight sinking into the couch. He sounded calmer now that his father was gone, despite the charged words. "And if you do, at least it won't be intentional."

"That's not good enough for me," I mumbled to my knees. "I'm sorry. I'll try harder on Dreamwalking. And to get along with him. I shouldn't have lost my temper like that."

"It's not just you who needs to try, my love. Of all of us, you've tried hardest. I see you calculating the best move. How to stand up for yourself without driving a wedge between me and him."

I lifted my head, and my heart squeezed. "You do?"

"Yes. Just know that if it comes to it, I will pick you. I missed him—still miss him—but I have to accept he's not who he was when I was ten. I'm not that boy anymore either. I'm what Omar made me. And who you helped me see I could be instead. He has to accept that as well and stop treating my affection like a prize that only you or him can have."

Tears jumped to my eyes as they had far too often lately. Side effect of not getting enough sleep: emotional overwhelm. I'd wanted to leave for Asheville tonight to make it there by dawn and catch the wolves off guard, but I was gonna have to try to sleep first.

Rather than answering Troy, I reached for the mug that was his peace offering or his reassurance that he wasn't mad at me for the argument that'd soured the post-hunt good mood.

"Thanks for this," I said.

He nodded, relaxing as I sipped.

I didn't want to drag the mood down further, but I had to clarify something before I left. "How long do we have before the separation is a problem?"

"Hmm." He leaned back against the couch and crossed his arms, his gaze searching the unlit fireplace. "I was okay for the three days you were on the gods' plane. Irritable but okay. The blood exchange should help stretch it out. A week, maybe two before you start feeling an itch in your bones. You'll feel agitated, like you need to run, but no amount of running or sparring will fix it. Then maybe another one to two weeks before detox kicks in."

"Detox?"

He nodded. "The pheromones and hormones that secure the physical bond layer over time. Get more complex. You start to need them."

Shit. No wonder the queens refused to let a hormonal bond settle. That was almost as good as letting someone they considered lesser control them.

"It might not be as bad for you." Troy shrugged. "Or it might take longer to get bad. I honestly don't know."

"Elemental, not elf?"

"Yes. I hope." He grimaced. "Mostly because I don't want to find out what happens if a primordial elemental detoxing from elf pheromones has a bad trip."

I noted he hadn't talked about how quickly he'd feel the effects on himself and decided to let it go rather than push. If he'd been fine for three days without a blood exchange, he should be good for the same now. I hoped, anyway.

Between that conversation, the Dreamwalking session, the refusal of the elves or the djinn to play ball, and not nearly enough sleep, I left for Asheville in a foul mood. I almost wished someone would try me when I got there. The drive was an easy one, a four-hour shot straight west on I-40. It was my first time driving that long or that far alone, and it was my first time seeing the mountains, for all I'd lived in the state my whole life. Despite already missing Troy and being worried about things back home, I couldn't help the lift my spirits got from both the pride in myself for breaking the habit of being a homebody tied to the land and river that nurtured me and my excitement to feel mountains. We had some hilly terrain at Eno, the foothills of the foothills of these rocks. But nothing like this.

I kept having to force myself to focus on the road and pull my magic back. Maybe for the first time ever, I wanted to roll in Earth, and I had Air extended to the max to taste the difference in these winds as they skirled over the hardwood-forested ridges.

These mountains were old, older than old.

Every time I let myself peek at them with Earth, I got honked at because I got dragged into their slow, sedate passage of time.

Which would be fine if I was sitting and trying to meditate. Not fine when I was meant to be going at least seventy miles per hour on the freeway but kept slowing down to forty because I was pulled into mountain time.

After the third time it happened, I reluctantly rolled the window up and put on some music. If I kept up like this, someone would call the cops or a state trooper would pull me over, and that would give Acting Director Lara Sinclaire exactly the opening she needed to fuck up my day. She'd already said I had a file. Files meant flags, and at the federal level, that would mean a big pain in the ass right when I needed to be most under the radar.

Troy might be willing to come and kick ass for me, but I couldn't put myself in a position where he'd feel the need to.

I finally reached the place where I needed to pick up the keys for my lodgings, a neat tiny house in the hills above Asheville. I think Troy would rather have put me up in whatever the fanciest hotel in the area was for security reasons, but he knew me. Knew I'd need as much nature around as possible to keep me grounded. I reeled my power signature in and kept my head down, hoping I didn't look suspicious as I tried to avoid the logical places for a camera and used the bill of my cap and my curls to hide my face. Then it was another short drive to the location of my actual rental.

As I got out of the car, the purl of a creek or stream made me smile. Troy had even found me a place with running water nearby. And it was...

I leaned back, gaping. It was a treehouse.

An honest to fucking Goddess treehouse, nestled partly in a massive oak and partly in the cliff face. Practically bouncing on my toes, I hurriedly gathered my things and let myself in. Small and quaint, with wood paneling and floors. All the fixtures were metal, glass, or wood, with natural fibers for any fabrics—no plastic or synthetic anything anywhere except where absolutely necessary. In the kitchen, a bottle of Malbec waited on the table, and the wooden box next to it held an assortment of my favorite teas. A balcony jutted out over a clearing, graced with two rocking chairs. I'd be able to see the stars after dark, if I was here for it, and the water I'd heard was a small waterfall tumbling down the rocks a short distance away.

I might be here alone, and the trip would probably end in blood, but Troy had somehow, in a matter of hours, arranged the perfect mini-getaway.

I got out my phone and dialed him.

"Are you—" He cut off at my wordless squeal of delight. "Ah. You're there. Good. I take it you approve?"

"Where did you find this? It's amazing!"

He was too far away for me to sense his feelings in the bond, but he let the pleasure come through in his voice. "Good. Have you unpacked yet?"

"No." I frowned. "What did you put in my suitcase?"

The smirk he must have been wearing was clear even on the phone. "Go settle in and find out. I'm about to be in negotiations with the Charleston Houses, so if you don't hear from me for a bit, don't worry. I'm fine."

There was an unspoken "for now" at the end of that statement, but he had Allegra nearby. He'd be okay. I had to trust his ability to keep his shit together and mine to get this done quickly so I could get home.

"Okay. I love you," I said.

"Love you too. Good hunting."

The call ended, and I ran back to the bedroom to throw open my suitcase.

On top of my clothes rested a small box of black wood. A piece of paper was tied to it with twine. I pulled the paper free and unfolded it.

I've been holding onto this for a special occasion, the note read. *You heading out on your own for the first time seems to fit. Don't be mad if there's some wishful thinking in how you choose to baptize it.*

There was no signature, but I knew Troy's handwriting. The word "baptize" made me frown; that was pretty clear in possibilities. But when I opened the box and found a beautiful little punchblade and a black leather sheath inside, all I could do was melt a little. The knife was silver—silver-plated steel, I amended to myself when I hefted it and tasted it with Earth—a scaled-down copy of his own punchblade. That one had always been too big to fit my fist comfortably, but this one...yeah. I could feel the savagery in the grin as I grasped it and made a metal middle finger.

Me and Troy weren't huge on gift-giving, preferring to show our love with actions and quality time, but I definitely appreciated this. I almost wouldn't mind testing it out on Sergei.

"You should really add a spell to that. Silver holds a djinn spell nicely."

With a swear, I jumped and whirled at Duke's voice.

He stood behind me, leaning against the door of the bedroom in his favorite human shape, grinning. "What are you doing so far from home, little bird? I was expecting to come out of the Old City in your house but..." Peering outside the window made him lift his eyebrows. "The mountains? Are you finally dealing with Sergei? Alone?"

"Yes," I snapped. "What the hell are you doing here?"

"Getting you your deal." Duke picked at long, black talons, pretending not to care. "Access to the archives was enough to get me a coalition willing to take a risk on your new Houses. But they want the elves on board first. Proof that everyone is appropriately serious about this whole mad endeavor."

"You're a day and a half late and several dollars short then." I pressed my lips together to stop from scolding him. It'd do me no good and only offend or amuse him. I wasn't sure which was worse. "We've got Keeya Bedoe. The rest wouldn't make a move without the djinn on board."

"Catch-22." Duke shrugged.

I heated at his nonchalance in the face of my feelings of defeat last night. "Go tell Troy, please."

"You're so cute when you're wrathful. Might want to work on that. Callista was even smaller than you, and she managed to be scary." He shifted planes before I could cuss him out.

Cute or not, I could beat his ass with elemental magic when he was in physical form, and he knew it. I gave myself another minute to be frustrated and disappointed that this hadn't come together sooner then forced myself to let it go. This was in Troy's hands now. Me getting pissed or upset about it all over again wouldn't help me do the job that was mine to do.

It was almost noon, and I needed to get out to the Volkov pack lands while the sun was high. Roman had been fine during the day, but his wolfy side had always ridden closer to the surface at night—smells and sounds got sharper, reflexes a little faster. A waxing crescent moon would give me a minor advantage, but the same at midday would give me the best chance of sneaking onto clan lands and doing some poking around.

I didn't bother unpacking. First, I planned to get this done as soon as possible and might have to make a quick getaway. Second, I was happy to live out of a suitcase. This wasn't my home. Home was 220 miles east, where my magic was sunk into the land and my bondmate had stayed.

I should probably make a tie here. But I hadn't been gone long enough for the absence to start aching, and while werewolves couldn't see or sense elemental magic, someone would probably sense a primordial's power signature. Tipping them off with that much magic would make investigating this case harder.

Grinning, I headed out the door. I had a case again. I might be alone, but I'd been alone and surrounded by enemies for a long time before Troy had come along. Omar had a Darkwatch informant somewhere in the area, but they had orders not to engage. The old man had almost had a conniption on hearing my plan, torn between the deeply ingrained responsibility to defend a queen and his personal opinion that, if I was finna be a jackass and go off alone again, it wasn't something he'd risk pulling the Triangle elves or the Darkwatch into a war over.

Fine by me. If I did this right, it'd be just like the best of the old times.

I refused to let myself dwell on what might happen if things went wrong, lest whoever was paying close enough attention to notice my thoughts and laugh at them got any ideas.

Chapter 19

My first stop was the Blood Moon clan hunting grounds not far from the Volkov mansion. Flashbacks to infiltrating Leith's boathouse—my boathouse now—at Jordan Lake distracted me as I navigated the narrow turn-off Omar's intel had pointed me to until I paused to take a breath and hold it.

"The best of the old days," I muttered to remind myself.

I had this. I might be rusty, but I'd infiltrated plenty of places before finally getting caught.

I pulled off, much like I had at Jordan Lake, and hid the car under the camo net Troy had stuffed in the trunk. Then I hiked in, following the musky scent of werewolves and another odd scent I couldn't place. Wolf but not.

Troy's nose might have the sensitivity to know, but mine didn't. It was still weird as hell following my nose as much as my eyes—an elf thing as far as I was concerned, given what Troy had said about how he navigated the world. But my senses had gotten better as my power grew, and there was certainly nothing to see.

At a small clearing, that changed. A low thrum against my magical senses alerted me to a tiny energy field above me. I froze, peering upward but couldn't see anything. I circled away from it, approaching from another angle.

There. A solar-powered camera pointed at the clearing. I'd barely avoided walking into its field of view. Fancy, from the look of it, but I'd have to get closer to learn much else. Fortunately, the tree was an easy climb with the lowest branches within my jumping reach.

As soon as I was up in the tree, I froze again.

It wasn't werewolf scent up here. It was earthy and a little sour—human, someone sweating hard in exertion and fear. Strong enough that whoever it was had been here observing something. And much stronger than any human scent on the ground.

What the hell?

There was no way Sergei or anyone else wouldn't have caught that scent, especially if they'd been in their wolf forms. So what was this?

Carefully, I shifted to dig out my phone and snap photos from a couple angles. Troy, Omar, and Etain would all be interested in whatever this was. I texted it to Troy with a quick note about location and general observations as well as a screenshot of the map with my current coordinates for him to pass along to the others. Then I shimmied back down the tree as quickly as I dared, not wanting to linger. More time meant more scent, and Roman and Sergei definitely knew what I smelled like.

Where there was one camera, there'd be more. If there'd been one watching the turn-off, I would have missed the energy coming off it amidst all that put off by my car. Someone might already know I was here. I'd brought my own car, preferring the comfort and reassurance of a vehicle I knew how to handle when I was so far from home. The Volkovs, the feds, or both might have been alerted already.

I'd only been investigating for an hour, and my plan was already going to shit. With steps as hurried as I could manage while moving as close to elven silence as I could, I made my way back to my car and got ready to go.

But go where? I reined in my desire to hurry off and tapped my fingers on the steering wheel, thinking hard.

The plan had been to gather evidence and confront the Volkovs only when I had to, given their numerical superiority. But if humans had cameras on the clearing, I had to find out why.

And it had to be humans; the camera and tree both smelled of them while the clearing and ground had only smelled of wolf. The human scent would have faded at ground level if they'd passed through that area quickly. Neither Omar nor Troy had mentioned the Darkwatch informant putting up a camera, and that informant wouldn't have been human in any case. The Bureau had been too quiet, given how many mundanes had gone missing during an attack on my land at home.

Had that been a feint? Something to keep me occupied while they moved on the werewolf blood?

The onyx ring on my middle finger heated and cooled then repeated the pattern. That wasn't quite it. Something was right, but something was wrong.

What would be the most unlikely thing in normal times?

Werewolves working *with* mundanes. Willingly.

The ring heated, and the Sight kicked me so hard I gasped as much from the physical clench of my stomach as the shocked outrage.

It wasn't just that Sergei wanted me gone. He was working with the humans too? For what? Something to do with the wolves.

Oh shit. Oh hell no. Was he really handing over werewolf blood willingly? Or worse, planning to turn mundanes as part of a deal with the Bureau?

This needed to be stopped. Right now.

One, because I had already decreed that no Othersiders were going to be telling anything to the mundane authorities, let alone working with them. Two, because if I came down hard on the Richmond elves for doing so and let the Blood Moon wolves slide, there'd be hell to pay with the elves.

And with Troy. I winced. I was more worried about his reaction than anything else.

I sent him another text, updating him on what I intended.

My phone buzzed almost immediately with his response: *Camera isn't ours. Eat something first.*

I'd been so ready to defend my decision that I couldn't help busting out laughing. Not for the first time, I reflected that with anyone else I'd be pissed at being managed. Because that's what he was doing—avoiding my temper and keeping tabs on my physical wellbeing. He was right to do so but still.

I shook my head and searched the Maps app for a restaurant nearby. I'd have to go back down the mountain, but the closest one would do. Burgers, fries, quick and simple stuff that'd keep me full for a while.

I got lunch to go, pulling off at a park to eat outside and get grounded. As I bolted down my food, equal parts hungry and anxious to keep up my investigation, I eased my shields lower as carefully as I could. It was a risk, but if the wolves were collaborating with the mundanes willingly, I needed to start anchoring myself in this area. I also needed to get myself as level as possible before dealing with Sergei and Roman again, and a land connection would help. I could do magic in an area without a tie to it, but I'd found having a connection made Water in particular easier for me to work with. The French Broad River wasn't far, and there were creeks and small waterfalls scattered throughout the mountains. I reached for the river, inhaling sharply at how old it felt. Kind of like the mountains it flowed through. It grounded me, oddly, rather than setting me on edge like some Water connections did.

Once refueled physically and magically, I tightened my shields again and headed for the Volkov family home.

It was a massive mansion tucked back in the woods on some private land off the Blue Ridge Parkway. I was sure the scenery was gorgeous, but I was too busy being on high alert for an attack to pay much attention. It'd be easy for an "accident" to send me off the mountainside. It was one of the options Troy had considered for dealing with the Volkovs in the last year after all.

Fortunately, I made it to pack territory without incident. The Volkovs were just one of several packs—family groups—in the Blood Moon clan, but they were the richest and oldest. Of course, they were now also at risk of dying out, with none of the three children of the old clan leader with children of their own on the way, as far as I knew.

For a minute, I felt bad that I couldn't bring myself to care about that. I should have. It was another Otherside faction on the edge because of all the change in the last few years. This one more directly my fault than some. Old Niko had been killed in a power play by the elves, and his wife Irina had fled and hadn't been heard from since. We didn't even know if she was still alive. From her failure to reappear when her sons had taken control of the family land, she was likely either dead or well and truly done with pack politics.

Omar's intel said Roman and Sergei were sharing leadership of Blood Moon, which sounded to me like the clan was still struggling to accept that Roman was, in their eyes, a magical "runt"—unable to shift fully. Sergei could, but he was technically too young and unproven to manage a clan. So the two brothers allied against challengers and had, according to reports, been winning. I kind of wished they hadn't been.

The tree cover got thicker and the road narrower as I got closer to the point my map said was the house. One lane, barely wide enough for the white Land Rover Sergei had been driving to make it. Easy ambush, if they were inclined to be offended that I hadn't called ahead.

Two massive wolves slunk out of the trees and showed me their teeth as I pulled up, so it seemed like they were choosing violence.

With this welcome, I was glad I'd made Troy stay at home. His protective tendencies would be in overdrive. I got out slowly, hands out to the sides, bumped the door shut with a hip, and took a few steps away from my car. If this went bad, I didn't need it trashed.

"I'm Arbiter Arden Finch out of the Triangle," I said. "I'm here to see your alphas."

Both wolves lowered their heads and growled.

"Y'all really wanna do this the hard way?" I asked. A year ago, this would have set panic creeping in at the edges of my mind. Now, adrenaline flooded in but not fear.

This was anticipation.

I smiled. "Okay then. I'll bite."

As soon as the words were out of my mouth, they rushed me.

Werewolves were fast.

Primordial elementals were, apparently, faster.

One wolf kept coming while the other split off to circle me. I sidestepped the one who lunged just enough to avoid the teeth and brought my fist down on their nose with all of my now considerable strength.

That wolf dropped with a startled cry, stunned.

Moving air told me exactly where the other wolf was as they attacked my flank. I dodged their leap and side-kicked so hard something cracked.

That wolf hit the ground harder than the first one had with a pained yelp.

When I turned back to the dazed wolf, they were dragging themselves to wobbly feet. I was feeling generous, so I let them have a moment to shake and orient.

"If you're smart," I said, "you'll show your belly before you get beat so bad your momma will feel it."

This wolf was either not smart or more afraid of something other than my beating.

So be it. I'd figure out why when I wasn't defending my life and reputation.

The wolf tried a fake-out, pretending to flank me only to set their feet and twist to come for my throat. I leaned in a backbend to let him soar right over me, twisting to punch up with a devastating blow to the stomach. If I'd been using my new punchblade, I'd've gutted him, but I was trying to do this without killing anyone.

A scraping claw drew blood on my right forearm, but that wolf landed badly, without enough air to howl as his left foreleg snapped.

I looked at the second wolf, who immediately rolled to their—his—belly and showed his throat. Wary of a trick, I bound him like that with Air before turning back to the bigger troublemaker.

That wolf was laying on his side, gagging.

I approached, hands on my hips to make myself look bigger as I did my best impression of Troy's threatening loom. "You done now? Or does your daddy need to feel a beating too? Maybe I could knock you into last week, and you could make smarter fucking choices when this day came around again."

Slowly, with bared teeth, he rolled to his back and showed his throat.

This one I definitely tied down with Air before turning back to the house.

The air eddied with the breaths from more bodies, low enough to the ground that I was willing to bet they were more wolves. I reached with all four elements to count bone structures and circulatory, respiratory, and nervous systems.

The clan knew I was here now. No more need to hide my magic, even if I'd stuck to physical attacks to prove that I wasn't easy meat.

Three more wolves.

"Sergei," I shouted, "you can call off your puppies, or I can consider this an act of war instead of a misunderstanding and level the house. Your choice."

The air rippled as the three wolves in the trees drew nearer. As I stretched a little farther, I found five more behind them.

I sighed, more annoyed than anything. If it was elves, I'd be worried. Stronger weres might be able to partially shrug off elven Aether and get inside an elf's guard with their speed, but if I didn't catch the spell and slice it with Chaos, the elf would get me.

Werewolves, I could take. At least now that I'd had Darkwatch training to complement my holding all four elements.

"Last chance, Sergei," I called out. "Or whoever's in the house. You call off the wolves in the woods, or I stop holding back. Blood was drawn, so blood is owed."

The door opened.

Sergei leaned in the doorframe with a smile that looked more like a sneer. His grey eyes were harder than they used to be, angrier. There were dark circles under them, giving his pale skin a bruised look, and his dark hair and beard were unkempt. He was still dressed in designer clothes, but otherwise he looked nothing like the sharp, cocky kid who'd come to the Triangle thinking to cross me and gain Callista's favor.

What the hell was going on in these mountains?

"Look who it is, big brother," Sergei said, calling deeper into the house. "Your little girlfriend finally decided to pay us a visit." He swept a mocking bow. "Your fucking Highness. I'd say be welcome, but you're not wanted here. Get the fuck off pack land."

Oh, this was not fucking funny at all.

Before I could reply, Roman came to stand beside his brother in the doorway. The older, slightly shorter, slightly more muscled Volkov looked almost the same as he had when I'd last seen him when I exiled him from the Triangle: lost and confused.

"What're you doing here, Arie?" he asked. "We didn't invite you. And lest you forget, you didn't seem too keen on seeing me again."

There was a note of something ugly in his voice. Hurt or betrayal.

I ignored it and pushed down the anger that he was both back to using pet names with me and, like Sergei, hadn't acknowledged that their people had drawn blood. "I don't need permission or an invitation to visit anywhere in the Carolinas demesne. Or the Dominion demesne, for that matter. Just in case the Farkas pack didn't get the memo."

Sergei snarled, a wolfish expression on a human face. "Even Callista had the sense not to come to Blood Moon territory. If you don't have her wisdom, it's your funeral."

I rolled my eyes, even as I kept half my attention on the wolves still edging in from the woods. "Callista was too busy planning her vengeance against the gods to care about y'all. I came out to see how things are going, since neither your sister nor I have heard from you in months."

No need to mention what I'd already learned just yet.

"My bitch sister needs to come home herself then," Sergei said. "And bring that whore Ana with her."

I glanced at Roman to see his reaction. Nothing, beyond looking at me like he couldn't believe what he was seeing.

"Tell your wolves to stand down. Or I'll take you down and deal with whoever is more reasonable," I said. "I have cause and I won't say it again."

The stand-off stretched. I was about to cause an earthquake when Roman squeezed his brother's shoulder.

"Let her up," he said in a voice low enough that I wouldn't have heard it when we were last together, before the Wild Hunt had boosted my senses. "Better to let her come in, see nothing, and send her away than make her think there's a case here."

Sergei half turned to sneer over his shoulder. "Lemme guess. Personal experience."

"Yes." Roman flicked a glance at me.

I made sure I was frowning like I couldn't hear what they were saying but was trying real hard. I might lack subtlety for an elf, but I had more than enough to deal with werewolves.

Roman refocused on his brother. "Trust me. You don't want her to start digging."

Good ol' Roman. Always underestimating me and everyone else. Asshole.

Useful asshole though, because now I knew our intel had been correct and that what I'd found in the clearing should indeed concern me. There was definitely a reason for me to be coming out to the Blue Ridge Mountains.

Chapter 20

S hit almost kicked off again when I reached the porch and Sergei tried to insist on patting me down before letting me in the house. From his leer as he offered to do it himself after my first objection, weapons weren't all he was gonna be looking for.

I pulled on Air to make my eyes flare gold. "You seem to be under some seriously bad misapprehensions here, Sergei. Nobody's touching me. Not your people. Not you. Not Roman." I smiled, making it as unsettling as I could. "Unless they want to deal with whatever consequences I see fit to deal out." I bit my tongue before the words "I'm the Arbiter" could fall from my lips. They knew it. Making me say it would only make me look insecure and undermine me.

A dangerous silence stretched before Roman broke it. "I'll vouch for her."

"Not smart, big bro." Sergei's eyes flickered to the silver of his wolf.

"Come on, Sergei. She hates violence. Let's just get this visit over with and let her be on her way."

"Hates violence so much she killed three queens and beat the shit out of our people at Jordan Lake?" Sergei retorted.

Roman rolled his eyes. "They attacked her first. She let me go, right?"

I was starting to regret that. Tempting as it was to interject, I kept my mouth shut. Let Roman think he was being the good guy here. I wasn't gonna promise anything. Not here, not now.

"Fine." Sergei turned back to me. "Let my boys up."

His boys, not *our*—his and Roman's. Interesting.

Roman's lips thinned but he didn't say anything, which hinted at a first-among-equals arrangement between them, probably based on Sergei's ability to shift fully.

All the same, I shook my head. "You don't give me orders. Neither of you. They stay where they are until our conversation is concluded to my satisfaction."

Roman opened his mouth, probably to say something ridiculous like "be reasonable."

I kept speaking. "If you have a problem with that, I'll pin all the wolves I can sense out there in the woods. Or maybe suspend them? How do wolves do upside down?" That was becoming one of my favorite tricks. I reached again, finding another five had joined the first set. How big was the clan these days? Something else I needed to find out. "Ten or fifteen is easy enough to handle, but if you need a demonstration, I'm happy to offer it."

Sergei stiffened, barely stopping himself from turning to where one set of five had gathered, and swept another exaggerated bow. "After you."

I don't know what I was expecting, but the inside of the house somehow managed to look expensively rustic. Wood finishing but gold accents. Marble floors and countertops, antlers and pelts on the wall. New money gone rural, a ridiculously ostentatious hunting lodge that didn't look anything like what Roman had done with his manufactured home over at Eno and had none of the simple comfort of my own woodsy hideaway.

I hated it, especially when I stopped to consider that Roman had wanted me to give up all that I had and was to move back here with him.

Sergei's lip twisted as he sniffed when I passed him. His gaze darted to my shoulder. "That's quite the love bite. Bet I can give you a better one."

I tugged my shirt aside to reveal it fully and prodded it gently. Almost healed, but with as many bites as that shoulder had taken lately it would definitely scar this time. I let my memory of yesterday's pleasure bubble up to tinge my scent as I smirked. "Nobody stakes a claim quite like Troy. Leave the bites to the kings, baby wolf."

Roman slammed his fist against the wall. "If that elf bastard—"

"*King* elf bastard." I barely kept a straight face, remembering Troy making a similar dry correction to Roman a few years ago. It'd been one of my first glimpses into Troy's sense of humor.

Apparently Roman remembered it too because he somehow managed to flush redder and glare harder. "If he thinks he can hurt you and get away with it—"

"Troy? Hurt me?" I rolled my eyes. "Please. Enough posturing, Roman. The only partner or ally of mine who's consistently tried to hurt me and get away with it is you. Calm down and shut the hell up before I decide to do something about it."

"So you can forgive that *elf bastard* for fucking drowning you, actually trying to kill you, but not me for only being involved in a messed-up situation because of *his* sister?" Roman snarled.

I just glared at him. I was not having this conversation here. Or at all, if I had my way. I didn't owe him this.

Roman had other ideas. "What makes him so much better?"

"Your big plan was to hook up with Evangeline, who actually fucking hated me and actively wanted me dead." I made sure the sarcasm was thick enough for even him to get it. "Brilliant move, Roman. Top-tier strategic thinking there. You really would have been the better choice."

Roman had known me when I was a nobody, so weak and powerless that I'd had to hide as a mundane and magical null from everyone, including him. I'd gone to him for help on cases or for comfort when shit got difficult. He was the first person I willingly outed myself as an Othersider to, and I was regretting that now.

He stared at me as silence stretched. "Who have you become, Arie?"

"Not who. What. I became an arbiter," I said coldly. "I'm not here as Arie, the girl you used to know and date. I'm here as Arden Finch Solari, Arbiter of the Carolinas and Dominion demesnes, High Queen of House Solari, and the Eternal fucking Huntress, to discuss the future of this territory. Oh, and your sister's imminent return to Asheville. Pick up your Goddess-damned phone the next time she calls."

Okay, so maybe the reminder was necessary. It stung though, that I was this out of control in my own demesne. Stung and made me anxious. The gods were watching. They were always watching. I couldn't help but feel like they'd find me lacking with all this. Would mentioning the loss of magic to the Volkovs get them in line? Or make them more determined to oust me and put a talking point straight into their hands to use as justification?

The two brothers exchanged looks. Sergei looked pissed. Roman was trying to stay cool, but anger furrowed his brow and anxiety pinched the corners of his mouth.

As far as I could tell, neither of them wanted Vikki back on this side of the state, which meant that, as Arbiter, I did. If she wanted to keep playing troublemaker, I'd clear out the territory and use it as a bargaining chip.

First though, I needed to make a point.

After a brief hesitation, both wolves headed toward what looked like an office behind gilded French doors, as though they expected me to follow. A quick pulse of elemental magic told me there was nobody else on the ground or upper floors, but there was something odd in what might be a cellar, an empty space belowground. Something that registered as halfway between mundane and vampire. It didn't feel like Darnell—he'd felt almost too alive—so I didn't know what it could be. But there were multiple instances of it.

I could only think of one explanation, given that we'd found werewolf blood at Verve and the odd scent in the clearing earlier. Shit. Could they really be fucking stupid enough to turn humans at the pack home? Drugged, maybe?

Roman started to turn, looking over his shoulder.

I covered my consternation by turning in a different direction, where my nose told me food had recently been prepared. There was no way I was gonna be here without the protection of hospitality, as thin a shield as the ritual of meat and mead might be.

"Where the hell are you going?" Sergei said. Heavy footsteps caught up to me. "You don't just get to—"

"Your manners leave a great deal to be desired," I said without stopping my quick pace to the kitchen. "Since you're not offering meat and mead or even salt and water, I figured I'd help myself."

A sense of movement made me duck, whirl, and come up with my hands in a block to sweep Sergei's reaching hand away.

Startled, he snarled and tried again.

This time, I caught his wrist and, to his surprise, held on. "I told you, Sergei. You don't get to touch me."

He tried to wrench his hand free and would have succeeded if I hadn't pulled on Fire and tried one of the tricks Val warned me about. One that I'd used to kill only a few days ago. This could not be allowed to stand.

Sergei dropped, his nerves so inflamed that he couldn't find air to scream.

Roman came running, and I threw a wall of Air up on both sides of him to keep him trapped in the hallway while I dealt with his brother. He hit the one in front and bounced, raising another flashback to the day the factions in the Triangle had agreed to the alliance.

"You always needed a hard lesson, Sergei. You appear to be in charge here, and one of your wolves drew blood from the Arbiter." I squeezed his wrist until his bones ground together. The feeling sickened me, but I couldn't keep being a pushover here. If Sergei wanted to play the same role his father had and be the domineering alpha, I'd have to dominate him in the only way he'd understand.

I could not let my authority be undermined and have Otherside fall into chaos. Not now. Not with the stakes so high. If being a protector meant compromising my personal ideals to defend the greater good...well, I guess I'd just gain a deeper understanding of the mindset Troy lived in.

I'd worry about it later, when I wasn't pouring nerve-degrading magic into a self-declared alpha werewolf.

A whimper escaped Sergei, more wolf than man, and his eyes silvered. Claws sprouted from his fingertips.

I wove a little more Fire into the chord I was feeding into his nervous system, trying for the deft touch Troy always managed with me. I probably failed, from the way Sergei's eyes were bugging.

"Arie!"

Lifting my eyes was the only movement I made.

The look I was giving Roman made him flinch. "A—Arbiter. Let him go. Please."

I looked down at Sergei. "When he stops trying to shift."

"The strain he's under will make that harder."

"He's supposedly an alpha. An alpha should have the control. *Will* have the control, if they want to remain alpha in my demesne." I knew it was possible to maintain control through acute pain.

Terrence had broken his hand sparring in the bar's basement studio with Troy last summer and, despite a bone piercing the skin, had remained completely cool and collected. Not a hint of his cat until Troy set the hand and Terrence intentionally shifted to heal it faster. They'd shaken on it and gone up to the main part of the bar to have a drink after.

"It doesn't work like that," Roman said.

"It does. For those who have earned the right to be alpha rather than simply inheriting it."

Frustrated, Roman slammed his fists against my barrier. "You're killing him!"

"This is nowhere close to it. This just hurts like hell." And it was turning my stomach almost to the point of vomiting, but apparently this was who I had to be to deal with these two. "Callista would have killed him, and the two idiots outside who attacked me. This is merciful."

With panting gasps, Sergei finally managed to reverse his shift.

I eased up on the flow of Fire with each sign that he was becoming more human, until he'd made it all the way back.

When I released Fire and his wrist, he dropped, retching. Dark patches dampened his shirt and pants, and the rank scent of fear and pain hung heavy in the air. His hoarse rasp seemed too loud in the quiet house.

"You will both submit to me as Arbiter," I said in a deadly soft tone. "Or you will be removed. I don't care how you two work things out with Vikki. But she will be coming home, and you will all submit to me."

Roman glared, jaw clenched, but slowly went to a knee and tilted his head to show his throat. On the floor, Sergei did the same.

"Good." I forced myself to relax slightly. "Now, I'm gonna give you one more chance to show some proper hospitality and respect. Or we're gonna have to do all this all over again. When we're done with the formalities, we will discuss sedition and treason."

Roman's head whipped up. He was nowhere near the actor Troy was, and I caught the tinges of fear and disbelief before he managed to hide them.

"What are you talking about?" he asked.

"Did you think I wouldn't find my own Watchers? My territory spans three large states. There's plenty of people in all of them who want to be on the right side of the woman who was chosen to ride with the gods and can control the weather with climate-change disasters on the rise." That was maybe more wishful thinking than anything else. But I had to appear to have both knowledge and magical strength, or shit would get much worse much faster. "Go on and fetch whatever y'all are using for hospitality these days so we can get this conversation over with."

Roman stepped over his brother and led the way to the kitchen.

I followed, close enough to be threatening but far enough that I'd be able to dodge him if he tried something.

Sergei limped in as Roman was pouring the third glass of mead under my watchful eye. The younger wolf was in bad shape—shivering, with a fine tremor in the hand that reached for his mead.

"With meat and mead, we greet our guest," both wolves said.

I ignored the resentment under their words and toasted them. "With meat and mead, we keep the peace."

Unable to help the ironic twist to my smile despite seeing how badly I'd fucked up Sergei, I downed my glass and helped myself to a piece of the brisket that must have just been cooked from the smell of the kitchen. Now that I was properly a guest, any move to harm me would be a severe breach of Otherside protocol for which I could claim all kinds of compensation.

Or simply kill them outright, given my rank and theirs and the blood already spilled, no matter how shallow the cut.

When they'd had their bite of meat and swallow of mead, they started to head back to the office.

"Where are y'all going?" I crossed my arms, tilted my head, and arched an eyebrow, letting them see that I couldn't believe they thought they were gonna retake control of the situation that easily. "This won't take long. We can talk here."

From their reluctance as they paused and turned back, they wanted me in the office for some reason. My private investigator's instincts flared. A trap? Recording devices? Or was there something in the rest of the house they didn't want me to see? Maybe it was those weird life signatures that were closer than before.

I wasn't going to figure it all out today, but I needed to get as much as I could outta them. Sergei would be mad as hell when he recovered and vindictive about it. Roman would probably get some bad ideas too. Where to start?

Maybe with silence.

I helped myself to another shaving of brisket, licking my fingers in what felt like a completely overdone way, but one that had Roman watching my mouth. Which told me that he'd only been acting the part of the submissive earlier. He still saw me as a woman to conquer and not his Arbiter to respect.

That told me still more: he had something he thought gave him an edge over me. That tied in with the camera and mundane scent I'd found earlier. But what did it mean?

Sergei was too busy supporting himself on the counter to notice what I was doing with my fingers, so I snapped them under his nose when they were clean.

"Well?" I prompted.

He jumped. "Well what? Arbiter."

His delay in offering me my title said as much as Roman's focus on my fingers. Not good. Not good at all.

"You were going to tell me why it is that I'm hearing rumors Blood Moon is finna break away from the Carolinas demesne. That sounds like a vote of no confidence to me." That was a stretch, given I had only werewolf blood in human hands and no rumors, but it seemed like a fit for the evidence and behavior.

Again, Sergei barely stopped himself from looking outside. But this time, his head half-jerked to the door leading from the back of the kitchen to the outside. "I don't know why you would have heard those kinds of lies, Arbiter."

I looked at Roman. "And you? Any ideas?"

"No. Arbiter."

I didn't need Troy's truthreading ability with liars as bad as these two. A decade of experience in private investigation was more than enough. "Fine. Then let's talk about treason. A mundane healthtech startup had werewolf blood. Explain."

"How should I fucking know?" Sergei's hands shook a little harder before he clenched them into fists. "It's not like we're the only wolves in this demesne."

"That's not an explanation."

"I don't have one. I don't need one."

The way his words were grated out in a breathy fear could be as much him fearing the consequences as lying. And those consequences could be the ones I'd already dealt out, or something he feared from the Sinners, who I was now convinced he was working with. I really had nothing here. Even with what I'd done to Sergei, both of them were still trying to hide shit from me. I was going to have to see if Zadie had managed to find more in the hacked data in the last night and a half.

Roman shifted from one foot to the other. "Arie—Arbiter. We know how dangerous this Supernatural Bureau is to Otherside. Believe me when I say we don't want the wrong attention drawn to the clan."

Entirely truthful words. Completely duplicitous intent. Compared to my dealings with the elves, the werewolves were child's play. I was tempted to push. But maybe I could get them to expose themselves in a way that would show everyone what they were up to, without having to put more blood on my hands.

"Fine," I said. "Then you won't mind me staying in town a few days to take in the sights. I've never been to the mountains. Gorgeous territory here. Almost inclines me to spend more time out this way."

Roman glanced at Sergei, who kept his gaze on me.

So it really was Sergei ahead of Roman. Interesting.

Sergei reached for another piece of brisket with such faux-nonchalance that it hurt. "Of course, Arbiter. Our territory is yours."

The ease with which all of that rolled off his tongue only made it worse. Heat flushed over me. How the hell could they think so little of me and my abilities that they would dare to lie so badly? Heat flipped to cold when another thought flitted across my mind: they might be that sure of their mundane allies, which meant the Bureau was in a better position than I'd realized.

"Excellent." I was glad for all my experience with the elves helping me keep my voice steady. "Then I expect a proper reception on my next visit."

"Yes, Arbiter," both brothers said.

Without waiting for their say-so, I made my way to the front of the house and out the door. When I was in my car, I freed the wolves who'd attacked me from their bonds of Air—and downed them again with the same nerve-searing Fire I'd used on Sergei. I tied the chord off, a short thread that would dissipate in a few minutes. If nothing else, it was punishment for drawing blood and would keep the wolves focused on their brethren rather than following me.

If a game was afoot in Asheville, I'd use every dirty trick I had to turn it in my favor.

Chapter 21

I was almost at the end of the private road when I spotted a partially obscured figure leaning casually against a tree. A large case was propped against it at their side.

"Who in the hell is this?" I squeezed the steering wheel, mentally preparing myself to run them down if they tried something. Most people forgot cars the size of my Civic hatchback weighed in at about a ton and a half and were therefore excellent weapons. Not me.

As I got closer, I realized it wasn't the tree cover that was making them hard to see. It was shadows.

An elf.

They dropped the shadows and raised a hand.

I stopped the car as much out of confusion as for the hail and rolled down the window. "Darius?"

Allegra's twin had shaved the locs he'd shared with his sister and gained some bulk, but it was definitely him.

"My queen," he said just loudly enough for me to hear. "Are you well? That meeting looked tense."

I had no idea how the hell he'd gotten out here, where he'd come from, or how he knew anything about my meeting with the Volkovs, but I couldn't leave an elf on their land. "Get in. Hurry up."

Darius stashed his case in the back seat before getting in the front with an air of reluctance. "If I may, my queen...first, I'm sorry."

"What for?" I rolled up the window and got the car going again, anxious to be gone from here.

"Everything? Hurting you, and Troy. And turning up like this."

"You weren't yourself." My stomach clenched. I believed that, but he'd really fucking hurt us when he'd severed the bond. Nearly killed us, probably. It was hard to be in an enclosed space with him and trust that he wouldn't do it again, but I couldn't leave him there, if only for my own sake. All the remaining Monteagues were mine, and everyone knew it. "Aside from that, what are you doing here?"

"Alli contacted me," he said with uncertain hesitance. "She said you'd lifted my exile."

"Yeah, so you could go home and help keep Troy level while I'm gone. What are you doing *here*? And where's your car?"

"I got an Uber to an overlook and hiked in from there. Figured you'd come this way eventually." He rubbed a hand over his head. "Asheville was on my way. Alli said T's okay for now and would probably stay that way longer if he knew you had backup. Everyone knows I was exiled, so if it comes down to it, you tell them I've gone rogue."

I took my eyes off the road long enough to give him a startled look. "You mean throw you under the bus. That would get you killed, given the current situation."

He shrugged, looking anxious as hell. "I know. But I owe you."

I bit my tongue to stop from saying that no, he didn't, because that was a reflex. But deep down, I felt like he did owe me. I owed it to myself to validate that feeling, even if only in my own head. Yes, it was shitty what Orion and the gods had done to him, but I'd been harmed. Troy had too.

Instead of denying it, I said, "Allegra is okay with this?"

"It was her plan. I don't know if the Captain knows."

"If he did, he'd probably agree," I muttered, assuming Darius meant his father and not Etain. I didn't love how Omar dealt with his kids, but that was between them. They were all grown.

"Probably." Darius seemed less distressed by that than he did being in the car with me.

"What's in the case?" I asked to distract us both.

"Sniper rifle."

"Excuse me?" That was definitely not what I'd been expecting. I really did not need an elf sniping a wolf and starting a war that would surely signal imbalance to the gods at the worst possible time.

"I posted up nearby to keep an eye on you."

Which was probably what Allegra, as the female and therefore dominant half of their twin pair, had ordered him to do. Darius might lack Troy's intensity, but apparently, they shared the complete acceptance that violence would be the natural answer if diplomacy failed.

I wanted to be pissed about that—I was trying to do things in such a way that people didn't get killed, and that would mean compromise—but I didn't have the energy for it. Besides, I'd blown Sergei's nervous system and that of two of his wolves, with only my title and their attempts to hit me first keeping it from being egregious magical trespass. "Just tell me where we need to stop to pick up your bags. You're staying with me."

"I am?" He winced when I gave him a firm look. "Apologies, my queen. I don't mean to question you. It...just makes it harder to say I've gone rogue if I'm staying with you."

"I don't fucking care. I'm overruling Allegra." When he just gaped, I huffed an exhausted sigh. "You're one of mine. You're family at this point. I'm not letting you or anyone else throw your life away like that. It's not like you were in your right mind before."

If anything, that made him more anxious. "My queen—"

"Shush. You've been gone for a while, and apparently nobody's told you that I'm ending the death cult. I've had enough."

"But—"

"Why is everyone arguing with me today? Goddess, will it make you feel better if I say there's been a marriage offer for you?"

"There has? Who? If I may ask, my queen."

"Sonia Bedoe. But I told her it's your choice. Neither Troy nor I will order you into it or guilt you or whatever." When Darius sat in shocked silence, I poked him with Air. "Hotel. Or wherever you're staying."

He gave me the address in a breathy voice that said I'd maybe dropped a few too many bombshells on him or had done something completely unexpected. This man was nothing like the arrogant conqueror of the governor's mansion, and I wondered if he, like Troy, had an inner darkness that he kept tamped down after a lifetime of abuse. One that had been pulled forth while he was under the influence of whatever spell had trapped him. Or maybe that arrogance had been the spell itself. Hard to tell.

I shook my head as I fed the address to my Maps app. That was neither here nor there. "While you were keeping an eye on things, did you happen to notice anything that might be a cellar door?"

"Yes, my queen. At the rear of the house."

"Ma'am will do." Awkward to be that formal with someone who'd be my brother-in-law, but whatever would keep the equilibrium.

"Yes, ma'am."

"The rear of the house." I tried to orient myself from my memory, which was difficult without having had a full tour and especially having been focused on whether I was about to be attacked. I'd have to check a map later, but I thought the rear might be in the vicinity of the kitchen. Was that why the Volkovs had been so anxious for me to be out of that space? "How big?"

"Big. Double doors, wide enough to let two men in shoulder to shoulder. They looked like reinforced wood. Heavy hinges so probably pretty thick."

"Big enough to carry a human body down."

Darius didn't even blink. "Yes, ma'am. Certainly and easily."

I thought fast. Darius's appearance offered me an opportunity I hadn't had before: to set someone on the mundanes I thought must be working for or with Blood Moon, without having to lose the scent of the clan's treason.

"Change of plans," I said. "I'll drop you off in town. I need you to track down any mundanes that look like government types. Do you know what I mean?"

"Yes, ma'am, of course. Bureau for Supernatural Investigation?"

I couldn't help my grin. For all I liked to work on my own, it was good to have help when I was truly alone. "That's my guess."

As I filled Darius in on our intel plus what I'd found and suspected, confidence and surety returned to his bearing. "Understood, ma'am. That also makes the car that's been following us more reasonable."

"What?" I glanced in the rearview mirror. I'd been so caught up in werewolf drama that I hadn't been paying attention.

"Black SUV, three vehicles back now, fast lane. They're good, but DC plates have to be front and back and that vehicle is obviously reinforced. Not much reason I'm aware of for a federal government vehicle to be here in Asheville unless it's for the wolves or for you."

Cold gripped me. I'd been so confident with reassuring Troy that I'd be fine, and I'd missed a glaring threat. Because now that I was looking, it was obviously not a local truck.

"When you get off this highway, make a loop of the first block," Darius said. "I'll jump out when there's a red light. You keep going."

"What are you gonna do?"

The darkness I'd suspected lived deep inside Darius peeked out in the small grin that curled his lips as he kept his attention on the rearview mirror. "Just cause an accident and steal a few memories."

I did my best to act like I'd known stealing memories was a fucking thing, but I was freaked out and had a feeling Darius could smell it. No wonder Orion or whoever had chosen him to attack me and Troy. Was that why I'd had amnesia afterward?

Cause a car accident—presumably by way of Darius himself getting hit by a reinforced SUV—and steal some memories. Like it was a trip to the grocery store. Troy talked like that sometimes when he wasn't thinking. Casual assassination or mind alteration. The more I learned about the Monteagues, the more they fucking terrified me. And I'd proposed marriage to the strongest of them, Goddess save me.

"I won't hurt you, my queen," Darius said in a soft voice. "I know what I did. But this is to make up for it."

"Yeah. Sure. Okay." I kept telling myself that Allegra, and certainly Troy, wouldn't have let Darius anywhere near me if they thought he might be a threat. That they had redirected him here had to mean he truly believed he wouldn't hurt me.

I had to trust them. All of them. Or I'd be alone again. As I was slowly discovering, I really didn't like that.

I pulled off at the next exit and joined the flow of traffic going downtown. The blessed light turned red, and Darius jumped out without another word when I stopped for it and checked traffic before turning right.

Stealing memories. What. The. Hell. Both Allegra and Troy had to have known about this and not only considered it completely normal but reasonable for me to be around.

Between the Volkovs and the Monteagues, Otherside family dynasties were quite literally driving me to distraction. I didn't know how I made it back to my treehouse, but I did, with Darius's sniper rifle just casually sitting in the backseat of my car and me with no permit in a part of the state where I definitely didn't want to be Black and a known Othersider with an unpermitted military-grade rifle and no way of altering minds or stealing thoughts.

I didn't even get a chance to hide that or call Troy before Harqil showed up.

It was a measure of what kind of day it'd been that I didn't do anything other than stare at them when they manifested in the kitchen, where I was prepping a cup of chamomile tea before committing myself to dealing with any of this.

They snorted. "That much fun today, hey?"

I just kept staring.

"Got it. Shell-shocked. Fortunately, I'm here to help. Your father wore a pendant. Do you know where it is?"

Frowning, I resisted the usual reflex to reach up and grip it. "Why?"

"Because certain members of our group have taken their nature to heart in a way that others consider excessive given the current circumstances."

Translation: there was a rift among the tricksters. Could I use that?

"You could at least manage it to an extent," Harqil said, addressing my unspoken thought. "If you had your father's prince's pendant and you convinced one of your djinn to turn it into a callstone for your mate. It would give you a leg up in your Dreamwalking experiments as well, since Cyrus is being Cyrus."

"Wait what? You can make a callstone to use between an elf and—"

"Arden, darling. You can make whatever you like when you're an elder djinni with celestial support. Do you have the pendant or not?"

I fished it out of my shirt. It clacked against the hematite callstone I used to call Duke.

"Perfect." Harqil waved a hand absentmindedly as they approached me and shoved a scrap of parchment at me when it manifested in that hand. "Give the djinni this. I was never here."

And just like that, they were gone. Not even a ripple of reality. I was standing alone in my rented kitchen with a screaming tea kettle and a piece of paper so old it felt like it'd fall apart if I rubbed my fingers wrong.

Terrified of that very outcome, I pulled the kettle off the stove then grabbed for my callstone with my free hand. "Duke?"

"Arden?" The voice that answered was feminine.

"Iaret! What are you doing with Duke's callstone?"

"Does it matter? What do you want?"

I hesitated. Iaret wasn't quite all there yet. But she was still the one who'd managed to re-enchant the stone that'd brought me and Troy back together. She might be the better option for this.

"I have something you might want to see. About enchanting a stone," I said.

I'd barely finished the words when the tug on my aura signaled a djinni trying to locate me. With Duke, it was a smooth, easy thing, something I rarely noticed until he had practically manifested on this plane on account of our blood tie.

Iaret was making a secondary connection, and it hurt, prickling like hot needles.

She came out of the Veil half in her natural djinni form and half in her preferred human form, a dark-skinned woman with fire-opal eyes and a lower body lost in smokeless flame. "Let me see."

I extended the scrap, wincing when she snatched it and hoping it wouldn't burn.

Iaret peered at it. "Oh! I haven't seen Ninlil's handwriting in ages. Where did you get this?"

My mother's handwriting? Harqil had casually handed me something my mother had written and failed to mention it? How many of her writings were going to fall into my possession via other people this month?

"Arden!" Iaret snapped her fingers.

"I— It was a gift."

"Harqil. Meddling as usual."

I frowned at the affectionate note in her voice. "I thought y'all didn't like each other."

"Nobody said that. We just have different goals sometimes is all, and the celestials are really the only ones worth competing against. Especially these days with everyone dying so much more quickly than they used to, ugh." She tapped my nose playfully. "Good of you to confirm it was them though. That means I can trust this piece of rubbish."

Despite the disdain in her voice, her fire-opal gaze sparked with excitement.

I tried to be patient but couldn't help myself. "Will it work?"

Her nose wrinkled as she peered at the scrap. "If you're intending to do something as mad as link an elf to anyone djinn-blooded, then yes. I mean, it should. A spell like this has been held hypothetical by the Academy for at least three millennia. Given Ninlil wrote this in early Sumerian text on Egyptian papyrus, she was having a laugh by concealing it from them. Delightful bitch. Always did like her. Let me see the stone."

Reluctantly, I handed it over. I hadn't heard of the Djinn Academy before. Hadn't even considered there might be a body aside from the Council.

"Don't get ideas," Iaret said. "The Academy keeps itself occupied with theory, not action."

There went that prospect. Still, it was good to know there was even more opportunity than I'd thought.

Iaret was still looking at me when I refocused. She traced the smooth surface of the onyx with her thumb. "Are you sure you want to do this?"

"What are the risks?"

"With you and your little king? Who the hell knows. That's why I'm asking if you're sure. You two are reviving what had been an entirely dead branch of auratic studies. Aetheric bonding was last a thing in the days of Atlantis, but I've never heard of an elf lodging some of his aura in someone else. Ninlil might have, but..." She shrugged. "For what it's worth, Harqil is one of the better celestials. You might even have an ally in them."

I scrubbed my hands over my face. "Okay, if I was a djinni and you were making me a callstone, what would you tell me?"

"Don't." She laughed. "But then again, I suppose you already have him living in your head. If you want to wedge yourself deeper into that trap, that's on you."

Anansi's words about being trapped echoed in my head again, and I shivered at a nudge from the Sight. I took out my phone to text Troy a warning. "Do it."

Chapter 22

I squawked as Iaret's taloned fingers abruptly squeezed the shoulder Troy had bitten, reopening the wound.

She held the stone against it. "Relax. Part of the spell."

"Warn me next time!"

She didn't bother to answer. The scent of lemon zest burst into the space as she read from the paper in a language I couldn't begin to make heads or tails of. As she finished the spell, a tingle rippled over me, and by tingle, I meant more like an extreme case of full-body pins and needles rather than the usual goosebumps.

"I thought you couldn't enchant people?" I gasped.

"I didn't enchant you. I enchanted the stone while it was touching you and bathed in the blood of a wound made by your mate. Subtle difference. Very convenient for this that you two follow the old covenants though."

I had no idea what she meant by that, but she was already phasing out of this plane.

"I'll just run this over to your lover boy. I can't wait to see how it works! You must take detailed notes as payment for my services."

"Wait! How do I hear him if he has the stone?"

She wrinkled her nose at me. "It's set up so that you're the djinni, silly. Really quite clever of Ninlil. Makes me wonder how long she knew she'd have a child by an elf. She always did downplay her ability with the Sight, the clever love."

Before I could respond, Iaret flickered, changing planes.

I clutched my neck and gagged at the pain of it, like someone had tied a string to the auratic point in my throat and tugged hard. By the time I recovered, she must have put the stone in Troy's hands.

"Arden?" Troy's voice came from everywhere and nowhere at once.

My skull seemed to split as I dropped to a crouch, instinctively covering my ears.

A poke brought my eyes open. Iaret was standing over me, grinning. "Ha! It works!"

"Is it supposed to hurt this much?" I asked.

Alarm came through the bond, searing the back of my skull as Troy said, "It's hurting you?"

"Not so loud," I whimpered.

"Hmm," Iaret said. "It usually takes some getting used to, but it might be amplified by your already having a bond. Rude of Harqil not to mention that."

"How long to get used to it? And can he see my end? Hear me?" I asked.

"I can hear you," Troy said. "Much more clearly than our mental communications."

From the looks of it, Iaret was doing her best not to fall out laughing. "You can mute it down a little. Like when Duke walls you out? Try whatever you do to mute your elf with the Aetheric bond."

I did, and immediately the sense of Troy at home dampened down to a level where I could breathe and exist in my own head and space. "Oh, thank the Goddess."

"That's quieter on my end as well," he said.

Iaret clapped. "Excellent! This will be so much fun. I've needed a hobby. Or better still, a project. This study will be my crowning work."

Troy snorted, and a deep sense of resistance tightened my skin. "I'm going to close this down now. I was on a video call with the Charleston Houses when Iaret popped in. We've almost got an agreement with all the Houses now that Duke has brought the djinn to the table. Stay safe, cariñamí. I love you. I'll check in later."

"Love you too."

The connection closed, and I was alone in my own head again.

No wonder Duke was always so pissy when I contacted him. Being the linked end of a callstone was fucking loud and uncomfortable as I was suddenly immersed in the other person's space. That would definitely take some getting used to.

Iaret was still bouncing. "I must go secure this and take some notes. Don't get killed!"

She disappeared, my mother's spell in hand.

This was all entirely batshit, but in a way, it was comforting. My mother's dream of uniting the elves and the djinn was coming about in slow, unexpected ways, but it was still happening. And most importantly, it would benefit me—and therefore, those I was trying to protect. I didn't know how yet, but apparently digging the "trap" deeper would help later. Maybe even with Dreamwalking, which given what Cyrus had said on his way out the door, was much needed.

I just hoped I didn't have to hurt too many more people before we got through to the other side.

That soured my mood, as did the consideration that Sergei and Roman would probably move whoever or whatever they were trying to hide from me and I'd have to thwart them while dealing with the feds. Time weighed on me in a way I didn't remember it doing before, like it was imminently running out. A clock that I couldn't see ticking down. Grains of sand trickling on me as I stood trapped and choking in an hourglass.

The more I thought about it, the more I was certain this wasn't like the Sunday scaries or some other kind of dreadful anticipation.

Something was wrong.

I didn't know what though. The Sight confirmed things for me. It might warn sometimes, but only when danger was imminent and immediate.

"Breathe," I whispered to myself.

I had to assume this was about the tricksters. Fine. Time was running out for me to get Otherside in balance. I didn't know how long. I didn't know what else I could do about it, other than deal with one faction at a time and delegate to Troy to handle another two.

The wolves. I had to get the wolves sorted.

Today.

As I was trying to figure out what to do about that, I reheated my tea water then took my cup out to the balcony. The cushions on the rocking chair were surprisingly comfy, and I tried to let the immensity of the mountains ground me.

I wished Troy was here. I didn't think I was experiencing withdrawal yet, certainly not after less than a day. I just missed him. Maybe I was finally starting to understand what Val had said about elementals being cast out as a punishment. I might have been alone my whole life, but now that I had people, being away from them hurt.

Neither here nor there. I sipped my tea, trying to figure out a way to deal with Roman and Sergei that wouldn't mean death and destruction. I knew what Troy would say. And Omar, Allegra, Terrence, Ximena, Duke, and probably Maria. The fae would certainly call for death on the hospitality breaches alone; you were polite and hospitable, or you didn't treat with the fae and live. Of the parliament, Doc Mike would probably be the only one calling for a peaceful resolution. Val or Laurel would probably abstain for the elementals.

But what was the right path for me?

More importantly, what would keep my people safe?

And had I drawn the feds here, or had the wolves?

I still couldn't escape the feeling that the wolves knew about that camera in the clearing. The Sight had confirmed my thought that they were working with mundanes. But were they working with them like Terrence was—turning willing volunteers, if against my orders and maybe using drugs to smooth the process—or was this something else? How involved were the feds?

Nothing came to me. The Sight had given me all it was going to give, or else my magical senses were out of calibration from the callstone spell. I was going to have to act.

My phone buzzed with a text to my personal number, rather than the public Voice number, from an unknown. I frowned and opened it, not sure if I should be relieved when I jumped to the end of the note and found it signed by Darius.

I've got something. Can we meet?

At the idea of leaving again, exhaustion washed over me. I'd driven four hours across the state, then around Asheville, then had a showdown with two werewolf alphas and some of their pack.

If you come here. I sent the address.

Perfect. Thanks.

Darius took longer than I'd expected to arrive, and I discovered why when I peered out the window at the sound of a car rolling up. He got out then went around to the trunk of a black Lexus ES hybrid and loaded himself up with grocery bags before approaching the porch.

"Lemme guess." I arched an eyebrow as I let him in. "Troy?"

"Alli, actually. But probably minding Troy more than anything. It's not like her to care about groceries. That was always my job. Sometimes Troy's, before he was sent on his initiation mission."

Funny how the elven pecking order would play out, even within the sibling relationship. I kept that comment to myself and led the way to the small kitchen and fridge. Darius frowned when I started helping to put things away but had the sense not to try arguing with me again. Everything was simple food, things that could be made quickly. Pasta, bread, frozen meals, shit like that. Enough for a few days.

I was still working out how I felt about Darius, but something in me wanted to trust him. Being naturally contrary, I wanted to fight it. Today though...today, I was too damn tired.

"Talk to me," I blurted when I couldn't figure out what else to say. "You don't look too banged up. Are you okay?"

Again, a startled sideways look, like he was surprised I actually cared. "Yes, ma'am. There's a way to get hit by a car that looks bad but doesn't hurt much. For a trained Darkwatch elf anyway."

"I'll take your word for it. How did the..."

"Extraction go? Fine. Easier than missions against other elves for sure. I was wearing a hat and sunglasses for the traffic cameras, declined medical, and mazed the police and the feds who hit me. No worries for being recognized by anyone who could do anything."

I wanted to ask what exactly an "extraction" entailed, but my stomach was already flipflopping. "What did you learn?"

"Definitely feds. Here for the wolves first, but then you arrived and became priority number one. Something about a field in the woods and a camera."

"Shit. I found that camera earlier today." My mood sank at having my fears confirmed. "That's why I went over to confront the Volkovs rather than keeping a low profile." I showed him the photos I'd taken.

"Fancy. I kind of want to go steal it for the Captain. He loves getting hands on new human tech."

"Everyone seems to know I'm here, so be my guest."

That got him to crack a smile. "Thank you, ma'am. Maybe I can buy my way back into his good graces."

I winced at that. "I can talk to him if you want."

"No. It was my screw-up. I should have known I was being compromised, celestial or not. I'll deal with the consequences. Besides, can't have the High Queen playing favorites."

Now he was making me start to feel bad for him. He was almost as chill as Iago, but less confident, somehow. Less alpha, maybe, now that he wasn't cursed anymore. I'd seen him fight, so I knew he could, but he might be the oddest Darkwatch agent I'd ever encountered. Almost like he would have been something else if his family hadn't pushed him into the Darkwatch.

I shook off the thoughts and tried to stay focused. "I'm pretty sure my visit today accelerated the Volkov's schedule. Did you happen to see what about the wolves had the feds here?"

"A glimpse only. A document, stamped confidential. Some numbers on it. Maybe a contract?"

"That could be anything."

"Yes, ma'am. I'm sorry. The target only glanced at it."

"Don't be sorry. You confirmed something I'd been debating." With the groceries finished, I dropped into a chair at the kitchen table and waved Darius to take the other one when he settled into a parade rest. "Stop with the formalities. I told you, we're practically family. You can be formal in front of other elves if it makes you feel better, but it makes me crazy if we're just talking."

Cautiously, he took a seat opposite me, sitting far more stiffly than I imagined was comfortable.

"I know," I said. "I'm an odd queen. But I've got enough to deal with trying to figure out how to deal with the fucking wolves. They've put me in a bad spot." My earlier frustration rose up again, and I traced the line of the wood grain in the table.

Darius inhaled then hesitated before blowing it out. "May I offer some advice, ma'am?"

I glanced at him, almost too grumpy for it but not wanting to shut him down after just having told him to be less formal. "Go on."

"Whatever Callista was and wherever she came from, I'd be willing to bet nobody went along with her at first either."

I started to snap at him, to ask what his point was, because Callista was dead and neither here nor there. Then I thought about it. "You're saying I need to stop beating myself up for having to hurt the wolves."

Some of the tension in Darius's body eased. "Yes, ma'am. From what I've heard, you have...beautiful goals. For all of us, I think. But nobody changes a society by asking nicely. Especially not when that society is Otherside, and especially not when it's in the United States."

My heart twisted. I knew that intellectually. But it was different when I had to be the one taking the actions to dirty my hands. The more I thought about it, the more my respect for Troy deepened. I'd been pitying him in a way, for being raised to see the world the way he did. At the same time, I'd been benefiting this whole time from both that upbringing—his unflinching willingness to use violence—and from his courage to turn his training to the service of our ideals at huge personal cost to himself.

Could I do any less, if I really wanted to be worthy of that? Of him?

I sighed. "You think killing one or two is better than letting this drag out into a full-blown rebellion."

Darius grimaced before blanking his expression as a flush darkened his features. "Yes. I can take care of it for you. Two bullets. Quick and clean."

"No." The idea made me half-sick. "We can't risk losing the bullets with the feds involved. And if I do this, I need to do it in a way that is undeniably Otherside and in a way the trickster gods can appreciate, rather than pointing at as a sign of imbalance. Some of Otherside still thinks I'm too human after living twenty-five years pretending to be one, and I need the tricksters to give me more time."

"Time? For what?"

I grimaced and filled him in.

He'd gone pale by the time I was done. "We can't—"

"I know. Nobody in Otherside can afford it and especially not the elves. The elementals are still debating whether they'd help, as far as I know, but they're none too happy with me."

The hard look I recognized from Troy settled over Darius. "Then, my queen, as your only advisor present, I have to insist on taking out the Volkov brothers. There's just cause, even if it wasn't your prerogative as the Arbiter."

Cold settled into my bones. "I know. I just wanted there to be another way."

"There is. You abdicate and resign your post."

I blinked, startled at the shift from meek to steel.

Darius's lips thinned, and he looked down at the table, like he was irritated with himself. "I don't mean to speak out of turn, but I know my brother. I know what he'd say and what he'd be thinking even if he didn't say it. Troy's ability to work in the interest of the House is hampered by instability in the territory and in the demesne. If he's dividing his energy between the House, the mundane government, and factional infighting, he cannot do what needs doing to keep us all safe. He can't do what's expected of him as a king. And that means Houses across the country are already looking here for conquest, with him as a prime assassination target."

"I know that." My stomach twisted as Darius spoke one of my late-night fears, that Troy would die and it'd be my fault. Agitated, I got up to open a window then pulled on Air to create a zephyr. I started to say that I wasn't a murderer, except that A, it wasn't true even if it was justified, and B, Troy killed people, but he wasn't a bad person.

So why was I so hung up on this? Was I as human as the rest of Otherside smeared me to be?

My attention fell on the bottle of wine on the table, and a nasty thought started trickling into a plan. "I'm gonna go back tonight. And it's gonna be a hunt."

Chapter 23

Apparently, the Volkovs' thinking mirrored mine when it came to dealing with territory threats—either that or the feds were putting pressure on them—because Sergei and Roman threw out a challenge before I could issue one of my own.

A dominance contest: a fifth of whiskey split three ways, followed by a fight. Midnight.

Roman knew I didn't drink more than the obligatory few sips of mead or a small glass of wine in company, even if he didn't know why.

The whiskey was an insult but one that gave me an opening.

I pulled up in front of the Volkov house again, praying to the stars twinkling in the tree-lined slice of sky that this would work. That Darius could do his part of the plan and both gain intel to confirm what Zadie had just sent over about contracts from the Verve files and keep the feds occupied by being up in their business while I dealt with this. That this was a challenge I could handle, that my acceptance hadn't been empty confidence, that I could hold my shit together after what had already been an eighteen-hour day on too little sleep, and that my maenad magic could take out at least one werewolf alpha and force the other to back down.

I hadn't needed Troy's frustrated arguments to tell me this had trap written all over it.

I had a lot to make up to him when I got home.

I refused to think of it as *if* I got home.

A half ring of wolves waited in front of the house when I stepped out of my car, more than had been here earlier. Sergei had cleaned up and looked more like the asshole who'd turned up in the Triangle than the ragged degenerate he'd been this morning. Roman stood slightly behind Sergei's shoulder, looking cocky as fuck. Not good.

"Midnight on the dot," Sergei called out. "Some people might wonder what you're afraid of to be so punctual."

"Some people might," I said. "Smart people would wonder what bigger shit I had to deal with tonight to make you the small-fry opening act."

"I'd say you were looking for another love bite." Roman's cockiness had a spoiled edge of disgust to it.

His petty nastiness hardened something in me, and I arched an eyebrow at him rather than reply. It was completely unnecessary. He'd lost, almost two years ago now, when he'd first turned his back on me for a chance at power and then joined an attack on me. But he was still trying to act like nobody else could have me. Nice to have him confirm that Troy had been right not to forgive or forget. It'd make the rest of tonight easier.

My silence threw Roman off. He was used to a different dynamic between us, one of venomous words and shouting.

"Fine by me." Sergei grinned. "Deposing an Arbiter early in the night means I have the rest for celebratory fun."

I let that slide as well, knowing he was trying to goad me. "Shall we then?"

"Let her through," Sergei said.

It didn't escape me that he'd done just about all the talking, certainly giving all the orders, and Roman was still playing second fiddle. Something about that seemed off. He'd been so determined to reclaim the leadership he considered his by birthright, but here was Sergei calling the shots.

I did my best not to smirk as I passed through the thin opening the wolves made for me. This trap wasn't just for me, not from the way Roman was keeping an eye on his brother from just behind his shoulder. Neither Volkov boy appreciated or practiced subtlety particularly well though, so whatever Roman was planning for tonight, Sergei hadn't seen yet amidst his excitement to get me where he thought he wanted me.

I paused in the middle of the ring, halfway to Roman and Sergei. "Quick formality before we get started."

Before they could object, I blended Air and Fire and fed lightning into every electrical line I could sense in the immediate area. Where the lightning encountered a transformer, generator, or anything else that would conduct or store electricity, I pushed harder and blew it. Darkness fell over a ten-mile radius.

Had to make sure there weren't any cameras or listening devices. Bonus points for making life very inconvenient for whichever of them survived this.

A pair of wolves leaped at me, and I slammed them away with Air then pinned them down with hardened chords. Spring was a sylph's best season, and this time of year was just getting into the conditions where a thunderstorm was ripe. I had no problem upping the humidity and the wind into a slow-moving storm that would sit over the area for a good hour and make it difficult to send a drone or a helicopter through if Darius's distraction didn't work.

"What the fuck is this?" Sergei shouted over the wind.

I smiled. "Just making sure our little get-together stays private. There were feds in town earlier, in case you missed them. Now, I just wanted to confirm what the agreement was." I wanted all this witnessed because whatever happened tonight would be the end of my troubles with the Volkovs, one way or another. "No elemental or werewolf magic once the contest starts, and winner determines leadership and direction of Blood Moon territory, right?"

"Yes," Sergei snarled to show wolf teeth. It was clear he'd rather jump straight to the part he was imagining about tearing out my throat, magical limits or not.

"To first blood or...?" I trailed off.

"To the death," Roman said, finally speaking up in a soft tone. "Unless the winner submits and abdicates."

"Giving yourself an out?"

His lip curled at the taunt, halfway between a sneer and a smirk.

Yeah. This was as much about Sergei as it was me.

"I don't need an out," Roman said. "But we also don't need war with your fuckboy if we can avoid it. Politics, babe."

I let my coiling rage at his casual dismissal of me as a threat and Troy as my partner fuel my inner huntress, keeping the adrenaline taut and focused. The punchblade Troy had given me rode in its sheath at the small of my back, where he wore his. I didn't want to baptize it the way he hoped I would. But I wouldn't allow myself to be killed.

I'd survived too much to let these two-bit curs take me down.

"Let's get started then. Unless y'all are scared of little ol' me," I said.

Mud squished underfoot as they led the way up to the dark porch and the table that'd been set out. A bottle of bourbon and three tumblers sat on it. No chairs.

This was gonna suck—other than rum or brandy, I wasn't a fan of spirits—but it would definitely let the maenad out. When that happened, maybe my reputation as someone who shouldn't be fucked with would finally be established.

Part of me hated it. I hadn't wanted it to come to this. But Sergei had been a power-hungry ass at every turn, one I'd had to humiliate earlier to even get him to show basic respect and hospitality. I was done making excuses for Roman, no matter how much I'd thought I loved him once. And I could not leave Terrence and Ximena, and their new pack member, with an unstable situation in the Triangle, worsened with Vikki's refusal to adhere to her agreement.

Sergei poured three fingers of bourbon in everyone's glass.

I raised mine in a toast. "Cheers, assholes."

At the scent of the booze, the maenad magic sparked to life. Rather than boxing it in and putting it away, I leaned into it, letting it consume all my fear and doubt.

We drank. And again, and again, until the bottle was empty and the night swam in my vision, creating two werewolves for every one in front of me. Both of them were much bigger than me physically, and if Sergei was like Roman, they were both much more accustomed to holding their liquor. When I squinted, both of them looked much steadier on their feet than I felt as my stomach sloshed.

I shook my head and closed one eye, trying to get four human-shaped werewolves to become two again. "Ready to lose?"

Both wolves smiled to show their other form's sharp teeth.

I smiled back at them, letting the maenad magic that'd been banging at my soul with every swallow of bourbon slither forth. "Come get me then, my dears."

My voice, deepened by the magic, or the words themselves made them hesitate. Or maybe it was that I was standing there in a ready stance rather than fleeing.

The maenad magic ate it up, delighting in the sudden spike in fear smell, sour sweat and rotted cedar. Even when Troy had insisted on practicing before the elven summit, I'd held back, too afraid of my first memory of unleashing the magic to fully lean into it.

This time? The maenad magic I'd feared my whole life was going to save it.

I freed all hold on it, laughing at the soaring feeling of freedom, and moved, elven-fast or faster.

My first punch took Sergei in the throat and landed with a crunch. He hit the wall behind him and dropped, choking, unable to breathe around a crushed trachea. Werewolves healed fast but not that fast. There'd be no surrendering from him. Only death.

The maenad magic drank up the inevitability of it and sang in my soul. It wanted chaos and death. These two weren't worthy of sex. They'd hurt us. They'd hurt our mate. We'd take blood as our due.

An eye for an eye and blood for blood.

Roman was making sounds—words? It didn't matter.

I blocked his hurried punch then grabbed him and hurled him over the porch railing. He hit the mud and skidded. Wolves scrambled away, yipping in uncertainty.

Werewolves had no long-range attacks, and I was faster than ever. Roman would keep while I dealt with Sergei.

I drew my new punchblade and kissed it, an acknowledgment of the love who'd gifted it to me, before pouncing on Sergei and sinking it in at throat, heart, and groin. That last stab I dug in as he writhed and screamed without sound.

"I know you raped Ana," I snarled. "And I know she probably wasn't the only one. Go to the ninth circle of hell, Sergei Volkov."

A sound did finally make it out of him when I dragged the blade across his crotch before twisting it and ripping it out.

The maenad magic roared, spiking even higher as it finally received a death. The first I'd ever given it. Power curled through me, a sensation almost like an orgasm, a reward for not just feeding the magic but doing it willingly.

I'd worry about how goddamn good it felt later. For now, I just groaned with pleasure.

The fast squishing of feet churning in mud pulled my attention. I spun and jumped down the stairs of the porch, planting my feet and stiff-arming Roman with a palm to the breastbone when he skidded in the uncertain footing and couldn't stop in time.

Something cracked, and he howled as he went down.

A sense of movement to my right pulled me around in time to drive my fist, punchblade in hand, down the throat of the wolf who'd thrown himself at me. He died before he could even register that he'd failed. His teeth caught on my arm as I yanked it free, and the pain and blood fed the maenad magic even more.

I wrestled it down enough to speak and turned my attention to the rest of the wolves in the circle. "Y'all were meant to be observers in this contest. Anyone else wanna join it?"

One by one, they all laid down in the mud as wind lashed their soggy coats.

As I turned back to Roman, he dragged himself backward with one hand, clutching his chest with the other.

"You cheated." He gasped and turned to cough then spit blood. "We said...no elemental magic."

"Oh, darling. This isn't elemental magic. It's something much more inclined to kill." I knelt and pinned him by the throat then leaned down to whisper in his ear. "But it never occurred to you to think about why it is I don't drink, did it?"

When I pulled away, his eyes widened. Pure fear filled them, and I drank it up. Let it slither through my soul and dance as it healed some of the pain of his past and present actions.

His mouth opened, lips already trying to form the words that would give him the out he'd insisted he wouldn't need.

I buried the silver punchblade in his throat.

Betrayal filled his eyes before they glazed over, confusing me more than anything else. Had he really still thought, after everything he'd done, that I would...what, leave Troy? Or that he could get Sergei out of the way, kidnap me, and keep me wherever they were holding the humans until he wore me down?

Insanity. I laughed, a wild, rippling sound, and stabbed him again. Someone that illogical couldn't be trusted to stay dead if they were only stabbed the once.

With three brutal deaths and a taste of blood though, the maenad magic was satisfied and started to fade, leaving me swimming in an impending adrenaline crash and a magical hangover.

Not yet. I had to pull it together and finish this. With an effort, I called the magic back and rose, needing its warm embrace for just a little longer.

It wanted a price. Sex or blood, my choice. I agreed to the magic's lingering call for blood and licked my blade clean as I met the eyes of every wolf still alive in front of this cursed house. "Anybody else feel like challenging me as Arbiter of the motherfucking Carolinas and Dominion demesnes?"

Every wolf rolled to their back with a quickness despite the ongoing downpour.

"Good. The Blood Moon clan is mine. Volkov land is mine." I paused, intentionally drawing out the drama to feed on their fear. "Viktoria ignored my last call, but I have a feeling this will get her attention. If she is a good girl and comes home as ordered and *if* she formally submits to me, I might allow the clan to stay here. Oh, and there's another condition. Y'all are gonna tell me about the deal with the mundanes and why there's a camera smelling of humans on the pack hunting grounds. Right fucking now, before I get thirsty again."

One wolf started writhing, and I gripped both the punchblade and the remnants of the maenad magic that wanted to kill him until he'd become a naked, mud-covered human.

He stood and bowed with the usual were nonchalance for nakedness, although exhaustion hunched him. "Arbiter, if I may?"

"Talk. Quickly. First, who are you?"

"I'm Mason. I was fourth in the clan." He glanced at the third wolf I'd downed. "I suppose I'm the ranking wolf present now, if it pleases you."

None of this pleased me except the woodsy zing of werewolf blood on my tongue, but I nodded so he'd keep talking.

"There was a split in the clan, Arbiter. Those who remained here after Miss Viktoria took her loyalists east had to choose: fall in with Roman and Sergei, with Sergei first among equals, or die." His gaze darted to the other wolves. "I'm not ashamed to say I wanted to live."

"Which two did I beat the shit out of earlier?"

"They're not here. They... Sergei wanted them punished for letting you through. He was powerful angry, ma'am, after you—after you humiliated him." Mason ducked his head, wincing.

"And the mundanes?"

"We had some in the cellar, to turn. Sergei ordered them killed and disposed of after you left. No witnesses, no evidence."

My heart sank, and it was all I could do to keep my knees locked and my voice steady. "I see. I know there was a contract between Blood Moon and Verve Health. Where do the federal agents who followed me today come into all this?"

"This was their program."

Shock pierced the last shreds of the maenad magic and the haze of alcohol. I'd been thinking Sergei had been an opportunist selling werewolf blood to Verve, but this sounded so much worse. "Excuse me?"

"They approached us. They'd ID'd Miss Viktoria and traced her connections." Mason shifted from foot to foot. "They offered political protection and money. Lots of money. But we had to give them werewolf blood and show them how to use it to make their own supersoldiers. They wanted it tested first, without a bite, to prove it would work. With bitten mundanes as a control group."

I closed my eyes in a long blink. I was too drunk for this, on both booze and magic. I wasn't even sure if I'd make it home or what to do about the bodies still laying all over the place.

Well. That last was easy enough.

"I want a full report," I said between gritted teeth. "Everything. Every detail. From each of you. And I want it by dawn. If there are any unreasonable discrepancies or if I even suspect that anyone in the clan has spoken with a mundane for any reason other than to cover up this fucking mess, I'll be back here for more of this."

My gesture at the house and yard made more than one wolf quiver.

"Get up and get the fuck out," I snapped, releasing the wolves I'd pinned with Air earlier.

They didn't need to be told twice. When they'd fled with tails tucked and there was nothing human or machine other than my car and Sergei's in the range of my elemental magic, I dragged all three corpses to the ground in front of me with Air and then destroyed them down to their elemental particles like I had the Sons of Seth. The plastic, I slagged and drove deep into the earth, deeper than any CSI team would bother to look.

That done, I staggered back to my car. There'd be no hiding that I'd been here. The power outage and storm would be pinned on me simply because I was in town. But if Mason had been telling the truth and the Sinners had been behind kidnapping their own kind to turn into werewolves for some fucked-up supersoldier project, they wouldn't be able to come after me publicly unless they found a way to spin it plausibly.

They might well do that, come to think of it.

But if we were talking about spinning, it was my own head that was doing most of it. I'd have to worry about this mess, and the nightmare of watching Roman elementally disintegrate, later.

When I leaned against the car to give myself one fucking second to breathe and try to find something resembling sobriety, a presence at my side made me jump.

"You keep surprising us, Arden," Harqil said. "It won't be enough, but it is certainly more than we expected. Roman's death will cause trouble for you though."

"Won't be enough?"

"Forget I said anything." They eyed me. "You need a designated driver."

"That'd help." I tilted my head back to face the rain. "What's the price?"

After a hesitation long enough that I turned to look at them, they said, "Call it a favor between friends."

"Are we friends?"

"Do you want to stay here if I say no?"

"No." I made my way around to the other side of the car and got into the passenger seat. A puff of Troy's scent rose when I collapsed into it, and I was suddenly glad we were too distant for him to get anything from the bond and that he was too busy to try the callstone again yet. I sent him a quick text saying, *Still alive and heading home*, so he wouldn't worry.

Harqil got into the driver's seat.

"Can you even drive?" I asked.

"Of course. Who can't drive an automatic vehicle?"

That sounded more than a little bit like a lie, but I didn't want to risk bringing Darius out here and had nobody else. Fortunately, they got the car going and down the road without incident. Great.

"Being trapped is being free." I rolled my window down and stuck my head out, hoping the cooler air and the rain would help sober me up. If nothing else, I'd be sick out the window instead of in the car.

"Indeed. Veles will be...unhappy."

"That the snaky fucker?"

"Snaky fucker." Harqil snorted a laugh. "Probably. Don't let him hear you call him that though."

I was too busy fighting off the rebellion in my stomach to answer.

Chapter 24

Harqil disappeared as soon as my car was parked at my rented treehouse. I dragged myself inside and made it to the bathroom but not quite to the toilet and was unbelievably sick in the sink.

Darius found me on the floor, shivering with a massive hangover. Booze mostly and just an echo of power. I wasn't used to using the maenad magic, although if I was honest with myself, this was as much mental upset as physical.

"What do I do?" He sounded almost as level as Troy would have. Small blessings.

"I need food. Something bland."

I blinked, and the next time I opened my eyes, Darius was gone. Stupid silent elven footsteps.

By the time I managed to shower and drag myself to the kitchen, he had a baked—microwaved—potato plated, topped with bacon baked beans.

"Protein without the stress that more meat would put on your stomach," he explained when I stared at it.

"Thank you." I looked up to find a pinch of worry between his brows. "It's great. Troy just always uses a lot of animal protein for power hangovers, and I'm a creature of habit."

"Goddess bless my brother, but Troy is about as elven as an elf can get and spent more time infiltrating other elven conclaves than human institutions. *I* was required to learn more about alternative protein sources."

I sat down and dug in, pausing as my stomach considered rejecting the food. I breathed through it until the mouthful settled. "Sounds like there's a story there."

Darius snorted. "There is. For another time. For now, I think I gave the feds enough trouble that they'll be focusing on their own business, if not outright leaving town with the blow you dealt to their program here."

"What intel do you have on it? I was only told the wolves killed the captives after I left." My heart hurt at that, but I'd killed the ones responsible. Otherside justice would have to do.

"It's not good. But I've forwarded everything in a report to Troy, as well as to your secure email."

"What?" I asked when he hesitated.

"I just...would recommend dealing with it in the morning, ma'am. The work we did here tonight will set them back enough that they'll need to re-evaluate their plans, and the Captain will have the Darkwatch on it as soon as Troy forwards my report."

"Yeah. Okay." The potato and beans had somehow disappeared from my plate, and I glared at it like someone had stolen them. "Any juice?"

Darius fetched a bottle of orange juice. "Do you need anything else to eat?"

"I don't know if I'd keep it down. I haven't had this much to drink or been this sick in a long time if ever."

"Hmm. Troy will be pissed if he hears I didn't get at least a little more in you."

"Troy's not here." My stomach lurched. "Please stop talking about food before I lose what I just ate."

"Yes, ma'am. In that case, I'll be on guard outside. Sleep well, ma'am."

I wasn't gonna argue with him. If I was being honest with myself, yeah, I was more than a little worried the feds or the wolves or both would try for me in my sleep. Sleep I desperately needed, even if the new fear of it was sending jolts of anxiety through my stomach. There was a question I needed answered first though, now that I was haggard enough to let myself ask it.

"Why do I feel so comfortable with you?" I asked.

"I wondered if that would kick in." Darius made the same wry, lopsided smile Allegra did sometimes, but with his lip curling up on the opposite side. "I'm a male blood relative of your mate. You smell like him" —his eyes darted to my shoulder, the one Troy tended to bite— "and I'm naturally inclined to protect you because of it. You sense that."

"Then why did I want to kill Allegra once? She's blood too."

"She is, but she's both strong magically and female. If you were injured, she'd almost certainly register as a threat."

"Sounds about right for the situation." I sighed, tired of navigating the layers of elvendom all over again. "I need sleep. See you when I wake up."

"Yes, ma'am. May the Goddess keep you."

I hoped She would as well because I had no idea what to expect.

Exhaustion pulled me under as soon as my head hit the pillow. I closed my eyes—and the bedroom around me disappeared, resolving into the windswept beach edged in tall pines and redwoods, the surf breaking against cliffs in the distance.

A Chaos sphere. Was this better or worse than the In-Between? And speaking of the In-Between, what had Harqil meant when they said Roman's death would cause problems?

Surely, it was what I was supposed to do, to restore balance?

At the thought, I was suddenly covered head to toe in blood. My curls dripped with it, my skin was sticky with it, and all I could do was stand there like a fool and stare at it thickening in the lines of my hands.

"Arden."

I spun. "Troy."

Before I could worry that my unintentionally pulling him here would be dangerous to him, he took a step closer, nostrils flaring. "Why are you covered in blood that smells like...werewolves?" Another sniff. "The Volkovs?"

Shuddering, I turned back to the ocean and knelt, trying to scrub it off. "Because I killed Sergei and Roman tonight."

"You what?"

I didn't answer. The blood wasn't going anywhere. Panicked, I grabbed a handful of sand and scrubbed harder.

"Hey!" Troy grabbed my wrist. When I tried to pull free, he squeezed and leveraged me to my feet, spinning me back to face him. "Stop that."

I couldn't look him in the eye, even as I opened my hand to let clumps of wet sand fall. "I didn't want to do it. It was a trap. Like you said. Like we both knew. They— There was bourbon, so much bourbon, and then they thought they were gonna kill me and—"

"Stop. Breathe, my love." Troy grasped my shoulders and gently pulled me closer.

"I used the knife you gave me," I whispered.

"You did?" He cupped my jaw in his hands and kissed both my eyelids. When he pulled away, he didn't bother being subtle about licking the blood from his lips. "I'm glad. I know it hurts you, and I'm sorry for that. But I'm glad it's done." He tugged me closer, blood and all, and wrapped his arms around me. "Tell me."

I didn't want to. Shame still ate at me for the violence the maenad magic had wreaked using me as a vessel—Chaos incarnate, made into death. More, for how much I'd enjoyed it while caught up in the magic. But in a Chaos sphere, everything was real, according to Cyrus.

That meant Troy was here. His scent was real. His strength was real. I was safe.

Buried against his chest, I recounted the whole day. It felt like a confession, but when I was done, I couldn't even find it in me to cry.

"Am I a monster?" I asked.

He grunted. "No more than I am. Almost certainly less. Monster or not, you're not a bad person."

My knees gave out with relief. I was doing all this to protect people, and protectors had to be good people. Right?

He caught me enough to guide me down, and we sat in the surf. "Let the blood go."

"I tried."

"You tried physically. Dad says everything here is real, but everything is also a figment of the imagination."

I leaned away to eye him. I hadn't thought Cyrus would be back anytime soon, after the way he'd left. "He did, huh?"

"He was worried this would happen. The Chaos sphere. Wanted me to be prepared. I agreed to a solo lesson to keep you safe." He winced. "And to learn more about that part of my own talents."

"That's fair." I bumped my shoulder against his. "Did Cyrus happen to say *how* to let something go?"

"It's here now because you're fixated on what happened. Feeling guilty?"

I flinched and nodded. "They both had it coming but yeah."

"So, if I understand it right, you can either accept that you did what you had to and let go of the guilt, or you can get yourself to think that it's not there and just dispel it."

"Is that all?" I said sarcastically.

"I could try licking it off." The deadpan tone had me questioning whether or not he was joking, and the bond didn't quite work here so all I got was an edge that said he might be a little serious. "But otherwise, yes."

The mental image of him licking me clean of blood was bizarre enough to shift my mindset, and the blood started fading.

"You did what you had to do," Troy said. "That's only a slippery slope if there was truly any other choice. Was there?"

I reflected on what'd happened, as much as I could with the holes the bourbon and the magic had eaten in my memory. "I don't think so. We finished the bottle. Sergei was ready to attack. Him and Roman both had wolf's teeth, even though we'd agreed no werewolf or elemental magic. I punched Sergei in the throat before he could get me. Roman said something though, or tried, before he died. Harqil said his death would be trouble for me."

"We'll deal with that if and when we have to." Troy's grim tone said he certainly didn't think there would have been any other way. "Now. You need proper rest. Let all this go here so you don't take this mess into the waking world with you."

Oh, now that would be a disaster.

Oddly, it helped by summoning the memory of another night I'd found myself coated in blood, after escaping the trap laid by Orion and a bespelled Darius. Troy had found me, despite the severed bond. Gotten me to trust him all over again. Cleaned me up. The memory was fucked up. But he'd fixed it. Or helped me fix it. Either way, there'd been no trace of the blood I'd woken up covered in by the time he was done.

Troy kissed my temple. "There. Well done, cariñamí."

I looked down to find myself clean and took a shuddering inhale, blowing it out hard in relief. "I don't know what I'd do without you."

"You'd manage."

"You have that much faith in me?"

"It's no less than you have in me." He turned my face toward him with a firm grip on my chin and kissed me on the lips this time.

The wet salt of the ocean blended with the taste of his mouth, taking me back to the day I'd proposed to him, and I smiled against his lips.

"That's better," he said. "Deal with the wolves. Let Dari help. Then get home as soon as you can. I miss you."

△▽△▽

The morning, or rather, the afternoon, brought me to Darius's report. It was as bad as he'd said, with the worst part being that Verve Health had been just the first of several facilities that would be involved in the program.

Fucking Verve.

At least we'd dealt with that particular threat. Maybe with what I'd done, the other businesses would back out.

Next was an angry call between me and Vikki, ended by my command that she take up her responsibility here in Asheville or I'd find someone who would.

In the end, it took a week to sort out the Blood Moon clan affairs, and I resented every minute of it. That Vikki seemed determined to drag her feet on coming home to a territory handed to her on a platter made it worse.

I made several ties to the land: at the treehouse, the hunting grounds, and the Volkov mansion. That kept the pinch of my magic at bay, but by the end of the week the sensation Troy had described—an unscratchable itch in the bones—had started. It made me short tempered as fuck, too much to manage using the callstone with Troy.

When I phoned him on my last night, the night before Vikki was due to arrive home, Troy sounded as grouchy as I'd been with the wolves.

"I've almost got everyone in line with the new Houses." From his tone, he was ready to kill whoever was standing in the way. "And I've given Viktoria a final warning to get out of the territory."

"Um. You did?"

"She was making noises about delaying again. We're supporting Terrence. He—"

Allegra's voice in the background interrupted. "Is that Arden?"

"Yes," Troy said. "What are you doing here? I told you to—"

"Lemme talk to her."

"No."

The sound of a brief scuffle made me pull the phone away from my ear. When it stopped, I caught Allegra's faint, "And I'll thump you again if you wanna try me, asshole."

I scowled. What the hell was going on?

"Arden, when are you coming home?" she asked.

"Soon as I'm done. You better not be hassling Troy. He's in charge."

"What he is, is an even grumpier fuck than he used to be. Kill Sergei and Roman and get back home."

Troy's growl in the background underscored her point even as he said, "I'm fine, Allegra. Give me back the phone." A pause. Then, louder as he spoke into the phone again, "Arden?"

"You didn't tell them," I whispered.

"It's for you to tell. Your victory."

Victory. The word was technically correct but still felt hollow. I was supposed to be uniting Otherside, not murdering its leaders.

"Victory?" Allegra said. "What victory?"

Another growl from Troy raised my hackles even two hundred miles away. "Allegra. If I have to tell you again—"

"Fine! Fine, I'm going."

When the sound of the door closing in the background suggested she was gone, I asked, "You doing okay?"

"I'm f—" He broke off and took a breath. "No. No, I'm not."

I waited, not wanting to crowd him if he was going to be honest about what he needed. He'd started to default to "I'm fine" because that's what his grandmother had beaten into him.

Warmth tingled over me that I was someone he could be honest with about something that would have gotten him punished for most of his life. Whatever I'd done wrong in my handling of Otherside, that was one thing I could look at and know in my bones was right. Other people might fear and vilify me because of what I was or what I'd done, but Troy? I was someone he trusted. Not just loved or was bound to or forced to be around. This was his best chance to be free of me in two years, and rather than trying, he was unburdening himself. Bringing us closer.

"It's harder than it was before," he finally said. "It used to be just an itch after a week of not being near you. Now it's a steady burn. I keep catching myself looking west. My heart hurts. Like glass ground into my chest." He paused to take a few more breaths, sounding like he was trying to settle himself after letting down the walls he was probably keeping all of this behind so he'd look in control while in public. "The Chaos spheres help. I don't know what Dad was so damn worried about. But the sooner you can get back, the better."

I tried my best to modulate my tone like he did when I was upset. "Okay. I still haven't found a few of the werewolves who were enthusiastically supporting Sergei, Roman, and the feds, but I think the example I made of the one I did ferret out will scare the rest into compliance." I hadn't enjoyed using the elements to scare the bejeezus outta the wolves, but I needed this lesson and my dominance to stick or I'd have to come out here again—and maybe do worse than I already had. I didn't know if I had it in me to torture like Callista had and I didn't want to start down that path. "I'll call Vikki again as soon as we're done and tell her if she's not back tonight, I'm turning the pack over to Mason and removing the Volkovs as the local dynasty."

"Mason? I thought you said he didn't want it."

"He doesn't, but she doesn't know that." I scrubbed my free hand over my face. "I'll see you tomorrow, okay? Hang in there."

"I will."

As we said our goodbyes, I prayed he would. Troy was too strong magically to risk him slipping, and his iron control hadn't been tested like this before.

That growl earlier had me worried about what state I'd find him in when I got home.

Chapter 25

The combined threats from both me and Troy finally got Vikki home. I'd taken to sleeping days, hoping that letting Troy shift to his natural nocturnal schedule would help keep him level, so I was still fresh enough to hit the road when Vikki arrived at an hour to sunrise.

Pushing it, the both of us. Her with my good graces, me with my own stamina and constitution.

I met her at the Volkov family mansion for a semi-formal ceremony, everything packed and ready to go, with Darius on standby in his car at the end of the private road.

Vikki wasn't stupid. She spotted the empty bottle of bourbon and the three glasses. Saw the churned-up ground, the mud now dried.

"Did you at least make it quick?" Dull, bitter anger flattened her tone.

"For Roman. Sergei, I hurt a little. For hurting Ana."

Vikki flinched at that, her lips pressing to a thin line. "I see."

"For what it's worth, I didn't want to do it. But I won't be attacked in my own demesne. You and I both know I couldn't let it stand. Not the unsanctioned turnings. Not the collusion with the mundanes. Not the threats or the assault on me as Arbiter."

"I get it. You had cause."

I studied her, wondering how much of our tattered friendship still held. "Are you gonna give me cause, Vikki?"

She gave me an equally long look then shook her head. "No. I don't get to invoke blood for blood and eye for an eye when their stupidity brought them their dues. I warned them. And for shit to get this bad around here..." She blew out a breath, and the lines of hostility in her frame eased as she slumped. "I want to be mad at you. Hate you. But I have no argument. All you've done is enforce the agreements other folks have made and do your job as Arbiter. They crossed a line with the mundanes, and with you. You uncrossed it."

"I appreciate that."

"Doesn't mean I want to look at you."

"That's fair." I turned to go then turned back. "You can send one wolf to the Triangle as a representative of the clan's interests. They can stay at Roman's old place."

Vikki stood a little taller, recognizing the bone I was throwing her. "Thank you, Arbiter."

I offered a tight smile then got in the car and hit the road. Hopefully, that would both stave off any rebellion that might have cropped up at being excluded from local politics and give me a way to keep tabs on the wolves.

Darius tailed me the whole way home, dropping back a few times. I paid enough attention to make sure it was a precaution and not a need for action, but otherwise, I just tried to stay awake and mentally order all the shit still waiting for me when I got back. I'd been keeping tabs on what was going on, thanks to reports from the Ebon Guard, the Darkwatch, and the faction heads, but it wasn't the same as being there.

The whole drive though, I kept feeling the weight of inevitability growing heavier. Harqil had dropped a few clues in my lap, but I didn't have enough of the big picture to assemble them into anything that made sense. All I really had was the sinking feeling that I wasn't doing enough or doing it fast enough, which frustrated me beyond measure. I was getting the djinn and the elves to end their cold war. I'd embraced the maenad magic and killed to stop the werewolves from doing something that would hurt and unbalance both Otherside and the mundanes. I was trying to bring the elementals fully into the fold. What more could I fucking do to regain control and restore balance to Otherside?

I didn't have the answer by the time I got home, exhausted and pissed.

Troy was waiting at the gate. I'd opened the bond as soon as I'd hit the Durham city limits, and the biting edge of agitation and need had adrenaline coursing through me. The sight of him sent everything else in me to flight.

He looked fine, of course. He could keep up appearances. But behind the slightly too brittle façade of his expression, he was a tornado in a bottle.

I wanted to open it and set him free like no one else could.

When he swung the gate wide, I pulled through far enough for Darius to come in behind me then waited for Troy to close and lock the gate behind us and get in my car.

"Arden," he said roughly as soon as the door shut.

I'd never heard anyone say my name like that, like everything good and necessary in the world lived in me and it was mine to bestow as I wished.

His gaze drank me in even as he held himself back. Waiting for me as queen—the dominant one in the relationship—to welcome him.

I leaned over and gave him as much of a hug as I could, shivering as he buried his nose at the corner of my jaw and inhaled deeply then twice more.

When he shuddered and exhaled hard, I let him go and got us the rest of the way up to the house with my fingers laced in his. The air seemed to zing with tension we'd need to do something about—after we'd sorted out Darius.

Darius or not, I couldn't help throwing myself into Troy's arms after we parked and got out. It was like a magnet pulled me to him.

Allegra came down the porch steps, wearing the blank expression that said she was nervous as her gaze darted between her brothers.

Troy squeezed me hard before loosening his grip. "Darius."

Darius hung back, keeping his head down and avoiding Troy's eye.

With a last kiss, Troy released me and went to him. "Look at me. What's wrong?"

"I didn't mean to betray you, brother," Darius's whisper was hoarse with pain. "I hurt you and your queen so much, when I was sworn to keep you safe."

"Oh, Dari." Troy pulled him into a hug that looked as tight as the one he'd given me. "Did you really think I could hold it against you?"

Allegra snorted, but it sounded forced. "T, your grudges are legendary."

Troy shook his head. "Not this time. This time, family comes first. There had to be a punishment so nobody else would think of trying what Orion did, but it's been served. You're home now. You're forgiven."

Finally, Darius hugged Troy back.

It was a touching scene, but I was too busy dealing with the flood of hormones that'd kicked in with Troy's touch after just over a week away. I shielded and walled up hard to keep from distracting him. But my hands were shaking, and it was hard to keep my breathing even.

I needed him. I couldn't look away from the way the black T-shirt stretched across the muscles of his back or the taut curve of his ass in his dark-wash jeans. Hunger pinched my stomach. Not for food though. I swallowed hard at the thought of tasting him, squeezing my eyes shut. I was an elemental, not an elf or a vampire or a were. I didn't need blood or flesh. I didn't.

I did. His.

Allegra noticed. "Family first but queen above all. Take care of your mate, T."

Troy whirled and hurried to me, bending slightly to peer into my eyes when I opened them. "Shit. She seemed fine."

"You know better than anyone she's good at seeming any kind of way until she crashes. Go on, give her what she needs. I'll get Dari checked in at HQ."

Where she, or some of the Ebon Guard, could keep an eye on him. Darius would probably go through the same hormonal readjustment period Troy had, but without a mate to anchor him, he'd need family.

I'd worry about that later. Right now, it was my own hormonal readjustment that needed to concern me because I was damn near ready to eat Troy alive or fuck him to within an inch of his life. Maybe both.

Both was good.

My mouth watered at his touch as he steered me toward the porch and I dropped both shields and walls.

He dropped his mask as soon as we were inside with the door shut and locked.

"Yes," I said to the hungry look before he restrained himself again.

I didn't want restraint. I wanted all the passion that was boiling in me reflected back. Not just to satisfy the callings of our bond but because deep down I was afraid I'd crossed a line I couldn't uncross in Asheville and I needed to know he still loved me anyway.

"Always," he said, responding to the unspoken fear. "I will *always* love you. Especially when you make a hard choice to defend yourself or us."

Breath whooshed out of me as my back hit the wall, and then I was drowning in his kiss, his scent, his taste.

More. I needed more.

I refused to question it. Not after a week of separation and bloodshed and loss.

With a growl, I hooked a foot behind his ankle and pushed, tripping him and riding him down to the floor, pinning his wrists. "Mine."

"Yes." As he had in nearly this same spot on the floor after the Thread of Thorns that brought back my memory, his body relaxed as he submitted, and the bond flooded with relief. "Please yes. I missed you so much."

I kissed him, unwilling and unable to deny him. I dragged my nails along the undersides of his arms to the dip of his clavicle then, in a move that surprised both of us, ripped his shirt off.

"Fuck," he breathed.

Relief, desire, need, validation...all of it swamped the bond as he lifted in a crunch and caught the back of my skull to maintain the kiss when I started to pull away.

He shifted, and the punchblade he kept at the small of his back was pressed into my hand.

For half a second, the memory of killing the Volkovs burst forward, and I hesitated. But the scent was right this time. It was my true love, not the one who'd sought to use me.

I dragged the tip under the scar on Troy's chest, making the point that others could try to kill him, to take his heart, but both his life and his heart were mine. He whispered prayers of thanks in elvish as I dragged my tongue along the cut and reeled from the burst of rosemary and sage and power in my mouth.

Still not enough.

I broke away long enough to cut his pants off with his own blade, thrilling him yet again from the spike in the bond and the quickly hissed inhale. He was definitely happy to have me home, and I was more than happy to strip hurriedly then take him inside me and demonstrate the same.

Both of us grunted with every rough rock of my hips against his. He was mine. Body, heart, mind, and soul. I was taking my pleasure from him until I couldn't.

I leaned back to take him deeper, my hands on his thighs and my body open to him as I let the knife clatter to the floor.

His elvish prayers switched to blasphemy as, with a mental push, he broke past the hesitation trained into him to take what he wanted in turn and skim his hands up my thighs, my hips, my waist. My breasts filled his hands, and he pinched my nipples to make me cry out, arch back farther, and ride him harder.

"Arden—"

I came, falling forward with a groan as his hands skimmed along my flanks and settled on my ass, squeezing to give him the leverage to go even deeper as I fixed on the cut on his chest again and pulled. Blood burst against my tongue anew as he filled me all over again down below.

We lay sprawled on the floor in a haze of lust and love, our minds as entangled in the bond as our bodies were in each other. If anybody wanted to attack the Triangle, now was the time to do it, because without Troy saying my name, I would have forgotten it—to the nine hells with magic or the gods or anything else.

There was only him.

I'd burn the world down for him. And in the unfocused inferno of his gaze following the trail of his finger sweeping down my body, I had no doubt he'd do the same.

"You'd hold my hand as the world burned," I whispered.

"I'd help you burn it. Down to the last circle of hell. Just keep me with you."

"Forever and always."

I think we dozed for a while, right there on the hardwood floor. The sun was past coming up, slanting at a sharp angle through the front window, and the air circulating through the windows

Troy had thoughtfully cracked tasted like morning dew rather than night's heady bouquet.

"I'm not done with you," Troy said.

The deep rumble of his voice vibrated against my ear, and I realized I'd shifted to sprawl across him. A thrill ran through me at the words. I'd learned elves had extraordinary stamina when motivated, and after a week apart, Troy seemed pretty damn motivated.

He nudged me. "Get up."

"Make me."

I might have underestimated exactly how motivated he was because I yelped in surprise at the speed with which he got out from under me, got to his feet, and dragged me to mine before throwing me over his shoulder and heading for the bedroom.

I'd barely gotten my brain rearranged before I was thrown on the bed belly-down, and our roles from earlier were reversed as he pinned my wrists and blanketed my body with his.

"Mine," he whispered against my ear, his breath as much as his words making me shiver.

We hadn't used magic the last time, but this time Aether skated across my aura and I couldn't help panting in anticipation.

He wanted a bite. I could feel it, taste the need he was trying to hide.

But I also knew him. He would never take me without consent. At the same time...he kind of wanted to. Or at least the illusion of it.

Easy enough to give him the fantasy.

I fought, trying to buck him off, free my wrists, wriggle out from under him. But he was too big. Too strong. And with the pinch of the sharp teeth in the meat of the shoulder opposite the one he usually bit, too dangerous.

"Yours." I took a breath, and as I let it go, submitted in the same way he had earlier.

Pure joy zinged through the bond, chased by triumph.

Troy's grip shifted from my wrists, one hand on my hip, one guiding himself into me. When he was as deep as he could get, he pinned me to the bed with the hand not on my hip. "We don't stop until one of us can't keep going."

"Do your worst."

From the savage pleasure curling through the bond, he was going to take me at my word.

Chapter 26

Waking hurt.

Not in a bad way. Just in the way that said I'd been well fucked multiple times and bitten in at least three places. But apparently, the intensity of my reunion with Troy had staved off the gods' interference because I'd slept from noon to sunset in a deep, dreamless slumber that did a helluva lot for my perpetual state of sleep deprivation.

I groaned, wrestling with elven hormones and djinn dream magic and my own body clock, trying to find the way to conscious lucidity.

A kiss under my chin anchored me.

"Arden?"

"Troy." I think I said his name anyway.

The bond echoed with the sense of protectiveness and the word *mine* as Troy stroked a thumb along my cheekbone. Then the bed shifted, and his weight and warmth were gone.

I didn't like his absence. It made my stomach twist.

Fortunately, he was back quickly. Firm hands drew me to sit up.

"Drink this," he said.

I tried to pull away from the scent of the weird-ass oral rehydration solution he mixed up whenever I was severely dehydrated. It worked, but it was just an odd taste and reminded me of nearly dying at Neith's hand.

"Arden." Warning was heavy in his tone.

I gave in and took the glass he pressed into my hands. When I'd finished it, he took it and set it on the nightstand with a light clack before getting back into bed, propped on his side.

"How do you feel?" He traced a finger down my neck, skipping lightly over one of his bites.

"You're in my head. You tell me." I curled closer to him, still half-asleep and beguiled by his scent. A week without it—without him—had been a form of subconscious torture, especially for someone as bound to their home and mate as I was. There was urgent shit to do today, but I needed this for just five more minutes.

Troy snorted and flopped to his back before pulling me in tight. For a moment, I thought he was going to launch into all the shit we had to do tonight, but he just curled one hand behind his head and the other around me. The bond smoothed out into pure contentment when I relaxed against him.

Seemed like we could both use a break.

I wasn't in the mood to argue. Yeah, there was shit to do. The werewolves might be handled, but there were still the Goddess-damned djinn, elves, and elementals, now a full week and a half late on my deadline. I'd have to do something about that, because I didn't want to be backed into killing another faction head to assert my control of the territory. Then there were the local weres, given I needed to see how the leopards and jaguars were holding up with the wolves gone.

But if I'd learned anything since first meeting Troy, it was that I could not go at an incessant pace until I dropped. Not for my health. Not for the good of anyone around me, pulled in to carry out whatever needed doing. And not for the stability of the territory. Because if I lost control—if my temper snapped or hunger or sleeplessness drove me to undue harshness—we might very well have war on our hands.

Or more wars. Matthias was still fighting Santiago for control of Florida even as I was, more diplomatically, fighting to bring the Charleston Houses under my control.

"Stop worrying," Troy murmured. "We have this."

"We have the weres sorted, for now. We don't have the new Houses. Something tells me that's kind of important for proving we can restore balance."

"Hmm." He was silent for all of three heartbeats before saying, "You're still not going anywhere tonight though."

"Excuse me?"

"Look inside yourself."

"Troy, what—"

"Just look."

Annoyed, I did as he said. "What am I looking for?"

"You don't see it? Feel it?"

"Feel what?"

"The emptiness." He sounded sad. "You need your land. This land." With a shift, he drew me on top of him. "You need me as well."

"Emptiness?" I looked inside again. Trying to do whatever metaphysical shit he was talking about was just frustrating me though. "I'll take your word for it."

"You really don't sense it?"

I shook my head.

Troy shuddered. "Any elf will. The well-intended would try to keep you company. Like Dari probably was. He mentioned cooking for you when Alli checked in with him."

Flushing, I grimaced. "He did. And stood watch. And sat and listened to me complain about the wolves."

No hint of jealousy came from Troy in the bond. If anything, he felt...comforted?

"Good," he said. "When Alli told me she'd diverted him there, I was hoping he'd fill a brother-in-law's role. He's spent a lot more time with mundanes than the rest of us though. Wasn't sure how much would come back to him on instinct."

I hadn't realized until then how much family care was built in under the intra-faction abuse and the general aggression elves displayed to other factions, or even other Houses. Kind of like lions, maybe. No wonder I kept thinking of Troy as being like a big cat.

"Okay," I said, "so what would someone not well-intended do?"

"The malicious...they'd either try to take advantage of the weakness to kill you, or they'd try to fill the emptiness. With a spell." He hesitated. "Auratic Aether users are especially good at it."

I went cold. Auratic Aether users like his father, who already had certain opinions and thwarted plans where it came to me, oath of protection or not.

"Understood," I said.

Troy relaxed. "Alli, Etain, and Omar have everything under control for the House negotiations. I sent word to Terrence that you'd be stopping by in the next night or so to check on his new leopard—he's just about managed the shift fully and safely. Looks like he'll make it. Maria has been busy negotiating with Renaud and Charity. Charity might bring us northern Georgia, by the way, if not the whole state. There isn't really anyone else to control in the rest of the territory, aside from a few smaller wereclans."

I frowned, confused. "Bring us?"

"Into the demesne."

Blinking, I pushed away from Troy's chest to stare at him. "Have you been empire-building while I was gone?"

His smile was hard and unapologetic. "Yes."

I waited for more of an explanation, brows lifted, but he just watched me. It was probably self-explanatory and obvious to him, but I needed to understand where this was coming from.

"I'm not mad, but I can barely handle the territory we already hold," I said.

A little thrill went through him at *we*, and his smile broadened. "Of course you can. I know you feel bad about how things went with Blood Moon, but it was what needed doing. You can do this, my love."

"That's just it, I don't want to do it like that."

Troy shrugged even as frustration flickered across his face. "Then you're going to have to find an equally thorough way to scare everyone into compliance with your way of doing things. I know you want to bring people around to a new way. But, Arden, we don't have time for it. Everything is on fire *right now*. How many more Othersiders are going to die if you don't take out the rogue elements and solidify your power now?"

I dropped my eyes from his and traced a finger over the burn mark where his House tattoo used to be, remembering my thought from a few days ago. Me being what I wanted to be was predicated on Troy making sacrifices—physical and moral—and working overtime to shore up political allies.

Like he had been the entire time I'd been away.

I couldn't keep doing that to him. I couldn't keep asking him to do it or hamstringing his efforts to keep me and everyone else in the territory safe. Especially not after how bluntly Darius had pointed out that's what I was doing.

"Arden?" His hands slid up my arms. "What's wrong?"

"You're right, and I hate it," I whispered.

"I know it's not what you had in mind when you found your role as protector."

I shook my head, still sliding my finger over the slick patch of skin on his chest. The cut I'd made was already mostly healed. I didn't want to talk about this anymore. I might have to stick around the house today, but as Troy had said, shit was on fire. Time to put something out.

"Charleston is still balking?" I asked.

He nodded.

"More than a week past the deadline? No," I said. "Fuck no. They're out."

Concern ripped through the bond.

"No," I said. "It goes to the elementals and a djinni. The elementals gain power because they're owed. The djinn because they came to the table to agree. The result balances Solari having an elemental High Queen and an elven king. I will not reward people who drag their feet and play games. I'll take Charleston by conquest if I have to. But this is bullshit, especially after that little call the new queens made to inform me that they'd killed their own mothers and grandmothers."

Troy pressed his lips together, and from his frustration, I was betting he was reviewing the last week of work—either looking for what he should have done better or because it was now wasted.

"So be it." He squeezed my arms before letting his hands slip from them. "I'm not happy about it. But I see the reasoning. And I obey my queen."

I studied him, trying to suss out if that was a good obedience or a bad one.

He offered a tight smile. "I can't tell you to get rogue elements under control and then not like how you do it."

"Thank you." I leaned down to kiss him.

Troy caught my face and lengthened the contact. "We will get through this. Together."

I wanted to believe him, but the feeling that we were running out of time still weighed on me. Yeah, we might get through it, but would we still have magic then? And at what cost?

Only one way to find out.

Both of us wanted a quickie, but we'd both gotten our brains running on managing the territory and the demesne. We got up, put coffee and tea in Thermoses, snagged a few citronella candles, and headed down to the river to work on our plans for next steps.

As the night wore on and the comfort of my land and Troy's nearness slipped into me, I became aware of a sensation like a cup filling in my heart. I just felt…better. Much better than I had in a week. The sensation seemed to flow into Troy because his short responses lengthened and his posture loosened.

When we'd hammered out an agreement between ourselves on the House situation, Arbiter to King, I stayed put on my rock while he moved a ways off to call the elven contingent. I had no problem playing the bad guy here and would have been happy to call the Charleston elves myself, but Troy had been handling the negotiations and insisted on being the one to tell them my decision.

I was kind of surprised when Val answered the phone on the first ring, having expected to be ignored again.

"What can I do for you, Arbiter?" she said stiffly.

"I have a proposition. One that gives the elementals a significant amount of power."

"I'm listening, but anything you tell me has to be taken back to the Collective."

"Tell them I'm offering them a House."

She hesitated, clearly having heard that I meant an elven House and not a building. "Um. What does that mean, exactly? We don't do Houses."

"But we did once upon a time. Which is the real reason behind Atlantis."

"What?!"

I explained everything I'd found in the materials Iago had copied for me. The elemental kings and queens of old, the origins of the Ebon Guard and the Darkwatch. The ancient queens' jealousy and their appropriation of elemental ways to give their rising power legitimacy. That elementals had been trying to thwart Darkwatch attacks on our homes and loyal Ebon Guard when we destroyed Atlantis.

After a heavy silence, she whispered, "And they knew all this? The elves?"

"No. It was buried in the restricted section of the archives. I learned it on the way to the elven summit last month. My Chancellor found it and sent it to me."

"Arden...this changes everything." Val blew a breath out. "They're gonna want to know why you didn't offer us this to begin with. Why you offered it to the djinn and the elves first."

"Y'all weren't speaking to me. Now you are. Call it a reward for good behavior."

Even if the only reason they were speaking to me was because I'd forced the issue. Troy was right. Everything was burning down right now, and I didn't have time for pride.

Val saw through it and snorted. "Right. But whatever. The elves aren't gonna be happy, and the elders aren't gonna put any of our people in their crosshairs."

"Let Troy handle the elves. Besides, this creates balance. Me and Troy, an elemental and an elf, rule House Solari. Keeya Bedoe and a djinni rule the second House. Another elemental and a djinn rule a third. Three factions, equally balanced between three Houses." Which had to up my chances for saving magic for Otherside as well, even if that weight of inevitability was still bearing down on me.

"Huh," Val said. "Okay."

"You gonna go tell them?"

"They're gonna want to know what their obligations are."

"Same as what I've put on everyone else in power in the territory. They help to the extent that they are able in terms of skills, powers, and resources."

"And that possible situation of losing magic?"

"With great power comes great responsibility," I said drily. "Anyone taking up a House gets the power and incomes that come with it. I'm talking multimillions, Val, so significant incomes. Life-changing money. But they're also gonna stand by me, publicly if necessary, if Otherside loses magic. I cannot do this alone anymore. I'm exhausted. You of all people know what happens when I get exhausted and try to manage too much elemental magic."

"Shit. Yeah."

A silence stretched, and I let it. This was a big ask, and I needed her to get all her thoughts, doubts, and questions out up front.

"Last question then," she finally said. "What are your expectations for the candidate who co-leads the House?"

"That they keep their people in line. They can disagree with me as Arbiter—I'm not finna be Callista, and you know that. But I will not tolerate selfish or unreasonable dissent that endangers the territory, the demesne, or Otherside as a whole."

"Won't tolerate as in..."

I gritted my teeth without meaning to, not wanting to admit this. "I killed Sergei and Roman. A week ago. Vikki has been sent back to rule Blood Moon and hold the western part of the demesne. Her people went with her."

She gasped. "You— Roman? But you—"

"Exactly. I will lay everything out to the parliament in the next few days. But I need the Collective, and whoever y'all choose, to know I am fucking serious about getting us united under one banner. The Volkovs didn't want to do that and attacked me." I inhaled, held it, then blew it out, trying to reconnect with Air to settle myself. "I don't want to kill to protect. But I will. That means in defense of the elementals as well, in case that means anything."

"Goddess. Okay then. I'll head over tonight and let you know as soon as I can."

I ended the call and stared into the night, willing the rushing Eno and the night breeze to soothe me. This was a good thing, but I hated who I was having to become to keep my people and my home safe.

Chapter 27

It took another two days of intense and exceedingly frustrating negotiations, but the elementals agreed. The frustration was almost worth it to have them working on the original timeline I'd given the elves and justifying my decision to change course. To my surprise, none of the elders in the Collective were the ones to take up the position of sovereign, although Rose came in as an advisor.

"We shepherded the past," she explained when I asked. "And we'll guide the future. But our old hands must relinquish the rudder and let those who will live this future steer it. We lost precious time as it is." Her scowl suggested she might have wanted to set Ben Pérez on fire, but I kept my mouth shut and accepted it.

A dea named Helia took up the role as queen. Helia was about ten years my senior, olive-skinned, with dark eyes and dark hair falling to her waist. With Rose accompanying her and Val already here, we were suddenly very Fire-heavy in the Triangle. Helia's younger brother Flint, an oread, came with her. They were all weak compared to me but among the strongest of the local elementals.

That was a relief at least. We'd need whatever strength we could get. I could only imagine what Val's granddad thought of it though, risking two of their strongest youths on this gamble.

Keeya had entered into a partnership with a djinni named Mansa, who seemed to be trying out a muscled, dark-skinned elven form for her benefit. Given the way she stared at him, I wondered if we might be seeing a new generation of trueborn elementals sooner than I'd hoped. A djinni named Ninos, who took a humanoid form that was small and a shade of brown lighter than Troy with reddish hair, agreed to join Helia.

Having the other two Houses re-established to form a full conclave again meant redistributing some of my own income to return the streams originally belonging to Luna and Sequoyah, but that was fine by me. Monteague had absorbed the incomes of Solari on top of their own, leaving them the wealthiest of the high Houses, and was mine by both conquest and my claiming of Troy as the ranking heir to the House. I still had more than I knew what to do with, and I couldn't demand other people give up some of what they had without setting the example myself.

With Keeya settling in at the rebuilt Monteague property in Chapel Hill and the elementals at the old Sequoyah mansion at Jordan Lake, the Luna property near RTP was left to House Solari. It was the smallest of the three, but that worked for me; it was most convenient to the whole of the Triangle, which could be useful for any negotiations with out-of-state elves or factions flying into RDU. Troy agreed and declared it open to any House adoptees or elves in transit but generally avoided all three locations.

I didn't blame him. I did the same.

All the while, the pressure grew.

It made me short tempered when I finally carved out time for a Dreamwalking lesson with Cyrus at home the night after settling the Houses.

"You're not focusing," he said. "I know theory isn't your strong point, but it's important that you know how to create and dispel things."

Something was off. Instead of being irritated with me, as he had been before, he seemed almost calm. On alert but not aggressive with it. He hadn't tried to guilt me once about pulling Troy into Chaos spheres while I'd been gone, after shoving the danger of it down my throat not too long ago. And while he usually gave off the air of knowing more than others in the room, tonight it pushed past a sense of amusement and into arrogance.

I swallowed down a snippy reply and glanced out at the moon. It was past midnight, and it'd be exactly full in a few minutes. As much as Troy was trying to suppress the irritation full moons lashed him with, I was still getting a prickle of it.

But no, it wasn't Troy's feelings in the bond or his subtly jittery presence on the couch that was the source of my distraction. If anything, mine was feeding into him and creating a feedback loop.

"Something's wrong," I whispered.

Troy's head snapped up. "I thought it was just me and the Goddess-burning moon."

"No." The more I focused on it rather than Cyrus or Troy, the more the feeling built in my gut and crawled over my skin. Was it the moon? Or was it something else?

I rose from the kitchen table.

Cyrus stiffened. "Where are you going?"

I didn't answer, some nudging of the Sight pushing me toward the bookcase and the lead-lined box where I'd dropped my callstone at the start of the Dreamwalking lesson.

"Arbiter..." Cyrus said.

Another oddity. He usually struggled or refused to use any of my titles.

Troy caught that as well and rose, slipping easily between me and his father. "What's going on, Dad?"

"What are you talking about?" Cyrus said.

The pure innocence in his voice set off alarm bells in Troy. "The last time I heard that tone from you, I was ten. The House Guard had just come to arrest you."

Oh fuck.

Dropping the callstone around my neck, I spun to face Cyrus even as the stone flared to life, almost burning hot against my chest.

Duke started shouting in my head. "Arden! Ishtar damn you, where—"

"I'm here." My stomach cramped, and I tried to keep my attention on a suddenly too-still Cyrus. "What—"

"I was at the bar drinking with Iaret and the djinn who joined the new Houses. The fae and the vampires just collapsed, and then...Arden, I don't know how to describe it. A spark left them. Visibly. I'm in Raleigh now, and Maria's unresponsive. Allegra and Noah are barely keeping the youngest of the coterie from going on a rampage through the city."

"*What?*"

My horror was echoed on Troy's face as Duke's mental communication came through to him as well via the bond and my hand on the nape of Troy's neck.

On the table, my phone rang.

"Duke, hang on." I rushed to grab it, not missing the small, satisfied curl of Cyrus's lip. "Vikki?"

"Arden!" Pure panic laced her voice. "We can't reach our selves!"

"What do you—"

"The magic is gone! It's the full fucking moon, and everyone who was a wolf is trapped as one. They just fucking fell over, and then poof! Some spark or flare or something came offa them. If I hadn't stayed human to see one of the teenagers through his first shift, I'd be stuck too. What the fuck is going on?"

Troy whipped his phone out of his pocket and dialed someone, an elven someone given he started talking in rapid-fire elvish.

"The gods," I said as much to Vikki as to Duke, still connected via callstone. "It has to be. They've taken magic."

"Do they have yours?" Vikki asked.

I sent a zephyr swirling through the house. "No. I need to go. I need to figure out how widespread this is. Keep your people calm. No fucking shenanigans."

"Understood," Vikki said grimly before ending the call.

"Duke? Can you get here?" I asked, squeezing the callstone.

"No." Bitter rage and shock made his voice harsh. "I just lost my magic as well. I'm trapped in a human form and can't cross the Veil."

Fuck. As a djinn, he had some non-magical powers. Now he was effectively mundane.

"Okay," I said. "I will figure something out. Keep yourself safe until I can reach you."

"I— Hang on, why do the callstones still work? I can't shapeshift or travel the planes, but I can connect with your stone?"

"I don't know, but I'm glad." If objects lost their magic as well as people, everything Otherside had charmed, enchanted, glamoured, or bespelled would be exposed. Including possibly decades of protections and coverups. "I'll check the rest of my items. I need to go."

Duke dropped the connection, and Cyrus, cool as ever, answered my question. "The djinn aren't of this plane. They'll keep enough magic to work with items, even if they can't shapeshift anymore. Any who stay on their own plane, as well as the fae remaining in the Summerlands, will keep their magic."

I looked at him, cold stealing over me. Everyone had mentioned a spark leaving them when they lost magic.

No spark had left me or Troy.

Or Cyrus.

"Enchantments on items or things like mindmazes won't go," he continued. "Yet."

"You knew," I said, shocked dismay keeping my voice at a whisper. "You *knew*."

Cyrus shrugged. "You did too. I know Harqil told you this was coming."

"But you knew what would happen and when. You knew it would be tonight." I swallowed hard, not wanting to let him know I'd noticed about the spark but needing the confirmation. "You knew you'd keep your magic."

He glanced out the window, where the moon bathed my front yard in silver. "If you thought about symbolism, you would have figured it out as well. The first full moon after the spring equinox, in Libra. A fresh start in a new year. Completion in the sign of the scales. Of balance." He smiled coldly. "Of justice. Which is what my patron offered me."

"And you didn't fucking think to say anything?"

"Of course I did. And I did tell you—that our goals weren't one hundred percent aligned." The amusement filtering into his grin was like a dagger. "One way or another, I was going to see the queens fall."

"And all of Otherside with them, you ass!"

He shrugged and levered himself up from the table with his cane. "That's what you're here for. Why I've been helping you with Dreamwalking and why I've explained what I just did. It makes you interesting enough to the tricksters that they'll let you live. For a little while, at least, which should keep my boy alive. It'll also give you time to fix this and help the rest of Otherside—after I've had time to take care of a few things. My oath to Ninlil is fulfilled. So if you'll excuse me, my part tonight is done, and my patron will be expecting a report. Then it's time for a few tricks and treats."

His part. Distracting me until my people were already thrown into chaos. Never mind that I had no idea what I would have done anyway. I thought I had done what I needed to do: get the Houses in balance, get the rest of Otherside back on track. I'd almost been feeling good, despite the confusing weight of destiny barreling down on me the last couple of weeks.

With a snarl, Troy ended his call and intercepted his father. Cyrus just leaned on his cane, unimpressed, in a bizarre contrast to his submissiveness the night before I'd left for Asheville. It really had been an act.

"I can go meet my patron, or they can come here, boy." He glanced at me. "They're intrigued by your queen after Asheville. You probably don't want them to come and meet her in person."

Troy looked at me.

"Let him go," I said.

Troy's lips pulled back, and his jaw shifted, dropping the sharp teeth in an open threat.

"Let him go, Troy," I repeated. "We need to get our people safe first. Remember what happened last time a god got interested in me and came here?" Neith had nearly killed me with one of her little tests.

He didn't move, but he didn't stop Cyrus from slipping past him out the door.

"I'll kill him," he snarled when the sound of Cyrus's new car starting and leaving reached us.

My heart broke. I'd wanted so badly for their reunion to be a happy thing for both of them. "No, you won't. If only because he knows more than us right now and might find it amusing to help us later."

Troy slammed a fist against the wall. Then fury abruptly melted into confusion. "Wait. Alli and Etain said elves have lost magic. But I can still sense you." The scent of burnt marshmallow flared in the room as he pulled on Aether and cloaked himself in shadows—not quite as dark as usual, but he still had magic. "If I'm wearing silver and lead or if you're wearing bronze, I can't feel you. Magic is gone. Why do I still—"

"The bond," I said.

He glared in the direction his father had gone. "Or something related to the auratic blending. *That's* why Dad was so insistent that I work on auratic magic while you were gone."

It made sense to me. Cyrus might let Otherside burn to take his revenge on every elven queen, but he wouldn't endanger his son. At least not until he was certain he could get Troy away from me. My heart hurt as I realized that made Troy leverage, both for the implications and for having thought of him that way at all.

"No," he said. "Don't feel bad. That's what it means to be High Queen and Arbiter."

I didn't have time to argue with him about it. "Your dad kept his as well. Part of his arrangement with his patron, I think."

"He what?" The bond grew taut as he looked at the door.

"Yeah. Leave it for now though. We need to figure out what's going on. We can't risk drawing everyone together for a parliament, but people here—shit, probably even across the country and around the world—are gonna be freaking out."

"You're going to be upset with me for saying this."

"Say it anyway."

My phone buzzed. Then buzzed again. I had a feeling it was gonna be going off like that all night as more people tried to find out what was going on and get direction.

Troy glanced away then back at me, straightening and settling into parade rest. "This is our chance to establish your strength and leadership. Completely. Not just in the local territory but nationally and globally as well."

I read into what he wasn't saying. "And yours as King and one of the only Othersiders who's not an elemental but who can do magic right now by virtue of your connection to me."

"I told you that you weren't going to like it."

"I really fucking don't."

He wasn't wrong though. If the shapeshifters couldn't shift and the djinn, maybe the fae as well, couldn't cross the Veil from this plane to the Old City or the Summerlands, that left a lot of people in the wrong place, in the wrong shape, at the worst time. The elves wouldn't be able to mindmaze or heal or cast aura-influencing spells. Who the hell knew what this meant for the vampires if Maria was down and the younger ones were trying to go on a blood rampage. No glamour definitely meant it'd hurt their blood pets and solidaires to be fed on, at the very least. The willing ones, that is. The unwilling would be able to remember their attackers now, which meant they'd have to be drained and killed. The witches wouldn't be able to heal or cast protection spells, and human sensitives like Doc Mike would find themselves in a world they might not know how to make sense of with their sixth sense missing.

It was an absolute disaster in the making. Otherside was completely reliant on magic to keep us safe, superior, or simply fed.

I could not let us fail in this moment.

Troy was still looking at me, waiting for me to think it through.

"The elves have a communications network," I said.

He nodded.

"It reaches across factions?"

"We have our connections. Enough to get the word spread, even beyond the Triangle."

"We need a few things." I paced as I thought, creating a ball of primordial energy and bouncing it from hand to hand. "Announcement. People need to know what's happened. Video of me and ideally Helia, demonstrating all magic is not lost. Hotline to report problems. What else?"

"Ultimatums," Troy said without hesitation. "You're thinking of the people scared by this. But there are going to be some who see an opportunity to take advantage."

Like his father. I had no idea what Cyrus was going to do after checking in with his trickster patron. All the queens who'd hurt him directly were already dead. But Cyrus had a big-picture mission, a capital-C Cause, not just an individual's eye for an eye and blood for blood revenge. Plus, he'd flat-out said he was off to make mischief.

This just kept spiraling, and my phone just kept buzzing. Deep belly breaths weren't really helping with the growing sense of panic. I was one person, and all of Otherside had just lost magic. There was a response and a fix, and I'd find them. But just this moment I had to wrestle my brain into submission first.

A spark of magic pulled my attention. With a shimmer and the faint scent of hot stone, it resolved into Harqil.

Shit. I hadn't noticed any tug on my wards, and as I stretched to look, they simply weren't there anymore.

My home was unprotected.

The realization hit me like a punch in the gut right as Harqil started speaking.

"Anansi sends his re—"

"Are you fucking kidding me?" I shouted. "Fuck his regards and everything else he wants to say if it's not related to fixing this!"

"Are you done?" Harqil crossed their arms.

No, I really wasn't. But they'd come to say something, so I'd shut my mouth and deal with it.

They nodded. "Good. There *is* a way to fix this."

"Do tell."

"Magic is returned the same way it was obtained."

I stared at them. "The fuck does that mean?"

"That's for me to know and you to find out. Just know that where the hunters had their Wild Hunt, the tricksters have...call it a riddle for you to solve if you don't want the world as you know it to end. A task."

It took everything I had not to throttle them.

They shrugged, looking genuinely apologetic as they glanced at Troy, then back at me. "It's all I'm permitted to say. If you find the answer, I'm permitted to help you. But, Arden, do not let things get to the point they were at in your dream. The apocalyptic one. If we get there, we are lost beyond fixing, given the gods have lost the primordial spark. That lives in you alone now that Orion is gone, and you're not a god."

Before I could answer, they vanished again.

Chapter 28

That night turned into the longest and hardest of my life. I had to set aside all my doubt, all my fear, all my anguish, and become the Arbiter.

Not just of the Triangle but of the whole Goddess-burning world.

After a quick call with Helia, we decided to keep the local elementals as a pocket ace for the time being. Troy was right. Someone would want to take advantage of this situation, and it would be easier to handle the territorial incursions if they were targeted at one person: me. Or rather, two people. Troy was insistent on making the point that his tie to me gave him magic as well, despite the risk that another elf might try to force the same bond he'd made with me once we got magic back.

I kept having to yank myself back from an "if."

With that decided, we recorded a video. I created a ball of primordial magic, shaping it first into a glowing white ball then into a miniature planet with land, seas, volcanoes, and fluffy white clouds.

I didn't just have magic. I had the power of creation. The making and unmaking of things. If we were going to get Otherside in line, they needed to know I could seriously fuck their shit up.

Troy called shadows, the one really visible trick elves had.

Neither of us spoke. The magic would make the point and the threat.

Etain, who recorded the video, tried to argue us out of sending it. She was afraid it'd make its way to the mundanes and put an even bigger target on us both.

The fear that might happen twisted in my stomach, but I'd already put down the first two dozen people to try me and my land. I would do it again if I had to, wards or no wards. Besides, that was half the point of not speaking. Anything we said could be used against us if the video leaked. Folks would read their own interpretation into the display either way. Maybe even blame us for the loss of magic. But the mundanes already knew too much. I couldn't give them or anyone allied with them more ammo. I had to leave the door open for them to write it off as special effects. The people the video needed to speak to would get the message.

Troy also pointed out that, without magic, anyone trying to ally with the mundanes at this point was too stupid to live and would be put down by their own people as a threat. I wasn't convinced—someone would always make a foolish choice thinking it would save them—but I couldn't control what other people were gonna do. All I could do was provide proof that hope wasn't lost and that someone would act.

Even if I didn't know what I'd do.

Yet.

With the video done and sent, I called all the people I was directly responsible for as Arbiter of the Carolinas and Dominion demesnes, starting with Terrence.

"We saw your video, Miss Arden," he said in clipped, precise tones that had to be a holdover from his military service. "What can we do to help?"

"Just keep your people calm," I said. His offer made my heart swell. It wasn't just me and Troy. "How's your new leopard?"

"He was human when magic went, thank the Goddess. He'd just completed his first shift to leopard and back successfully, so that helps. But other than that, he's really not good. This is a critical time of bonding to his cat, and it's trapped inside him. We had to sedate him."

"Anything I can do?"

"Keep the mundanes busy. I know those feds have been nosing around Durham. I can't afford someone sticking it here."

"Got it. That's top of my list, next to figuring out how to get magic back. I'll let you know when I have something."

The conversation with the rest of the factions went similarly. Maria was back up, fortunately. It seemed any vamp over two or three centuries had passed out from the shock of effectively being mortal again. Still stronger and faster than human but definitely no glamour. Maria complained that she could feel herself aging again, and I didn't know if she was joking or not. The elves were in a similar situation—still stronger and faster than human, still with very sharp teeth, but no Aether.

Troy put a hand on the phone as I stared at it after the last call, to the Farkas pack in western Virginia, trying to figure out what to do next as the sky started to lighten toward dawn.

"You need to eat something." He pulled the phone away.

I let him take it and crossed my arms on the table, slumping to put my forehead on them. "I'll eat. Then we need to get to the bar."

"No. Then we need to sleep."

I lifted my head to look at him and see if he was being serious. The bond said he was, but I needed to see his face.

His expression gave me nothing. "I mean it, Arden."

"We're in a crisis—"

"And you tend to crackle lightning or blow trees down when you haven't had enough food or sleep and add stress to the mix. Do we really need to have this conversation again?"

That stung. I didn't want him to be right on any count. But my brain was starting to fog, and my stomach chose that moment to growl.

Troy gave me a knowing look, lips thin and brows lifted.

"Fine," I whispered. "But then I'm going to the bar. I need to be accessible."

"The spells and wards will be gone. We might find ourselves with mundane visitors."

"I told Zanna to put up the closed sign when I spoke to her."

The bond said he wasn't happy with this plan. "The house is more defensible."

"I can't hide here, Troy. I know queens move in the shadows of Otherside. I know there are gonna be multiple parties gunning for me. But I hid myself away all of last year and nearly fucked everything up in the process."

"That was different."

Goddess damn it, of course he was going to choose now to be stubborn. I refused to debate him on this. I was Arbiter and High Queen, and right now he was reverting back to what'd been trained—and beaten—into him: defend his queen at all costs.

Rather than continuing to argue, I got up and went to the fridge. There were some leftovers, roast beef and potatoes with some zucchini that'd be heavy enough to keep me going for a while.

Sensing my resolve in the bond, Troy sighed. We prepped our food and ate in silence then went to bed.

It took a long time for me to fall asleep.

△▽△▽

Noon found us up, showered, dressed, and on our way out the door after another round of check-ins.

"What's your plan for the day?" I asked.

"Staying with you."

"Shouldn't you be heading to Chapel Hill?"

He grunted a negative and pointed at his car as we trotted down the steps. "I'm delegating management of elven affairs to Omar and Allegra until this is resolved."

Well, shit. Possible translation: he thought the situation was so unstable that the revered Captain of the Darkwatch and our high-blooded declared heir would be the more reassuring option for all the new elves coming into the territory than a goldeneye King claimed by an elemental High Queen. Either that or he was really that concerned about threats against me.

"What about Helia?" I asked as I climbed into the passenger seat.

He slid into the driver's seat and got the car going, squeezing the steering wheel. "Etain has tasked a detachment of the Ebon Guard with keeping them safe. We are keeping our word." He turned and held my gaze with one that was utterly implacable. "This is not just about maintaining stability in our new conclave. It's about protecting you and you alone. There is nobody better suited for that than me, and we both know it."

I opened my mouth to argue. We were the only two with magic. Surely, we'd be more effective if we split up to handle different fires.

He spoke over me before I could get a word out, and the icy slash of his power signature, though weakened, was enough to make me shiver as much as the emptiness in his eyes. "You stay in my sensory range—sight, hearing, or smell—until we have this under control. Do you understand?"

The command in his tone put my back up even more than the words themselves did. My natural contrariness kicked in, and I lifted my chin, ready to tell him off. He'd gone into full-on Darkwatch mode and turned it on me. This wasn't a training exercise. I wasn't his subordinate here. I was the motherfucking High Queen and Arbiter. And in any case, we had a callstone

between us as well now, in case one of us got hit with either
bronze or lead and silver and lost magic. He'd know where I was.
There was no need for all this.

If anything, his expression grew even harder at the little signals
of my dissent. He was the man I'd met on a cold January night,
demanding I walk away from the Sequoyah case as he trapped
me on a dark street and stole my camera memory card.

"Don't fight me on this, Arden." The deadly softness of his
voice raised goosebumps on my arms. "Do. Not. The more
I have to fight my instincts to keep you safe, the worse it's
going to be for everyone. You can have me at your side and
focused on finding a solution. Or you can have me distracted
with wondering if my mate is secure amidst the greatest threat
Otherside has ever faced. I'll accept responsibility for the fallout
when I'm pushed too far. But you choose now."

I started to snap at him. To cut him down and tell him I didn't
need all this. The air in the car shifted, but it wasn't the air
conditioning. It was me. I was so pissed I'd grabbed Air without
realizing it. And still he stared me down, knuckles almost white
where his hands gripped the steering wheel, like if he took them
off, he'd do something he'd regret.

That was what caught my attention. That, the scent of rotted
herbs filling the car, and realizing he'd shut the bond down to
the barest slip sometime between waking up and getting in the
car.

"Open up to me," I said.

The walls in the bond dropped without hesitation, and I
jerked back against the door of the car like he'd slapped me
at the piercing intensity of what was going on inside him.
Gut-wrenching fear. Soul-deep determination. Love so strong it
threatened to drown us both. Churning rage, probably directed
at his father. More telling, he didn't hide it away at my reaction.

His face didn't change under my scrutiny. He really was fully
in Darkwatch mode—the general, commando, and assassin.

Or more accurately for the current moment, the bodyguard. In control of his more deadly instincts and reactions as long as I was safe. This had to be another reason the queens didn't allow bonded mates. The only control I had between the two of us right now was in how I responded, and no elven queen would let a mate, especially a male, be that free.

"I won't fight you," I whispered, accepting it. I'd signed up for this when I'd claimed him. I'd navigate what we both needed. "I will stay in sensory range. And together, we'll find a way to fix this."

Troy yanked the walls back up in the bond, again only leaving just enough of a crack that he'd be able to keep tabs on me with magic as well as physical senses. "Thank you."

As he put the car in gear and got us down the driveway, I tentatively put a hand on his thigh.

He gripped it, hard. "Don't be afraid of me. Please. Not you. I couldn't bear it." The words seemed wrenched from him, like he was dipping into reserves to keep his hard mask on.

Startled, I squeezed back and leaned over to kiss the corner of his jaw. "I'm not afraid of you. I was pissed at you giving orders, but I get it. Right now, I'm afraid of what's going on and what we might have to do to stop it. I'm afraid of where this road will take us before we reach the end of it. But never you. Not anymore." I slid free to get out and open the gate as he pulled up to it. When I got back in, I gave him my hand again. "Will you be okay?"

"Yes. Just stay in sensory range." His expression pinched for a bare moment. "I think I'm still recovering from you being gone. But I will help figure this out. I just...I need to know that you're safe. And I don't trust anyone else to do the job."

I left it there, letting him focus on the road.

Halfway to the bar, a black SUV pulled up behind us, and a temporary police light flashed.

I twisted in my seat to get a better look. It looked just like the vehicles that'd taken me from downtown Durham a few weeks ago and like the one Darius had noted in Asheville. They'd gotten smarter about the DC plate though. There was nothing on the front.

"Shit," I said. "Feds, has to be."

"How do you want to play this?"

"Pull over. We can't give them a reason to look closer at us or Otherside. Mazing them will do that if they've logged this stop."

My heart pounded and my mouth dried as Troy obeyed. We both stayed still and kept our hands visible as a small man in a suit got out of the truck that'd parked behind us. Two bigger guys, clearly muscle, joined him. The driver stayed put.

The small guy flashed a badge as he knocked on the driver's side window. When Troy rolled it down, he leaned over and made to put his hands on the car.

"Stop there," Troy snarled.

To my surprise, all three of them did. From the scent in the breeze, fear was a big part of it.

Small dude straightened, anger flashing across his features, and cleared his throat. "Mr. Monteague?"

Troy didn't acknowledge them, just kept them under his stare. The two big guys didn't appreciate that one bit.

"Ms. Finch?" the guy tried next. He held up two packets of folded papers. "You're being served. The both of you."

Shit. Let me see those please, I sent to Troy.

He extended a hand for the papers and passed them both to me after a quick sniff and a crackle of Aether that raised eyebrows on all three mundanes. I couldn't blame them. Troy was usually more careful about seeming human.

I opened the packet with my name on it and read the first page, my frown deepening with every line. "A subpoena? Are you fucking kidding me?"

"Your testimony is required," Little Dude said.

I laughed, mostly in disbelief, as he backed away. "I think the fuck not."

I pulled on Fire, ready to burn the silly things. Contempt of court would be the result, but there was no mundane jail cell that could hold me and I could pay any fine. This was outrageous.

Troy directed a thought my way. *Don't give them a reason to try arresting you now. Otherside first. Or there was no point in stopping in the first place.*

"Your move, Finch." The small man's smile twisted into something nasty, like this was just the opening gambit in a high-stakes match. It was a good thing I was wearing sunglasses, or the glow of my eyes would have inspired an entirely different expression.

We waited until they'd gotten back in their car and were on their way before Troy started for the bar again. North Carolina plates this time. They were trying to be tricky.

"What's it say?" he asked.

I scoffed. "We're to appear before a select committee organized by the US Senate for a special congressional inquiry on supernatural activities and threats in the United States."

"You refused to speak to them voluntarily. So, they think they can compel us."

"That's what it looks like. Maybe especially since I suggested we'd follow the law." I flipped through the pages. The word "werewolf" caught my eye, and a sinking sense of dread dizzied me.

"Arden?"

"There's a schedule. They want to discuss the properties of werewolf blood. And the disappearances of Roman and Sergei Volkov, as well as four other people from Asheville and the surrounding area in the last month."

"How much time do we have?"

"One week."

Chapter 29

Downtown Durham was emptier than usual as Troy shadowed me to the bar. A heavy don't-see-me working got us there without any further interference.

The main space was in an uproar, despite the bar supposedly being closed. Zanna was grimly serving drinks while Sarah hustled to deliver food to tables. We usually got a lunch rush—early breakfast, for Othersiders not on a human schedule—but this was unusual.

Conversation silenced as I made my way through the room, Troy tight behind my left shoulder, which raised eyebrows on a few of the elves present.

I stopped in front of the bar. I had to say something.

"I understand you're all scared or angry. Confused. Uncertain. But there is a way to bring magic back to Otherside."

Joachim, Ximena's second, was tucked in a booth with a few other werejaguars. "Rumor has it you never lost it," he said boldly.

I let a cold smile slither across my face and made lightning crackle over my left hand. "I didn't. I have been in contact with the tricksters. We *will* restore magic, if I have to steal it back myself."

A kick of the Sight hit my gut so hard that it took every ounce of Troy's Darkwatch training for me not to react.

That was it. It had to be.

In many of the trickster legends, they had stolen the gifts they gave to humans and Othersiders. There would be no giving of magic a second time.

I would have to find it and steal it.

That was neither here nor there though. I met as many eyes as would meet my gaze, trying to look firm and capable as I hardened my tone. "I expect all of you to be on your best behavior until magic is returned. No fuck-ups and no fuckery against other people or factions. There will be no warning on the consequences, and believe me, there will be nine kinds of hell to pay if you try me."

With that, I continued through the door to my back office, ignoring questions and muttered comments. That was more than Callista would have given them. I had to strike the balance between knowledge as power and power as my only means of controlling this very messed-up situation.

"What happened back there?" Troy asked the moment the door was shut behind us. "The bond went funny. And you sounded like—"

"The Sight. We have to steal magic back."

Even that didn't get a reaction from him.

He took the seat opposite me. "Before or after dealing with the subpoena?"

"Before, I think. But that's not all."

"It never is with you." Not picking at me, just observing. "What else?"

"Harqil had asked me to look into the Nightmare Court. Wouldn't say why, only that it was a personal favor and that they were, or might have been, responsible for that fucked-up dream I had."

Troy's expression hardened. "'Comes and goes, goes and comes. That which is given is taken and riven. Fire goes out, crow goes home. All that's left is dust and bone,'" he quoted back. "You think magic going is the first part."

I nodded. "I think it was a warning. Whoever or whatever this Nightmare Court is, maybe they've only been held off by Othersiders having magic. Maybe we're not the only ones who didn't lose it. Maybe this Nightmare Court still has it too."

"We can't know that. Any of it. We don't even know who they are." His gaze went distant as he worked through the possibilities. "Either way, restoring magic might be the best way we have to avoid that outcome." His attention sharpened on me again. "And that means you need to be ready to put someone else down like you did the Volkovs. There's too much opportunity for chaos right now."

A pang hit me, despite my threat in the bar a few minutes ago. Roman's death was fogged by the bourbon we'd drunk, the edges of the memory dulled, but I still felt the sticky wetness of blood and the way the rain had channeled through it as it dripped over my fingers. Having literal blood on my hands had made this real—made what Troy considered normal real—in a sickeningly visceral way.

Troy stayed quiet, giving me space to deal. To mourn, really. In that silence, I found another truth.

"Nobody ever gave you the space you're giving me right now, did they?" I whispered.

He shook his head.

As I stood there, craving his touch but not sure if I could ask it of him, he leaned back in his chair and opened his arms. I came around the desk and sank onto his lap, seeking the scent of him at the corner of his jaw.

"I know what I'm asking of you is hard." His arms came around me, a firm, steadying embrace. "I know it feels wrong. And inconsistent with what we've done so far. But we cannot keep using the same strategies and tactics when the objectives, the resources, and the players have all changed. Setting aside the Nightmare Court, the US federal government is like an Otherside faction head: they will only change course when they are shown that not doing so will result in more blood and economic damage than their people, and especially their donors, can stomach. We already took out Verve, a small but crucial facility. Now we need to follow up with strong action on this subpoena—early in the war—as a warning. And to manage that, our people need magic back."

My mind swam with the implications and possible consequences. "Sinclaire's call and the investigation mean they know it was me at Verve. They can't let that stand. What if everything we're doing makes it worse?"

"It will."

His blunt words were a hammer blow to both my heart and my optimism, and I stiffened.

Troy's arms tightened to keep me where I was. "You need to be prepared for things to get much worse before they even look like they can begin to get better. I can't make that pretty for you, Arden. I can't fix that or mitigate it or determine which of the people we care about might get hit and which might get saved."

I thought I'd understood what the side of him trained to be a general looked like, but apparently, I'd barely seen the surface. Part of me was horrified and wanted to deny everything he was saying. Reject it and maybe even him.

But a bigger part of me was relieved. Grateful, even. I had someone at my back—better, at my side—who would tell me the hard truths. Who would make sure I didn't bumble though this and get more people hurt out of ignorance and naïveté. Who would be honest about his own capabilities. Not out for glory but for the safety and preservation of as much as what we could save as possible in the face of unprecedented danger.

I leaned back enough to rest my forehead against his. "I love you."

He grunted and pulled away to search my face. "That's not the reaction I was expecting."

"You thought I'd be mad."

"I thought you'd be furious. And stubborn."

"I told you, I need one person who will hold my hand as the world burns. You've just shown me once again that you're it."

The bond cracked somehow, like my words were a vine piercing a stone wall. Still, he held up his mask.

"We'll see how you feel about it when bodies start hitting the ground," he said softly.

I flinched. He hadn't meant it to hurt me, but I couldn't help but worry who we might lose. Etain? Haroun? Maria? Val? Which of my friends wasn't going to come back from this or come back from it whole?

Regardless of my feelings and fears, I couldn't dwell on this.

I rose slowly, reluctant to leave him. He wasn't the only one still suffering from our separation. "Let's figure out what the damage is and what we need to do to get everyone into a reasonably stable holding pattern."

He nodded, pulling out his phone to make calls.

I settled behind my side of the desk and got my laptop going. He'd been right. Some Othersiders were taking advantage of the chaos and crisis to settle grudges, make moves on territory, or claim justice for old wrongs. And it wasn't just information from the Carolinas or Dominion demesnes coming in. Half the demesnes in the United States now had a folder with at least a case or two in it.

My heart sank. A lot of these Othersiders were going to die. I had a feeling silver, lead, and fire would be just as deadly as they always were, and without magic to speed healing, recovery would be partial if at all.

How the hell was I going to fix this? How could I bring Otherside and the mundanes together when my own people were hell-bent on taking the first opportunity to wipe each other out? I was focused on the elven death cult, but all of Otherside had long memories and longer lives. Some of these grudges were centuries old, and the original parties were still alive. It wasn't even history to them; it was their lives. Their justice—or their vengeance.

I couldn't fix this. Not right now. I had to focus on the main goal for right now: getting magic back.

Before I could turn to doing that, my phone buzzed.

Acting Director Sinclaire.

I flashed the phone at Troy then waved a hand for him to stay put and wove a sound-dampening chord of Air between us, floor to ceiling.

He frowned, not having seen that kind of working from me before.

I shrugged. I got the idea from the Lunas and their Aetheric soundproofing spell. This would allow us to stay in visual range without Sinclaire hearing what Troy was saying.

He pointed to the desk drawer. *Get the scrambler.*

I did as he said, barely getting it on in time to catch the call before it went to voicemail. "Finch."

"Ms. Finch. Sinclaire here."

"What can I do for you, Director?"

"I hear you've been served."

"That so?"

"It is." She sounded pleased in a petty sort of way, like she'd won something. "I have a proposition for you."

"What's that?"

"Come in and testify to me. Personally. Quietly. We could handle this murder investigation out of the public eye."

I snorted. It was apparently in both our interests to keep our antagonistic engagements quiet then. "We've already discussed this. I don't snitch."

"Even if it will keep your precious Otherside secrets from being aired in a public special inquiry?"

Troy finished his call and tapped his ear.

I dropped the soundproofed wall, put her on speaker to be sure he could hear, and kept talking. "Seems to me like you might have orchestrated all of this to set up this very outcome."

"What happened in Asheville, Ms. Finch?"

Nah. She wasn't gonna throw me with that. "I'm not sure what you're referring to exactly, but that sounds like the opening to an accusation. I'm gonna have to refer you to my lawyer for any further conversation. Again." Iago would probably be busy as hell right now but holding off whatever the feds had planned was the number one priority.

Troy swiped a message, probably to Iago. My Chancellor was a bar-certified lawyer, and the territory had several good elven and vampiric lawyers. Just one more benefit to the alliance to pool the resources.

"Lawyering up?" Sinclaire said. "That doesn't look innocent. Especially after that business with Verve and the ongoing investigation into a number of missing humans."

"I don't give a monkey's ass what it looks like to you. You've been coming at me for weeks. Threatening me at home. Don't think I don't know what games you're playing."

Sinclaire hesitated, maybe taking the accusation of threatening me at home literally rather than thinking of Durham in general.

Good. I knew it was her who'd sent the Sons of Seth to attack me and Troy.

When she did respond, her voice had gotten colder. "Maybe the Eads were right. Maybe Solari does mean terrorist."

"Pot meet kettle," I snapped.

Cool it, Arden, Troy sent. *She's probably recording this. That can be taken out of context. Badly.*

Shit. And I'd forgotten to record myself. Goddess damn it. I was too rattled by everything going on.

"So you're not going to cooperate?" Sinclaire asked.

"As I've stated multiple times, I will not provide information about Otherside. Especially not while the Sons of Seth and other human supremacist terrorist groups continue to carry out vigilante attacks on my community, both locally and nationwide."

My mentioning the Sons seemed to hit a nerve because her tone went from cold to heatedly venomous. "We'll see, Finch. You might wish you'd chosen otherwise when the special inquiry starts."

The call ended.

Feeling sick and angry, I clicked off the scrambler and tucked it carefully back in the drawer.

It looked like Troy was right. I was out of options, and playing nice or civil or by the rules would only dig me deeper.

I needed to give Sinclaire something else to worry about. "I think it's time to bring Jo in."

"Jo?"

"My journalist friend. From the Durham Hotel."

"Right." That mean little smile came back. "Infowar. Good play."

Despite the bad feeling spoiling in me and pulling my skin tight, I couldn't help feeling proud. This was a non-lethal play—at least, on the surface, it was. I couldn't determine what would happen after my little leak went out, but neither the murder investigation nor this special inquiry had hit the news. Neither the Ebon Guard nor the Darkwatch had picked up on anything either, although to be fair, they were overtasked and stretched way too thin, even with the new arrivals from Lyon and Richmond.

Whatever was going on here was something nefarious. Queens weren't the only ones who preferred to move in the shadows.

I was just gonna have to be better at it.

Chapter 30

I fished Jo's card out of my wallet and dialed her number.

"Ms. Finch!" she answered. "This is a surprise."

"A pleasant one, I hope?"

"Getting a personal call from the Queen of Otherside? Hell yes! Whatcha got for me?"

Troy's brittle mood cracked into something more amused at "Queen of Otherside," and he shook his head, rolling his eyes.

I couldn't help a smile of my own. "This line secure?"

"Yes, ma'am."

"Great. Might be worth your while to do a FOIA request." I rattled off the number on my subpoena.

"Is that a docket number? Is there going to be a trial?"

"An investigation. Apparently into supernatural activity."

"Juicy." The sound of a keyboard clattering. "In the interest of getting the full and unbiased story—why are you calling me with this? I would think investigating Otherside would be against your interest?"

I glanced at Troy.

Partial truth, he advised.

"It might be. It might not be. All I know is that I've also been threatened. If I go missing, it'd be a shame if something important got buried."

The journalist in Jo got sharp. "Threatened? Can you elaborate on the nature of these threats?"

Troy's lips thinned. *Hunt carefully, my love.*

I considered what and how much to say. I couldn't talk about the attack on my home, or I'd draw too much attention there—and possibly to the investigation I'd been threatened with. I wanted as much as possible to keep people away from my land. Virginia though...that might be enough.

"I have evidence of an attempted kidnapping. And I know who was behind it," I said. "That stays off the record please, Jo, unless something actually does happen to me. My security team is concerned that if it becomes public knowledge there could be further, perhaps more elaborate or dangerous attempts."

"I see." More keyboard clattering. "This could be big, Ms. Finch."

"Tell me about it. And like you said, it's probably not all gonna turn out well for Otherside. But I meant what I said when I told you productive relations are important to me. We're in a brave new world. We're all gonna have to adapt."

"That's...very noble of you. How much of this can I quote you on?"

"None of it, for now. I just thought it was interesting that I'd be served with a subpoena to appear before the Senate, apparently for a public hearing, without any kind of announcement having been made. Tax dollars at work, but how?"

Jo snorted. "You don't fool me, Ms. Finch. But I can appreciate a good tip when it falls into my lap. You should know though, that I will investigate this without bias. If it turns out bad for Otherside, that's not on me."

"I understand."

"Okay then. I'll be in touch if I need a comment on the record."

"Thanks, Jo. I'll let you know if anything else of interest crosses my desk."

She laughed. "Oh, I'm sure loads of interest crosses your desk, but it's just not in *your* interest to share it publicly."

I grinned. It was good to have a cordial understanding with a mundane. Reminded me of the old days with Doc Mike. "Speak soon. Bye now."

With a last amused snort, Jo ended the call.

I slumped in my chair and looked at Troy. "Thoughts?"

"Sinclaire will know it was you who leaked that docket number, but it will throw her off. She's counting on your refusal to speak to her about Otherside meaning that you won't speak to anyone."

"Yeah." I sighed. "My one worry is that all of this is intended to push us to do something drastic. Something they can use to paint us as terrorists for real."

"They're already doing that. It's time we took control of the narrative. Flipped it from terrorists to freedom fighters."

My stomach twisted. I hated that whole dichotomy. I hated even more that I'd been pulled into it. Lying to mundanes, I was fine with, but this world of high-stakes spin and optics made me feel like I was drowning again. If I wasn't careful, it would be blood I was drowning in. I couldn't have that, not for the Goddess-damned optics and not for my sense of right and wrong.

I rapped my fingers in a pattern on the desk. "If that's the optics game, then we need to do something public to generate goodwill. Not just money. Actions."

"Gerard Ead is an option."

I frowned. "In what way?"

"Get him to publicly discredit House Ead."

"No." I grimaced. "He and his family have been through enough."

"Then we have your and Maria's actions to defend Raleigh—"

"Or the storm." I sat up. "You said there were tornado watches."

Troy nodded.

"So, we do the same thing I did with the Charleston Conclave. Leak a news report to your contacts. Help people see the connection between us being left alone and my availability to help with shit like that."

His tight features probably would have told someone else nothing, but they spoke volumes to me. "That sets you up to be available for any natural disaster on the Eastern Seaboard. No."

"But—"

"It's too much, Arden." At my frustrated glare, he raised a hand and added, "It's a good thought. But you'd follow through on it. And the current acceleration of human-driven climate change means you'd have time for nothing else."

I huffed a sigh. He was right. Again. "Then we have to shore up relations with Otherside. Make it clear that I can only continue making big moves to defend us if I have them unified behind me."

"There will be some who reject it for the obvious power play it is. But I think most will see they don't have a choice, especially with magic gone. Certainly in the demesnes of the Eastern Seaboard. Maybe some in the Great Lakes and the Gulf as well, given they border our region."

"Then that's what we do. Agreed?"

"Agreed." This time, Troy's grin was pure satisfaction. "This is nice."

"What is? Planning the effective takeover of the Eastern half of the United States after magic disappears?"

"Yes. But more doing it together. You're not giving me orders. You're not blindly taking my advice. We're working together. I never thought I'd have something like this." From his tone and the heat breaking through the cold focus in the bond, that was decidedly sexy for him.

I reached across the table and took the hand he dropped in mine, bringing it to my lips to kiss his palm before scenting his wrist. "This is a deeply fucked-up situation. But you're the only one I could imagine navigating it with. Now, let's get back to damage control."

△▽△▽

Two hours later, I was back home and on a video call with the parliament. After introducing the heads of the new Houses, I launched straight into the point of the call.

"I've called you together because I need your help with a gamble."

Terrence, looking sleep-deprived but still focused, asked, "Gambling for what, Miss Arden?"

I smiled tightly. "Time. So that I can steal magic back from the tricksters."

Vikki blanched. "Steal? Magic? From the gods?"

Glancing at Helia's small square on the laptop's screen, I said, "Yes. Me, Helia, and the elementals who came with her can't protect the Triangle indefinitely, let alone the demesne. We'll be the strongest territory for now because we had forewarning and organized accordingly, but we can't rest on that."

Ximena, always looking for the angles, leaned back in her chair and crossed her arms. "You wouldn't be telling us this just to keep spirits up, would you, Arbiter?"

Before I could answer, the smell of hot stone burst into the room.

Recognizing the scent of a celestial in transit, I jumped out of my chair fast enough to send it clattering backward, a primordial ball at the ready. At my movement, Troy was up and out of his chair with longknife drawn, somehow angled in front of me but with enough gap that I could throw my little ball of elemental destruction if I had to.

"Harqil," I said when I saw who'd come through. "What are you doing here?"

They waved at the laptop from where they'd manifested in the short entry, behind the screen. "That seemed interesting. I wanted to join in."

"What happened?" Allegra's voice called from somewhere in the background of Maria's screen. "What the fuck is going on?"

The others had similar sentiments from the sound of it, but I kept my attention on Harqil.

"Interesting how?" I asked.

They tilted their head at me. "You're going to need help."

I didn't deny it.

"Who is she talking to? I don't hear anything," Janae said.

"Bloody Harqil," Duke muttered, also from Maria's screen.

"Who the fuck is Harqil?" Maria and Allegra snapped at the same time. It would have been cute in another situation.

Arching an eyebrow at Harqil, I dispelled the ball of primordial energy. "Well?"

With a huffed sigh, they slunk around the half wall. As they did, something about them solidified. They still appeared vaguely masculine and largely nondescript, but it was easier to keep my eye on them and see that they wore a loose orange T-shirt over baggy silver-grey trousers. No shoes, which I held myself back from commenting on.

Troy sheathed the longknife and shifted to keep them in sight as they moved to stand behind us.

Harqil waved at the screen. "Greets."

A chorus of uncertain hellos came back.

"Told you it was Harqil," Duke said.

I crossed my arms. "You wanna introduce yourself properly?"

"Ah, I suppose I ought to. Harqil, celestial, messenger-class." They straightened and smiled broadly, spreading their hands in a gesture of beneficence that forced me to lean away, lest I be hit. "I bring glad tidings!"

"Here we go again," Duke muttered.

Maria turned around and slapped at him, showing her fangs when he danced away to avoid it. She turned back to the screen, pupils wide. "Enlighten us then, sweetcheeks."

"My patron," Harqil said, "aggrieved by what they perceive to be a gross miscarriage of justice, has sent me to assist your Arbiter and the King of Solari in restoring what has been taken from you all."

I blinked, both at the flowery speech and at the offer. "Are you serious?"

"Deadly." Their smile widened. "But that's for more private discussion. Not for little monsters with pointy ears."

None of the Othersiders present had pointy ears, so I had no idea what that was referring to but gave a firm nod.

"Okay then. Let's wrap up this meeting." I gave the rest of the parliament the highlights of what I'd discussed with Iago, adding, "I need all of you to keep your people in line. No excuses. No second chances. All of the mundane attention needs to be on pulling together whatever this special inquiry is for now. Definitely not with gaining more evidence or discovering that we're currently easy meat without magic." I hardened my tone and my expression, even though it hurt to address people I considered friends, maybe even family, like this. "We have an opportunity to be an example to Othersiders all over the world here, y'all. But if that's not enough to convince you and inspire your people, know this: the Volkov brothers are dead. I killed both Sergei and Roman in three-way ritual combat and turned all Blood Moon properties and incomes over to Viktoria, who's now back in Asheville."

Shocked expressions and gasps filled the video call, even as Troy's approval curled through the bond.

I met each person's eye before continuing. "They made themselves targets in more ways than one and lied about working with the mundanes. If you force me to make time to deal with your people, your problems, or you, I promise you will regret it. If I find out anyone under my jurisdiction is collaborating with the mundanes, they will regret it. Don't make me be the bitch. Or the executioner, for that matter."

A chorus of serious-sounding, "Yes, Arbiter," echoed.

"Good," I said. "Keep sending reports as you can. But keeping your people in line comes first. I'll be in touch when I have more news."

One by one, they all exited. The last screen to disappear was Terrence and Ximena. They both gave me a solemn, approving nod before leaving the call.

I almost blew out a breath, but Harqil was still here.

"What's this assistance Anansi is offering?" I asked.

"Knowledge," Harqil said. "Of a loophole."

"What kind of loophole?" Troy didn't bother to hide his suspicion.

They smiled slyly. "The kind that lets your queen travel like a celestial. Even when she's technically not one. Yet."

Surprise stunned me.

It fell to Troy to ask, "Travel how?"

"Her dreams, of course. They're not called Dream*walkers* for shits and giggles, little king."

I shook myself. "But Cyrus—"

"Wouldn't know to tell you," Harqil finished for me. "He's working off a partial elven translation of a djinni manuscript, and he has his own agenda. You were right, Arden. About how you ejected him from the dream. He misread the passage." They looked at their nails. "Or maybe he just wanted you doubting yourself to get you away from his son and please his patron."

Troy scowled. "Then why leave it to him to train Arden?"

With a shrug, Harqil crossed their arms and let their gaze wander the main room of my house, pausing to appreciate the glass bulbs with air plants suspended from the ceiling. "We let him do the difficult part: unteaching some of Grimm's more malicious lessons and laying foundations for a better practice. He wasn't hurting her, and it kept him busy. The tricksters needed to see if Arden could reach a balance point, of any kind, on her own."

Kept him busy? That pissed me off. "So I'm a tool? Again?"

Harqil tipped their head. "You're not a celestial, let alone a god. Just as you exert power over your parliament, the gods—and the celestials—shall exert power over you. It's the way of the world, little bird."

"Don't call me that," I snapped. "You don't know me well enough to get to call me that."

"Focus on the matter at hand," they replied with a flick of their hand. "You have quite the task ahead of you. Sutekh took Otherside's magic."

"Sutekh?" I didn't know that god.

"I think mortals call him Set now."

Oh. Set, the Egyptian god, not Set*h*, the son of Adam and Eve from whom our homegrown terrorists had taken their name. I vaguely recalled reading about Set in association with Neith but couldn't remember the details.

Harqil sighed impatiently. "Ignorant children. Sutekh. The divine embodiment of chaos and confusion. Most of us just want to have a little fun, but that one..." They grimaced. "He wants violence with his tricks. He's been delighted by your actions these last few days. Those desert storms in your dream? Sutekh took notice of you."

"Wait, are you saying it's my fault Otherside lost magic?" A pit dragged my stomach to the depths and my head spun.

"Not directly. The gift was always going to need to be reciprocated, and that was looking highly improbable given the current state of affairs even if you did technically meet the initial criteria required to give you an extension. Sutekh disagreed, rejected the agreement, and went rogue. Always impulsive." Harqil rolled their eyes. "Probably trying to impress Isis again, for all the good it'll do after he dismembered Osiris and with her being Great of Magic and all. Bloody mess all around. Anyway. I digress."

Troy held up a hand to stop the torrent of Harqil's words. "Hang on. That's all Egyptian pantheon."

Harqil nodded, their expression saying that Troy was stating the obvious.

With a long blink and a heavy sigh, Troy scrubbed a hand through his hair. "The Duat."

"Precisely!" Harqil brightened. "Not completely ignorant then."

I looked at Troy. "What am I missing?"

He waved at Harqil to continue.

"The Duat is a liminal space much like the Crossroads or the In-Between," they said. "Some think it's an echo of the primordial darkness that was before all that is."

The pieces fell into place. "You've got to be shitting me. Set—Sutekh—used primordial Chaos to withdraw magic from this plane and, what, carry it to this Duat?"

"Glad you're catching on." Harqil's expectant look told me I should keep going.

"Okay," I said. "Primordial magic can only be countered by primordial magic. So, it's definitely me who has to go. And the Duat must be reachable by Dreamwalking. So me again."

Troy stiffened. "She's not doing this alone. I know she's capable of it, but I'm going with her."

Harqil's smile took on an edge. "Good. I'd recommend that. Sutekh is only partly aligned with the tricksters."

Cold gripped me at that. "What's his other alignment?"

"The warriors. Nasty fighter. And those chaos snakes and sha monsters he has. Not fun. You'll need a squad."

I just stared, trying to reconcile all this new information. "How long have you known this?"

"Oh." They waved a hand like it was no big deal. "We just pinned him down on it. We're not the most cooperative lot."

At least there was that. But that still left me in a tight spot.

"So you want me to Dreamwalk to the Duat, with a squad who can fight off whatever in the nine hells a sha monster is, and steal magic back. Do I have that right?"

"My want doesn't come into it," Harqil said. "What do you want, Arden? To rule Earth as the Eternal Huntress with your Hunter at your side, the two most powerful beings on this plane? Do you want an elemental queendom of your own, now that the djinn and the fae are barred from here and your people are the only ones with magic? You could rebuild Atlantis, if you wanted. I'm sure I have the original plans laying around somewhere. Or the twins might. Hermes and Mercury have all kinds of information, for a price. Just don't speak of them like they're one person. They hate that."

When neither Troy nor I had an answer, Harqil's grin became sly. "You could prove the tricksters wrong. Show them up and steal back magic. Finders keepers after all. Magic would be yours to give or withhold. The choice is entirely yours. Think on it overnight. I'll be back at sunset tomorrow. Try not to get yourself assassinated in that time. The tricksters allied with Anansi only let him send me because you might join the celestials one day, so it's not technically breaking any rules. If you die and your Hunter with you? Everyone here is shit outta luck."

And with that, they twisted reality and disappeared.

Chapter 31

I t was too much.

Just...the very fucking idea that I had to use Dreamwalking, a skill the djinn feared badly enough that Duke had been avoiding me so that he wouldn't have to deal with the fallout, scared the hell outta me. Because of it, I'd dumped sand and a desert storm in my bedroom. I dragged Troy into Chaos spheres every time we slept at a distance from each other. I didn't trust myself to sleep these days lest I hurt him or myself. That he accepted it as part of the price of being with me scared me even more.

Now I had to figure out how to get not only myself but also Troy and a whole group of people—people who wouldn't be able to use magic—to a plane of the ancient Egyptian afterlife? Having the abstract idea that I'd need to steal magic was one thing. I'd thought it would be like, tracking it down to some remote mountaintop and playing at riddles with a Sphinx.

Not going up against "the embodiment of chaos and confusion," fighting his army of gods-knew-what kind of monsters, and escaping with my prize.

What could you even contain magic in? A box like Pandora's? How big was it? What did magic look like when it was removed from supernatural hosts? All the reports had mentioned "sparks," but I had no idea what that meant in practical terms.

My head spun. There had to be another way. Maybe I could get Sutekh to bargain.

Or what about Hermes and Mercury? Harqil had implied one might buy information from them. What did they have, and what would it cost?

"Hey," Troy said. "You okay?"

I stared at him.

Tentatively, he reached out and grasped my arms. When I didn't move to shake him off, he skimmed his hands up to my shoulders then cupped my jaw in both hands.

"It's a lot," he said. "But it's not all on you. We'll do this together."

Words wouldn't come.

"What's scaring you the most right now?"

My insides jolted. I swallowed hard, trying to clear a lump in my throat, but my mouth was too dry so I answered him in more of a croak. "Dreamwalking."

"You're doing fine with that. I'm still in one piece, right? And you weren't doing it wrong. My dad was being an asshole on purpose."

I just looked at him. I was tired of repeating that "fine" wasn't good enough. I had to be perfect. It wasn't just me at risk. It was him and whoever else signed up for this—this heist.

Stealing from the gods? I hadn't really let myself think about what that meant or where magic would have gone before. Or who had it, for that matter.

"Arden." Troy peered into my eyes, and a flicker of magic skated over me like he was checking me. "Talk to me."

"I can't." I needed to stop this maelstrom of thought and not think for an hour. I didn't want to make a decision. I didn't want to put on a smiling face and manage this mundane special inquiry, exposing myself to the world so that everyone else could sleep soundly.

But not me. When would it be my turn to rest? What did I have to do for it to be my turn? Maybe it was what I signed up for when I decided not to step down, but the pressure was threatening to undo my sanity.

I needed an outlet.

Troy was here. He would help me not think. Help me find space and grounding.

Pushing against his grasp on me, I caught his throat with one hand and pressed against his chest with the other. We slammed back against the wall, and I kissed him like there was nothing else in the world.

"Arden?" he whispered when I pulled away to breathe.

The softness of his tone broke through my need.

I looked for the right words, I really did. All I managed, though, was, "Please."

He knew. I didn't know if it was logic, instinct, or scent, but he knew.

"Take me," he whispered. Everything dropped—his Aetheric shields, the walls separating us in the bond, his mental and auratic defenses. Even the taut muscles of his abdomen eased under my hand when I slid it down.

I wouldn't second-guess him. I couldn't. I needed one fucking person to accept all of me, and I needed a few hours to just be a woman and not the only hope of the entire plane.

Chaos consumed me as I relinquished control over my magic.

He grunted with the force of it combined with me spinning us and tackling him to the floor. But he stayed open, drinking in everything I poured into him.

My love, my need, my desperation to just *be*.

Time passed strangely. Clothes were there and then gone, his weapons there and then gone. We were on the floor, and then we were on the bed. Desire was the constant thread twining through it all.

Our kisses seemed to last forever as I straddled him.

His grip on my hips, pulling me closer and then, as he entered me, deeper, was all that existed. At least until he moved. Then the friction and pressure of his hips against mine, his desire sparking mine, pulled me away from thought and thoroughly into feeling.

Unable to help the roar of magic, I bit him. Hard. Copper and iron, rosemary and sage, marshmallow and smoke. All of it burst onto my tongue and jolted through my brain.

He hissed. "Fuck, Arden."

Horrified, I pulled away in a panic, afraid I'd hurt him in a way he didn't like. I should have asked him first. But Troy caught my arms and pulled me back to him, one hand on the back of my skull, guiding me back to the meat of his shoulder.

"Do it again," he growled, even as he thrust up into me.

Well shit. If he wanted it...

I bit down.

His growl at the pressure of my teeth pushed me to keep going.

"That's it," he panted. "Take all of me."

Magic and blood. Body and soul. With all of me, I took all of him, and he submitted. Gave me everything I needed and more.

I came so hard that everything stopped.

And in the gap, Troy surged to keep us moving. He flipped us, putting me on my back.

I gasped his name, only for it to be drowned in his kiss as he drove into me. One of his hands tightened around my throat, squeezing as I panted, rasping for breath, while the other steadied my hips for his authoritative push into me.

Queen to king. King to queen. Round and round, a carousel that could only end in death. A little one—orgasm—or a greater one, when both of us left our bodies.

This. This was what I needed. Release.

I tried to stop the scream building as I came, but Troy trapped both my wrists alongside my ears as he kissed me. All that I was burst out as a buffeting wind or poured into him even as he pushed into me. No Aether. No bond. Just pure chemistry and need. Trust that the other would give everything and yet hold back what was too much.

Trust I'd only find with Troy.

Then it was over. Movement slowed, stopped.

Both of us crashed, utterly depleted by the intensity.

Some time later, I blinked awake again, forced out of contentment by heat and weight.

"Cariñomí," I groaned. As I crawled closer to consciousness, I found us thoroughly entwined, the sheets still damp with sweat and other fluids.

He groaned and burrowed closer, the sharp teeth he hadn't retracted scraping along my collarbone.

"Troy," I whispered.

With a shudder he pulled himself to consciousness. "Arden?"

"I'm good."

He nuzzled even closer, and this time the scrape of his secondary teeth was more of a pinch.

I settled into it, relaxing both my mind and my body.

The pinch sharpened before Troy pulled back just enough to create space to breathe against my neck. "May I—"

"Go on." I wrapped my arms around him. We were both still on the edge from our separation. I needed it as much as he did.

The dart of Aether Troy flooded me with drew echoes of our earlier pleasure. He took blood and power from me as I had comfort and strength from him.

Lust.

Power.

Balance.

All ever so slightly tipped in my favor, making me feel safe. Making Troy feel powerful with his ability to both subdue and protect me.

We lay sprawled side by side when he'd taken what he needed. The herby metallic taste of him coated my tongue, and the maenad magic in me stirred again before deciding we'd been well satisfied.

"Feel better?" Troy asked.

"Mm-hm. Thank you."

"It's my pleasure to serve."

When I turned my head to look at him, the smirk in his voice was painted across his lips as well.

"Yeah?" I asked.

He shifted enough to look at me. "Just in case you're not trusting the bond again, I love that it's me you turn to, in every capacity, when you're feeling in over your head." His expression shuttered a little as he turned back to look at the ceiling. "No matter what I did or how hard I tried, Keithia used to tell me I never served the way I ought to. Then she'd punish me to make the point. But you need me. I can feel it. Not in the sense that you're incapable but in the sense that you're finally learning you don't have to do everything alone. And it's me you choose to help you."

I blinked as hot tears threatened to fall. Not just that he was healing that much more from the bullshit and abuse his grandmother had put him through but also because he had that much faith in me. Because he could accept and handle and love all of me.

A soft smile curled Troy's lips as he turned back to me. "It's an honor I never thought I'd receive. And for doing my duty to be this much fun?"

His sudden rolling pounce made me shriek, half in surprise, half in delight as he peppered me with kisses. He kept going, wrestling with me, tickling until I started giggling like a fool.

"That's more like it." He let me go, resuming his position next to me.

As we lay together, each of us lost in satiation and our own thoughts, I kept thinking about the last parliament call. Nobody had argued with me. Nobody had thought I was being mean when I told them about the Volkovs and threatened them, or if they did, they kept it to themselves. Was it because magic was gone and they were scared? Or was it because I had finally stopped playing the people pleaser and established what I would and would not accept?

Whatever it was, maybe Troy was right. About a lot of things.

Maybe it was time to embrace my own inner monster, instead of trying to manage his. We were Othersiders, after all. We were meant to go bump in the night. We were meant to rule under the moon as the humans ruled under the sun. The stylized eclipse symbol that represented Otherside was supposed to be a perpetual reminder of the overlap between our two worlds. Worlds that blended and collided...but eventually separated again.

It didn't have to be Iago's separate but equal solution. But it did need to be something more than Othersiders living in hiding and forced to obey human laws, or living outside of the broader society we all found ourselves in.

I had some decisions to make. Restoring Atlantis and ruling Earth as a primordial queen appealed only in the sense that I might finally feel safe.

But people would be hurt. A lot of people. People I cared about. And I didn't want the weight of managing the whole Goddess-burning world when it exhausted me simply managing my rapidly expanding territory here on the Eastern Seaboard.

At the same time, the idea of leading a squad into battle—in my dreams? Imposter syndrome soured my gut as my earlier troubles rushed back. Could I do that? Cyrus had shown me how very wrong my former understanding of dreams had been, even if Harqil had pointed out where he'd been playing me. Aside from that, he would probably do whatever he could to defend Troy, maybe especially if it got Troy away from me.

And what would I do if—*when*, I corrected myself firmly—I did get magic back? If I could really give or withhold it as something I'd stolen for myself, how did I act in accordance with my principles while keeping my people safe and offering justice to those in Otherside who'd been trampled?

"We'll figure it out," Troy said gently. "This obsessive sinkhole I'm sensing in your thoughts isn't going to help you. It feels like the same place I go when I'm starting to spiral. You always have to pull me out if I let it get much further than where you are now."

I sighed. He was right. And that'd been the whole point of distracting myself with him.

"Okay." I grabbed my fears and smashed them into a mental box then shoved it into the dark recesses of my mind. I didn't have time for it now. "Action plan: We clean up. We come up with talking points for this special inquiry and the inevitable media circus. You grill me. Ask me the hard shit you know I'm not gonna want to answer. We get Jo on board as a distraction, we deal with the reports that have come in in the last..." I tilted my head to check the blinds, finding it was just past sundown. "Few hours. And then we decide, together, how we rule Otherside."

Troy rolled to his side and propped his head on his hand. "Rule Otherside, is it?"

"Or at least the Eastern Seaboard." I flushed. "I was tired of territory squabbles, even before Matthias and Santiago decided to make them my problem. I'm shutting it down after we finish with the magic heist, assuming this Nightmare Court doesn't come out of whatever shadowy pit they're hiding in to challenge us. All of this keeps getting worse because I'm terrified of what it means for what I thought I wanted. But I think it's what it's going to take for me to feel safe."

Troy's smile surprised me.

"What?" I asked.

"I'm just enjoying this." He leaned over to kiss me. "Two years ago, I enjoyed watching you jump at shadows, acting like prey. Now, the whole world is *your* prey. You'll run it down to secure safety for *our* family, whatever that ends up looking like. You've come a long way, my love. A very long way."

It was easy to forget that, the distance between where I'd started and where I was now. Probably because a lot of the time I still felt scared or unsure or like I was an absolute fraud standing in Callista's big, nasty boots.

But in Troy's words I heard another truth: I was on a healing journey of my own, and I was still growing into my potential.

I might not be doing as well as I wanted to or as well as I was pressuring myself to. But I was meeting the challenges that needed to be dealt with.

So, in a way, I was doing just fine.

And sometimes, fine just had to be good enough.

With me being the only one who could get magic back from one of the more dangerous trickster gods? It was definitely gonna have to be damn good enough.

Either way, I'd rise to the challenge.

I owed it to myself and the future I wanted to build with Troy.

I just had to get everyone either playing nicely or off my back long enough that I could gather a team and plan a heist.

A plan. I needed a plan.

That more than anything boosted my spirits. I'd never broken into a place with the intent to steal, per se, although Callista had had me infiltrate targets as a Watcher back when she held my Arbiter title. But this had to follow the same principles as those I'd known as a private investigator.

Step one: research.

Step two: observation.

Step three: action.

Step four: don't get caught with the damn payload.

Just because the payload was usually information—and just because there were a few extra steps this time—didn't mean I couldn't handle this.

Magic would be mine. And so would Otherside.

Acknowledgments

The nature of the Shadows of Otherside series seems to follow the nature of the gods it focuses on. The Huntress Cycle was a relatively linear story to tell, but this Trickster Cycle is proving a very different process. There's less planning and more discovery—tricks, even. As a result, this book needed a much heavier rewrite than usual, so I'm grateful to my beta readers and my editor, Jeni Chappelle, for providing the necessary feedback and guidance.

I also want to thank the indie bookstores continuing to make space for Otherside on their shelves or offering opportunities for readers to get signed copies, notably Resist Booksellers in Virginia and Flyleaf Books in North Carolina. Indie bookstores are so important for helping to get the word out about books that aren't on the big bestseller list, and I appreciate indies supporting indies!

A big thank you to libraries as well. *Elemental* is now on audiobook and most of the sales are to libraries. I'm so glad that readers have that option!

Last but not least, I'm forever grateful to the friends and family who help me keep my head on straight with the ups and downs of indie publishing. Thanks, y'all.

Also By Whitney Hill

The Shadows of Otherside series
Elemental
Eldritch Sparks
Ethereal Secrets
Ebon Rebellion
Eternal Huntress
Tempered Illusions
Talion Rule
Temporal Gifts

The Otherside Heat series
Secrets and Truths
Curses and Faith
Menace and Memory

The Flesh and Blood series (as Remy Harmon)
Bluebloods

About the Author

Whitney Hill is the author of the Shadows of Otherside fantasy series and the Otherside Heat paranormal romance series. Her books have won the grand prize in the 8th Annual Writer's Digest Self-Published E-Book Awards and made Kirkus Reviews' Top 100 Indie Books list. You can find Whitney hiking in state parks or on Twitter and Instagram @write_wherever.

Learn more or get in touch: whitneyhillwrites.com
Sign up to receive email updates: whwrites.com/newsletter
Get bonus content on Patreon: patreon.com/writewherever
Instagram: instagram.com/write_wherever

Ingram Content Group UK Ltd.
Milton Keynes UK
UKHW040828030723
424469UK00004B/360

9 798987 378540